Percy Wyndham Lewis, painter, novelist and essayist, was born of English and American parentage at Amherst, Nova Scotia, in 1882. He came to England in early childhood and was educated at several schools, the last of which was Rugby. He then studied at the Slade School of Art, where he won a scholarship, and afterwards spent some years travelling in Europe, with a period of Bohemian living in Paris. By 1914 he had emerged as the leader of the 'Vorticist' group, of which some of the main figures were T. S. Eliot, Epstein and Gaudier-Brzeska, and with Ezra Pound he founded the periodical *Blast* (two issues, 1914–15) which Lewis edited. Wyndham Lewis always regarded himself as an artist first, a writer second, and was one of the most advanced English painters of his time, influencing both his contemporaries and other young artists after the Second World War. Lewis's satirical and polemical writing was largely directed against the cultural and literary movements of the 1920s – as represented by D. H. Lawrence, James Joyce, and the Bloomsbury Group. His first novel, *Tarr* (1918), drew on his life in Paris. It was followed by *The Childermass* (1928), the first part of his great trilogy *The Human Age*; the two subsequent parts, *Monstre Gai* and *Malign Fiesta*, appeared in 1955. In 1930 he published his extraordinary satirical novel *The Apes of God*, a gargantuan demolition of the cultural life of the 1920s, of which T. S. Eliot said, 'It is so immense I have no words for it.' His other works include *The Lion and the Fox* (1927), *Time and Western Man* (1927), *Men Without Art* (1934) and two volumes of autobiography, *Blasting and Bombardiering* (1937) and *Rude Assignment* (1950). In 1949 he began to lose his sight and he became totally blind in 1953. Wyndham Lewis died in 1957.

Paul Edwards teaches at Bath Spa University College, where he is Professor of English and History of Art. He has produced several critical editions of Wyndham Lewis's work, and is the author of the most .... *wis: Painter an*...

comprehensive study of his work, Wyndham Le-
and Writer (Yale University Press, 2000).

Wyndham Lewis

THE REVENGE FOR LOVE

⤙⤚

With an Introduction by
Paul Edwards

PENGUIN BOOKS

PENGUIN BOOKS

Published by the Penguin Group
Penguin Books Ltd, 80 Strand, London WC2R 0RL, England
Penguin Group (USA), Inc., 375 Hudson Street, New York, New York 10014, USA
Penguin Books Australia Ltd, 250 Camberwell Road,
Camberwell, Victoria 3124, Australia
Penguin Books Canada Ltd, 10 Alcorn Avenue, Toronto, Ontario, Canada M4V 3B2
Penguin Books India (P) Ltd, 11 Community Centre,
Panchsheel Park, New Delhi – 110 017, India
Penguin Books (NZ) Ltd, Cnr Rosedale and Airborne Roads,
Albany, Auckland, New Zealand
Penguin Books (South Africa) (Pty) Ltd, 24 Sturdee Avenue,
Rosebank 2196, South Africa

Penguin Books Ltd, Registered Offices: 80 Strand, London WC2R 0RL, England

www.penguin.com

First published by Cassell & Co. Ltd 1937
Reissued by Methuen & Co. Ltd 1952
Published in Penguin Books 1972
Reprinted with an Introduction by Julian Symons, by Martin Secker & Warburg Ltd 1982
Reissued in Penguin Books with a new introduction 2004

3

CONTENTS

INTRODUCTION

The Revenge for Love has a fair claim to be regarded as Wyndham Lewis's best novel, and it is certainly one of his most readable. Like most of his work it has a strong satirical side to it – mocking the deluded self-indulgence of the fashionable left-wing intelligentsia of the thirties – but unusually for Lewis it also tells a story involving characters whose fate the reader can care about. What happens to Victor Stamp and Margot (particularly Margot) matters to us. This was new in Lewis's work. As a pioneer modernist in painting and writing, he had programmatically left no room in his previous work for empathetic response from his audience. His writing was cold and apparently alienated from its subject, syntactically eccentric and sometimes confusing, focused minutely and at length on the visual exterior of things and people. Any human story it was supposed to serve had to wait its turn – which could be a long time coming. Lewis was a stylistic virtuoso ('the greatest prose master of style of my generation', according to T. S. Eliot), but his style is definitely an acquired taste, and critics who have not acquired it dismiss his writing as clumsy and exasperating. This stylist is the Lewis of *The Childermass* (1928) and *The Apes of God* (1930) or, more accessibly, the Lewis of *The Wild Body* (1927). *The Childermass* and *The Apes* are in almost open competition with Lewis's drinking partner of the early 1920s, James Joyce, and have self-conscious ambitions to be masterpieces of modernism. But by the 1930s, stricken with illness, burdened with debt and beset by lawsuits, Lewis was more concerned simply with writing a novel that would sell, and *The Revenge*, though it starts in the slow motion of Lewis's harsh cinematic vision, takes on some of the narrative excitement of the thriller genre it pastiches for its own purposes.

Lewis seems to have taken himself by surprise in writing this novel. Appealing to his reluctant publisher in November 1936 not to 'visit [his] displeasure' on the book, he explained, 'as I was reading my proofs I realized that the book that is thus to be contemptuously flung upon the market is probably the best work of fiction I have written'. And he retained this high opinion when he wrote his intellectual autobiography, *Rude Assignment*, in the late 1940s. In a chapter devoted to his more celebrated *Tarr*, he calls *The Revenge* a better novel, but says that it will not be republished until after his death 'when all the dust of these present conflicts has settled'. (In fact, thanks to a new relationship with a sympathetic publisher, Methuen, it was reissued in 1952.) Lewis himself was besmirched by clouds of this dust, much of which he raised himself by his political pamphleteering of the thirties. The conflicts he refers to are the great wars between the great power blocs of the twentieth century, with their accompanying ideological battles. In the mid-1930s the cockpit for these battles was Spain, which was also the site of a rehearsal of the Second World War itself, as Communist Russia and Nazi Germany (supported by Fascist Italy) fought out a murderous proxy war through the opposing sides of the Spanish Civil War, from 1936 to 1939. The war began with a rebellion of Army chiefs in Morocco against the Republican Government, and for many European intellectuals it quickly became an issue of crucial commitment: a clear choice between progress and reaction, the people and their oppressors, the forces of good and the forces of evil.

The reality, of course, was more complicated, as George Orwell famously found. Having committed himself to 'progress' and revolution in Spain, and fought with the army of the P.O.U.M. (a libertarian socialist movement involving some Trotskyists and former Trotskyists) Orwell found himself on the run in Barcelona, effectively under sentence of death from Communists who had denounced the P.O.U.M. as traitors in league with General Franco's Fascists. His account of these complications (and of the survival of his own commitment to socialism in spite of them), *Homage to Catalonia*, was published in 1938. His mistrust of Stalin and the Communist Party also survived along with his socialism.

When *The Revenge for Love* appeared (May 1937), the Spanish Civil War had already been in progress for nearly a year, and its author had already made clear his own preference for the Nationalist (Fascist) side, in an intemperate book-length pamphlet entitled *Count Your Dead: They Are Alive! or A New War in the Making*, which had appeared the previous month. Unlike supporters of Popular Front politics, who allied themselves with Russian Communism as a bulwark against the spread of the evil of Fascism, Lewis advocated appeasement of the Fascist dictatorships as a bulwark against the evil of Communism. Franco was for him (bizarrely) 'an ordinary old-fashioned anti-monarchical Spanish *liberal*' reacting against the interference of Russian Communism in his native land. Following on from his sympathetic exposition of Nazism and Hitler in the 1931 *Hitler* (written and published before the Nazis came to power), Lewis was by now regarded by the majority of British intellectuals as a Fascist apologist. This was a simplification, but not an altogether unfair one; Lewis didn't really begin to roll back his support until after a visit to Germany and Poland made just after *The Revenge for Love* was published in the summer of 1937.

The 1937 publication is misleading, however, for Lewis actually wrote the novel well before the Spanish Civil War – during late 1934 and 1935 – as the third in a three-book contract with Cassell. The publisher regarded the book as an embarrassment, however, and tried to persuade Lewis to take it to Jonathan Cape. The first of the contracted books, *Snooty Baronet*, another novel, had appeared in 1932, but its sales had been badly affected by Boots's and W.H. Smith's lending libraries' decision to buy only a few copies. It was too coarse and free in its expressions for their subscribers, they decided, and could not be placed on open shelves. Cassell submitted the manuscript of Lewis's new novel (at this stage entitled *False Bottoms*) to Boots for prior approval, and the publication delay was due to the long process of revision needed to satisfy their demands, as well as to Cassell's own desire to offload this politically embarrassing novel somehow. It could be argued that the novel was distorted more by this long delay than by the actual censorship, which mainly consisted in a toning down of some of the only mildly salacious detail of Jack Cruze's sexual fixation. So, although it was published in 1937, the novel does not take sides on the Spanish Civil War, but uses the Spain of 1934 as the place that reveals the real consequences of commitments, self-delusions and deceptions the characters take there from England. Some, but not all, of these commitments and deceptions are political.

In the course of detailing the lying tactics of the Communist Party in eliminating its rivals, George Orwell singled out a smear on the P.O.U.M. militia:

In the *New Republic* Mr Ralph Bates stated that the P.O.U.M. troops were 'playing football with the Fascists in no man's land' at a time when, as a matter of fact, the P.O.U.M. troops were suffering heavy casualties and a number of my personal friends were killed and wounded.

It was this same Ralph Bates (1899–2000), a cultured man and himself a novelist, who provided a model for one of the central characters in *The Revenge for Love*, the Communist 'agitator' Percy Hardcaster. In January 1935 he published two admiring articles about Lewis in *Time and Tide*, and the two men met. Lewis also read Bates's 1934 novel, *Lean Men*, which assisted him in his portrayal of Percy. The biographical note on the flap of the dustwrapper of the 1938 Penguin edition of Bates's novel speaks of the author's having engaged 'in the more colourful side of political life' while working as a docker in Barcelona before the Civil War (during which he was a 'Commissar of the International Brigade'). Percy's attitude to truth, his preparedness to embroider facts and issue lying propaganda in the service of the Communist cause, is signalled as an issue in the novel more than once, and we are told that 'in Percy's professional make-up he never quite knew what part of bluff went to what part of solid belief'. Percy begins the novel as a blustering, somewhat contemptible character, inclined to infantilism, for which he is punished by the loss of one of his legs. But our respect for him increases, not least because of his willingness to deliver a few 'home truths' about Communism to the upper-class party-member Gillian Phipps: 'if it ever comes to a showdown and if there's a bit of a shoot-up, it will be a matter of complete indifference to me *which* of you – whether you "Communist" intellectuals, you fancy *salon*-revolutionaries, you old-school-tie pinks, or on the other hand your fascist first-cousins – are wiped out'. Even these 'home-truths' have an element of bluff to them, however: plain speaker is at least partly just another role Percy adopts as occasion demands. But by the end of the novel he will begin to be aware of the cost of his posturing, and will act, for once, to help the innocent people he has led into danger. He is, in his way, a decent and humane man.

The falsity that runs through Percy's nature is by no means unique to him, however. As I have mentioned, Lewis's original title for the novel was *False Bottoms*, and in a variety of forms these are a recurrent motif, from the false-bottomed basket in which instructions for Percy's escape from a Spanish jail are hidden at the beginning of the story, to the false-bottomed bootlegger's car in which machine guns are supposed be smuggled into Spain at the end. Nothing is quite what it seems, or what it claims to be; the grounds on which anything purports to be real are always suspiciously hollow. This is, of course, a convenient scepticism for a satirist, and it can lead to an unattractive species of self-congratulation: everyone but the author is a foolish dupe or a malicious hypocrite. In this novel the pretensions of Communism, of Bloomsbury feminism, of Victorian chivalry and of any number of cultural constructions of nature and art are all shown to be false-bottomed. But Lewis the satirist is still enough of a modernist to realize that his universal scepticism also undermined any claim of his own to a privileged access to a reliable 'reality'. Besides, *The Revenge for Love* is far from being simply a satire, just as it is far from being merely a political thriller. It is an exploration, through imaginative narrative, of what 'the real' actually might be, and an attempt to find grounds for action and commitment of some kind when only provisional answers to such questions are available. As Lewis wrote in the publicity material on the dustwrapper of the 1952 reissue of the novel, 'if the events of the story are turbulent, that is, as it were, its outer crust. Its kernel is another matter. It has a metaphysical centre.'

This is not the place for an exposition of Lewis's metaphysics. It is perhaps enough simply to record the fact that this extraordinary man – novelist, cultural critic, modernist 'abstract' painter, portraitist and political theorist – actually had a worked-out metaphysical position on 'reality'. He had outlined it in a work of philosophical and cultural criticism, *Time and Western Man*, in 1927. But the metaphysical position he reached was not a secure one, and left the surface world of common sense – that world to which as a visual artist Lewis was committed – as a precarious construction masking a dangerous void: 'with bridle and bit we ride the phantoms of sense, as though to the manner born. Or . . . camped somnolently, in a relative repose of a god-like sort, upon the surface of this nihilism, we regard ourselves as at rest, with our droves of objects – trees, houses, hills – grouped round us,' he wrote in his conclusion. This 'nihilism', or the 'nothing' so often invoked in the narrative of *The Revenge for Love*, beneath the surface of ordinary life, constantly threatens to reveal itself and by doing so to reveal the fundamental absurdity of the human condition. As the word 'absurdity' indicates (it is Lewis's, used by him in one of the expository essays in his book of short stories, *The Wild Body*), laughter also – what *The Revenge* calls the 'screamingly funny' joke – affords a glimpse into this nothingness. The grotesque antics of the Spanish dwarf disconcert the sensitive Margot Stamp because they reveal to her her own strangeness and force her to recognize her own part in 'this system of roaring and spluttering bestial life of flesh and blood'.

Lewis's metaphysics are theoretically 'timeless', but he was more aware than most of the way that modern science, modern technologies and ideologies had played a crucial role in undermining the classical stability of the commonsense world he valued. In *The Revenge*, the man of action Victor Stamp becomes another kind of creature as he drives the bootlegger's car, transformed into an extension of the violent energies of the machine that rushes him on to a deadly encounter with the Civil Guard in the road before him, rifle raised. Margot, Victor's passenger, finds her perception of both herself and the outer world paralysingly undermined by the effects of speed. 'Time and space died yesterday!', exulted Lewis's old Futurist master, Filippo Tommaso Marinetti, celebrating the transforming experience of speed in fast motor-cars. But speed reveals to Margot what lies in wait beneath the surface, and she tells Victor 'I saw nothing. Yes, I saw that – at least I think I did.' Percy Hardcaster sees 'nothing', too, when he is subjected to a horrifyingly violent assault that reveals to him the absurd logic of human behaviour inflamed by 'natural' desire.

Margot is Victor's 'mate' (passing as his wife), and apart from her genuine passion for him is an imperfectly real product of the 'sham-culture outfit' her time has foisted on her, the '"highbrow" feminist fairyland' that is *A Room of One's Own*, for example, 'purchased for five shillings from the local Smith's'. Nevertheless she shares with her creator a Foucauldian or Nietzschean consciousness that arguments about what is 'real' are not simply harmless academic matters. Some people have the power to define what reality is, and thereby have power over others who are denied power themselves. Margot and Victor are two such powerless people, driven by economic injustice to participate in criminal activities. At the nightmarish party given in honour of Percy Hardcaster (the wounded

Communist hero returned in triumph from Spain), Margot senses the hostile manoeuvrings that are taking place behind the false panelling of the room:

> It was *their* reality, that of Victor and herself, that was marked down to be discouraged and abolished, and it was *they* that the others were trying to turn into phantoms and so to suppress. It was a mad notion, but it was just as if they had engaged in a battle of wills, to decide who should possess most *reality* – just as men fought each other for money, or fought each other for food.

Simply by being flesh and blood Margot has to participate in such struggles – indeed much of her energy at the party is expended on securing food for Victor. But the novel seems to intimate that she also represents a reality and value that originate outside the power struggle that victimizes her. She is, in fact, partly a victim because she does represent a value that transcends flesh and blood, and that is resented by malicious swindlers who themselves are rendered slightly unreal by their lack of it. Margot is throughout associated with images of birds, which for Lewis are symbolic of the non-bodily soul. For Victor there is something supernatural in her ability to outstrip his car and flag him down near his Spanish destination despite his having left on his gunrunning expedition before her: 'She must have chartered an aeroplane! For how had she done it, if not by air? Or she must have arrived like the Egyptian symbol of the psyche'. Margot has a 'second self', Victor realizes. Bird-like symbols of the psychic double, the *ka*, are depicted in several of Lewis's paintings of the thirties. It is in this non-material dimension that Margot's unconditional love for Victor has its origin. And it is upon this love that the false masters of material reality will have their revenge.

Paul Edwards, 2003

A NOTE ON THE TEXT

The Revenge for Love was subject to considerable censorship before publication. But Lewis usually revised his work extensively at proof stage, so it is not always possible to establish the reason for differences between the published text and surviving manuscripts and typescripts (the disappearance of the proofs also adds to difficulties). There are two options for a reissued text, therefore: reproduce the text that the author finally allowed to appear under his name, or attempt to reconstruct a text that is as close to his intentions as can be conjectured from the available evidence. This latter is the route taken by Reed Way Dasenbrock in his invaluable edition for Black Sparrow Books (Santa Rosa, 1991). But this text must remain to some extent conjectural, and needs to be read alongside the table of variants and editorial justifications that Dasenbrock supplies. Anyone wishing to make a full academic study of *The Revenge for Love* and its history of composition cannot afford to ignore Dasenbrock's work (nor that of Linda Sandler in her unpublished University of Toronto PhD thesis, '*The Revenge for Love* by Wyndham Lewis', 1974). The aim of this Penguin Modern Classics edition is simpler: to make Lewis's novel available again in as accessible a form as possible to a new readership. For this purpose the text as Lewis originally published it and reissued it in 1952 is still the most suitable and is therefore the one followed here, with minor corrections of printing errors.

PART I

THE CIVIL GUARD

Chapter 1

'CLARO,' said the warder, 'Claro, hombre!' It was the condescension of one caballero to another. His husky voice was
modulated upon the principle of an omniscient rationality.
When he spoke, he spoke from the bleak, socratic peak of his
wisdom to another neighbouring peak – equally equipped with
the spotless panoply of logic. Deep answered to deep – height
hurled back its assent to height! 'Claro, hombre!' he repeated,
tight-lipped, with the controlled passion of the great logician.
'We are never free to choose – because we are only free once in
our lives.'

'And when is that?' inquired the prisoner.

'That is when at last we gaze into the bottom of the heart of
our beloved and find that it is false – like everything else in the
world!'

His prisoner laughed.

'You have been unfortunate, that is evident!'

'Claro, hombre!' argued back the haughty voice, indulgent
and unperturbed. 'Like everybody else.'

'That is too sweeping, Don Alvaro, is it not? Not *everybody*!'

'Si, señor! Everybody.'

There was a flash in Don Alvaro's eye that made it clear that
on certain points he would, as between gaolbird and gaoler,
brook no contradiction. The prisoner bowed his head.

'I must disagree with you, Don Alvaro, in one matter,' he
said, after a conciliatory breathing-space. 'Men are free more
than once in their lives. There *are* other occasions!'

'No, señor. Once and no more. Only one thing can set them
free, and that only for a moment. Free, to kill – or to forgive!'

There were two crashes in rapid succession, a third, and then
an outbreak of demoniacal cries. The Andalusian evening shed
down its brilliant operatic light upon the just and the unjust

alike. At a long table in the centre of the large concreted patio sat a dozen unjust men. Twelve of the most unjust in Spain, at the moment. They were unsuccessful politicos. They had been caught red-handed, with arms in their hands. Now they were awaiting trial – while other politicos, those who had triumphed over them, disputed in the Cortes Constituentes, Ateneo, and elsewhere, as to what was the best thing to do with them – whether it was a case for the firing-squad or for a magnificent Spanish pardon – should they be convicted, when at last they were brought to trial. They played cards, sweated and spat. Their furious shouts, harshened by extreme catarrh, as they crashed Joker and King down upon the table, alarmed the pigeons patrolling the skyline of Baltic-blue over their heads – who made themselves into perambulating fans, to receive the coolness of the evening breezes into their overheated wing-pits, their button eyes cocked towards the remote sierra, from whence the coolness came in irregular bursts of gently-flowing air.

'*All things are lawful for me, but all things are not expedient!*' the prisoner remarked, in passable Spanish, rolling a cigarette.

'What is that?' asked the startled warder. It was the 'me' in this half-muttered saying that principally excited his attention, as if some personal claim to a lawless immunity had been advanced.

'You want chapter and verse? It is from the epistle to the Corinthians.' The prisoner, however, as he spoke, gave a wary look over at the ruffled dignitary, who was stretched out in the shade of the cloister, his eyes hidden by the peak of his military cap.

'What is that?' Don Alvaro asked stupidly.

'The Apostle Paul.'

'The Apostle Paul?'

The prisoner nodded. Don Alvaro pushed back his cap. Stuck up upon one gaunt elbow, he planted himself more firmly yet, and socratically inflating himself, a finger wagging, he exclaimed in his deepest organ-tones, vibrant with rich expostulation:

'No, señor!' He paused and drew in through his nose enough air for a full-dress exordium. 'No, señor!' His eyes flashed with all the calmly-embattled rationality of the Castilian, as well as the didactic dignity of the prison-guard. 'All things, señor, are *not* lawful. You cannot say that! All things are not lawful – it is impossible to say that. You are not free to put *expediency* in the place of *law*!'

'You can!' the prisoner replied, against his better judgment. 'Although it may not always be expedient!' he added, and he grinned over in a friendly way, soliciting a cynical English laugh from the argumentative mask of authority before him. It was not forthcoming.

The warder was on his mettle. As proud as Lucifer in this particular, where his rational prowess was concerned, he was now thoroughly ruffled. He looked haughtily at the English convict, and spat before replying.

'Señor Hardcastér!' he announced (*ar-car-stair* was his pronunciation), with a threatening look upwards at the seated Briton. 'It is *never* expedient to replace law by anything else! We live by law – where should we be without law?'

'We live by law – that is true.' But the prisoner allowed his gaze to rest upon the limb of the law with a shade too heavy a burlesque significance, and Don Alvaro blinked like an offended owl before continuing:

'Bueno, bueno!' at last he retorted, with the dignity of the sphinx. 'But remember that anyone – *anyone*, Don Percy – dispenses with law at his peril. He substitutes his private law for the law of man only if he is mad. And the mad always end by being put under lock and key – whether here or in England, it is all one.'

The prisoner lowered his eyes, and bowed his head.

'Now I've torn it!' he said to himself. 'Hell!'

But a spirit of contradiction seemed to be possessing this caged man, and he reared his head pugnaciously, holding the official with a blue and vicious eye.

'In England the law is not the same as it is here in Spain,' he said, in a somewhat schoolmasterly manner – that of laying down the law with a backward class. 'There is a certain amount of justice in my country. Not much. But they do *pretend*.'

Don Alvaro pulled himself abruptly up into a sitting position, and then, recognizing that this was inadequate, he rose to his feet stiffly, with the movement of a lanky cat. Fixing an angry eye upon this English malefactor – who murdered in the name of foreign freedom, with the help of foreign funds – he exclaimed with considerable violence:

'Señor Hardcastér, *haga usted el favor de no faltarme!*' He ran his tongue along his lip as if along the gummed edge of a cigarette paper. 'If, sir, the laws of your country suit you so much better than the laws of Spain, why do you come here at all? We did not ask you to. You have received no invitation from us. Your sort is not the sort we are most anxious to have amongst us. We can well do without your sort of Englishman, allow me to inform you of that! *Englishmen* means nothing to us! And if you behave here as if *all things are lawful* for you, you must expect what you get. And, let me promise you, it will not be particularly pleasant! It will be a *mal negocio* for you, believe me, Señor Hardcastér, to attempt to impose your laws upon us!'

'But, Don Alvaro, I did not mean to offend you – I was speaking to you as man to man.'

'*Basta!* I am not a fool. We understand one another!'

And scouring his throat, to the remotest mucinous crypt – a bloodshot eye still bracketed upon the red moon-face in front of him – he spat, the dust spouting beneath the percussion of the saliva, as if it had been a bullet, half-way between himself and the lawbreaking *inglés* – that 'Don Percy' of just now, but of never again, for he washed his hands of the English too!' – the sullied English, the New White-trash of post-war Britain – bearers, yes, of His Britannic Majesty's passports, and sheltered everywhere by their *shameless* consuls (*sin vergüenza – sin honor!*) but whose name was mud for all true men!

He stalked away along the ambulatory, his lips moving as if in prayer; but such litanies as are appropriate probably to the celebration of the Black Mass, not to the offices of the catholic and apostolic church.

His face as he left him was not a reassuring sight for the British prisoner – for *any* prisoner, however privileged, with however many well-paid consuls at his beck and call (without shame, and without honour!)

When level with the card-players, Don Alvaro flung at them

10

one glance for form's sake, as if to show that he had taken note that a dozen toads were engaged in a game of chance, but that, not being a naturalist, it was no business of his: immediately he averted his face, darkling but impotent, in all its grandiose lines and ascetic pits and hollows, as tanned as the Berber – for Don Alvaro knew he could do nothing to spoil their sport. They had the whip-hand of the mere janitor. Their sport must go on. What matter! He spat – a narrow shave for two prisoners who were huddled in the shade, like corpses parked upon the roadside in the fields of battle. There were handkerchiefs over their faces to keep off the flies. (They were part of the recent capture – they had a hundred of them here.)

These sham politicos, what a burden for the shoulders of an honest servant of the law! The Spanish pistolero was not innocent until he had been found guilty, or any humbug like that (if indeed it were true for English law and assuming the unworthy Don Percy had not been lying), but *that* made no difference. A politician must always give himself airs (*como no!*), even when held for homicide. All crimes of politics were potentially condoned as soon as committed – by *other* politicos of whatever colour, who understood that their own skins might not always be safe and so were quick to pardon, and every ruffian knew it – who shed blood or robbed the bank, or bombed a passer-by! And if he was shut up for a spell, to show him he'd lost the *parti*, why, everyone understood that the fellow would soon be out again and ruling some fat roost or other to his own great profit, and to its undoing – there was no help for *that* in Catholic Spain! So *that* one over there – that squinting deathshead of a man in a crimson shirt, open at his throat to allow his Adam's apple to jump up and down at will, as if it were some petted parasite domiciled in his gullet – bald except for a black patch over his left ear, like the last irregular tatter of a moth-eaten carpet – a week's blue piratic stubble to give his eating-hole a coloured border like a sink – *he* who had sawed up a Jesuit and sold his lights for catsmeat – he was as much at home as if in the patio of a seaside casino during *el veraneo* – the devil incarnate! – and there he was now clapping his dirty hands for another bottle of the best Rioja, the shameless assassin – as if that were a waiter and not a warder!

11

'*Pobre España! Pobre España!*' muttered Don Alvaro in his black moustache – rolling from one side to the other, once, his big, faithful and fierce, toffee-black eyes, for his private satisfaction. And as he turned in at the door that led to his official quarters, he turned his head, and glanced once in the direction from which he had come.

The English prisoner still sat smoking, his big red forearms sticking out along his stumpy thighs. He was chatting with another warder at present, who had come up as soon as his superior had taken himself off – Serafín, a subordinate of whose principles Don Alvaro was unable to approve – a Catalan importation, a good-for-nothing, a dog from a city of dogs! Saliva shot from under Don Alvaro's moustache, back over his shoulder, a parting salute for all that was gathered there – as he stood a moment, with his head reversed.

Forgetting what he was lately doing, Don Alvaro reflected how these foreigners enjoyed much honour under the Spanish sun, and were much talked with as if they were of some importance – por Dios! This was a new outrage – that all these foreigners should have been admitted into the domestic politics of Spain, upon equal terms or worse – given a carte-blanche to kill! Always he had respected the English, from afar. A great nation, of portentously rich caballeros! But here was a new sort of Englishman, of a darker and dirtier feather! *That* it was important to get fixed in one's head – the confederate of Russian and German gunmen – a rat who hid in archways and shot a man in the back, or sniped the officers of the law from roofs and ran away down the skylights and wastepipes. A new sewer variety of the English kind. Odd – or perhaps not! – that England should go the way of Spain. Two countries with a splendid past, of piratic achievement, of glorious blood and gluts of gold – yes, two countries going rotten at the bottom and at the top, where the nation ceased to be a nation – the inferior end abutting upon the animal kingdom, the upper end merging in the international abstractness of men – where there was no longer either Spanish men or English men, but a gathering of individuals who were *nothing*.

Don Alvaro's high and gaunt shoulders levitated a fraction with an airy disdain at the thought of the bottlenecked breed that had taken the place of the races of great gentlemen. And he saw the bottlenecked thickness of Señor Hardcastér, the New Briton of his bilious fancy. He had been willing, yes, to converse with the pink English rat in a way that he would not have consented to do with a compatriot, fed with Red Russian gold. *Mala gente* of the pestiferous Red Syndics. He muttered to himself maledictions as he trod the stone passages. *Pobre España!* went up his customary sigh. He was an ex-Civil Guard, of that legion of incorruptible police-soldiers. He had never taken money, where everyone else (except his fellow Guards) took money as backsheesh. He had belonged to a great kid-gloved military élite, with power to shoot all suspect citizens at sight, after a formal challenge. Once that, always that! One does not change. *Basta!* One does not become as other men once one has been *that*.

Chapter 2

THERE was no sound in this part of the prison. Don Alvaro passed the armoury. The door stood ajar. He closed it with an angry bang – which reverberated like the faint roar of a bomb out among the card-players: causing one to wink his eye at another and remark, as he slammed down a court-card, 'Vultures of Franco's! Have they followed us here? Take cover!'

Farther down the corridor was another door, this one standing wide open. Stopping again, Don Alvaro thrust in his head, remaining half in and half out. It led into a square, vault-like hall, of formidable size, and very dark. He suffered his eyes to travel round from spot to spot, as the bull's-eye of a careful constable is flashed impartially upon all the house-fronts in a street in turn. Don Alvaro was satisfying the habit of prying round and spying out, nothing but that. It was the hunting instincts of his calling. And that was the reason for his head being on one side of the door and his heels on the other, the feet ready to rush forward across the threshold, or the head to dart back, as occasion might require.

13

It was the hall that he had stopped to inspect, a section of which was a cage – where the prisoners might be interviewed by visiting friends and relations, conversed with through bars like dangerous wild animals. At present it was deserted.

At the farther extremity of this reception hall was a door which led out into the street. It was the door at which the visitors presented themselves, at the appointed time, and it was now open. There was nothing against its being open; the hall had to be ventilated, and no outsider could trespass beyond the massive bars of the cage. The street without was a panel of solid sunlight. Slowly into this panel a figure moved. It was a peasant girl, and she passed across the luminous panel and out again at the farther side, carrying a large basket.

Idle but attentive, his eye fastened upon this lazily moving object, Don Alvaro studied the profiled countenance, as you watch an advertisement flashed upon a safety-curtain before the beginning of a play. Since it is presented to you, you lend it your attention – all is grist to the mill of the senses, there is nothing that is refused in a vacant mind.

The girl was nothing. She was a mountain-girl. *Una serrana de la sierra! Somewhere* he had encountered her, however. It was curious that he knew her at once. But *where?* – for a crowd of images reported before him, but no identification resulted from the parade. So *interrogation-mark* against the passing girl as a matter of course. That was necessary, for everything must be accounted for; and things that could not account for themselves at sight were suspect. So down went the question-mark, against the young peasant X – of the female sex – belonging to the *pueblo* X – passing the *carcel* upon her lawful (or unlawful) occasions, at such and such an hour of the day.

The girl did not see *him* – girls see *nothing*. They go through life as blind as bats, except for the Man their bed is waiting for. Old prison-warders lost in the deep shadows of a jail they have no eyes for, *claro!* – that would be absurd.

But as the result of her ignorance of his presence, it was suggested to his mind that he had this figure *under observation*. To resist the suggestiveness inherent in seeing without being seen – that was not to be expected of a cop. So – attempting to place his passing hill-girl, in her flowered party-shawl – Don Alvaro withdrew noiselessly from the door.

Very thoughtfully proceeding on his way, Don Alvaro bit the extremities of his pungent moustache, flavoured with garlic and rank Spanish tobacco. He drew in his breath with a gastronomic hiss, exercising suction upon the resistant bristles, which (arched inwards like a system of black fishbones) made a glossy sheath for his lip. He frowned, sternly reflective. A face – a face – that called up something! Of no importance. What were the things faces called up, or that were called up by faces? That was it. It was the sort of thing this face attempted to call up – it was perhaps the sort of *people*. An unimportant puzzle, that taxed his recording machinery, like a question of mislaid finger-prints. However, hammer at this little enigma as he would, it remained a little jigsaw of a profile – sticking out there in the bright panel of sunlit emptiness, defying identification. The angles of it fitted nothing that mattered. But they stood out all the more in consequence. He was at a loss. He tasted his moustache; and the taste was bitter.

Strolling forward along the passage, Don Alvaro had reached the street door which terminated it. Inside it he stood still. What was this? He recalled himself to the significance of what he did: instead of turning off to the right, he had continued in a straight line. Like an animal! *Claro, como las bestias!* He smiled – his moustache left his mouth as he did so, and resumed its customary military sweep towards the extremities of the jaw. But accepting the logic, such as it was, of these streetward movements of his, with an amused grimace, he turned the handle of the door, and stepped out.

The lofty domestic wall upon the opposite side of the street, or lane, might have been in Fez or Cairo, for in intention it postulated an Asiatic secrecy. Its architect had thought in terms of the harem! The lazaret was immediately opposite the spot where he stood. As if to advertise its identity a bloodstained bandage lolled like a red tongue out of one of its ventilation slits. Don Alvaro looked up at it. The blood of Pedro Casas! He had gone in that morning. A *cuchillada* in the shoulder – a nothing. He would be back in a week. Don Alvaro, bending from his hips, spat into the dismantled gutter, in which there was a trickle of thick yellow water.

Then he looked up the street, in the direction taken by the peasant girl with the basket.

She had gone some distance, and now had almost reached the confines of the prison, where a larger street passed at right angles, down which once an hour ran, with the clatter of a cash-box down a rock-studded declivity, an electric tram, out to the first village of the *campo* and back. She was walking very slowly: she was walking with the orthodox majesty of the women of those unspoilt districts – their skulls flattened with heavy pitchers – with a hieratic hip-roll that bore her away no quicker than a tortoise showing off its speed at the mating season. And it was plain enough she had time to burn, apart from that.

She and Don Alvaro were the only people in sight. Don Alvaro spat and waited for a few more revolutions of the hips to bring this slowly-ploughing traditional vessel of Old Spain (built to accommodate, in capacious quarters, the fiery man-child down below, and at the same time several pints of water up on top – incubator and caryatid at once) to the tramlined thoroughfare for which it was headed.

At the corner this slowly trampling contraption turned, on its own centre, with a sultry swirl of the skirt, and started to walk back. Then she stopped. Don Alvaro continued to look at her. She started to advance again: when, as if thinking better of it, she came to another halt; but less abruptly, as if in some hesitation as to whether to go forward or not.

Don Alvaro signalled to her with his head, peremptorily, to come down to him. To come down at once! And, slowly as before, she began to move forward, her eyes fixed upon the chief warder now – with a movement that was suggestive of some dance of courtship in a primitive ballet: the reluctant, bashful, and voluptuous approach of the bride.

Without taking his eyes off her, his hands clipped in upon his meagre hips, his back as stiff as pasteboard, he awaited her without movement. With the woman, as with the bull, atavism steps in – the repertoire of attitudes, for the male waits upon prescriptive technicalities, more especially in these lands that

16

have been touched by the sloth of Asia. Don Alvaro, of the stuff of which Spanish wife-killers and bullfighters were made – before mattresses were strapped under the mount of the picador or women plucked from the conjugal shambles by transatlantic sex-ethics – Don Alvaro was not the man to conduct himself as if a woman were a boxer in petticoats, or to depart from the strict male canon. And, right foot advanced, the angle of the instep at ninety degrees, his pose was a model for just such a dumb show, and was worthy of those studied sideway-tosses of the oncoming hips – though it was at her eyes he looked, as you look at the eyes and nothing else of the oncoming bull. Her eyes were lowered – they were milk-blue slits. She might have been a concubine of Tachefin's. She might have been reporting for some misdeed, at the tent of her overlord, in the deserts of the Niger.

As she had drawn nearer, he had begun examining her features with attention. Suddenly a light broke upon Don Alvaro's mind. A slight smile came into his face. It was very slight, and very unfriendly.

With a nervous smiling grimace and a flash of white animal teeth, the girl came up; nodding her head up and down at him, as if to say, 'Well, well! So at last we meet!' muttering *'Buenos dias!'* Having wished her good day, he pointed at the basket.

'For one of the prisoners?' he inquired.

'For one of the prisoners!' she smiled. 'I was a little early.'

'So you were walking up and down?'

'Yes, up and down a little!'

Her eyes, when she opened them, gushed, with a massive coquetry – her 'up and down a little!' was charged with the full weight of the walking-exhibition which she called 'little' only to tease with a palpable understatement; and she drooped two fans of inkblack lashes down upon her cheeks, and heaved a sigh to provoke her bosom into voluptuous action.

'Why didn't you sit down on the basket?' he asked. 'Anything precious inside it, may one ask?'

'Nothing! Food!'

She wailed *'Comestibles!'* at him as if she loathed to disabuse him and refer to anything so vile, before a strange caballero like himself.

17

'Who is it for? Señor Hardcastér? I have seen you before. You bring him provisions every day.'

'Every day!' she echoed him mournfully – no day passed but what she bore this heavy basket, full of mere provisions, to this ill-omened spot!

'Very well.' Don Alvaro stroked a moustache. 'Very well.' He looked meditatively down at the basket.

'Here – come in a moment,' he said, turning towards the door of the visiting hall. 'Come in here.'

The girl hesitated.

'In there?'

'Follow me!' he ordered, wheeling round on her and changing his tone with the suddenness of a thunderbolt, fixing her with the irascible eye of the law. 'At once!'

'I come!' she said, shrugging her shoulders to herself. '*Vaya!* I come!'

A frightened contraction of the brows showed that these events were not to the taste of this sauntering girl of the people. But she followed him into the gaol-hall.

Seating himself upon a table, in the absence of a chair, Don Alvaro held out his hand for the basket, his index finger pointing at it. She handed it to him slowly, and he placed it upon the table beside him.

Lifting the napkin, which protected the contents from dust or insects, lazily he withdrew, one after the other, the objects within, and placed them in a row upon the table – a melon, *cerveza*, bread, a cold fowl. Having done this, he stared into the empty basket for some moments without moving. Then he thrust a hand into it, and picked with a fingernail at the bottom. Noticing a wicker strand that stood up a little from the surface, he pulled upon it, and the bottom of the basket came away in his hand. He lifted it out. Leaning over, he peered in once more, subjecting it to official inspection, but careful at first not to disturb what was there.

'Ha! What is this?'

'*Por Dios, hombre!* How should I know? How can I tell?'

'No? There is a false bottom to your basket. A peculiar basket to bring to prisoners.'

'I have never seen such a basket – it has a false bottom! I do

18

not know what to think. It is not as I thought it to be! It has two bottoms in place of one!'

'Even so! Two instead of one!'

The eyes of the girl were stretched open, staring with insane fixity at this extraordinary man – as if he next might be expected to accuse her of sporting bogus pockets or having *caches* in her shawl. Her eyes would never shut again, they were so distended, so as to miss nothing that fate might have in store with such a man as this. Tears, collecting under the lids, ran down her face unnoticed.

'What have we here, señorita? Foreign newspapers, I see. Excellent. And here – a letter. For Señor Hardcastér. It is most interesting. A letter too!'

Packed tightly at the bottom had been three foreign newspapers; and as Don Alvaro had lifted them out a sealed envelope had fallen to the floor. Opening this, he took out a typewritten note, and held it up against the light. Beneath the plausible typescript might lurk other messages, or faint markings to pick out a code. The girl followed his every action with the same fixed dramatic alarm.

With dignity he desisted from his scrutiny of the sheet of paper against the light, and spread it out beside him, upon the table, proceeding to the more prosaic inspection of what was visible to the naked eye, and relatively straightforward.

Por Dios! what tongue was this? Doubtless the English, seeing its destination. Don Alvaro held it sideways – it might give up its secrets, at an unaccustomed angle. Por Dios! What a barbarous tongue! He spat on the floor in protest at this jargon.

The note consisted of a half-dozen typewritten lines. But there were several words which Don Alvaro could understand. There was, for instance, 'Serafín', and there were the words 'Paseo' and 'Calle Pimentel'. And there was '12.30'. Serafín was the name of the young Catalan warder with whom the English prisoner had been in conversation as he had left the courtyard. And as to the Calle Pimentel, that was a street which led out of El Paseo. And 12.30, it must be supposed, was 12.30 in every tongue.

Taking a strapped notebook from his hip-pocket, Don Alvaro copied out, letter by letter, the contents of the typed note.

19

Having done so, he replaced the note, without its envelope, between the two uppermost newspapers; and returning its false bottom to the basket, pushed it down forcibly into place. When satisfied that it was as neatly adjusted as before he had disturbed it, he replaced the other things, one at a time, and last of all the napkin.

'Bueno!' he said.

'Bueno!' came in despairing echo from the staring peasant, one of whose hands, clutching a corner of her shawl, had been twisting tighter and tighter around the fingers of her other hand – bandaging the intact flesh against all the threats of disintegration, which hovered in this stormy and electric air.

Don Alvaro could not have moved more slowly off the table had he been demonstrating some exercise to a slow-witted beginner in gymnastics: first he uncrossed his legs with a languorous slowness that suspended the leg he was thus translating for an appreciable accretion of seconds in mid-air; and he dropped it down beside the other with as much deliberation – as much inch by inch – as if the floor which was to receive it had been a hot brick, or an uncomfortable icicle. And he rose to his feet with a studied indifference to speed that would have done credit to the most pompous contortionist, recovering the upright position after having turned himself successfully into a human corkscrew.

'Listen with great attention, señorita, to what I shall say!'

The girl could have done nothing to convey a greater attentiveness than already was pictured in her staring eyes, at the full stretch of mesmerized alarm. She clutched the basket to her slowly heaving waist-line and waited, with perhaps an extra dash of dismayed stupidity upon her dusky face.

'Listen with great attention!' His voice took on the argumentative modulation of the indulgent lecturer – a master of his subject, resolved that no pains shall be spared to make his omniscience accessible to the most benumbed intellect which could possibly be brought up against him by the perverse destiny that delights to obstruct the path of the teacher. 'When the time comes – when the time shall arrive, señorita, to go in, go in as usual! Go in just as you have on former occasions. Just as before. As upon former occasions, go in as if nothing –

20

you understand *nothing* – had passed! Understand – nothing!'

No understanding at all was betrayed in the glazed expression of settled alarm upon the young peasant's face, thrust more and more forward in the direction of her captor.

'Go in as usual and deliver this into the hands of Señor Hardcastér – without comment, you hear me! Not a word – not a look! I shall be observing you all the time. Nothing you do will escape me. Do not attempt to communicate to him what has happened. You will be sorry for it if you do. I can promise you, you will regret it, señorita! You have heard what I say? It is enough!'

He had taken a step towards her as he had warned her of the consequences of a omission to observe his instructions, raising a flat hand in the air as if in the act to strike her. A moan that was half a growl breaking from her crimson lips, she had stepped back, bowing her head, but still sustaining his threatening gaze – the big arabesques of her expressionless eyes revolving upwards as her head sank, beneath tightly knitted brows. Large tears detached themselves, and crashed down her cheeks.

'To weep is excellent!' Don Alvaro exclaimed harshly. 'But it is better still not to lend oneself to things that must result in tears – and worse! Far worse! Tears are nothing. See that you do not do anything that will bring upon you *worse* than tears!'

The tears flowed faster, but her eyes did not wink.

'When you have delivered this, return to me here. If I am not here, wait for me outside.'

'Sí, señor!' came the girl's husky response.

'Wait for me here, or outside.'

'It is understood, señor. Here or outside. I shall be here.'

'It is better outside.'

'Outside it shall be.'

'Before you go I will take down your name. Where you live, too. Where is it?'

He opened the notebook again. She gave him a name. Josefa de la Asunción, and an address, in a pueblo.

'Now go. Do as I have told you! Or you will suffer for it! Go!'

Occupying the centre of the large sunless hall, there stood

21

the bright panel of the street, at their backs, as it had been when he had first caught sight of her. Painfully had the male will made its way into her body, compelled with all the potency of Spanish eyes, taking over all its nervous centres with an iron control. Her eyes still stared, with their hypnotic animal glaze. And now like a sleepwalker the girl wheeled in front of him, as if in ceremonial dumbshow; and the great clockwork hips, setting up their sleepy swaying, in a stately slowtime march bore her out of the hall. She entered the panel of sunlight, almost blotting it out for a moment as she passed into it. Don Alvaro watched her with the grave approval of the *aficionado*. If women had been collected into herds like bulls, she would have belonged to a great herd, beyond question! So he felt about it. He felt he could trust this instrument, upon which he had played – *como no!* – as a master, and dismissed it to its fatal tasks full of the awful music of his deep implacable voice, to subdue it to his will.

Once more the-girl-of-the-panel, Josefa de la Asunción, wheeled to the right, and the last rhythmic agitation of her skirt had in another moment, as she moved off, been plucked out of sight.

Chapter 3

THE warder who had stepped over to where the English prisoner was sitting was sallow and young. He was ten years or more the junior of Percy Hardcaster, and he had come up with his left eye squinting and winking at once, a cigarette drooping from his teeth. His mouth was depressing. His underlip hung down limply in front of his chin, as if permanently put out of action by a homeric cold in the head. As a result the red beef of the lower gum was generally in evidence. The gums were not good, they were ugly scarlet roots. A small mustard moustache lay dankly upon his upper lip. His lower face was in a decline in fact, as everything about it slumped. But his amber eyes sparkled with confident effrontery – that of a pragmatical *chulo*, ready to match his wits against the world – which

22

was not much anyway, *estúpido* from pole to pole! So he was
ready for it, with much *cafard*, with much hispano-gallic Bar-
celoneta *phlegm*. And his father in Perpignan was the same as
himself, only with more *cafard* and if anything more phlegmatic.

'*Qué pasa?*' he inquired, slightly amused. '*Qué pasa?* What
is the trouble?'

'*Nada, nada!*' the prisoner crossly and shortly snapped back,
staring at the ground – *not* amused. Very much the reverse of
amused! Don Percy was exceedingly displeased with himself
for having succumbed to an impulse of romantic aggressive-
ness. He saw the sort of mistake he had made, and he knew the
reason that caused him to make, on occasion, that order of
damfool mistake. A weakness he had to watch out for very
much, that! He had driven off his principal gaoler in an alarming huff. It was definitely worrying. His big fat face of bold
baby-scarlet – with the soft fretful pleats of the teething-time,
and a portentous pianist's frown of the bib-and-bottle epoch on
top of that – scowled at Serafín, who continued to be amused:
he even shook lazily with a little dry laughter, a very little,
mirthless and thin.

'Are you *de puntas* with the chief now, Don Percy?'

'I'm on bad terms with no one except myself!' Don Percy
answered forcibly. The great man had failed him – Percy was
not the man to spare Percy! Him least of all! Spare the rod
and spoil the child! And Percy was always the schoolmaster,
with himself as with others.

'With *yourself*, Don Percy!' mocked the warder softly. 'With
your *self*!'

'Yes, with Don Percy!' violently answered the great English
sindicalista. 'Very angry indeed.'

The young turnkey, indulgent always to this big fat English
kid of forty, in the Revolution game – his charge for ten days
past – looked down at him, contemptuously amused, leaning
against a buttress of the cloister, his arms folded on his chest.

'Have you been talking politics with Don Alvaro? Have you
done somethng to offend this old fool?'

'I hope not. I did not intend to.'

'I thought I heard your voice, Don Percy – it was raised I
thought. You were annoyed?'

'No, mine wasn't raised. He is a little cross. I said some damfool thing that's put the old devil's back up.'

'Oh, is that it? That's not much. What did you say?'

'Nothing. I passed a remark or two about the rotten laws of this rotten country, if you want to know!'

Serafín laughed at the vehemence of his spoilt child of a charge, as he saw he was expected to, and shrugged his shoulders.

'That can't be helped, hombre! Don't worry about *that*.'

'I hear what you say. But I am very much annoyed with myself. Very.'

'No matter. He is nobody. Why worry?'

'He will be apt to be troublesome now.'

'It is nothing.'

'He will be keeping his eye on me.'

Serafín sneered, turned away and spat.

'He keeps his eye on everybody! It is nothing,' he said.

'Perhaps. But I should have been more cautious.'

'You won't be here much longer.'

'That may be. Or it may not.'

Serafín shrugged disdainfully.

'You leave that to us, Don Percy!'

He parted with a terrific wink, displaying his full complement of teeth, which could bodily have gone into a dental museum as a model of superb caries, and which suggested, in some roundabout manner, all the comforts and advantages of extreme corruption of a *moral* order as well.

'Don Alvaro will be none the wiser!' he said. 'He will wake up one morning and find the bird has flown.'

'So.' Percy was dubious as to this slick flight of the caged bird in question.

'What can he do?' Serafín inquired in querulous disdain.

'All right. You had better not be seen talking to me too much, Serafín. He looked back at us just now.'

'That is nothing! He can do nothing. He is nobody – he is an old fool. *Guardia civil* – ah-ha!'

'He's a lynx-eyed old devil.'

'Bat-eyed – bat-eyed! He couldn't see his own navel at midday – he'd think it was a pockmark!'

'I should have buttered him up more, Serafín. I have been a fool.'

Don Percy got up and stamped, as his fat legs stuck to the trousers on these hot afternoons. He was so much the picture of blond Midland well-being – so stocky and sturdy, with his little walrus moustache – that he was such a figure as might be seen any day in a roadmenders' squad in some English city tarring a road or working a rockdrill: though his lobster-red suggested a hotter sun than that of the 34th meridian. In his shirt-sleeves, his stout arms bare to the elbow, with silver-rimmed spectacles, large feet, he was conspicuous among the Spanish prisoners – a British navvy turned Marxist school-master: and as he took a few steps out now into the sunlit court several voices exclaimed at once:

Chorus of Terrorists

'Olé – Percilito!'
'Percy, chico, ven acá!'
'Mira – Percilito!'

*

Complacently breasting this spontaneous ovation – for which his private qualities as well as Britannia were plainly respon-sible – this little plump miniature lion that had crept out of the belly of the big stuffed British Lion whose roar rattles the Seven Seas, strolled forward, his two brick-red paws stuffed into his trouser-pockets. The card-players with their backs to the popular Percy had all turned round as they heard he was coming. The red-shirted priest-butcher caught him round the waist as he came up, and drew him in against the table with profuse proletarian affection – hugging him low and leering up in a flattersome fashion at this man-of-action whose govern-ment possessed Gibraltar.

'Play!'
'Take a hand!'
'Sit down, old Percy!'

Don Percy basked without speaking for three or four minutes in this comradely crepitation. Shaking his head – his eyes half-closed, an indulgent-superior simper upon his sun-flushed face, he declined, with carefully disinfected dignity, all offers to drink, join them at cards, or sit down and commune. Dragging himself with gentle violence and sweet force away from the cordial gang of high-minded hold-up experts, with a sturdy little buttock-swagger he moved off, continuing on his way to the *excusado*.

Percy's standing would have gratified any man in the Left-wing game – he stood high with all these eminent Partymen of the Peninsula. He was one of them. He was looked up to as an organizer of parts, a man of good party-brains. And they knew he did not funk a shot or two on the quiet, at need. They had all heard how he had potted at a tax-collector from a tree-top. He had told them. He was the only Spanish 'gunman' who had come out of Edgbaston. And there was no bourgeois shame or uncivilized modesty about old Percy – he betrayed a robust disregard for civilized decorum while yet far short of the place for which he was making.

When Percy left the 'Excuse-me' and came out into the courtyard again (same sterling disregard of convention as on going in!) the scene had changed. There was a stir. The comrades of the card-table were standing up and stretching: a dozen or more less outstanding comrades who were not of this potential junta of the élite were crowding out into the court-yard, as chickens start to swarm in a chicken-run on the arrival of the figure with the bird-seed. The rank and file, such as were not in the class of politicos – not the speech makers but the journeymen *saboteurs*, the true gunmen – were confined more strictly in crowded cells, sustained on bread and soup.

Those who had food sent in from outside the prison were most of them the card-players, the brass-hats of the class-war. The messengers with the food-baskets or trays were now approaching the centre of the court.

Percy spotted, by the proud carriage of the high-combed head, by the stately tread of her, the sumptuous bearer of his daily supplement of food. And she had observed Percy, too, as he issued from the *excusado*. But whereas Percy gave a waggle of his fat fist, just snatched out of his pocket to signal, and a benevolent glimmer out of his glasses to show he saw her, the girl with the basket betrayed no recognition, otherwise than by

26

directing her rhythmically swaying person towards the spot where he had appeared. However, Percy sauntered towards the table; and she altered her course again, so as to encounter him there; her eyes still lowered upon the ground before her, over which she was about to walk, as if it had been a surface of uncertain ice, demanding watchfulness.

Don Percy and the madonna of the basket reached the table at the same moment. She did not look at him, nor for that matter did he pay any attention to her, for he was again called to acknowledge cordial outbursts of camaraderie, and was not behindhand, as befitted a courteous Communist from the land of Wellington and foster-land of Karl Marx, established among the dago descendants of Ferrer.

The face of Josefa de la Asunción wore a mask of austere modesty as on other occasions. Her beauty alone must have imposed this upon her, among strange men of so fiery a sex-urge as was to be expected from those among whom her lot was cast. But the habits of the Mohammedan veil, out of the Berber past of the southern provinces of the Peninsula, must still govern the conduct of the face among the illiterate poor, who are scarcely as near to the aviator as they are to the Cid.

Nevertheless, this downcast face suggested so much the imminence of tears, and was so tautened up into the traditional Latin grin of affliction, that, although Percy was not observant in such matters, and although accustomed to impenetrable reserve on her part, he 'passed a remark' all the same.

'You look as if you'd lost a pound and found a sixpence!' he said, or its equivalent in her idiom.

Her response was so extremely depressing that he gave her a second look – sharp enough, indeed, his attention focused for a moment. For with a deepening of pessimism in all her person – as she realized he was speaking and that further this *inglés* was addressing himself to her – she flung at him a glance that was a terrible dumb expostulation. It was indignant – it flashed out its outraged feelings as a thunder-cloud disgorges its rain with sudden unrestraint. It said as plain as words: *'How can you indulge in these pleasantries, sir – you know your number's up! If you don't know, others do! If you refuse*

*to notice the black fate that is hanging over you, the fault is
yours!*' This *inglés* might have been smirking at a funeral!
That was the sort of look she had flung up in answer to his
joke. And Don Percy – unable to penetrate her strange displeasure – saw all this, but asked himself what on earth he had
done to the disgruntled Carmen.

He could not imagine in what he had been found wanting.
For it was plain that it was *he*, Don Percy, who was supposed
to be at fault. But he felt innocent – he was a little piqued:
seeing how popular he was being with the other Spaniards just
at the moment, it got him on the raw. A discordant note in an
otherwise highly gratifying situation. And Don Percy as a
matter of fact did not exclude the possibility that it *might* after
all be because of his socially compromising position, as a man
under lock and key, that this brutish daughter of the people –
with the terrifying respectability of the Masses – had not a
smile for him, and answered his fair words, and condescending pleasantries, with dour looks. He was offended in spite of
his hard-boiled 'outcast' shell. This was the tightest corner yet,
that, as a salaried official of political lawlessness, he had
known. Such was the penalty of failure. And as his British
respectability was his long suit now, a certain obscure touchi-
ness as to 'appearances', as to criminal status, was perhaps to
be expected. His freedom to come and go at will – to chat with
an official, to saunter to the *excusado* – was of some significance. To languish in the penitentiary of the Rio de Oro, or
something worse, was not to his taste. Things that at other
times would not have affected him, discovered the power to
annoy.

The touchy, the somewhat unbalanced Percy underwent a
change.

'*Qué hay?* What is it? Speak!' he barked, very tough – in a
good imitation of the back-block Spaniard, as if addressing a
refractory animal that would understand its master's voice and
nothing else – taking a quick step towards her, in serio-comic
menace – flashing out at her through his schoolmasterly
glasses a good upper-dog glare, tempered with contemptuous
humour. 'What ails you? What has disturbed you? Don't you
like coming here? Speak, *mujer*!'

He thundered the 'moo-hhhair!' in a shortwinded pant, as if the African aspirate was too much for his sedentary flesh and there was a shortage of wind in his paunch, exhausted by the calls upon it made by the hurtling *jota*.

She stepped back as if he had slapped her face, and without hesitation burst into a torrent of tears.

Several of the Spaniards nearest to Percy and the girl turned sharply upon them, very astonished, and discovered their English colleague with one foot advanced, apparently menacing a woman who had just brought him his basket of provisions, and who had fallen back before the aggressive Briton, and dissolved into tears (of mortification?) at something he had said.

'What is it? What is it?' exclaimed the most influential Partyman of them all, Don Agustín, a revolutionary magnate of fanatical aspect, with prominent moist-blue eyes, and a cicatrice in the form of a boomerang connecting his mouth and ear.

'What is it, *chica*?' asked another, coaxing and compassionate. 'The poor thing! She is unhappy! Don't cry, kiddie!'

To say that Percy was taken aback would poorly convey his discomfiture. He was exceedingly confused. He stood blinking at her, blushing deeply. His attitude was that of a person surprised in some unbecoming action. Rooted to the spot, he continued to stare at the sobbing messenger, as if hoping that an access of homeric laughter might succeed to her access of passionate tears. For the former even could not have been more irrational than the latter. She had put Percy wrong with his comrades: and perhaps, who knows, she might put him right. It was possible: with this child of nature surely there must be some principle of poetic justice! He waited pathetically upon it – to declare itself, and to clear up the misunderstanding.

'I don't think she likes coming here!' was all he could find to say.

'She doesn't like coming here?' demanded Don Agustín in amazement – as if to come to a prison was a privilege that must be patent to the least educated.

'I think not,' Don Percy said.

29

'Don't you like coming here?' screamed Don Agustín, in incredulous and angry appeal.

The girl burst into a fresh cataract of tears. Now that somebody else had done the same thing as himself, and brought on an incomprehensible storm, blowing out of the eyes and mouth of this beastly woman, Don Percy regained a little of his composure.

'She evidently thinks we are dangerous!' he remarked, and – still very red in the face, and his neck still hot from the heavy blush he had given – he smiled a little naughtily at the big noise of the Common Front.

'She thinks we are dangerous!' Don Agustín croaked shrilly, in great excitement. 'It is impossible!'

'Not at all!' said Percy.

'But it is incredible! Did she say she thought that we were dangerous?'

'No, she didn't say it,' Don Percy admitted. 'She didn't say it as far as I can remember.'

'It is impossible.'

'Of course it is!' said a young Catalan Communist, called Ramón (or 'the Fashion Plate') in a smart shirt and glazed shoes, who had shown sympathy just now, and had since then been observing the madonna of the basket with a swiftly waxing sexual appetite. To the organ-notes of grief and the great female billowing of her doubtless milky bust he had tuned-in his dapper organism. He was already in no condition to be non-partisan. 'The poor kid's in love!' he exclaimed, with reproach in his glance at Don Percy. 'She has been deserted by some reptile – probably a coast-guard!'

'Or a prison warder!' said another ex-card-player, with a great juice-laden chuckle in which most of the others joined.

'Or a *guardia civil*!' another suggested at once.

'Or a *guardia de asalto*!' another said, who had lost a finger to the bullet of a *guardia de asalto*.

'Or an aviator!' said yet another.

'Or a priest!' snarled the priest-butcher.

'Was it a priest?' demanded Don Agustín, fiercely of the shrinking girl, as if, had it been so, he would have required an explanation of her immediately.

'No! A fine girl like that would have nothing to do with a black crow!' the young Catalan Communist assured all present. 'Would you, *chica*? Not you! You'd knock his teeth out if he came any of his funny business! Wouldn't you, baby?'

'Of course she would!' came a croak from behind the table – a chorus from a passing malcontent, on his way to the *excusado*.

'Stop being funny with the poor creature!' an indignant voice broke out. It was a jealous young Bolshevist from León, who was a little hostile to the popular Percy. 'Can't you see how upset she is? She's all in!'

Serafín had come up while this was in progress, and had stood for a moment, watching – fuller of *cafard* than ever, glum and dank, his cigarette dangling in front of his nerveless lip. It was with a dull distaste that his eyes rested upon the tearful trollop, out of the chorus of *Carmen*. He now made a salacious remark, which caused an outburst of catarrhish chuckles, to the effect that the girl's condition was the result of a feminine disability of a recurrent nature and in effect was *nothing*.

Don Percy had entirely recovered from his embarrassment. He should, perhaps, he reflected, affect to defend his employee against the further attentions of the onlookers. He could not seal her up, but he could attempt to screen her. So, in the manner of a broadminded but compassionate gentleman, he stepped in, British and bluff.

'Let's give the poor girl a rest, boys! She has her troubles, I expect, like the rest of us!'

'Ah!' said Don Agustín. 'Who have not their troubles in these times?'

'Who, indeed?' Don Percy agreed.

'*Pobre gente!*' Don Agustín exclaimed. 'Hereabouts they are robbed by everybody – everybody fleeces them! I doubt if the poor animal has enough to eat. Her parents are probably being evicted for rent at this minute. Poor people – poor miserable people!'

Don Agustín turned fiercely upon her, as if she had been holding something back, of value to the Social Revolution.

31

'Are your family being turned out into the street? Speak!
The miserable wolves! The brute-beasts of rack-renters!'

'Devils incarnate!' hissed Tomás Madrigal, whose work was
mainly agricultural agitation.

With a ferocity that made the girl step back a pace and fling
her arm up in self-defence, Agustín pressed her, in screaming
reproach:

'Why don't you kill them? Speak! Why don't you *kill* them,
instead of coming blubbering to this prison?'

For answer, as it seemed, she pointed to the basket on the
table.

'What do you want, *chica*?' asked the youthful Catalan,
Ramón, in a caressing, confidential undertone, going over to
her. 'Do you want something out of the basket?'

Violently she shook her head, and a fresh rain of tears
ensued.

But Serafín had been observing her with aloof suspicion:
for people did not usually conduct themselves like this, and he
was not the man to be taken in – where there is smoke there is
fire, and here was a lot of unnecessary smoke.

'When did she start this?' he asked Don Percy. 'What was
she like when she arrived?'

'She started just now. I noticed nothing before that.'

'What is it all about?'

Percy flushed with annoyance, for this was still a very tender
spot.

'How do I know? I didn't do it. Ask *her!*'

Serafín left Percy and went over to the girl, motioning to the
young Catalan prisoner to leave them alone. He said nothing
for a moment, but contemplated her with his eyes screwed up
in a mocking scrutiny, composed of equal parts of scepticism
and disgust.

'What is the matter with you?' he suddenly rattled out at her,
in his best police-voice delivery, for dealing with the toughest
female pickpockets. 'Come over with it, Bessie! Why have you
been making an exhibition of this sort of yourself? What is the
big idea?'

Speaking with his face close to hers, the cigarette still suspended from his lip, he seemed ready to pounce upon anything

that, under pressure, she might disgorge, of value as evidence. It was impromptu third-degree.

She threw her head up and, stepping out of his way, made a truly imperious gesture of a tragedy-queen in the direction of the basket, her eyes flashing angrily at Don Percy.

'She wants her basket!' said the young Catalan Communist – also giving Percy a rather hard look, as if that gentleman had been convicted of attempting to subtilize a poor girl's basket. 'It's her basket she's asking for.'

'Well, she can have it!' snapped Don Percy, in a most indignant injured voice, turning to the basket, and – pulling one hand pettishly out of his pocket – removing the napkin.

From the shadow of the cloister, behind this group of people, Don Alvara made a sudden appearance. He stepped forth, and stood still: he was holding himself in readiness, one would have said, for some event which had not materialized, but which might call for his presence. The girl's eyes, however, widened to their full distension as she caught sight of this ill-omened form. Following the direction of her terrified gaze, the knot of a half-dozen men looked at him too, with eyebrows raised in contemptuous query at the hackneyed figure of the not very popular turnkey.

In his most portentous and penetrating tones, Don Alvaro addressed himself to Percy's rather formless back, bent over the basket.

'Don Percy!' the voice tolled out.

Percy turned round, more astonished than anybody.

'Yes?' he said. His face took on its most engaging expression: but the demeanour of the disaffected turnkey had in it so little that was reassuring, that the feebler the smile upon the prisoner's face became the longer he looked over at the other.

'Don Percy! This is the girl who brings you your dinner every day?'

'It is. Quite correct.' Percy was very genial and helpful.

'What is the cause of her distress?'

'I am sure I can't tell you!' Percy bridled at once. It was no use: he could not keep his temper when *that* subject was broached. *Any other question* – and, in order to make it up

33

with Don Alvaro, he would have bled honey. But his face immediately darkened and reddened at this. 'Don't ask me!' he barked out at him, before he could stop himself.

'Not ask you?' inquired Don Alvaro, with smouldering irony. 'Not ask you, sir?'

'No. I am not responsible for her behaviour – oddly enough.'

Don Alvaro took a step nearer at this – a threatening step, for he was quite near enough to make himself heard without raising his voice, and his voice did not diminish in volume or intensity after it; on the contrary, it increased in a startling way.

'Do I understand you to pretend, sir, that you do not know for what reason this woman has had an attack of tears?'

'Yes, that *is* what I pretend. I do *not*! I have not the remotest idea why she is so nervous.'

'You are not speaking the truth!' Don Alvaro shouted suddenly.

'What do you mean, Don Alvaro?'

Percy was purple with highly-repressed indignation. But his antagonist advanced another step forward as he retorted:

'What I say, sir! I have been watching all the time. I saw what you were doing! You are lying!'

The chief warder's face had become very pale and his eyes very large and black, altering the pictorial values of his large black moustache; in fact, Percy experienced with great force the odd sensation that Don Alvaro's face had changed to somebody else's – it was no longer the same person that was before him but another man: like him, but younger – more frivolous, as it were, and irresponsible.

'I don't understand you, sir, at all!' Percy blurted out, biting his nails, in an endeavour not to repeat his mistake of earlier in the day.

'You don't understand? You lie! You were threatening her – I saw you doing it!'

'I threatening her! You are mad, Don Alvaro.'

'Si, señor! It is not part of the rules of this prison that prisoners should conduct themselves in this brutal fashion – it is a lock-up for brutes, *claro!* like all prisons. But they have to leave their brutishness outside.'

A mutinous muttering started among the prisoners.

'Don Alvaro –!' began Percy.

'In the country you come from – a by-blow from its gutters!' – and he spat – 'that may pass. Not here! Yours was the action of an anarchistic pig. Yes, sir – to impose upon a woman's weakness – the action of a cochino!'

Percy, as a porker, scratched his head, acting the poor fellow at a loss for words, in the face of an ignorant tirade. He smiled, curling his lip in scorn, and was silent, looking over at his friends, for confirmation of his refusal to do battle with the likes of this grim dependant of the oppressing classes.

'No, sir,' persisted his enemy. 'No, sir! It is of no use. I have watched you. You are a prisoner. Do not forget it. A prisoner, in a prison, cannot behave as he chooses. Before the law – for me – you are no more than a cutpurse – if as good as that! I doubt it.'

Pandemonium, at this, broke out among the other prisoners, who had been listening with folded arms and sneers on their darkening faces while their British comrade was denounced, with occasional exclamations of disdain and resentment. Don Agustín called out roughly at this, with a furious gesture of dismissal towards the outrageous turnkey:

'Be off, old ruffian! What are you threatening us about? Mind your own business!'

'Shut your mouth, police scum! Dung of a civil guard!' bellowed the priest-butcher, Juso Radio, springing up from the table upon which he had been sprawling. 'Take yourself off – quickly, quickly! – or we shall kill you! Go!'

'You drivel! You are an old madman!' roared Percy – ashamed suddenly of the cautious rôle he had been playing. 'You are a police faggot! You are a jack-in-office, with a swelled head! You are unacceptable to me as a prisoner! I shall report you for behaving like a Cossack!'

'Yes, you are unacceptable to us! As prisoners, we take exception to you!' several exclaimed.

Don Alvaro's eyes lit up like beacons, to which he had just put a match. They were in a blaze. But they gave out no heat, and they were wary. They were almost light-hearted – almost mocking. Their flame was almost mischievous: a hollow, a

35

false, flame. Again Don Percy felt that he had before him somebody else: a cleverer, somewhat unscrupulous, brother of his old friend, the socratic turnkey.

But the black moustache drew in and flattened itself against Don Alvaro's jaw, in an alarming fashion, in the way that some men's ears, when they grow angry, become flattened against their skull. He placed his hand upon the holster of his official pistol. He meant business, you would have said. He seemed swelling – or rather shrinking and elongating – with offended dignity. It was a capital imitation of an angry warder, if no more.

'Silence, you insubordinate British louse!' he roared, in the trumpet-note of those who set out to cow with their ringing tongue.

'Insubordinate!' jeered back the prisoners in raucous chorus. And they flung themselves back on their haunches in ironical attitudes, their arms akimbo, and wagged and tossed their heads at him on all sides.

Don Alvaro took no notice of the others. The English prisoner was his solitary mark.

'Understand you are here, sir, on a charge for which you will have to answer!' he remarked.

'How – *answer*? Be off, poor fool!' Don Agustín wailed at him with ineffable disdain. He did not notice Don Agustín at all: but he sent over another shot at Percy.

'If you do not answer for it, all Spain will want to know the reason why!'

'All Spain – all Spain! What is *all Spain*?' the Sindicalistas all shouted together. 'What *is* "all Spain", *por Dios*?'

'*You* will answer for *this*!' thundered the now thoroughly uncautious Percy. 'You see if you don't!'

For he understood the magnitude of the forces, overt and covert, that were ranged against this ex-praetorian guard, where the latter did not.

'Don't threaten me with your Consuls! Address me as you should, you foreign mongrel!' retorted Don Alvaro at the top of his voice. 'See that you do that, or I will make you!'

'*You* make! Ah, police bastard, wait a week or two till we get you outside!' screamed the priest-butcher, grinning with every fang in his head at the prospective victim of the Sindics. 'You have signed your death-warrant, Don Tom Thumb!'

But they all came into action at once. Don Agustín pointed his forefinger at the common enemy, as if to take aim, his finger trained upon his man. Then with all his force *he spat* – as if a slingstone had parted from its sling: but it was a *word* he spat – a big percussive back-block epithet – his skull flung forward at the end of his long neck. This verbal missile should have plunged plumb down the other's gullet – if a vocable could have weight – could drip, and stink. His moist-blue eyes (at the best of times like projectiles – an asset for the platform) almost left his head along with it. Some minutes had to elapse before they went back into their sockets.

Several of those with the biggest reputation for fierceness, put on their mettle by this, made a rush in the direction of the contumelious turnkey, who drew his revolver – a slight grin peeping out from under his severe moustache – a glitter of false teeth.

'Stand back!' he called out. 'Rats of Sindicalistas! You will not have to ask me *twice* to rid the earth of you!'

Don Agustín flung himself before his friends. His long arms spread out upon either side, he held back the toy tornado with no great trouble – indeed they all accepted his arms as an impassable barrier, throwing themselves against them and against his back with one accord.

'Go back!' he ordered. 'Let us leave this scarecrow to himself – he would like an excuse to drill the lot of us! Don't let us give it him! What does he matter? An ignorant village bumble! Come – let us eat our dinners. Enough of this!'

At first Serafín had not moved. He was watching Don Alvaro. To start with he watched him with amazement; afterwards the same clouded contemplation, full of dry suspicion, came back into his face, as that he had levelled at the eccentric girl. For here was more of the same stuff – behaviour that did not fit the facts, as they were disclosed to the casual eye. A lot of bother out of nothing! What was the matter with all these people (he was disposed to ask himself) this afternoon – that one after another they took leave of their senses? There was *something* at the bottom of it! *Aqui hay algo!* But *what* was the hidden spring?

When the Sindicalistas charged, he set himself in motion, dissatisfied and sluggish. But other warders were approaching rapidly from different directions, drawing their Mausers, and he was the nearest to this inexplicable scene. He stopped at once when Don Agustín placed himself in the path of the insurrection – spat, and turned on his heel.

Growling remarks over their shoulders, that were the coarsest libels upon the fine body of men the republican government of the Middle-clases employed to restrain idealists and dreamers, the Sindicalistas suffered themselves to be turned back for the present into the paths of peace by Don Agustín – the priest-butcher shaking his fist at Don Alvaro as he retreated, and shouting:

'Wait a bit – wait a bit, old dung-pie! Wait a little, Agrippa! We'll skin you alive yet! Your old black thatch will go to make a fine fur-collar for one of our girl-friends! You will see if we forget you! We have long memories, depend on that!'

Percy had taken a few steps with the others, or behind the others, in the direction of the waiting turnkey. But this was after all not entirely his country – he could not, for instance, even if he wished to do so, hang up a priest's ribs for sale in a gutted shop, during an outbreak, and pretend to be engaged in the meat trade – even in the height of a provincial revolt. In a word, there were limits to his freedom of action. But in the present instance his handicap was of a different order. He had been cowed: when he considered the disagreeable nature of the events that were occurring, for all of which *he* must be held ultimately responsible, he did not feel easy in his mind. He was serving his masters badly, it would seem as if he had deliberately upset the discipline and good order of a prison. So he now turned very firmly indeed to his food-basket, glad that at least *that* was at an end and blood had not been shed.

Next minute, glancing up, as he was in the act of removing the last article, ready for use, he saw that Don Alvaro had disappeared. Percy was isolated at his end of the table – indeed as his Spanish colleagues swore and gesticulated at each other violently discussing the events, for which they had been quite unprepared, he reproached himself for having allowed his temper to master him, and for bandying words with the principal warder – again. The action of the other prisoners had been in his support, and following upon his, Percy's, offensive. He would not be *blamed*, of course – he should not give a hoot if he *were*! But he should not have allowed this to happen. He ~was extremely annoyed with Don Percy.

After looking around a second time, just to make sure, Percy wrenched up the false bottom of the basket, and quickly drew out the English newspapers, thrusting them into his trouser-pockets. Then, having adjusted the interior of the basket, he handed it to the girl, without looking at her. He could not bear to have looked at her again; and besides who could guarantee, if he had so much as glanced in her direction, that she would not let off a scream or throw a fit. He must take steps to secure a new messenger at once. This one, decidedly, was one of the most enigmatical lunatics that it had ever been Percy's lot to encounter. So he sat down to his supper in a very ruffled state of mind, and when the priest-butcher sat down near him to settle the hash of some tinned *bacalao* it was a busy man, a busily feeding man, who replied to him with his mouth full – cheerily but shortly, with little more than a *yes* or a *no*.

'Don Percy!' muttered a quiet voice behind him: and he found Serafín lounging at his side. The young warder sat down on the table beside his plate and began rolling about his melon.

'*Lo quiere?*' asked Don Percy, indicating his chicken.

Serafín sawed his forefinger backwards and forwards in the air, to express refusal.

'There is something that puzzles me,' said Serafín.

'What is that?' said Don Percy, without interest.

Serafín played football with the melon with his finger.

'What did you say to that girl?' he asked.

Percy put down his knife and fork with a bang and sat back violently, roused at last in very truth.

'Will you not, you misbegotten glue-eyed jail-rat, ask me that damfool question again?' he roared. 'Haven't I told you *nothing*? NOTHING! Is that good enough or *not*?'

39

Serafín was watching the retreating figure of what was by now Percy's bête noire, with a scowling face of dark inquiry, without its cigarette.

'She just went off bang like that – for *nothing*?' he asked with studied incredulity.

Percy did not answer – he addressed himself to the savage dismemberment of the tiny fowl.

'Don Percy!'

'Go to Hell!' bellowed the enraged Percy, his head down over his food. 'I don't wish to discuss that, or anything else! Get me? Hop it!'

Serafín shrugged, slightly amused, and strolled away from the sulky British baby – whom he was paid, from two sides and twice over, to safeguard, succour and bear with.

Chapter 4

THE cell appropriated to the British prisoner was a double-barrelled compliment, at once to the majesty of that land of hope and glory that was his material home, and that Marxist one that was his spiritual home. Both Moscow and G.B. were names that held forth the promise of fat tips to the staff of the lock-up. He was well-housed, if plainly – it was not Sing-Sing.

Built for coolness, the convent-room turned cell possessed no window, in the European sense. There was only a vertical slit upon the street-frontage. This was a ventilated recess, as it were; widened within, for the diameter of the wall, into a triangular niche, in which a figure of a saint might have featured. And at present Don Percy occupied it, cooking his hot buttocks upon its stone sill. The dangling sausages of his lockram-clad legs established contact with difficulty with the stone floor beneath.

Two candles standing upon a table in the centre of the cell were the most reliable illumination, and Serafín was examining, by their light, the typewritten message, which Percy had discovered when he had opened the newspapers taken from the basket.

'In three hours' time,' said Serafín.

'About that,' said Percy.

Holding the paper limply, before his stomach, Serafín turned from the table and stood opposite the prisoner, crouched in his recess, contemplating him as if sullenly sizing up this fleshly revolutionary personage, and seeking to reach some decision, partly dependent upon the results of his scrutiny.

'Well!' said Percy, looking up over the top of his glasses.

'Don Percy!' began Serafín in a faint pant, and stopped as though to weight his apostrophe with a minute of ominous silence.

'Yes?' Percy slipped his hands inside his braces, using them as slings for his wrists.

'I should not go tonight!' Serafín said at last. 'I should pay no attention to this note.' He took it in his hand, without looking at it. He gazed at his British charge dully, without interest, prepared evidently for any response that might be made to his proposal, perfectly indifferent one way or the other. Take it or leave it – he had given his opinion.

'Pay no attention to it!' Percy got down quickly at this from his niche – very disturbed by his confederate's remark.

'Why not?'

'Because!' The suspended *porque* quavered lazily in the cell for some moments. 'I should neglect it entirely! I should not go. You can do as you please. But it would be better to wait.'

'But for what reason?'

'No reason. I think it would be better. I have a feeling that everything is not as it should be.'

'Do you doubt that this is a bona fide note? It is in perfect English. What's the matter with it?'

'Nothing – nothing!' Serafín shrugged. 'It isn't that. The note's all right. But I should not go tonight.'

Percy took the note from his hand, went over to the candles, and read it through carefully.

'It is an Englishman who has written this. Probably it is Roger Banting. He thinks it's better for me to skip. He knows what's going on outside.'

'There's no danger. For an Englishman. You're all right, Don Percy. We don't shoot Englishmen in Spain.'

'That we must leave to my friends to decide.'

'Perhaps.'

'They would not risk a moonlight flit if they did not think things looked sticky.'

Serafín was silent. He lounged back against the wall now, his eyes on the floor, smoke coming from between his ruined gums.

'It's only thirty miles to the frontier,' Percy said.

'*Claro!*' said Serafín. 'Of course!'

'It's the get-away. Otherwise there should be no difficulty.'

'It's the get-away!' said Serafín.

'Is there likely to be any trouble?'

Serafín smiled, just enough to show that such a question put things upon a basis that was unreal, and even laughable.

'No trouble,' he said, 'all other things being equal. At the end of this passage is a prison guard with a carbine. I have fixed him. He is a friend.' He shrugged. 'We can get out all right. All other things being equal.'

Percy fidgeted, biting down into a hangnail with a nervous preoccupation.

'What is the obstacle then?' he asked.

Serafín again shrugged at the question and spat near the foot of the wall at his side – a discreet jet.

'I can only tell you what I should do, Don Percy. I should not go tonight. I think there is danger.'

'Have you heard anything that makes you think –?'

'Nothing! I have a hunch. *Basta!* I advise you to stop where you are.'

Percy had grown very nervous: he had never thought of *danger* as a possible factor in this situation. This was something quite new. Danger indeed! He was a little indignant with Serafín for speaking of *danger*. He began moving restlessly about the cell. He stopped in front of Serafín.

'You mean you think that old devil Don Alvaro has got wind of something. Is that it?' he exclaimed. 'Speak!'

Serafín threw out his hands in a gesture that deprecated the mention of names, or of anything so concrete.

'But you must have something in your mind,' Percy grumbled at him. 'Can't you say what it is?'

'How can I do that? It is nothing – it is a feeling I have. I should not have selected tonight. Alvaro tomorrow is going to try to have you disciplined – he wants you moved from here.'

'What for?'

'For causing a riot in the prison.'

Percy made a gesture of contemptuous impatience. At the mention of the episode of the mad peasant girl his face darkened with a dash of the furious frustration of that afternoon.

He glared at Serafín for a moment.

'What riot?' he asked pugnaciously. 'I don't understand.'

'Oh, the trouble in the prison yard. That's all.'

'But if I am going to be moved from here tomorrow, there is no time to be lost! All the more reason to get out tonight!'

'Certainly!' agreed Serafín. 'That is why I have left it to you.'

Percy, the onus on him, bubbled up, and the die was cast.

'But there seems every reason to take this chance. *Of course* I had better make my get-away tonight!'

'All right. If you are prepared to take the risk. I had to say what I thought.'

'But why should there be any more risk tonight than any other night?'

'All right,' Serafín agreed. He walked towards the door lazily, rolling a fresh cigarette as he went, between fingers hennaed with tobacco, as if everything had been arranged and settled and he had already forgotten the matter.

'Serafín!' Percy called after him; his face was strained, he did not take these events quite so coolly as did his fellow-conspirator. Sweat had collected on his forehead, and he took a handkerchief from his pocket and dabbed at his brick-red brow. Serafín turned round, a small tongue-tip protruding above his depressed lip, as he licked the paper of the completed cigarette.

'Serafín. Couldn't you manage to see Pascual and find out if everything's O.K.?'

'What's the good of that?' asked the warder. 'They will be there all right. It's *here* things may go wrong.'

'But didn't Pascual send you a message?'

Serafín shook his head, and sighed.

'Why should he? I told him that, whenever the order was given, I would see you safely out. There's nothing to see *him* about!'

Percy scratched his head.

'All right, Serafín.' Percy was becoming much more friendly and civil with Serafín as the moment approached to put himself in his hands. 'But how about it? What are you going to do?'

'Nothing,' said Serafín indifferently, leaning against the door.

'I know, but how about the get-away?' He smiled pleasantly, through his perspiration, at the imperturbable master-mind who made him feel like a fussy old lady embarking on a steamer, and asking everybody on board if it was going to be rough. 'What am I to do?'

'Nothing,' said Serafín lazily. 'I will fetch you.'

'That's what I wanted to know. Shall I bring anything with me?'

'Nothing,' said Serafín again.

'Good,' said Percy. 'No luggage. Nothing, well, so long, Serafinito. You will be here then round about midnight?'

'Round about,' said Serafinito.

'Good. I shall be ready,' said Percy amiably. '*Hasta la vista!*'

'*Hasta la vista!*' said Serafín negligently, as he passed out of the door, locking it on the other side.

*

On the opposite side of the prison to the lazaret was the river. Don Percy's cell was on that side. Through the ventilation slit a faint coolness reached the perspiring Briton. Glaring through this tenuous opening, he could see the moonlit water, of bronzed milk, in the path of the moon, with an oily shimmer reminiscent of the bottom of a sardine tin; and in his ear was the buzz of a mosquito, which he had just driven off. The buzz was like the vibration of the bronze element – a dull, brazen growl. There was no other sound – unless there was a vibration in the firmament, which, when all men were blotted out in sleep, maybe had a buzz of sorts.

It was midnight by his watch, and Percy felt none too comfortable. *Danger* – that was a novel sensation in revolutionary politics: for Percy was not a *front-fighter* or anything of that nature, but rather a careerist of the propaganda section: wielding the pen, not the pistol. The technique of the general strike, of the *coup d'état*, he had at his finger-tips: but he was a brass-hat in the class-war. The three sticks of dynamite found in his pocket when arrested were *somebody else's* dynamite. He had supposed himself immune from arrest.

As it was, the misgivings expressed by Serafín had had three solid hours to take action, tending to liquefaction, upon cuticle and upon intestine: then the oppressive heat had not improved matters. Liquefaction was complete. Percy was an aqueous shell.

The very coolness with which those misgivings of the phlegmatic turnkey had found expression, the personal detachment of their author, had made them more impressive. They at least could not be discounted on the score of *panic*! The most that could be said was that Serafín was not, at the best of times, conspicuous for credulity: a suspicion would not have to knock twice to find a home away from home in his bosom. A tap would suffice! But this peculiarly disturbing conjunction of sublime indifference with emphatic anticipation of danger had so worked upon Percy's mind that had he been able to communicate with his confederate in the meanwhile, he would have countermanded the escape. Fighting the mosquitoes had been his only relaxation, for he could not sit still. He had almost asphyxiated himself with *Flytox*, and the wall was mottled with the discharges from his pulverizing squirt.

And of all cursed things, there was the beautiful night – a source of profound irritation to Percy, as was beauty upon all such occasions, he had invariably found. It was rather as though, serene and self-confident, a beauty-queen had been sent into his cell to capture his attention by an inopportune display of her attractions. He could not support the placid night outside! There was not only the fact that Nature was blind to the intellectual beauties of the Social Revolution, and deaf to the voice of Conscience; there was also the fact that Nature, especially in these sumptuous climates, required a spartan watchfulness on the part of the revolutionary, tending to clip the wings of Percy's more civilized muse, and non-party mind. If he was not, in short, to be lulled into forgetfulness of social injustice, he must never allow himself to play *the artist*. And Percy liked playing the artist. Percy the 'gunman' insisted upon Percy the 'artist'! It had been very awkward at times. He had even incurred suspicion – there was something bourgeois about Percy's dealings with bel canto, and oratorios were a perennial source of misunderstanding. Did not Lenin say that he *hated* violinists, because they made him feel he wanted to stroke their heads, and all the time he knew that it was in fact his duty to bash their brains out?

So he glared out of the ventilation slit, watching the lotus-eating Spanish night, frowning upon the absolutely aloof surfaces of its magic elements, of earth, air, and water – the latter of which would go on being 'beautiful' if a whole colony of splendid proletarians were starving upon the foreshore. This velvet night of southern nature was as detached from mankind as is the cat.

He was eaten up with a cross impatience, too, on account of Percy. There was *danger* – Serafín, at least, thought so. And here was Nature typically indifferent as to whether Percy was in danger or not!

As the key began cautiously revolving in the lock of the cell, Percy sprang away from the window. His heart was beating a bubbling tattoo. At the same time he was intensely relieved at the thought that his tête-à-tête with Nature was at an end. Perforce he must turn his back upon this cat, this 'sphinx' – this devil! He would now be able to exchange all these treacherous appeals to Percy the artist for matter-of-fact appeals (or commands) to Percy the man-of-action. The Social Revolution would be there once more, in place of the static make-believe and seductive deceptions of the objective universe. Thank God for the good old *subjective* world! all Percy's instinct intoned in chorus.

46

Serafín stood in the doorway, his pendent cigarette sticking to his extravasated lip, in every respect the same as when he had disappeared three hours earlier. His expression was profoundly bored, but not more so than before. He beckoned to Percy.

Rapidly pulling on his poplin jacket and slouched hat, Percy obeyed him without speaking.

'Do we start now?' he asked, in a low voice as he reached the door. 'Is all set?'

Serafín nodded.

'If anything occurs,' he said, 'you are my prisoner.'

'Right!'

'I am returning with you to your cell.'

'Quite.'

'Say that you lost yourself. The door was unlocked, you went to the lavatory. Anything. It doesn't matter what you say.'

'No.'

'You are my prisoner. The rest is nonsense.'

'I get you.'

He turned, and Percy followed him out into the corridor, closed the door behind him. Pushing the swing door, leading to a minor stairway, they passed the sentry. His carbine reposed upon his knees, he was, to all appearances, fast asleep. They moved down the stairs, treading softly, and, at the bottom, there was a small door leading into the street. Serafín took a key out of his pocket and unlocked it. He stopped.

'This is the street,' he said.

Percy smiled.

'If anything occurs –'

Percy smiled again, a little, but not much more broadly. The notion of 'danger' had departed from his mind.

'If anything occurs, I am taking you, you understand, round to the lazaret. You are ill.'

Percy grunted.

'Take my arm!' said Serafín. 'You are ill.'

Percy took Serafín's arm.

Even to Percy this device seemed a little too infantile a simplification. Why, it might be asked, had they let themselves out with a key? Why had they selected the longest road round to the hospital? But he supposed that *anything*, as Serafín would put it, was good enough as a story, where *everything* would be disbelieved. One excuse was much the same as another – none would be believed. If they were to be condemned, they were to be condemned – should they be caught! And if they were to be caught, they were to be caught! But there was no likelihood of that, as Percy could see. So fatalism was out of place, and Percy smiled accordingly.

They stepped out, upon the quay, and certainly the affectionate manner of their exit, arm-in-arm, gave such a buffoonish turn to their actions that Percy's inefficient nerves caused him to chuckle a little explosively against Serafín's shoulder. Chuckling, he noticed, afforded him an added sense of security: also undoubtedly conveyed the impression of gallantry. He chuckled again.

Percy thought of the Babes in the Wood: and, seeing that *he* was the one that was broad-in-the-beam, he supposed he was cast for the Principal Boy! But Serafín did not share his matinée memories; and, far from feeling that he was participating in a Christmas pantomime, he had all the air of a person called upon to play his part in a melodrama so utterly boring that he could not even smile as he said his lines. They were too silly – something for children! And he even frowned very slightly as he heard the muffled outburst of nervous mirth at his side. But he said nothing.

Tripping as they did so and lurching into each other – Percy again smothering a hysterical mass of chuckles – they stepped out upon the moonlit quay. There was a border of black shadow for a few feet out from the wall, to which they kept as near as possible, though Percy was fully disclosed, his back brilliantly exhibited – of which he was unpleasantly conscious. They started walking up towards the main thoroughfare. They had gone only a dozen yards or less when Percy thought he heard the sounds of spitting behind them and turned his head. To say that Percy's blood froze, that an *escalofrio* ascended his dorsal cord, would be to insult his sensations. His spine became an icicle, his blood *boiled* with alarm. And his fingers closed upon his guide's forearm in a grip that caused the unresponsive Serafín to gasp and start.

48

Outside the door through which they had just passed a man was kneeling, half in and half out of the moonlight. He wore a black military cape. He was taking aim with a rifle, and before Percy could absorb more than this fact, there was a crashing report, that yanked up the vegetative night by the roots. Serafín's body tore itself out of his grasp in a spiral movement – Percy hurling himself round in pursuit for half of its tactical diameter: and then, as his companion, his arms thrown up in the air, plunged down upon his back, he was knocked sideways by his fall. A stone revolved under his left foot, and Percy came down hard upon his left knee.

There he knelt, in a dazed abstraction, for a moment, half turned to the river. He had been rooted up, too, along with the night – rooted up and flung roughly down. Was he in the middle of an action, or at the end of it? Was that *all*? No, that was not all.

As he knelt, a second crack bisected the sultry stillness, and as it began – as the event of which it was a part first touched him – Percy began to draw in his breath as if to meet the on-rush of a shower-bath. But his right leg, which had been stuck awkwardly out, received a terrific blow. It was carried away, as it seemed, from beneath him, and he rolled over violently upon his face.

Percy did not move. Half his face, shining with sweat, was bathed in moonlight. It seemed that he desired time to cogitate. Something had 'occurred'. There was an effort on his part to remember his instructions, in the event of anything 'occurring'. He was to be *sick*. That was all he could bring to mind. And as a sick man he must behave, that was the agreed procedure. He was sleepy, however. He was in quite unexpected harmony, all of a sudden, with Nature – with the shimmering sardine oil of the waters of the river, and that sunburst of diamonds that spattered the velvet sky.

A cloaked figure, pointing a carbine at him, had come up. He was bending towards him. From a long way off came a familiar, a friendly, voice. It said:

'*Buenas noches*, Don Percy! *You* here!'

Percy winked his upturned eye.

'A law-breaker!' the voice said – and he perceived the

familiar black moustaches that belonged with the well-known voice. 'Please do not move! If you move I shall have to finish you off. Plainly you are a dangerous person. You are probably armed. No? Found with three sticks of dynamite on your person. And *now* you are discovered corrupting your guards – he has paid with his life for his falsity. Attempting to escape!'

Don Alvaro coughed – he threw his cloak up on his shoulder, against the attacks of the night air.

'Why, Don Percy, did you never propose to *me* a little deal? Every man has his price! Did you think I should ask too much?'

Don Alvaro shook his head reproachfully.

'I am offended, Don Percy!'

Objectively Don Percy considered this apparation, as he lay, right eye uppermost, and he was able to examine him with so inordinate a detachment that he saw what he had never seen before. He saw that this man was *false*. His moustache was stuck on – it did not grow there! When he had coughed, he realized that it was a goat that had coughed, not a man. Yet he had always believed that he had been dealing with a gentleman! He was nothing of the sort. It was doubtful if he was even a man. He was, of course, a Civil Guard. That was it. He should never have been off his guard – not with an ex-Civil Guard!

It was astonishing how thoroughly he had been mistaken in Don Alvaro. Percy did not *mind*. He had been relieved of all responsibility. He had become like unto a little child again: and he lay there weak and ready to be petted – a Babe in the Wood, in fact. About the other Babe he could not bother, for Babes ceased to bother about each other once they were out of sight and out of mind. But Don Alvaro! How curious that he should have been deceived in this man! He had the face of a sindicalista. Percy was damned if he hadn't! – with apologies to the comrades and all that – for this was in fact a murderous Civil Guard! But he was not the man he had taken him for. And as he idly examined the stern, traditional features under the warder's cap they began to dissolve into the stars around them, and Don Percy became one with that vast and beautiful neutral system, of the objective universe of things, which cared nothing for the Social Revolution but flattered him into thinking – upon moonlight nights – that he was a Beethoven who had been forced into politics by poverty. And he hoped his mother would air his shirt against his return – for he was going home after this, to his mother in Edgbaston. Percy was definitely tired: so he thought he would go home. And the flash of the carbine a foot from his face and the tremendous roaring of it in his head made no difference at all to his plans for immediate withdrawal from these troublesome scenes – a man's world, yes, but he was through with the whole business.

Chapter 5

DON PERCY, as he grew stronger, grew more irritable. And the Sister found his mock-proletario vocabulary assembling itself against her in ever rougher combinations. Percy did not take the prospect of lameness for life at all well.

But the impatience of the convalescent was not disciplined by any traditional charity. It was aggressively the reverse. And as for humanitarianism – that, with respect to inefficient, fat, perspiring Spanish nuns was unthinkable: humanitarianism begins at home – if it is not *everywhere* out of place. And as an obedient apologist of terrorist revolutionary power, Percy saw it as taboo *everywhere*. Was not the humanitarian the confederate of the despot (meaning the hereditary despot of Western Feudalism – there were *other* despots, but they had no connection with the humanitarian – indeed no humanitarian could exist in their shadow)? He spat on kind hearts as much as on coronets. Indeed, was it not the 'kind hearts' that kept the coronets on people's blocks – and the mitres too! That was so – kind, silly, hearts! How did the priests get so fat? The silly, bead-muttering, Spanish housewife gave them her pennies – her husband's pennies!

'*Ama al prójimo como a ti mismo!*' sneered Virgilio, from the next bed – when Percy was thus painfully perspiring, in his invalid impotence, the pillow saturated where his shoulders

51

discharged into it, pint after pint of the best water of his glands.

'Love? I couldn't love that bitch as much as she loves me, however much I tried! So what's the use?' Percy blusterously complained, very *proletario*, waving a still fattish arm – glaring at the doorway through which the good Sister had just silently vanished, with her hands crossed upon her stomach. 'I don't love *myself* a tenth as much as *she* loves me, blast her! This Christian love gets me down – it's more than I can bear – with the thermometer at a hundred and ten in the shade. And the sooner she understands it the better! I don't *want* her love! It comes from a place I regard as putrescent! It is criminal love!'

Virgilio chuckled, a guttural runculation, of racy mischief, and his squint eyes twinkled with lazy malevolence.

'Yes, it is criminal!' he agreed. 'You are her passion, Don Percy.'

'Oh!' Percy protested.

'Yes! Her big love!'

'But someone is *robbed* every minute of the day in order to supply me with that love!' boomed the perspiring Percy, short of breath. 'It makes me feel like a receiver of stolen goods!'

'You shouldn't show her you feel that way, it's stupid,' Virgilio said – after a pause, to get his breath back, on Percy's part.

'Why not? Why shouldn't I?'

Virgilio laughed indolently at his big boob of a co-partyboy.

'Because it pleases her so much! Of course it does: you are manufacturing a martyr, Don Percy!'

'How do you make that out?'

'You give her a fresh *cornada* every half hour, don't you?'

'Do I?'

'She *suffers*! What comes next? Canonization, that's what comes next. You can see the halo bobbing about already back of her lousy head. You, Percilito, are responsible!' he muttered slyly.

'I don't care if I am!' shouted the reckless Percy. ' I don't care if I am.'

He mopped his brow and neck.

'I am a *bigger* martyr!' he said.

But as he said it a cloud passed over his face. 'Many a true word is spoken in jest!' he said to himself, with the stabbings of a deeper *misericordia* than any nun could inflict. And he fell silent, and most abruptly quieted down. It was Percy who was the martyr. Yes – if you were going to talk of martyrs there was no question where you would have to look for them. On Percy's bed of sickness.

'You are a martyr – yes!' Virgilio replied, with unexpected gravity – looking over at him (as if to make sure of his facts before pronouncing). Percy did not like this, and turned away his head.

Neutrality – that was anathema. It was a cardinal principle, forced upon the revolutionary, whose adopted country was Spain, that in the matter of religion *neutrality* was impossible. At the outset that had been recognized by Percy – as the most conservative attitude for the proper Red. Neutrality was out of the question. Spain was Catholic more than it was Spanish. Agnosticism was not enough! You could be neutral about bull-fighting. You could not be neutral about a papal bull. Ignatius Loyola was more Spanish than the matador. This was the motherland of the Inquisition. You could not be *neutral* in this country when it came to the Jesuit. This racket asked and gave no quarter. So *écrasez l'infâme!* or it would make short work of *you*.

And perhaps, as a foreigner, in the effort required of him to master this lesson, Percy had been if anything over-thorough. He saw red whenever he encountered the black frock of the papal matador (the bull, of course, was Spain –'*pobre España*' – as much for the imported communist as it was for Don Alvaro), or pretended to; for, of course, bluff was the tactical basis of the latter-day revolutionary personality. (We all know too much today to be plain blunt men.) Bluff stood in the same relation to the revolutionary expressionism as does sangfroid to the pugnacity of the duellist. The *bogus* in the bursting up-lift it was that made it intellectually bearable. It made it a game – as a game only was it acceptable, once you'd got used to it. 'Be on the winning side!' whispered, with a wink, the hard-bitten revolutionary, to such people as were not susceptible to unadulterated uplift (unadulterated with a pinch of bogusness). In Percy's professional make-up he never quite knew what part of bluff went to what part of solid belief. And in solution neither bluff nor belief remained quite the same as they were in their natural state. Bluff was mixed in as you went along – like the comic element in the Shakespearean tragic technique. *He* could not have put his finger on this attitude, or on that, and said: *This is Bluff* or *Here you have an authentic bit of Belief*. He just knew that there was plenty of bluff to swell it all out to imposing dimensions, and he left it at that. – *He who goes out to save a fool, must do so as an impostor*. And Percy Hardcaster was as honest a fellow as any in the Party: and having learnt a part, he really played it *con amore*. The Jesuit *was* his enemy – as much as anyone in the world. Since Percy was a good-natured man, it was not *much*. – This basket was not in reality of simple manufacture. It was most of it honest *false bottom*.

So outwardly Don Percy was a little rugged, as a matter of dogma – his tongue was a little rough. And at present, poor fellow, he was an angry man, a very angry man indeed. His bogus rage was real rage – but diverted from its true object and made to play upon a stock Aunt Sally of the dogma of Spanish revolt.

*

However, Sister Teresa was the most aggravating lunatic of all her detestable communion, that he would swear. Unhappy Spain might never shake off this incubus of reactionary papal power, or it might: but Sister Teresa, whatever happened, would still be the most exasperating nun on record.

When Percy observed one afternoon that she was crying at something he had said, he flung himself in the opposite direction in an outraged sulk. He refused to lie there and tamely contemplate such gratuitous hypocrisy – intended to punish him, helpless as he was, for being justly snappy. And in so doing, bouncing angrily over with too little regard to his condition, he had disarranged his system of splints and clinical jambeaux. Complications followed. He was put back a week or more on his convalescence. Martyr or not – a profane martyr, suffering for Anti-Christ – or just a common-or-garden casualty – Percy passed through a period of renewed pain, and much anxiety.

But at last, sorely wasted by his six weeks of immobility, Don Percy was able to get up and to crouch in an armchair for three or four minutes, his head spinning. The two sisters, Teresa and Inés, hissing at each other like a couple of pledged conspirators, in stage-whispers, made his bed. But he felt very sick. And again contact with Sister Teresa was imperative – which made him more sick than ever.

Be touched by this woman he *must* on occasion, that there was no avoiding: though sometimes he would push her hand away and curse under his breath. Yet half-fainting, there was no way out. He was picked up out of the chair, in which he was sinking, and lifted back into his bed, by these tenderly compassionate women – vowed to such insidious tasks; who handled their English patient as if he had been made of some precious substance – especially marked in the handwriting of the celestial Carter Paterson: *This side up – With Care!* Percy's humiliation fought for first place with his nausea. He would as soon have found himself in the arms of a Blackshirt. Sooner!

*

It was a day of suffocating heat. Squadrons of mosquitoes, in close formation, manoeuvred in the air of the ward, and advanced, in a hysterical drone, to the attack. The Briton and the Basque ate their lunch beneath their mosquito-curtains; they conversed with each other like a couple of heavily-veiled brides, peering at each other's shadowy head short-sightedly through the vestal netting.

A groaner had got into the neighbouring ward. Since the evening before he had been heard there. His groans were the deepest and grimmest either of them had believed possible – and both knew what a groan was when they saw it. Percy had been wounded in the war, and had served his apprenticeship in that pandemonium orchestra. As to the Basque, he came from a country of keeners and groaners, and as a stripling had been a keen groaner himself.

'I once heard a snorer who was nearly as bad as that,' said Percy. 'But I've never heard a groaner who could touch him!'

'Nor I, Percilito!'

'Ah well! I suppose it pleases Sister Teresa! She must really feel she's in Dante's inferno. So it probably makes somebody happy!'

'I don't believe it could make anybody happy.'

'I believe you're wrong. Teresa has looked ten years younger this morning. She's a new woman since he's been here.'

Altogether it had been a bad day up to date. And after their lunch they started an argument about *classes*. It was a hot day for this subject. But where the marxian *class* counter was in question – and who brought it up neither quite knew, they seemed to have done so together – neither Virgilio nor Percy would allow himself to be daunted by a spot of heat.

'The vertical classes of Capitalism,' Percy had strongly contended, 'are better than the horizontal classes of Fascism.'

'Better still *no* classes! *No* classes are better still,' Virgilio had replied hotly and mournfully.

'*Claro!* That is self-evident.' Percy was by this time a little cross. He found it difficult to digest his food in the horizontal position, and he had to get a little cross in order to shake it down. It had started to go down quite nicely. A belch or two had announced its downward drift. 'But class, Virgilito, of *some* sort there always *must* be.'

Virgilio squinted at him suspiciously through his white bridal veil – as one bride might at another who had been guilty of too flippant an observation.

'No, señor!' he said a little violently. 'If you permit *that* much class' – and he measured off a fraction of a class no longer than a half of his fingernail, the dirty half – 'you let in *all* classes!'

'Give Class an inch and it will take an ell!' said Percy pleasantly.

'That is so.'

'I agree with you. In principle, Class must be banished from the new communist society. But you cannot in practice abolish class. Stalin and his great commissars after all constitute *a class*. An administrative caste. We know that.'

'But they are not hereditary.'

'We cannot even say that. They are not supposed to be. A century hence that would be easier to answer.'

'I don't understand you.'

'You never do. What I am saying is only common sense. Class, in some form, *must* persist.'

There was a restless movement from under Virgilio's mosquito curtain.

'And it is better,' Percy concluded, with rugged dogmatism, 'that class should be frankly – *starkly* – vertical!'

'No, sir! That is impossible!'

Percy shrugged his shoulders loftily.

'You want a *horizontal* classification – like that of the sexes – upon the political plane, and that sort of class is no use.'

'No, sir! I want *no class at all*!'

There was a finality in this expression of the desideratum of Virgilio, of the syndic of postal workers, reaching him from the shrouded bed next his own, that caused Percy to pursue the subject no further. What was the use in talking to a brute? The lunch was where it should be, well down the trunk. Closing his eyes, he went to sleep.

Waking, and opening first his right eye, Percy perceived that Virgilio had removed his mosquito-curtain, and was smoking a cigarette. He had his history open. With a bloodshot eye he was following the flight of the king to Varennes. He rode with Baillon on the heels of the fugitives. He knew that they could not escape him. Percy closed his eye again. He passed into a half-conscious doze.

'Percilito!' he heard. 'You are awake?'

He grunted angrily.

'What is it?'

'Nothing. Something has occurred to me.'

'Something is always occurring to you!' Percy muttered. He lay there without moving, and for a moment there was silence, except for the mosquitoes. Then he could scarcely believe his ears – for he heard Virgilio say, with great deliberation:

'I sometimes believe, Don Percy, that you are really a Fascist.'

Percy stiffened. Slowly he turned his head upon the pillow

until both his eyes were trained upon the face of his neighbour.

'What is that?' he said heavily – still by no means sure that he had not after all been dreaming.

'I said sometimes I felt,' Virgilio repeated, 'that you were a Fascist.'

His ears had not deceived him, then! Now he had all his wits about him. In the face of an unprovoked charge of such gravity as this he must step warily. He cleared his throat and licked his lips.

'How do you make that out?' he asked off-handedly and in a thickish voice intended to convey that he was still more than half-asleep.

'I don't know. The things you say.'

'I talk a lot.'

'You don't seem to feel things, Percilito, like us. Not like a *sindicalista*!'

'No?'

'No. You feel them more like a Fascist.'

'Thank you, Virgilio! *Muchas gracias! Muchas gracias!*'

'*No hay de qué!*' responded placidly the prim-lipped Virgilio, from the syndicalized purlieus of Bilbao. Percy had always felt an invincible dislike for the Basques. And Virgilio was not a nicer Basque for being an ill-paid revolutionary agent.

One of the oddest things about Revolution was that it did not attract the *less* offensive national types. Nationality remained. It did not transform by magic this offensiveness into an acceptable something divorced from race and from nation.

'In what particularly do I *betray*' – Percy was ironically dignified – '*fascist* principles, my friend? Your idea interests me.'

'In what?'

'Yes – to come down to brass tacks, Muntán! No *feelings*, you know.'

'No feelings?'

'Yes. Something concrete, for once, if you don't mind.'

'You will not be offended, Don Percy?'

They had started *donning* each other, and going back to

58

surnames – Percilito was to be a thing of the past, for the present.

'Not at all. Why should I be?'

'Are you sure? I feel you may.'

'You feel wrong,' Percy said energetically. 'Come on now. No wriggling out of it!'

There was a slight pause. British bluffness was nonplussing – Virgilio had nothing to meet with it, so it had to be isolated and left behind by an interval of silence, during which smoke poured out of the Basque's nose and mouth.

'Mirabeau was a freemason,' Virgilio remarked, as if imparting unwillingly a piece of disagreeable information, which he would have preferred to withhold.

'Well? What of it?'

'He is the type of man that you praise, Mirabeau.'

If this had not been such delicate ground, Percy would have smitten this devil hip and thigh, with a great onrush of withering words: as it was, he took a deep breath, and answered smoothly:

'But many of your leaders are freemasons.'

'No. None.'

'They are. I could name half a dozen.'

'None.'

'I could name a dozen.'

Virgilio waited for a name, or a dozen names. None were forthcoming. Percy knew better than that.

'Are you a freemason, Percy?' Virgilio asked.

Percy smiled, with easy scorn.

'No, I am not,' he said.

'You are not a mason, then?'

'No. What next? Get off the freemason lay. The only organization I belong to is the Communist Party,' sternly and proudly he added.

Virgilio considered this statement very gravely.

'You have not the Communist mind,' he said at length.

'You think not?'

'I do not find in you the hatred I expect of the bourgeois.'

'I don't wear my hatred on my sleeve, as do some of my colleagues.'

Virgilio shrugged his shoulders.

'Your ideas of revolution are bourgeois. Administrative.'

'I am a practical man.'

'You believe in boss-rule. You are contemptuous of the people.'

'I will not have you say that!' Percy exclaimed, inflating his chest ominously, and panting a little. 'I *belong* to the people!'

Virgilio shrugged his shoulders again.

'All who are born in slums are not *proletarios*.'

'You do not need to tell me that!' exclaimed Percy. 'I was born in a slum.'

'I was born in a hospital for venereal diseases!' hissed back Virgilio. 'My mother was the lowest of prostitutes.' Virgilio's eyes flashed. He seemed to be accusing Percy of having connived at this situation. 'She had not even a name. I had *to steal* a name, to go about the world with!'

Percy was crushed. The wind had been completely taken out of his sails by this. He did not suppose it was true for a moment. But there was nothing more to be said. And his chest went back to its normal peace-time expansion – forty-two in place of forty-six, to which 'the slums' had carried it (*proletario* and proud of it!).

'Hardcaster is not *my* name either,' was all he could find to say.

'I didn't suppose it was,' said Virgilio contemptuously.

'It is Hardcastle. *Castillo duro*.'

'*Castillo?*' What had a 'castle' got to do with the social revolution, Virgilio seemed to want to know.

'Yes, I had to change it so as not to prejudice my mother's position in her slum: in case I "dishonoured" it!'

He tried to put great bitterness into this, but it fell flat. Virgilio pretended not to hear.

These biographical sallies and excursions had led them into a cul-de-sac – a cul-de-sac in a slum, dominated by a Lock Hospital. The Lock Hospital was an unassailable trump-card. There was no getting away from the Lock Hospital. And Percy gave up the attempt.

'You are an Anarchist at bottom, Virgilio,' said Percy at last in a palpably lame counter-attack. 'That is what you are. It is the old, old Spanish difficulty – you can never get away from it. The Spaniard spoils his socialism with his anarchism.'

'The Spaniard desires freedom. Not a new sort of slavery. He has had enough masters.'

Percy heaved himself impatiently upon the pillow.

'How often have I not heard that? You resent discipline.'

'You are English!' Virgilio retorted, with enough force to cause Percy to eye him warily, and resolve to bring this unprofitable conversation to an end. 'The English are not like us.'

'In what way do our problems differ?'

'The English are *"una nación de tenderos"*! You have the spirit of the little bourgeois. You cannot understand the Spanish.'

Percy laughed, a short bark of superior disdain. Whenever, upon one of the desiccated paths of Communist controversy, he encountered Don Quixote, he barked in his dry, unpleasant, fashion. For political purposes Cervantes' old lunatic must be bracketed with Saint John of the Cross and the Little Sisters of the Poor.

'We are climbing up on to our Rozinante, are we not? We become *nationalist*, I am afraid. I shall begin to think it is *you* who are the Fascist, Muntán – Go to sleep, chico! Your brain needs a rest. You have begun contradicting yourself!'

And Percy crowed quickly, to clinch the matter. His face wore an expression of polite distaste, the lip curled up a little. He was displeased in the extreme. After this they talked less. The British syndicalist adopted a rather haughtier attitude towards his Biscayan ward-mate. He, too, had his Rozinante. (Britannia ruled the waves!) But he avoided certain areas of controversy. And he refused point-blank to discuss Thermidor – or the Mountain as against the Plain. And *l'infâme* came in for more crushing and brow-beating than ever, now that others refused to take their reasonable share of sitting-on – by the big British big-wig of an imported politician; and indeed defied him, entrenched in their Lock Hospitals and armed with their false names.

Chapter 6

PASCUAL came in several times to visit Don Percy. It was Pascual who had been supposed to organize his escape from outside. Serafín had not been killed at the first shot, so Pascual insisted with forensic fury. It was incontrovertible – he had been murdered upon the ground. He had been plugged, as he lay wounded, a second time. *That* was the fatal shot. A bullet had been fired into his throat. Another Guard, who was a friend, had seen it happen from a window. The savage had plugged him in the windpipe, standing with his foot upon his chest, the unthinkable thug! Pascual insisted that they had proof of this. Evidence that was watertight! Three doctors had testified to it. Three respectable doctors. *Not* Party-doctors.

Slipping down upon a stool at the side of the bed, a pale new hat perched lightly upon his knee, Pascual would rattle on in a hoarse whisper at top speed – his pockmarked face close to that of the patient, feeble from shock and loss of blood – exciting himself with atrocity-propaganda until the veins stood out like black blisters on his temples.

On the occasion of his first visit, Pascual was trembling all over. Disinculpations tumbled from his lips and expressions of extravagant regret: and inculpations were not absent. He excused, and he accused. The whole catastrophe was attributed by him to negligence and worse on the part of Serafín. Darkly, in a passionate whisper, he asserted that Serafín had been *false*!

'He was a false guard!' he argued violently. 'Like all of his calling he was double-faced. Had Serafín done as he was told – had he got in touch with me that evening – ah, Don Percy, *then* you would not be lying here at this moment! I would answer for that – I swear it! The fault was his. You would be as sound in wind and limb as any of us!'

'Perhaps.'

'Serafín was a traitor.'

'That astonishes me.'

62

'We knew nothing. They locked the girl up.'

'Who did?'

'Alvaro.'

'Ah!'

'Yes. We did not know what had happened to her. How should we? Serafín did nothing. We could not know what had happened. It was Serafín who was to blame. Nobody else.'

But Don Percy listened as little as possible to all this, as he did not like talking about what had happened.

'I expect it would have been all the same, anyway,' he said.

'No. You are wrong, Don Percy! It could not. We had arranged everything. Nothing was forgotten. Nothing!'

'What's it matter?'

'What's it matter!!!'

'What's done is done.'

The fatalism of Serafín seemed posthumously to have passed over into his unlucky charge. He was unwilling to hear anything against him.

'I discussed it with Serafín,' Don Percy said. 'He told me there was no object in seeing you. You could do nothing.'

'*Es mentira!*' shouted Pascual, springing from his stool, beside himself at this. '*Es mentira!* He said I could do nothing? He lied! It was his *duty* to do so, to come to me! I was expecting him.'

'That was not his view of the arrangement, that's all I can say.'

'He was lying! Ah, miserable dog of a good-for-nothing *agent provocateur*! But he got his deserts. Alvaro shot him because he double-crossed him – that is plain enough. We know it – we have proofs. Alvaro had been promised fifty-fifty.'

Don Percy shrugged. The seamy business side of the Revolution fuss repelled him just at present. The pay-roll of the rank-and-file – the price of bombs – the cost of inflammatory pamphlets (for penman and for printer) – pistols and informers' fees – such matters were the abracadabra of the machine-life of an hysterical, half-conscious, underworld – out of which he had been plucked and temporarily abstracted, to lie in an olympian sick-bed, above the battle – and very, very sorry for this outstanding casualty.

'Fifty-fifty!' Pascual hissed in his averted ear: 'And *that* would have left him a good wad of greenbacks too. But he thought he would do it all by himself, the fool, behind Alvaro's back and keep the lot for Number One – and say afterwards you had escaped while he wasn't looking, on your own account, and so there was no money.'

'That sounds nonsensical. I don't understand.'

'That is how he planned it. He was a fool.'

'He must have been, if that was his scheme.'

Don Percy was staring into the distance – into the temporal distance. There he perceived two little figures talking in a cell. They moved hither and thither, one lethargically and one impetuously. The impetuous one, the one who was a little stocky, perhaps even on the *stout* side – nice-looking, but very fresh-complexioned – *he* moved swiftly and nimbly (if a little heavily). For he had *two* legs. That was the two-legged Percy! – And he turned his eyes, away from this disturbing scene, and down upon the perspiring face of Pascual, with a gaze of bitter impatience. Here, if anywhere, he felt sure, within a bare foot of him was in fact the culprit! He would have *both* his legs under him today in all probability if it were not for this fool.

'It's nothing!' he exclaimed peremptorily, in a querulous pant. 'Shut up – I'm tired! The man is dead anyway.'

'Dead! Death is too good for such garbage!'

'It would all have happened just the same anyway. It was Banting's fault, if anybody's. Why *escape*? Stop telling me about it, *chico*. I don't want to discuss it any more, see? The subject bores me. Go away and come back some other time. I feel rotten. Adiós!'

Pascual withdrew, casting such glances as an emotional poisoner would openly throw at his prospective victim, at the recumbent source of all his business difficulties: indifferent as a Lord Mayor as to whether he – Pascual – was sacked by the Syndics for bungling, or not! The foreigners all over! One was as bad as another. He only wished this objectionable *inglés* had got it (literally) in the neck in the place of Serafín, who at least was an unvarnished rogue, whereas this individual was an arrogant simpleton. His lips still violently moving – rapping out soundlessly a cataract of words, belonging to his truncated address for the prosecution against Serafín – he quitted the lazaret and dashed to the nearest telephone. For he had to speak to *somebody*. And a few minutes later he was breathlessly informing a personage in a neighbouring city that Percy Hardcaster had said he had attempted to delay his flight but that Serafín had been obdurate. Also Serafín had tried to hide behind him when the shooting began. That was why the English prisoner had been hit in the leg. Percy Hardcaster perfectly realized that it was Serafín who was *alone* responsible for his misfortunes.

*

Percy would certainly denounce Pascual as soon as he was up and about, he promised himself – if only for giving him a headache with his hammering tongue! Had Alvaro been bribed? Had such a man an itching palm like the rest of them? Why should it be supposed that he hadn't? Percy recollected with great vividness the warder's remarks, made while Percy was lying wounded upon the quay. 'Every man has his price!' the old ruffian had told him. Could that have been mockery and nothing more; or had Alvaro expected a tip he never got, because of that air of incorruptibility that had taken him in? Percy dropped this, a problem for a well man – and of no importance at all. 'And I thought he was a straightshooter!' Percy sneered at himself off-handedly, and left it at that.

Alvaro Morato had left the prison. They could not find out, Pascual had said, what had become of him. His case was before a committee of the Cortes. The deputies of the Left and their papers agitated continually. The nationality of the outstanding victim of his professional marksmanship made it likely that this police-murderer (unlike many of his colleagues) would have to suffer for his act. The governor of the prison had been scandalized by such savagery – that was public knowledge. He was a half-Red, though reputed to be in the pay of the Catholics.

'When we have found out where he is,' Pascual constantly hissed, sweating and threatening to spit, but pulling himself up, 'we will attend to him, Don Percy. We'll make a clean job of him. We'll cut out his eyes!'

Don Percy fanned himself, wishing that the eyes of Pascual,

without being 'cut out', could be hamstrung, so that their perpetual idiotic muscular distension might be put a stop to at
once and for all – and if his tongue could cease from troubling,
too, as a result of a similar operation, so much the better!

*

Pascual's last visit occurred towards the end of Don Percy's
convalescence. Don Percy Hardcaster was sitting in a chair,
reading a copy of *El Sindicalista*, looking like the British working man enjoying his Sunday read of the *News of the World*.
And like the British working man under such circumstances he
did not seem to relish any disturbance of his well-earned repose.

Virgilio was sitting upon his bed, the third and last volume
of the French Revolution in the pit of his stomach, a rain of
ashes falling upon it from his cigarette. He frowned languidly
as he read. He had got to a very unsatisfactory part of the
French Revolution. It was the epoch of Thibaudeau. For
several days he had been, without intermission, in a very bad
humour indeed. Napoleon was on the horizon of his history. It
was as if Hitler had been there.

Pascual came in, nodded to Virgilio, and sat down beside
his English patron. Don Percy looked over the top of his silver-
rimmed spectacles at him but did not put down his newspaper.

'Ah, Pascual? How goes it?' he called out. 'Good?'

'What heat!' said Pascual.

Percy resorted to the habits of the traditional Victorian gram-
pus, to signify his gruff agreement.

'That poor devil Juan!' said the visitor.

'What?'

'He's going to be buried today.'

'Juan what?' asked Don Percy, putting down *El Sindicalista*.

'Santaló!'

'Ah, Santaló!'

The manner of the great Don Percy Hardcaster conveyed
that he recognized Santaló as an abstraction to be reckoned
with. He frowned a little to confirm this, and stared at the
crucifix which hung upon the wall before him (an abstraction
of another and hostile order).

66

This local anarchist was dead. Santaló was to be buried by the priests. A dead anarchist always meant more than a live one, even when he had died in his bed. But this one had died under dramatic circumstances. He had died of over-eating, at the height of the heat-wave. That, and no more, crudely announced, would have done little to enhance the prestige of Anarchy. But that was not how it had been announced by his fellow Partymen. They had announced that he had died of food-poisoning. A different matter, that. For why was the food of the public such as to be a death-trap for budding *anarquistas*? He had eaten half a tin of cheap caviar, among other delicacies, cheap but delicious, to celebrate his *fiançailles*. An imported capitalist foodstuff. No Castilian connected caviar with Communist Russia – they would think, if they thought at all, that it came from the land of the Czars. But such details anyway are unimportant – details are *nothing*. Santaló had been killed by the capitalists! He eats out of a tin – he dies. It was simple. Either the middleman was guilty, for keeping the food too long: or the canned-goods magnate was the culprit. Either way, Santaló was no more – killed by the capitalists – struck down in the clash and clangour of the class-war by canned goods as well and truly as if a Mills bomb had been levelled at his head.

The sound of a church bell – a languid and heat-stricken bell – became audible in the breathless hush of the post-siesta, and steadily impressed itself upon the sense of those present as a more purposive pulsation than that of a mere outburst of Time's clockwork voice. But a few strokes, perhaps not yet a dozen, had sounded, when Sister Teresa was remarked by Don Percy standing in the doorway – seeking, as it seemed to him, to attract his attention, with her head on one side.

'*Tocan a muerto!*' she said, crossing herself. '*Tocan a muerto!*'

Pascual sprang up.

'It is Santaló!' he exclaimed, and went over to the open window.

Sister Teresa, now joined by another sister, moved over to the window too, noiselessly, in single file. The bell continued to toll. Percy turned his head away: for he now clearly perceived that Sister Teresa was about to annoy him very much. Head drooped and hands clasped, she was seizing the opportunity: death was to be exploited, it was to be anticipated that her worst characteristics were on the point of being deployed, under that awful authority, with impunity. Don Percy turned his head as far as it would go, in the opposite direction to the window.

Pascual, turning round, hissed back at him.

'They pass! They are passing now, Don Percy!'

'Who?' said Don Percy, heaving himself about on his chair, as if not his head alone, but his whole person, had been directed away from the source of the disturbance, But he knew quite well that 'they' meant the cortège of the comrade Santaló – a caviar tin on the coffin, doubtless, and the name of the exporter probably on a banner at the head of the procession.

The chanting voice of a priest arrived suddenly from the street, nasal and strident, and Don Percy suffered a mild convulsion as he heard it.

'Ave Maria Purísima!' he muttered. 'Why did that man want to have his carcass droned over like that, dear God? The women wanted it, no doubt. Always the women – in this God-forsaken country!'

A God-forsaken country that could not shake off the nightmare of God!

'The *prometida* of Juan is following the body!' Pascual announced, breathlessly.

Don Percy got up from his chair. Something must be done about this funeral – to give it an air! To *disinfect* it! Noisily he clumped over to the window, thrusting himself in roughly in front of Sister Teresa. Then he stood, in full view of the street. He raised his clenched fist in the salute of the Red Front, frowning down at the passing procession. – A horse chuckle of sardonic raillery came from his rear, from where Virgilio sat, who had been a silent witness of this scene. Don Percy clenched his fist still more formidably, and raised it on high a farther inch or more; but the back of his neck was suffused with an angry brick-red flush.

PART II

VICTOR STAMP

Chapter 1

THAT morning Victor Stamp had risen late. Margaret woke him at seven, but Victor played possum. Like a signal-gun the bed went off bang as she sat up. But he absorbed the harsh report without stirring a muscle.

As Margaret ceased to move, the cymballing of the dilapidated box-mattress came to a stop. Stealthily she adjusted herself upon the ruins of their thirty-shilling love-nest (second-hand, in the Bell Street market), in an awkward squatting position – so as not to anger any further the stupid springs. So she remained for a while, unwilling on her side to make the next move. That should have come from Victor. The springs had spoken – it was for him to salute the day. But Victor played possum, in a sly sham-stupor, cut off from the crass daylight by a husky shoulder. He was having no truck with *this* day!

Two taut lines of an extreme fatigue went down to the extremities of her mouth, which was well shaped and gentle, and of a youthful red. Her eyes were charged with the same painful uncertainty as was betrayed in her hesitation to get up.

Having half got up, apart from the desire to spare Victor the crashing of the ambushed springs, when she should next move on them, she procrastinated. There was something in her dully-beating heart that sent out waves of apprehension from one end to the other of her halted body, awaiting the order to march. It was a counter-order. It told her to stop where she was; *not* to march, but to leave the day to look after itself. But it was always doing that, pretending to clairvoyance, and challenging the active spirit, alleging laws of its own. She had learnt to disregard its invitation – to refrain, or on the other hand to execute, under the compulsion of some mechanical superstition. But today she submitted to its interference, feeling too weak to resist.

She had been crying, muffling the bitter spasms lest she should waken Victor. She had been saying to herself that love was in vain, that love could do nothing, that the gods had a hatred for love; that love, in short, was unlucky! What could love do against events? She felt herself a frail contraption, to stand up to time and what each day brought forth and had in store! She was of no use at all, to anybody whatever – without money as she was, without talents, or anything worth having – except *love*: which made everything worse, not better. Far worse – if you looked at it in cold blood. If she did not love Victor so much, then things would not have turned out so badly. All the evil and misfortune that came their way was sent there expressly by destiny, because it knew that love was there, where Victor and she were, and it wished to play upon that – to crush out by torture – *love*!

If she could have hidden her love away from fate, then fate would have turned elsewhere, have been kinder to Victor! She was the cause of all the ill-luck that came his way. It was because *she* was there that no pleasant thing ever happened. It was *the revenge for love*! This, on the part of fate, was the revenge for love. There was no way out, unless she could kill love. And to do that she must first kill herself. But even then love would not die! Once to have been loved as she did Victor was enough – it was compromising to the *n*th degree. He was a marked man! Even if he did not return it, fate would never forget. Victor would always be, whatever happened to her, *the man who had been loved*, in the way she had done (it was *the way* that she had loved was at the bottom of the matter). She *knew*! But there was no help for it.

The notion of death always – in spite of the fact that she saw how it was quite impracticable for her – brought rest to her mind. For when she had first considered it – before she had realized the catch, from love's standpoint – it had deeply impressed her with its beautiful Journey's End effect. It was *The Heart of the Sunset* – as the girl had written who killed herself up among the skyscrapers of New York.

Her head of a small wistful seabird, delicately drafted to sail in the eye of the wind, and to skate upon the marbled surface of the waves – with its sleek feathery chevelure, in long matted

wisps – arched downward on its neck to observe Lord Victor.
The rhythm of his heaves, in his sulky imposture of sleep,
certainly approximated to the ocean. She hovered over him in
her ecstasy of lovesickness, her eyes full of a dizzy gloating,
rocked by the steady surge of his chest. Her eyes were almost
popping out of her skull in the intensity of her desire *to settle*
– to skim down and settle: to ride there and to be at rest!

But why had he not woken up? He was surely only pretending to be asleep after all, for she had made a great deal of
noise! Victor, except for his lungs working, was quite still. He
kept his back turned, with a shoulder jutting up, his face forced
into the pillow.

Victor wanted to avoid her! A tear slid down her cheek.
That was because when he looked in her eyes he would see
nothing but his own misery there. So he wanted to keep out
of her way – who could wonder at that? – especially the first
thing in the morning – the first thing was always the worst time
for nervous men like Victor! What would they be saying to
each other if he showed that he was awake? Nothing very
cheerful, this morning, she was afraid. – And a breath that
would scarcely have stirred a feather, which deputized for a
sigh of flesh and blood, escaped her lips.

But love was too strong. There was its tousled heaving object! There was Victor! She could hold back no more. And
she touched him with a little nervous hand, saying in a small
and rather throaty voice:

'Vic-tor! Are you awake, darling?'

An attractive foreign accent – say the last vestiges of aristocratic French on the tongue of an émigré – made her speech
pleasant and a little 'quaint'. It was not a foreign accent, however. As she had been born poor, she had taught herself
English, and so had evolved a composite speech of her own.
It was flavoured with American talkie echoes; but on the
whole it suggested a French origin, and was extremely pretty,
though her voice had gone a little hollow with the constant
effort cautiously to shape the words correctly.

Victor rolled in one movement, banging upon the box-
springs with his revolving body; and flinging his arm out, behind Margaret's shoulder, drew her down so that her face got

hidden at once under his granite chin, and in the he-man hollows of his collarbone, as she fitted herself in beneath the pressure of his arms. He did not say anything at all as he did this, and they lay there without moving, Victor glaring up at the plaster scrolls of the ceiling, like a picture of an Orang defending its young, his eyes full of the light of battle.

After a while she stealthily lifted her head, uncertain as to what was going on. She stamped a series of impulsive little kisses upon his chin and cheek. Then his arms parted – there was a vacuum, a chasm, where there had before been a plenum: and the small girl stiffly stepped out of bed backwards, as débutantes withdraw from the presence of their sovereign.

'I think I will go home,' she said huskily and hollowly, 'after I leave the shop, and get the address of the man from Nellie.'

'What man?'

'Oh, you know, the man who wanted a canvasser.'

'Right-ho.' Victor rubbed his eyes with his big white workman's hand. 'He's found one I expect by now.'

'I shall find out from Nellie; and then I will come back.'

'Rightyho,' said Victor.

'Shall you be there, Victor?'

'Yes.' He frowned at her as she dressed. 'Benjamin's coming at five.'

'Was it five? Well, I shall be back at seven, or just after.'

She went into the kitchenette and Victor circled over till he was in the same position as at first, with his face flush in the yellow pillow, his back turned on the daylight. He could hear the mild splashes from the sink as Margaret washed her face and the low buzz of the gas was just audible in the silence, when she was attending to her make-up. A big windy groan broke from him unexpectedly – he himself was surprised and coughed.

'Did you speak, Victor?' she called from the kitchenette.

'No, Margot. I didn't speak.' She came into the room. 'I must have been asleep,' he said, as she approached with the tray. 'I could go to sleep on a clothes line!'

'Could you, darling? Well, why don't you turn over and go to sleep again when I have gone?'

'Man must work!' he said, with a Clark Gable smile telescoping one side of his face, and with a sardonic corrugation of the brows.

There was a double knock, cold and perfunctory. It came from downstairs in the hall, where it had thudded faintly: a half-hearted reveille. She cocked up her head, in bird-like attention.

'I will see if there is a letter,' Margaret said – with a voice dying away at 'letter' – rising, at the same time as she spoke, to her feet, with her wraith-like noiselessness. She waxed wanly, indeed, very nervously but airily – becoming a full-length, also, with a certain loss of ground, giving away a foot or so as she drifted upwards. As a plant, as it rose into the air, falling away from the prevalent quarter of the wind, so she fell away before the face of her recumbent lord – with eyes inevitably lowered, and hand behind her upon the back of her chair.

'What hopes!' said Victor.

A few minutes later she came up again from the hall, and Victor could hear her saying in her small hollow accents: 'Yes, isn't it?' in reply to the buoyant rotarian shout of Mr Higham, going down to fetch his morning milk – 'What a glorious morning, Mrs Stamp!'

She came in with several letters in her hand. There were three, which she put carefully upon the bed, near to his hand, and sat down. He picked up the first: having glanced at it, he handed it to her. The People's Art League notified him that the three pictures he had lent them for exhibition were that day being returned to him. In the P.A.L.'s travelling exhibition these three works had brought Art with its Victorian capital letter to thirty cities of England and Scotland. The cities had examined them with a healthy provincial distrust. They had not been tempted by the deliberately low prices. On the contrary. The low prices had only confirmed their feeling that this 'tripe' had no value whatever (and the hire-purchase facilities offered were perhaps even more convincing testimony): and that six pounds could buy many things more worth having than the unsightly stunts in oil-colours and gouache initialled (not even *signed* – not worth it!) V.S.

As on former occasions, Victor had played his part, at the request of the organizers of this sentimental picture-circus, to bring Art to the People. And the People had returned him his goods without comment. He did not blame the People. He would not have bought a Victor Stamp himself, if he had been the People. The P.A.L.'s uplifting announcements, and the perorations of Miss Hyde, the itinerant saleswoman, would have been more than enough to stop him. He loathed the P.A.L. He did not give a damn, one way or the other, for 'the People'.

But the second letter (and he laughed at the jokiness of Chance, which had plugged it in at his letterbox at the same moment as the other one – he was a great admirer of Chance) had a direct bearing upon the P.A.L.'s typical communication. It was from Joseph Griffith, Framemaker, Shepherds Bush. Thirty shillings of the amount claimed by this impatient trades-man was accounted for by the framing of two of the pictures which were coming home to roost in the course of the day. He threw this down in front of Margot.

'And then he'll wake up!' he said.

'What, darling?' she asked.

'Griffiths wants "my cheque" by return of post!' he said. ' "My cheque" is good!'

'I'm afraid Griffiths will have to wait,' she said, pushing away the bill with a finger, quietly but firmly.

'I'm saying Griffiths will!'

In the case of the third letter, he merely looked at the bottom of the page where he at once saw the name Sean O'Hara, and in the same moment allowed it to flutter down to the floor, unread. Margaret picked it up.

'Sean is throwing a party,' she said, as she looked at it.

'Is he? Well, he can throw it.'

'Tomorrow. I vote we go, Victor!' she fluted, with a prim precision.

Victor said nothing. He swallowed with a loud bushranging relish a strong and large kitchen-cup of black-brewed pungent tea – the cheap ash of the tea leaf.

'Who, Victor, is Percy – what is it? – Hard-caster?' she asked. 'Percy – Percy Hard –'

'Hardcaster.'

'What a strange name.'

'Somewhat.'

'Who is he?'

'Some bloody Red. One of old Sean's Red Men. I've heard of him.'

Margaret looked steadily at the note. She very seldom smiled. Poised upon her Dresden China pedestal, exquisite, impassive as a mannequin, she belonged to a 'period' – of her own manufacture – in which no smiles were sanctioned, in which the reserve must be absolute. Only Victor was able to make her smile, she smiled for no one but Victor. But the smile was always a little painful, as if extorted from her by violent means – the violence, of course, of her love, since it was Victor alone that provoked it.

'Oh, yes,' she said. 'This man has just come out of prison.'

'The best place for the swine. Why did they let him out?'

'He landed yesterday, Sean says. From Spain. Cadiz is in Spain, isn't it? Has he been in prison there? I suppose he has.'

'I suppose so. It doesn't matter to me.'

'It matters to him, I suppose.'

There was the slightest, the coldest, passage across her face of something like smiling. It was a lofty half-concession to the British taboo on the 'straight face'.

'If they jugged him, he bloody well asked for it, I expect. Being jugged, for his sort, is like being hung on the line at the Royal Academy. Just about that.'

'Or having a one-man show at Tooth's,' Margaret suggested.

'Yes. Or being seen at parties – the way women feel about that. But old Sean's getting a bore, with his Reds – he *always* has Red bores round with him now. Always.'

'Yes. He has.'

'Always. It used to be Blackshirts. You remember his Black-shirts?'

Margaret nodded, as she bit at a small biscuit.

'I must say, if I had to choose, I prefer his Blackshirts,' she said – with hesitation though. For both Reds and Blackshirts were very gross material for her to have to pronounce upon, or even to recognize as fully contemporary – as inhabiting the same world as that in which her quietist spirit of ascetic genteelness dwelt. That she should plump for a Blackshirt – *that*

75

testified to the fact that, as far as she could feel anything of that sort strongly, she entertained something approaching aversion for the 'Red.'

But Victor shrugged his big workman's shoulders – with the instinctive scepticism of the cannon-fodder, regarding all wars, of Class or Nation.

'It's six one and half a dozen the other.'

'I suppose it is,' said Margaret. 'But I did think his Blackshirt was rather sweet.'

It was a fact that she had said to herself more than once that this Blackshirt bore a *distant* resemblance to Victor. There was the same jaw. Then the shoulders were in both cases atlantean. There was a *something*, too, she could not define. There was enough, at all events, to endear him to her, in a reflection from her cult. But now they fell silent. Percy Hardcaster was to be thrown a party. The fact lingered in the air for a few minutes longer and then sank into the drabness where it belonged, and out of which Margaret had believed it might be usefully abstracted. But in its futility it faded out.

Margaret was in no hurry to move off. They both sat silent over the empty tea-cups, she with a droop and he with a sag, mutually deflated, not a word suggesting itself to either, each avoiding the other's eye.

She got up slowly upon her feet at last.

'I think I'll go and do a little spit-and-polish business before I go off,' she remarked, walking towards the kitchenette.

'I shouldn't worry!' he said.

'But my shoes are dis-*gust*-ing, Victor!'

He flung himself back upon the pillow, a large sultry athletic lock falling over one of his eyes. He set his jaw and remained completely still.

'If that man Blackie comes I should tell him you are expecting a cheque at any moment now.' Margaret, having returned, stood by the bed looking down at the closed eyes and determined jaw with painful attention. 'Did you hear what I said, Victor?'

'Blackie?' he said, looking darkly up at the name Blackie as she said it. 'I shan't go down.'

'You don't think it's better?'

'He's had it in for me ever since I ticked him off about ring-ing. I don't want to have a knuckle-fight with a lousy dun on the doorstep, do I? I shall take no notice. I shall be working.'

She bent down and kissed him as she was about to go, and he took her small round head in his hand with the action of a man warming his fingers upon a teapot.

'Do you love us, Margaret?'

'You know how much I love you, Victor!' she whispered precisely, dipping her head to say it with the action of the cere-monial dipping of a flag.

All of a sudden he began shouting violently.

'I'm a rotten useless bum of a man!' he holloed, sitting up, and she sprang back as if she had been struck. 'No one should waste their time on *me*. I'm only fit to be a cattleman, while I'm still young, and then pass out. I'm a bloody washout! Take that from me! I know myself – shouldn't I?'

'Why do you talk like that, Victor?' She was trembling. 'I didn't think you were a quitter, Victor!'

'Yes, I am. I'm a quitter. It's no use. That's just what I am, a quitter. You've said it.'

'I wish you wouldn't talk like that, Victor!'

'It's the truth, isn't it?'

'You know it's not, darling.'

'Yes, it is.'

'I shouldn't mind even if it were. I should love you just the same. I should love you all *the more* if you were what you say, Victor.'

He called a halt as he heard this, irony driving out the direc-ter movements of his ruffled spirit; and he came down with a spell of silence, during which with one eye he stared at her blandly, as if what she said had dazed him a bit.

'The more out-of-luck or good-for-nothing I was,' he said slowly, 'the more you'd like me. God!'

'I didn't say –'

'You did – what's more, it's true!' He laughed, curling a lip. 'All right. But you forget *me*!'

'How, Victor?'

'I'm not quite so mean as that, Margot. Think what it must feel like to be me – if *that's* me. And it is!'

77

'Darling, you don't understand!'

'Yes, I understand.'

'You're quite wrong.'

'I'm not after all such a lousy sneak as to accept *that*. I hope you don't think I'm quite so bad as *that*!'

'You'll break my heart, Victor, if you talk that way!'

'I can't not talk.'

'Why do you say all this, just as I'm going off? You don't really think what you say, do you, Victor?'

'How can I help it?'

'But we're all right, Victor – we'll get over the present, you know we shall: things *are* sticky, as you'd call it, now, darling, I know. Just *now*.'

'Ay – take the good times with the bad!' he jeered.

She began crying, with little soft pants, into a pocket handkerchief. His jaw softened its lines. A mellower light was seen in his eyes. He reached over and hooked her towards him; dragging the small weeping creature up against his chest – reared up upon the edge of the bed, rampant as a figure in a frieze, all in the two dimensions.

'I'm sorry, Margot. I'm just a wild Australian! I just feel as if I was alive with cooties jabbing at me day and night, and don't know what I'm doing or saying half the time, believe me! Call me batty – leave it at that. Don't listen to what I say.'

'I know, darling. I know that, darling!' she stroked his head, with clinging downward strokes of her small hand.

'I shouldn't mind if it wasn't for you,' he said. 'You make me ashamed because I can't get us out of this – and I *can't*, or so it seems. I'm a failure. Let us face up to that.'

'You're not to say that, Victor. At your age how *can* you say that, anyway?'

'Time is moving on!'

'But you haven't started, hardly.'

'Haven't I?'

'You're a baby, Victor, in some things. Promise me you'll stop thinking as you are doing. I can't bear it.'

Her tears began to drop again as she exclaimed she couldn't bear it.

'All right, Margaret,' he said, patting her to suggest the providential return of optimism: 'I know – I'm not the first man to be handed a raw deal.'

And he laughed, a little hollowly, to encourage her.

'Of course you're not, Victor,' she eagerly agreed, but with dispirited eye.

'I'll see it through – I shouldn't have talked like that this morning. I've had a rotten night. Oughtn't you to be going? What's the time?'

Margaret wiped her face with her handkerchief, with some of the businesslikeness with which she would make-up. That the female headpiece was ill-plumbed was for Margaret a fact of a different order – the cosmetic mind did not, with her, totally prevail. The eyes, as a cosmetic phenomenon, were one thing, but when they ran over with tears, why then it was the heart that was breaking. So her businesslikeness was a trick of the wrist: from tinkering at her face, the wiping away of a tear was perforce very deftly done, with an expertness that had a callous look. Realizing this, she made a desperate and clumsy sweep of the handkerchief and a parting jab at her eye and, throwing her head up, smiled in a strained way; and he smiled in a strained way back.

'Yes, I must go,' she said.

Her going was not easy for her, and when she had passed again into the kitchenette to attend to her face she stood without movement for some time, the work done, meeting her image eye to eye. Breaking off this heartrending staring-match, she returned to the bed.

'Promise me, Victor, not to worry.'

'Of course I shan't, Margot,' he droned up roughly at her.

'You won't, will you?'

'Of course. I'm just tired.' He stretched out and closed his eyes.

'Sleep it off then. That's the best. Bye-bye, darling!' She kissed him. A minute, and he heard the gentle bang of the front door.

79

Chapter 2

Two hours later Victor Stamp was attacked where he lay with a great current of unlooked-for energy. The bed suddenly shook, the blankets were torn away, and the next minute a large young man was rushing in all directions – dressing excitedly, splashing water over his neck and face in the sink, and announcing in all his movements the resurrection of the animal will.

What had occurred? It was the effect of a dream – if Victor Stamp had indeed slept. He was under the impression that he had not slept, but it was impossible to say. Suddenly it was as though Margaret had been there. As palpable as a touch he had experienced her presence; and he had been stabbed with the suggestion of her uneasy care. This dream had masqueraded as a miracle. Its effect partook of a supernatural compulsion – he was standing on his feet before he knew what he was doing. This was not an animal but a spiritual spark; but how much more powerful it was, to galvanize the flesh. It had been as if Margaret had come back into the room, with her wistful, peering, sweet-lipped face, and told him not to worry, that he was young and vigorous, and that everything would come all right in the end: and whatever he might think about that – and it was a girl's way of talking, for there were things that *could* not be righted – he must not fail her, whom he loved. And as he had said *loved* he had sprung up, although he was not susceptible to this word as a rule. Now he was up, of course, the stern reality challenged him. He had to face it, toe to toe.

A very hell of a lousy situation, he granted you it was that. It seemed like somebody's hoodoo. This room got on his nerves as well, and that was another fact. Yes, he was jammed on a lee-shore this time right enough! But there was never any telling. Until the water was over the Plimsoll mark it was best to carry on as usual. And they weren't there exactly yet.

Margot was his mate, Margot was his *love*, who had never reproached him – who was as gentle as a young wallaby, who

reminded him always of that lovely and strange-plumaged bird
that had floated down into the water, covered by his gun, but
he could not fire on it because it seemed too mild a thing to
bludgeon with a bullet – just where the Gentle Annie Creek
runs into the Sandy Elvira. (And a great current of homesick-
ness besieged him, like a storm of scent in the centre of a frigid
breeze, as he remembered his days upon that tropical stream.)
Beautiful Australian names, soft and wild, mild and desolate
– the English mildness masking, or giving an absurdly homely
contour to something hot, vast, and empty, which had no contour of its own, and so had to borrow an eyelash from the
Gentle Annie. A label lisped in the hush of the stark noon of
the 'great open spaces,' jeered at by those who had never
crossed to the colonies, but elected to stop in this damp little
doll's-house of a country, with a perpetual cold in the head!
And Victor Stamp took a deepish breath – to inhale the far-
away spaces, which compared so favourably with Maida Vale.

But the room was full of discreet footsteps of his mate. It
was haunted by his darling, in her absence – who had come
back, as it almost seemed just now, because it had looked as
though he might never get up again, he had gone on lying there
so long, in a malignant stupor. In her spirit had she seen him
dead, and hastened to his side? But only her anxious spirit had
ventured to return – out of timidity, lest otherwise he might
have rounded on her for her gross interference, with a cross
word or a rough look.

Not to let down another creature, who had brought her life
over and cast in her lot with yours, what sort of a fool's dream
was that? But maybe it was a question of good luck, if nothing
more: just as you would not willingly betray the trustfulness
of a bird that makes its nest against your window. A rugged
unrevolutionary principle, founded upon sentiment, not intellect. But Victor Stamp was prone to accept it, because of the
simple life that was his natal background. It was the pact of
nature; but with the human factor it became more. Was it not
the poetry of the social compact too? Here was one of the elemental things in life. Why, it was the psychological analogue
of the 'great open spaces' upon the geographical plane. He
reflected that he was poor Margaret's universe. What he did not

give her she would never get. No! He must not stop in this inert condition, but begin furiously moving round upon his axis – even if only in the void and in a blind spin, and to no useful purpose (though this hateful qualification was added in a sotto voce to the more energetic preamble).

Margaret's last day of work had come round. The Twopenny Lending Library where she had been employed had gone phut and this was the day of the final winding up and they would be lucky if she got her money. Both were now unemployed, instead of one, and on all sides they had debts. But the rent was five months overdue, and a rent that had got so far as that might go on another month at least before eviction set in. That was how things stood. But everyone Stamp knew was in much the same case. Did they all live on their women? No, all did not. But some had to *keep* them, on the other hand: things *might* have been a little worse. He had no real foundation for such extreme depression, as he felt. As he whirled about he told himself all this, fighting off the great melancholic bat that hung upon his flank.

That he felt sanguine was not true. But he felt big and strong and young. He was physically strong anyway, twenty-six was young still. While the physical movement persisted, and he charged about, to dress and wash, all was well. He was back in the chin-high buffalo-grass of his native continent, as a young chap just out of school. He was back in the noisy nothingness of his whoopee days. If he did not feel fine, he felt the next best thing. He felt good, in a mechanical way. He felt good up to a point.

And an odd hopefulness stole over Victor Stamp. It insinuated itself unperceived at first into the hurly-burly of his strange love-dance. Reaching back in one way he reached back in another. He encountered his first ambition, not as if for the first time, but yet with a sort of spurious freshness. And that got into the dance with him too, imparting to it a factitious mettlesome abandon all its own. He felt the Artist now! He had that Artist feeling – he'd be lost without it. The bustling lover vanished in this new measure.

This deluded man could have been seen to cast a glance in the direction of his painting table, where the tubes and brushes

82

in tidy arabesque revealed the housewifely hand of Margot. Almost it might be said that his nostrils dilated above the heady fumes of the turpentine, as the heavy tubes exuded their limpid faeces upon the surface of the palette – as in the old days when they were playthings for a raw schoolboy and he had not yet understood that art was more than a vocational romance, common to adolescence. He felt back into the days before he suspected that the dice were all loaded against him, as an artist – when he was an innocent youngster 'of promise,' in a dud art-school in a colonial town.

In any event, the old hankering seized him, or at least he returned to his vomit with a vamped-up appetite. His mind took the direction of his neglected 'work' once more, without any warning repulsion. He experienced the good old normal itch: he felt it would be good to get on with this, and to explore the possibilities of that, in the game of pictures – trying his hand at the tricks of the tricky Paris maestros. A circus horse reared up in his mind bedizened and white-bellied (started a year ago, the thing was, in gouache): he forgot that the power of a Lautrec or a Picasso was not there to confirm his enthusiasm. Indeed, there was scarcely any power there at all! Nothing but a clumsy smudge would come of it. He forgot that!

A landscape he had started came to mind. He saw a couple of cows: and they were as he had *first* seen them – before he found out his mistake. They were, in fact, two cows of Vincent Van Gogh's. They were not the cows *he* had produced with the sweat of his back-block brow and, try as he would, he had been unable to produce any others! He had had three tries.

With eagerness he boiled himself a kettle (shades of the billy, for this good swagman!) he must have tea again before finally striking camp. All his canvases, on which he did his pictures, were in a wide recess, with their faces turned to the wall. A fortnight had elapsed since he had last gone near them.

Victor Stamp was consumed with curiosity: he was on tenterhooks to see what would be revealed, to a fresh eye, no longer tired and harassed by irrelevant problems of bohemian economy, when they were brought out to be examined, in the light of this new urge to 'work'! For the thousandth time he was so consumed: from the greatest to the least of workmen these sensations of mounting expectancy are familiar, down to the cobbler who approaches his workbench in the morning: he was now merely reacting in the best tradition of his, or of any, craft.

Setting the teapot down upon their domestic table, he brought out and placed against the wall which faced the two windows a half-dozen of those oil-paintings in which his expectations had been particularly centred. One he placed upon a chair: one he hung upon a long nail protruding from the wall.

Then he sat down by the table and poured himself out a large breakfast-cup of the blackest tea, to which he added a small clot of Nestlé's Milk and stirred it as he carried his gaze from one to another of the six canvases.

The revulsion of feeling was not immediate: though from the word go, as he confronted the pack of his recent creations, the reaction made itself felt. Only slowly it gathered momentum, and, becoming the full thing, assailed his digestive centres like an emetic.

Noisily sipping, he fastened his big intelligent eyes upon one in particular out of these six pictures, a small still-life. There a portion of the surface, owing to a happy (or unhappy) accident, had approximated to a passage in, perhaps, a second-rate Braque. He always went to this little canvas first, to warm himself at the spectacle of this highly satisfactory mistake. And today it sustained him for several minutes without faltering. A half-dozen *more* accidents of that nature, and such things might become a habit!

But the energy slowly ebbed from the husky, half-crouching spectator of his own ponderous handiwork. It was a losing battle Victor Stamp was fighting with these maddening things. In ten minutes he was as despondent as just now he had been the reverse. But there was one picture in particular which accounted for at least fifty per cent of his lost guts – namely, the one he had propped up against the back of the chair. This finally reduced him to the lowest ebb. Against that he was quite unable to stand up, it was no use!

It was a largish composition, representing Margot in a summer hat of azure straw and a biscuit-green jumper.

84

How these things can mean anything to a man it is difficult to see, maybe. They are silly smears and blotches only, things that schoolchildren do to while away the time, and think no more about it. But to Victor it was as if he had put his life into these painted imitations, bit by bit, brushstroke by brushstroke; and they had proved a death-trap, as it had turned out. He had drawn upon the life-blood in his body, a drop at a time, as all these artists do. It had all gone over into what he did. It had been transfused, especially, with considerable pain, into this particular image. He had put his shirt on this dud object.

The stake was Victor Stamp, Esquire, no less. And there it stood – not worth the sail-cloth it was painted on: a thing outside himself that *would* not do what he wanted it to do: a monument of his inability to bring anything to life outside himself at all. The thing literally shouted *Second-rate!* at him. *Art-student* yes! but *Artist* not! it kept up its offensive heckling, and it cowed him every time. He never answered back. He bowed his head. He knew that it was true.

Yet he knew in a sort of way how the thing *ought* to look (though as to why it ought to, of that he had but a faint idea). But make it look that way he could not, and what's more he knew it. There was nothing doing. There was something so irresistibly final in its mere incompetence – in its dull imitation of the celebrated modern models of how to paint to win – that there was nothing further to be said. His animal energy wilted in front of it. What was the use of animal energy? He sat morosely gazing, his head between his hands.

He had seen, even as a student, well enough what was what – so long as the brushes were not in his hand. Or he had been visited by intelligent vision in a flash, that had faded out the moment he had started. Margot had sat patiently in front of him for this picture, as he had placed her; the hat, the jumper, the face, made a pattern that reminded him of a picture – probably by Matisse. Even, when he had started, he had known what he had to do. But he had reckoned without his *hand*. For his hand had proceeded to do something entirely different from what his eye had told it; or the eye and hand in partnership had stultified the irresponsible, merely spectator's clearsightedness, of the eye alone.

So it always was. A depressing and oafish caricature of what had stimulated him to activity was all that came of it. So it always had been! And a big groan echoed through the room as he shifted his position. A big groan came out of his big body, because his education had betrayed him and caused him to think of his bovine aptitudes bovaristically, and led him into behaving as if he were an artistic star.

Victor Stamp would never make his mark. He was no good as an artist. He had never been able to draw properly: and his rugged assertion at the art-school at Sydney that *colour* was his long suit – in order to mask his formal shortcoming – was not borne out by his subsequent practice. But it was even worse than that! It was far worse than that.

An ineradicable *prettiness*, of all distressing things, obsessed his responses to the colours of this world. This chromatic sweetness was designed to match, perhaps, the rather meaningless roundness of his halting linear transcriptions. This was his culminating misfortune. It was a really diabolical trick of nature. And against it he could do nothing.

The almost monochromatic severity of the French never ceased to impress, to tempt, and to elude him! As to the well-nigh pathological sobriety of the Spaniards, Victor Stamp gasped in simple-hearted admiration whenever he encountered it. But when he attempted to emulate it, his cheerfulness *would* keep breaking in – if the gushing of his posterish sunset palette could be described as that.

Why should this big rough fellow, so good a specimen of the stockman breed, taller than most over here, with his large bony good looks – why should such a fellow possess this taste for the silly sweet, where the colour question was concerned? In one form or another such a question suggested itself to all those who saw what he did, and then, side by side, saw the man that had done it. The tissue of his senses might have been coarse, and no matter; they might have been infantile – they might have been elephantine: pictorially that might have stood him in good stead. But why should they be *doucereux*, dulcet and vapid, like the sweet-tooth of the immature or the girlish? It was against this painful conundrum that Victor Stamp dashed his skull in vain – seeing that he had been taught first in Australia, and then in the European academies, how unsatisfactory, indeed how scandalous, this saccharine type of seeing was.

But it was really no use at all. That the more intellectual rigours of design should have escaped him, have been plainly beyond him, he understood (very unwillingly). *But this colour business!* It was the last straw – he knew his back was as good as broken. It was such a much more intimate, and as it were ultimate, shortcoming. Against that there was no appeal. He was undone by his vulgar oranges, his saponaceous blues, his queasy purples – just as some men are undone by women and some by wine and a very few by song.

There was, however, a consolation for these things. But it was a consolation with which he passionately refused to have anything to do. It was this.

Most Australian or English artists were little, if any, better than he was himself. When first he had been obliged to give hospitality to this disgusting reflection, so insultingly consolatory, he had almost thrown in his hand. Then he had been forced also to admit (it had to come to that, sooner or later) that there were no good artists in Australia at all. Australia had never produced a single good painter (except it might be for a Nineties fan-decorator). It was futile to deny this self-evident fact. But what had that got to do with him? A lot, something told him, quite a lot. But he *would* not listen. Furiously he banished the outrageous opinion. If anyone had *said* that to him he would have socked them one: but it was *himself* that had arrived involuntarily at the discouraging generalization.

*

At length Victor Stamp rose from the chair, a grin upon his face. It was an almost ruffianly grin, the Botany Bay effect much deepened by his unshaven chin. He returned the pictures unceremoniously to their recess: then he went over to the work-table where his colours and brushes were.

Stamp was a good Australian, he was fond of a game of chance. A good gamble was just what the circumstances demanded – if there had been two Stamps instead of one, a pack of cards would have made its appearance at this juncture. He picked up slowly a big tube of Venetian Red. He put it down again – but apart from its all-red mates. Now he picked up a Red Ochre: he sized it up, supporting its little leaden carcass in his palm awhile. Then he put it down alongside the Venetian Red. Stirring the tubes with his big index finger, he selected three or four more. They all went to join the first two. All belonged to the red end of the spectrum.

With that lazy hip-swagger that distinguishes the men of the Great Open Spaces of Anglo-Saxony, he went over to a second stack of canvases in the recess, and picked a new one, about two foot by three. Placing it on his easel, he took down a small palette from the wall, squirted the red and the ochre, and the rest as selected, ranging them in a crescent of glistening mounds: then provided himself with a dozen brushes, stuck several down below the thumb-hole of the palette, and sat down to paint.

Stamp painted from then until about one o'clock – a matter of two hours or more. It was like a game of poker: and he had on his poker-face from start to finish. It was a good game.

Stamp enjoyed himself. He was quite unhurried, rolling a cigarette occasionally, and lounging back against the sash of the window from time to time, thinking out the next move from afar.

The subject was a still-life. It was a selection of yesterday's debris upon the domestic table – two empty Watney bottles, a tobacco pouch in oilskin, three mystery-novels, a cutty pipe and a blue handkerchief. He did it as a red monochrome. He chopped it all up into big and little blocks of heavy red.

They all moved upon a small fork of yellow, as upon a pivot, in the left-hand corner – away off to the right, in a Noah's Ark herd. He peppered the left-hand of the system of red blocks with a shower of ash-grey flakes – a jagged confetti. Braque would have built it twice as well. There was too much confetti. But it was a muddy red: Victor Stamp *had* mastered his desire to turn it into orangeade and strawberry-cream. He had allowed nothing on his palette that would make his favourite milk-pink punch.

This flight-from-self had been undeliberate, of course. Intuition had been his prompter, telling him that what would come off best would be what would remind him *least* of Victor Stamp. Even his hand, in building up the blocks and chopping them out, called upon his help as little as possible.

His unusual poker-faced approach to the problem, on this occasion, resulted in something semi-automatic, that was the fact of the matter. The red blocks really *had* a spice of intoxication in them. It was one of Stamp's best efforts, unquestionably. Or by one o'clock it was that – up-to-date, and as far as it had gone.

Downing tools, he stretched. He yawned – a long lip-lifting yawn. Swaggering into the kitchenette, he boiled himself a cup of strong tea. Sipping it with a rasping relish, he contemplated his picture as it stood, at the end of two hours.

Normally he would have felt an ungovernable enthusiasm at the sight of such a surprisingly successful upshot to a morning's work. As it was, keeping faith with his idea, submitting to the gambler's fatalism, an extremely grim, not to say ascetic, satisfaction might have been detected at the very most. He *did* know a good thing when he saw it – his training had taught him that much. And this was a good thing. As such things went, this was moderately good. He eyed it sardonically. In a sense he recognized that it was not his. He grinned at it over the rim of his breakfast-cup. He was *amused* at what had happened, tickled quite a lot. He chuckled.

Victor Stamp had been cheated by fate, as it were, that was the meaning of this. He had accepted this last hand as decisive, as a *to be or not to be* wager. And fate had fooled him with a *To be!*

He had painted without effort a passable picture! Irony of ironies, it had been granted to him to do the trick. It was worth nothing – from any point of view; for of course no one would give anything for a picture of that sort today, unless it had a Name attached to it (and Stamp was not a name) and not much then. But it was amusing it should have turned out that way. It altered nothing – he had wasted two more hours, that was all. He was *not* going to put his head in the gas-oven, however.

And that was that. He croaked out a short guttural growl of laughter.

*

Victor Stamp stood up slowly, his expression changing, until at last his face was set in the most solemn lines, as if disciplined to take part in some formality, such as a masonic investiture or an execution.

Well, he had had his game! He had been tossing red blocks with the Devil for his life. He had had a run of luck. Since the way the red cubes had fallen (and so composed themselves quite well) was a matter of pure chance – instead of any personal skill on his part – it *had* been a proper game of chance, and of *course* the bloody things fell right way up! A stupid game! Had the Devil won or had *he*? It was hard to say offhand, but he was pretty sure it was the Devil.

He looked down at the table beside which he was standing and fidgeted with the things upon it. He picked up the blue handkerchief and examined it. It had been blue to go with a blue costume of Margot's, when they were first together and there was a spot of money moving round. As he held it in his hand he smiled his Clark Gable smile – one side of his face all sardonic half-mirth, the scalp muscles ploughing up the forehead to make it all go careworn, so as to embitter the one-sided smile down below still more. The blue handkerchief, in its day, had caused him a spot of·bother, it had led him a pretty dance! Did he remember how as a blue patch in a picture it made life not worth living for him for a full week? Did he not! It was an ill-omened piece of blue! He blew his nose on it noisily, and replaced it on the table. This trumpeting in the blue handkerchief rang down the curtain for this act. He laughed an ironic, scornful laugh and went into the kitchenette to boil more water, for his shaving mug.

*

While Victor Stamp was shaving – using a most formidable blade, a perfect pocket-scythe, which he flourished as he bore down with it upon the field of snow-white lather – the bell rang in the passage, outside his door. Thrusting his head out of the window, he saw in the garden below his friend Tristram Phipps, and shouted, hailing him. Running down, he let him in, and they stamped up the stairs together, Tristram with a dreamy tramp, tramp, tramp.

'I was on my way to the Zoo,' Tristy said. 'I can't stop long. How are you?'

'Fine!' said Victor with a dramatic excess of heartiness. 'How are you?'

'I've had invisible 'flu. But I'm better now. Jill's had it too.'

'Too bad. It's that cellar of yours.'

'I know!' Tristy replied, smiling eagerly.

'You ought to get some other place.'

'Oh, I don't know.'

'It's a rotten hole.'

'Not so bad as all that. It gets wet when it rains.'

'And it's damp when it's dry outside.'

'It never gets *dry*!'

They entered the room and Victor went back into the kitchenette to finish shaving. Tristram Phipps sat down on the corner of the table and contemplated the still-life upon the easel. There was complete silence until Victor came out of the kitchenette, his chin bleeding as a result of his tendency to bravura in the handling of the razor.

Tristy continued to gaze at the unfinished picture, in the attitude of a man in a 'brown study.' He quietly went on gazing with an expressionless attention as he answered Victor, who sat down to clean his shoes with a paint-rag, and said:

'Why are you going to the Zoo, Tristy?'

'To draw a toucan,' Tristy muttered.

'A toucan? What's that for? Is someone advertising six-week trips to the rain-forests?'

'Not that I know of. No. It's not in my *professional* capacity that I'm going to draw the bird. It's merely as an artist!'

Victor laughed, with a sympathetic rumble, as he polished the tip of his shoe with Kiwi.

'It's on the side. For pleasure, so to speak,' said Victor.

'Exactly. For pleasure.'

'Ah.'

'I thought of a scene in which a toucan occurred. I've got a biggish picture started. So I have to go and get the bird. I don't know how he fits his beak on to his neck.'

'I like toucans.' Victor was all for a toucan or two; for two pins he'd have gone off to the Zoo.

'They're jolly beasts. Their personalities are *so* romantic that I can never see them without feeling that it is lucky men's characters are not expressed externally, in that hard and fast way.'

'Aren't they? I think they are,' Victor laughed, aggressive and short, like the crack of a whip.

'Not quite so bad. Toreadors are just like other men underneath the brocade. If our uniforms *were* our skin!'

Victor laughed again, in a deep roll straight from the chest.

'What then, Tristy? Supposing they *were*?'

'Well,' said Tristy, hesitating a moment, as if not really desirous of dotting the i's and crossing the t's in such a desultory talk: 'all men-toucans would have to be put to death, I fancy.'

Victor laughed loudly. He saw a flock of romantic men rocketing in the tropical tree-tops, and an Ogpu hunting party of *anti-romance* inspectors, getting ready to put them to death.

'They *will* be, anyway!' he said.

'Perhaps they will!'

Tristy left it at that. He was content to suppose that that might have to happen anyway, although deploring the blood-thirsty issue.

Victor rose and stretched, his big romantic head thrown up and taking on an heroic look as his body strained upwards following the skyward aspiration of his uplifted arms.

Tristy had continued to gaze with great steadiness at the still-life, not even looking up to discuss the toucan.

'When did you do this, Victor?' he asked at last.

'Just now.'

There was another pause in which Tristy slowly scratched the back of his head, and Victor lounged back against the mantelpiece, both elbows supporting his bunched-up shoulders, while his back pushed against the marble shelf, as if snuggling into the stone by *force majeure*.

'I like it very much,' said Tristy slowly, as if the words, of which he was somewhat ashamed, had been dragged out of him against his will. They might have been some damaging admission, his voice had dropped to so low a key.

Victor who had pushed off from the mantelpiece, stood with his hands in his pockets now, at some distance from his latest work: and the Clark Gable smile had made its appearance, up one side of his face, and his brow had suffered the rugged contractions without which the Clarkly mask would be incomplete.

'Do you? I'm glad.'

Victor stood his ground, his detachment stuck out a yard and was at last remarked. Tristram Phipps looked up for the first time – not directly at his friend, but at the wall behind him. But he was enabled to remark the almost contemptuous expression upon Victor's face, which he had not expected, and for which he was unable to account.

'How is Margot?' he asked at that. 'Gillian wondered if she and you were going to Sean's tomorrow. Hardcaster is to be there. You know, I expect?'

'Yes. Sean wrote me,' said Victor. 'Is Hardcaster out of jail?'

'He's just got out of hospital. In Spain. He was shot, you remember.'

'Oh ah, of course he was.'

Tristy's knowledgeableness regarding the individual known as Hardcaster seemed to impart to Tristy's voice, not the pomposity, but certainly some vestige of the self-importance that in another man an inside knowledge of the movements of a great statesman would bestow. It was a self-importance so disinterested, if one can say that, it was quite evident one would have to look elsewhere than in the amour propre for the origins of this emotion. It was ceremonious – it was devotional. A hierarchy was implicit in this pomp. He remained where he was for a few moments longer, as if expecting to have to reply to some question or other. Victor did not speak. Hardcaster remained suspended between them, as it were, for an interval. Then Tristy removed the seat of his trousers from the corner of the table.

'I must be off,' he said.

He did not look at the picture again. Hardcaster had taken

its place in the centre of his consciousness. It was after all only a thing of paint and canvas. It had, as a matter of fact, shrunk into relative unimportance the moment Hardcaster's name had passed his lips.

'Give Margot my love,' he said. 'Tomorrow, then. Nineish, I suppose?'

'Right!' said Victor. And he swaggered forward to see Tristy out, his eyes ironically lighted to show this man who had been taken in by what he had done off the premises – and slightly offended, on behalf of his colony of red cubes, by the intervention of Hardcaster.

PART III

JACK

Chapter 1

JOHN CRUZE was known as 'Jack' to everybody, much as Falstaff is in Shakespeare's pages; and 'Jack' he was to himself as well. Or it would be better to say that because he had always thought of himself as 'Jack,' others did the same. The fact that 'the Garbo' is the accepted way of describing the Swedish Queen of Hollywood must just mean that she saw herself as that, rather than as 'Greta.' That sort of impersonal style she must have carried about with her – shutting out the familiar, the diminutive, or the fond. But old Jack Cruze was the opposite of that. No one could be above a half-hour with him without dropping the 'Mr Cruze.' He was a natural 'Jack'!

To be standoffish you must have dignity, and you cannot have dignity if you are as fond of the girls as Jack Cruze was – or as fond of liquor, if it comes to that, as Falstaff. The habits of the pothouse made the one into a born 'Jack,' and it was the habit of low gallantry that made of the other a born 'Jack.' Otherwise there was not much resemblance between them.

Jack Cruze was a throwback to an older sort of Englishman, a sport as it is called: he was full of an animal life that you get from contact with animals only. Men don't induce it. It grows to its full stature in the stink of a stable. He was not tall but built on heavy country lines, thick like a dwarf bull: a fair man (now losing his thatch, the remains ruffled up on his head in an untidy saffron crest); with a merry but not entirely friendly eye and a somewhat long upper lip. He hailed from an eighteenth-century Wiltshire village, brought up among horses, dogs and cows – with a soft downland wall overhead, remarkable for a white nag picked out in chalk, and a long valley of water-meadows, complete with hawkweed, stretching away to the woods of a Georgian park, dating from the great building time when squires had become small parish kings, upon the extinction of the Stuart monarchy. But the civil parish of Blackton de la Zouche was his birthplace. Jack was not of The County though; he came from a handy little cottage, and his father was a constable.

From catapulting squirrels and thrushes Jack had grown up to be an eager hustling youngster with a bright eye that darted straight into people's faces, whatever their station, like a shower of irresponsible spring rain – stimulating their attention, and compelling them to pick him out of the herd and exclaim 'There's a bright lad, my word!' And soon he was behaving in a quite eighteenth-century fashion all over the township, and even down in the adjoining valleys for quite a distance, seeking out the shy short-skirted fillies and tiny flappers, and bringing blushes to many a small dimpled cheek with his unbecoming remarks and enterprising habits.

With the bolder girls he disappeared into shrubberies, from which astonished squeals would issue. Everyone soon knew, for miles around, what Master Jackie Cruze was like. No one could fail to note it. He had a bad name, such as that particular precocity brings; and he was always ready to fight if anyone wanted to bar his way to his quarry. His young fist would jump out and draw blood, if anyone should be found to object to the direction his attentions took. And this budding amorist, too, was by no means of the patient sort, it was said. He was a rough boy. Jack was a very rough boy; but the girls laughed when they saw him coming, with his dancing eye, down the road, or out of the hedge, in a Jack-in-the-box scuttle, this limb of nature – whether they were disposed to fall in with his tricks or not. He was too small to be a scandal yet. He was a joke cracked by Mother Nature, the old witch – that fair made you split your sides, if you were on the distaff side of life, with *hysteros* at your heart. You quivered then till your eyes watered, whether matron or maid. 'A dirty piece of work!' more than one stern man had muttered, however. And he had his eye cut open with a paternal fist, and limped for a long while because of a blow from a stick from the grown-up brother of a kid who went crying home about him, and no wonder. In fine, he was *so* natural as to be strange; and he belonged from the start rather to the order of nature than to the human order – a fawn in schoolboy's clothing. Every man's hand was against him in a sense: but to counterbalance that you must conjoin the adage 'A little touch of Nature makes the whole world kin.' The only trouble with old Jack was that he was rather *more* than 'a touch.' He was a proper handful.

*

So much for the *backgrounds* of the offices of Cruze and Manners; but many long years had passed and old Jack was a prosperous man in the outskirts of the City. In Jack's line of business they see all sorts and the great Mr Tristram Phipps came into his office one day, on the off-chance of finding him in, sent by young Hailes, about his income-tax.

'Tristram Phipps is about the biggest artist in this generation,' were Hailes's words, in the letter of introduction of which Phipps was the bearer. He'd properly got the wind up, it seemed, about a demand note from Victory House.

'Is Mr Cruze in?' in a fatigued whisper the artist inquired of one of the girls in the first office he entered. She was a big, dark and dimpled, smiling young lady, with sex-appeal written in big luscious, sinuous capitals all over her quivering person; and when some minutes later young Tristram Phipps followed her up three stone staircases, it was at a pace – set by her – so obligingly dilatory that he was the involuntary spectator of what seemed to him an interminable upward revolution of well-tailored hips, and of slow-motion calves – of the *Ballyhoo*, the American, order – of flesh sheathed in skin-tight silk; and up from those bulging surfaces a skirt alternately raised itself and slid back towards the elegant ankle – unkindly obscuring the view, and then again withdrawing the veto upon the indiscretions of the masculine eye.

An impalpable well-kissed look, as it might be described, that clung about all the stenographic staff (impossible as that was not to observe, upon casually entering these offices) was the *first*, though it was not by any means the *last*, impression made upon Tristram Phipps in his acquaintance with Jack Cruze. The girls who now clustered about good old Jack to type his letters, reconstituted, in some sort, the scenes of his earliest rustic essays in self-expression. They were encouraged by their employer to dress in such a way as to leave no doubt as to the nature of their several charms; for if he had exchanged the lonely lanes of the countryside for the sidewalks of the East End, it was not in order to see fewer nymphs, but more, and more seductively turned out. He had plunged up into London head-first as if into a dense forest of women: he never wanted to see a horse, or dog, or cow again, although deriving from them, or being confirmed by them in, his animal attitudes; he had brought the woods into the city, or at all events a wildness that translated itself into a sort of pioneer dream of metropolitan bliss – a perfect ocean of resilient Sex, as hot as the Gulf Stream when it first rolls out of the Gulf in a boiling tidal wave.

And so now, knocking gracefully upon a glass-topped office-door, the back-block dream of lovely woman stood aside, deftly withdrew her by-him-untouched but only looked-at person. With a brilliant and sex-searching smile she said to Mr Tristram Phipps, pushing the door open:

'Won't you go in, Mr Phipps? Mr Cruze is expecting you!'

And Mr Phipps swam past her upon a soft and southerly breeze of Parma violets, to discuss his income-tax inside.

Chapter 2

JACK CRUZE got up from his desk, young Hailes's letter in his hand. 'Tristram Phipps is about the biggest artist in this generation' – such was the description in the tone.

'Sit down, sir,' said Jack, 'and tell me what the trouble is.'

Tristram Phipps explained that he had received an abrupt and incomprehensible demand for a hundred pounds odd; and of course it turned out he hadn't got any income and didn't owe anything, to His Majesty at least. He'd got even less than one would think, for an artist. They soon fixed all that up for him, and he was as grateful as anything to the firm for doing so, and especially to Jack. He seemed to take a special fancy to Jack. They palled up straight away. It must have been a case of attraction of opposites.

Like all artists, Tristram had a good opinion of himself. Oh, his *art* of course, that was everything, and he looked on Jack and what he did, when first he saw him, as so much dirt. Tristram was a good-looking young fellow and he knew all about that, all right, as well. He dressed the part of the blooming young genius – he looked as though he hadn't washed for six months and probably he hadn't, it's always been the pose of the artists. But Tristram was the sort of lad who knew how to get on the right side of you – he didn't show to Jack's face, of course, that he considered him an inferior biped to himself. It was quite the reverse. He said it must be wonderful to know so much about income-tax as Jack did. 'Our Mr Meopham,' Jack told him, 'he knows twice as much as I do.' Jack thought no doubt he was being buttered up, and he just waved the ruddy butter away like, or rather passed in on to his clerk, to show this young gentleman he didn't want any of *that* dope.

'Now if I could paint pictures!' Jack said, and he gave a kind of grin at this to show him that he mustn't expect too much of him in the way of looking up to those who did them.

'Ah, if I could only paint them, too!' says Tristram at this.

At the time old Jack couldn't make this out. He thought he was having his leg pulled, else he was probably fishing for his compliments. Anyway, Jack wasn't going to say 'If *you* can't paint them, no one can, Mr Phipps!' or anything soppy of that sort. Later on he came to know his man and understood what he meant when he talked in that way. At the time he puzzled Jack quite a lot. But he was a bit of a puzzle all round.

They'd never seen the likes of Tristram in their office before. They went into his earnings, and what surprised them (in fact they didn't believe him at first) was how little he made. They couldn't figure it out at all. All the papers and magazines, too, said he was the coming man. He showed them what the papers said about him. His oil-paintings were 'beautiful,' nothing was too hot and heavy for Tristram Phipps, genius of the first-class, made of no common clay.

'That's why they won't believe I'm not rich,' he said, 'because of the papers.'

'I can understand that,' said Jack. 'I'd think the same myself.'

'At first I thought it would mean I should make money,' said Phipps, 'but now I know better. No one wants pictures. How many do you think I've sold this year?' he asked.

'Oh, a hundred or two,' said Jack, in a half-joke.

'I've sold *three*!'

'Go on! That's not many.'

'No,' said Tristy. 'It's not – nor what I got was much neither. I did not do much more than get back the cost of the canvas, frames and paint.'

This surprised Jack very much.

'Then how do you live? You don't mind my asking you, Mr Phipps.'

'Live?' said he. 'By doing drawings of motor lamps or of ladies' and gents' underwear for the advertisement pages.'

And the expression upon the face of the young genius plainly demonstrated what a degradation he considered it to provide the hosiery and other trades with drawings of ladies' and gents' underwear, sports outfits, motor lamps and vanishing creams.

Jack Cruze laughed, a hearty bell-like peal of laughter, such as would issue from the chest of a Rowlandson agriculturalist, disporting himself at the Hiring Fair.

'Ladies' and gents' underwear?' he repeated, interested at once. 'Ha ha ha! sir. That's not a job I should object to, Mr Phipps. I think I should take that on if I was in your place, I shouldn't be too particular, you know.'

'Oh, it's not so bad. Don't think I'm complaining.'

Tristram Phipps's income-tax returns took on a quite different complexion for Jack thenceforth and he warmed up to his task with a will.

'Let me see,' he said, his eyes full of a novel light that astonished Tristram, transforming this little business-man on the other side of the table: he did not know what it was, of course; he did not know that the Spring woods had entered into the office with all their sweet scents and exciting noises, and that an agent of Pan was now sitting there instead of an interpreter of the mysteries of the Inland Revenue. He had struck a spark, he was aware, and smiled indulgently (for he guessed that lewdness was afoot); he heard the joy-ring in the voice's note, all right, alert and strident, but he did not really see at all this fawn who was a fisherman in springs and pools, and who had detected the heavy white shape of a swimming woman, a 300-pounder of a muscular nymph, and had put himself on guard behind a bush to catch this slippery human fish as soon as it emerged, and have it wriggling on the bank in his strong clutches.

'We ought to be able to knock a bit off there!' said Jack. 'I suppose they're the sorts of things you see in the illustrated magazines?'

'Yes, that's the kind of thing.'

'Camiknicks, step-ins?'

'Yes.'

'Ah – and *corsets* – and yarn undies – I like *yarn*!'

'Quite – all that beautiful woman wears next to her skin – that's the idea.'

Jack laughed, with the full savour of the intimate life of his fair obsession upon his thoughtless countenance.

'They send you the things along, Mr Phipps, I suppose? But how do you do them? Do you employ girls to pose as artists' models? I suppose you do. You must need nice girls to do it.'

'Oh, I can't afford that.'

'Well, you can say you do – you *ought* to have girls really, to pose as models, shouldn't you, Mr Phipps? Most artists do.'

'I have a lay-figure.'

'Oh ah! A wooden thing.'

'Yes. And then there's my wife, of course.'

'Does you wife put them on? Well, that's handy. So you are married, Mr Phipps.'

Jack made a note upon a piece of paper.

'Married man's allowance,' he noted. 'That is a hundred and forty pounds off straight away. Any children?'

'No; no children.'

'What's the dummy cost?'

'I beg your pardon?'

'What did you pay for the dummy?'

'Oh – you mean the lay-figure?'

'Is that what you call it – lay-figure? Right.' He noted 'lay-figure' on his scribbling pad.

'I paid thirty shillings for it, as a matter of fact – I got it second-hand.'

Jack pushed the pad away from him. He began to think of artists' wives – unclothed, of course, most of the time. As he thought of artists' wives he grew pensive.

'The wife poses as your artist's model! You're lucky, Mr Phipps, to have a wife who is – well, you know.'

He clapped his large hand upon his face, and massaged it downwards hard, then looked up again a little flushed and sheepish.

'Willing to sit,' Phipps suggested.

'Well. Beautiful! I suppose to be an artist's model –'

'She has a very good figure, certainly. I work a lot from photographs too.'

'Photographs of girls?'

'Sometimes girls. Sometimes stout elderly ladies! And men as well, you know. Everyone wears underclothes.'

'Oh ah! Pants and vests.'

'And suspenders.' Tristram smiled.

'You never have had girls for the work anyway.'

'I have had models, of course. But they are very expensive. I've never been able to afford them. My friends sit sometimes.'

'Girl friends?'

Tristram smiled again and nodded. He began at last to see that the four walls of this office were by way of being a conventional framework only. He recognized a force of nature that had burst its way into this city office and had consented to assist at the assessment of his income-tax.

'Young ladies, I suppose?' wistfully Jack inquired.

'Friends of ours. Girls we know.'

Jack quizzed this cold and grave young fellow (stuck-up, long-haired blighter), who spoke of these things upon a tone of such detachment; and he saw him in his mind's eye surrounded by a group of real live young ladies (*a bunch, say, of 'Girton Girls'*) and his eye took on a brooding look as it rested upon this unresponsive face. Some people didn't know when they were in luck's way and that's a fact, thought he. Jack Cruze decidedly had chosen the wrong job! *Why* had he not turned to the palette and brush?

102

Jack Cruze sighed and turned to other details of artist's expenditure, of a less interesting order.

'Paints, I suppose, and brushes, Mr Phipps?'

'Now and then; when I can afford them.'

Jack stared a little doubtfully over at this celebrated down-and-out, who had strayed into his office: but all this subsequently Jack found to be correct. All that this rising man, the great Mr Tristram Phipps, got for his *art* – for which he lived, of course, they all do – was fair words when you came down to brass tacks – beautiful printed words of praise, but no ruddy money! As he said himself, the only people who made any cash out of *his* art were the artist-colourman and the art-critics – and even they got less space for their stuff and less pay at that, every day now, he said. This was an eye-opener for Jack. He'd always thought that when you got known in the art-game there was money in it.

As Tristram talked to him Jack's feelings changed somehow, from feeling as he did at first. At first he'd felt, he was open to admit it privately, a little in awe of this blooming young celebrity who had been sent to him in such a flourishing sort of way by young Hailes. In the end he couldn't help pitying the poor young devil. This great young Mr Phipps said he'd never make any more, either, than he did at present – that no one he knew made enough to live on by their pictures. Jack soon saw he was telling the truth. But he didn't seem very upset about it somehow; he was a placid-looking young chap. He almost seemed *pleased*, as Jack described it, to be so poor as he said he was, and quite bucked that it was so hard, so *very* hard, to make anything!

However, this was how these two first came together. Phipps went to Jack about his income-tax and they took a fancy to each other. Or if they did not do that, at least Tristram was amused at Jack; and old Jack began thinking about the studio life and wanted badly to get a glimpse of the inside of a studio, of the studios where ladies' and gents' underclothes were sketched.

'That will be O.K., Mr Phipps,' said Jack, ringing a bell on his desk. 'We'll fix all that up for you. Leave it to us. We will get in touch with the collector.'

103

A radiant platinum version of the first young lady appeared in reply to the bell just as they were moving towards the door.

'Now there's a girl, Mr Phipps, you ought to get to pose for you as an artist's model,' Jack exclaimed. 'This gentleman is an artist, Doris, and he sketches ladies' underwear. Will you be his artist's model?'

'Oh, I'm sure I shouldn't be beautiful enough!' the girl replied. 'I know I shouldn't be beautiful enough!'

'Don't you listen to her, Mr Phipps. She's got the finest legs in the office. Haven't you, Doris?'

'I wish you wouldn't be so personal, Mr Cruze!' the young woman said with shining eyes, moving away, out into the passage, as Jack was too near and inclined to forget himself.

Tristram threw his head up into the air like a distinguished and rather unearthly horse, and gave a faint laugh like a neigh.

'Will you sit for me? No, will you really?' raising his eyebrows, he inquired of Doris, with a smile that just curled his mouth a little, with his eyes half-closed in what appeared to her superciliousness or worse.

'I'm afraid I couldn't – I shouldn't be beautiful enough,' she said.

'I'm sure you've got a very beautiful figure,' said Tristram indulgently. 'It must be.'

He had to play up, he felt, to his professional status of beauty-doctor to whom 'figures' were the breath of life, as well as bread-and-butter.

'She's got a figure in a thousand. She'd sell any pair of cami-knicks she put on!'

Swaying her hips from side to side as the great Stars do in the pictures, she swung down the passage before him, in clockwork rhythm, and Tristram followed, after having shaken his deliverer warmly by the hand.

'It is extremely kind of you to take all this trouble,' he said.

'Not at all, sir!' Jack replied.

Chapter 3

WELL, Jack first went to Tristram's flat soon after that. Tristram had asked him round and Jack lived in the same postal district. It was a basement flat and Jack stood in the area a long time listening to what was called, he thought, the *Swampy River*. They were always putting it on at that time. In looking back Jack always connected that damp cellar flat, which always smelt of the mudflats upon which that part of London is built, as they both pointed out, with the *Swampy River*. They seemed to be as bucked as anything, Jill as much as Tristy, by the fact that they were half buried alive in a bally bog, in two coffins of brick, crushed as you might say by the upper apartments of a four-storey tenement-mansion of converted 'flatlets' – packed to the roof with underfed black-coated proletariat, hawkers and bandsmen, old maids that are 'geniuses', and remittance men.

Whenever Jack thought in the days to come of that household under the gutters of the street as he first came to know it, he seemed to hear the *Swampy River*, which was a pretty hefty piece of musical sadness as it appeared to him – 'Yes, a sick song,' Jill said, 'a very sick song, Jack!' – when he said how it gave him a hollow feeling in the pit of his paunch. It suited the basement to a T and that was a fact: they had nothing but records that were rotten sad – they lived in these clammy quarters under the street – the rain flooded out their scullery in the winter – and turned on hour after hour the most moth-eaten music. Where they got it from Jack was blessed if he knew. Mr Shandy used to go down the Commercial Road for the worst of it (black horrible stuff it was, that seared up the gizzard) to some shonk-shop by the Tower of London. When he once brought them a cheerful jazz they never played it but once, it seemed to make them mournful.

Well, when someone came to the door at last, Jack saw Jill! She said:

'Mr Cruze? I thought as much – *what* an eye Tristy has, it is uncanny!'

Jack was pleased but puzzled.

'Tristy described you,' she said.

'Oh ah!'

'He can make one see anybody as if they were standing before one – it's uncanny. It's devilish!'

'Are you Mrs Phipps?' Jack asked.

'Yes. Please come in.'

'Is this the studio?'

'The studio? Yes this is it. This is *all* the studio!'

Jack was pretty much taken aback. The sweet vision he had had of the bunch of young ladies posing in pink underclothes, upon leopard-skinned ottomans, was killed dead forever at the first glance. And a sultry grimace set in upon Jack's face, as he took the measure of this mournful place. It was a disgusting travesty of his romantic mental picture. His erotic fancy had been let down – with a bump.

Several people got up from the butter-and-eggs boxes and kitchen chairs as he went in, geniuses like himself (Tristy, I mean) who bowed to Jack – young painting chaps and their molls. If ever a fish felt out of water it was Jack.

But young Tristram was all over him. He took him into the back room and showed him his canvases – his oil-pictures he called his *canvases*. Jack got quite into the painting ways during his time with them, he used their expressions. But I don't suppose he would have gone back much to their nest-above-the-sewers as they called their basement-flat, if it hadn't been for Gillian. With Jill and him it was something at first sight. It was not *love*. I don't know what it was, but it was there. Maybe it was love.

Tristram's canvases were on a par with that *Swampy River*, they made Jack feel as if he had a great black cave in the pit of his stomach. 'I must believe Tristram was very clever,' said Jack to his partner, Joe Manners, some months later, talking over how he came to do what he did. Everyone thought that young Tristy was. 'I could see the cleverness, too, come to that, but he was *clever-mad*, if you follow me, for the things he did pictures of were so downright ugly and worse that they made me feel quite bad.'

Well, in this old waterlogged crypt at the back, where the

106

genius worked, there was only a single gas-bracket, whose raw blue flame sawed the air three sizes too big. Jack felt that he was dreaming. Yet Tristram, although he was untidy, did not somehow look as if he belonged in this Black Hole of Calcutta, and his nightmares of pictures were out of keeping with the beggar. For he was a healthy-looking chap. He stood quite six inches taller than Jack. He must have been as strong and fit as anyone to start with, as Jack put it. You would never have picked him out as a genius if he had not been dressed in the way that he was, was Jack's summing up.

But it wasn't only Tristram who would have surprised the outsider in that respect. Most of the half-dozen young chaps who were there looked as healthy and capable young men as you could wish to meet. There was a young Canadian who was a fine sunburnt young hiker-like lad, with a little girl-friend by his side. He was a young poet, Jack was told by Gillian. But he looked like a farm-hand or lumberjack, to a simple-hearted raw accountant, to whom the Café Royal was a closed book – open-necked but smartly tailored. And so on with the rest. None seemed to have been *born* in cellars. They were a rough out-of-door lot in a way. But they all had good opinions of themselves and didn't let you forget they were *artists* for long, and most were Oxford men as well. One it seemed had pots of money even. He'd just come back from Moscow, he was a proper Red, as Jack saw it then, before he got the hang of it and changed his opinions.

When Jack and Tristram Phipps came back, Tristram said to them: 'This gentleman is an actuary. He has consented to manage my affairs.'

They were having a great argument and Jack sat down. It bore upon the politics that interested them, although it meant damn-all to old Jack at the time. Most of those present seemed agreed and it made them very grave, that the General Strike had been a great chance thrown away, never to be repeated, until a blessed war came, perhaps, and was lost by Great Britain, with a mighty slaughter on the home-front, and everywhere else, and if possible sinking all the Fleet.

But they shook their heads mournfully quite a lot. For all were agreed that no war was yet in sight, though one lived in hopes even if one might die in despair. He had always privately sympathized with the Reds, had old Jack. 'I may be a "thug" (one of the pretty names among others that he'd had used about him) but I shouldn't be averse myself to making mince-meat of a good few "capitalists" I could mention,' he said, 'and I don't mind who knows it!' But when it came to what they said about the Strike, well, a man has to think of himself first, after all. That was Jack's attitude. It would bother him *just a little* and he didn't mind owning it, to see Meopham come upstairs with a gun in his hand and push him out of his office. He was a capitalist when it came to *that*. But he thought the better of these young fellows for wishing to get back on those at the top, though some were at the top themselves, it seemed, and he couldn't fathom that. Good old Jack! He's no politician but his heart's in the right place.

'The capitalist doesn't even know his own dirty business,' said one. 'They destroy the artist.'

'Yes, as they don't support art they certainly destroy it.'

'So they help to show themselves up. Art covered their beastly nakedness for them once. It's not covering them *now*. The fools have killed it. They don't know their own dirty business, as Frank says.'

'Yes,' said another, 'they scarcely advertise their own régime, do they, our blind old bosses?'

'They almost seem to *want* to show how hideous the world can be under capitalism, one would say,' said Gillian, who was a keen debater, and could talk Red politics with the best.

'They are good communists at bottom!' a third grinned over at Jack – as if to say that *he* was one, Jack thought. 'They are their own worst enemies, as the saying goes.'

But Jack couldn't help thinking to himself what a beautiful sort of world it would be, *I don't think*, if Tristram's pictures were the 'pictures of the year.' He smiled to himself, he couldn't help it. The capitalists were not such dumb-bells as all that, thought he! Such advertisement to 'a régime' as Tristram's pictures might be dispensed with without danger.

But putting aside the rights and wrongs of what they said, about which he cared very little, to drop in on – just to *happen in on* – this was a pretty grisly lot of dismal Jimmies. About

108

that there were no two ways, thought this great keen-eyed kid from the outer darkness. There they sat or sprawled, sucking their old pipes, and egging each other on as it seemed to the astonished outsider, to give each other the blues. Any looker-on would have seen it that way, Jack said. It was a case of the blacker the brighter with this bunch – they only seemed to get really happy when they had proved up to the hilt that everything was as hopeless as anything and you might as well go and lie down and die. If it hadn't been for Jill talking away and he liked watching her – as she flared up against the presents at some Bright Young Wedding or the high price of vegetables – Jack would have got pretty down in the mouth.

After having jawed away for half an hour in their grand Oxford accents and Park Lane drawls, and proved, to their *own* satisfactions, that is, that there wasn't anything left under the sun worth living for, they turned on the *Swampy River*. They all dropped into a dead silence by mutual consent. It made Jack think of a chapel. They sat gripping hold of their pipes and hugging their great gloomy thoughts – you could see it almost, as it seemed to Jack. They were sort of congratulating themselves on being upon these mildewed premises, squatting between these old walls sweating with good Thames-side damp, with their shoe-leather planted on wet floorboards from the last cloudburst. "I know it sounds stark crazy but that is how it looked to me coming in from the outside like,' said Jack to Joe. And Jack was not the craziest man in that room by a long shot.

Well, after half a dozen more records, each more of a midnight tomcat fandango than the last, they started again about 'their old social revolution,' Jack's words again : and Tristram, it seemed to Jack, got fairly worked up about it more than the rest. He tossed himself about, clenching his fingers and ruffling his hair which was in great black locks like a coster's. He was a pretty boy, if he had cared to look after himself.

It was then Jack first heard the name Hardcaster. One of them had a newspaper he had brought out of his pocket. He handed it round to the others, and several leant over to look at it and they read it together, in a frowning group. A grim group,

109

of frowning proletarians, in one of the roughest billets of the class-war front, with a low-watted filament casting a romantic high-light in their cellar-refuge.

'It's the only account I've seen,' said the one who had brought the paper. 'They shot him "while attempting to escape." As usual!'

There was a fierce growling murmur in the throats of all present, at the phrase 'shot while attempting to escape.'

'What are we doing about it?' asked Gillian suddenly. But 'we' didn't seem to be doing anything, for nobody answered. They were huddled up and gazing dourly at it in their minds, as if it had been an object-lesson, supplied them as an exercise in appropriate response to propaganda. Gillian's remark startled them, as if a jackdaw had barked out a slogan for a more advanced class than theirs. Gillian turned to Jack, to explain what was going on.

'It's the fascist formula – "attempting to escape,"' she said, looking very determined. 'They always say that when anyone is shot up. Rosa Luxemburg was shot that way.'

'Who was it was shot?' asked Jack.

'A communist. A splendid man. Percy Hardcaster.'

'Was he killed escaping?'

'No, he wasn't *killed*.' She fixed on him a dull eye, of half-doubt. 'And he wasn't escaping.'

'Oh!' Jack looked mystified. He had understood that some Red had been killed while escaping, by Blackshirts.

'He was very badly wounded,' said Gillian severely, frowning at him. 'I don't expect he'll recover. He's not expected to.'

She looked very grave and Jack put on a grave look too. He was wondering if he'd heard aright and if the name was really Hard Caster. That must be communist for something. He heard someone else say it, and he heard it again. It certainly sounded like Hard Caster.

One of them was reading:

'"Percy Hardcaster is in the prison at Fuentes." That isn't where he was, is it? They've moved him!'

Their comrade had been moved. There was a guttural stirring of larynxes.

' "No one is allowed to visit him. Our correspondent asked if he might send him up a note. He was informed very curtly that it was out of the question. The doctors, reporting his condition, say it 'gives no cause for anxiety.' But 'absolute rest is essential.' There is reason to believe, however, that his condition is graver than would be gathered from their statement. Our correspondent gives it as his deliberate opinion that it is doubtful if anyone will ever see Hardcaster alive again – except the prison authorities! That is certainly the impression he carried away with him." '

Mocking guffaws greeted the reading of the doctor's bulletin. It was obvious Hardcaster was being murdered by the fascist doctors.

'But he can't be allowed to die like that!' said a pretty girl, whose mouth looked all the better shaped for its expostulatory distension – just as a chest is none the worse for being charged with indignant wind. And Jack joined in, trying to catch her eye.

'What is the British Consul doing about it – does it say?' asked Tristy, rolling in a dark agony upon his egg-box.

'The British Consul? No.'

'He's doing nothing, of course – why should he be doing anything?' said Dick Toland, the biggest 'Moscoutaire' present, a thirty-year old don from a northern university, where he had a big noisy left-wing cell. 'What an extremely odd question!'

Tristy looked as if he had been caught out in an elementary mistake, and hung his head, discomfited and disconsolate.

'I meant, of course, why wasn't he?' he muttered apologetically.

'Why? I think we can guess *why*!' said Gillian with extreme scorn.

'Can't the ambassador in Madrid be made to do something?' the Canadian artist asked. 'I mean, through the Foreign Office?'

At the words 'Foreign Office' several who had been about to explode at 'ambassador' changed their minds and held their peace, with one accord.

But Gillian jeered, in a bitter drawl (in spite of 'Foreign Office'):

111

'The ambassador! If you had been born in a legation, young man, you wouldn't talk about ambassadors doing anything in a case of this sort!'

'But he wasn't!' retorted the Canadian's girl-friend tartly.

'I know!' said Jill.

'What!' exclaimed Dick Toland. 'Interfere in the internal affairs of another country! Who was it made that extraordinary suggestion!'

Everyone laughed.

'Do anything that would impugn *the sovereignty* of a "great and friendly neighbouring state"!' he exclaimed. 'So much as *hint* that it was anyone else's business if a foreign government kills and tortures its minorities or shoots up a few of His Majesty's subjects! That is a very ignorant suggestion, sir!'

'The Foreign Office might do something,' was all the Canadian could reply to this, a rejoinder that was allowed to lie.

Jack, who was under the impression that they had begun talking about Russia now, laughed as he caught Jill's eye and said – as she lent her ears to him, smiling patronizingly:

'It's a fact they're none too fond of us British in those parts from all accounts.'

'It certainly seems they're *not*!'

'A business pal of mine nearly got put in a slave-gang.'

'A slave-gang?'

'Yes – they have slaves. He went nosing round a bit – sort of souvenir-hunting; and the next thing he knew he found himself locked up with two or three dozen other chaps – a proper lot of hobos – in a cell about ten foot by twenty. Or thirty.'

'Twenty probably.'

'Yes – you're right, it was twenty.'

'Was he tied with ropes to other people?' asked Toland.

'I don't think he was *tied up*. He said the stench was enough to turn you up.'

'You bet it was.'

'They took his passport away – he never saw that again. And all his money too.'

'Was that in Valencia?' Toland inquired.

'No, that wasn't it,' Jack said. 'What do they call it now?

Petrograd. Yes, that's right! Petrograd. He said *the pauperism*
– it had to be seen to be believed!'

Noticing blankness – a sort of amazed petrifaction – come
into the face of Toland, he hastened to add:

'But there are some classes there it seems who are quite well
off with cars and servants!'

'Really?' Gillian said, who had not been listening.

'That was only the folks in the streets he meant. He didn't
like them because they gave him a raw deal. – But it's not the
capital.'

Geometrically in the centre of the blankness that had driven
all expression from Toland's face a light broke, an intelligent
spark appeared. This spread, or crept, with a direct slowness
outwards, until a slight smile – still hemmed in by the stony
blankness – stood out a minute, and faded again, as he glanced
at Jill – sitting and flushing, with surprise, beside her stammer-
ing protégé. Then he turned his back upon Jack, and joined
again in the Hardcaster racket – the name was conversationally
held aloft as a cornucopia at the christening of the classic
crops.

'Who told you all that stuff, Jack?' asked Jill angrily frowning down at him. 'You are an old nitwit to be sure! Can't you
see that's all a pack of lies? Someone has been telling you
fairy-stories about Russia, Jack.'

'I know the fellow *went* there right enough!'

'That may be. But that wasn't what happened to him.'

'I daresay not,' said Jack – saying in his heart 'all men are
liars,' and remembering that old Fred, who had told him this,
had more than once departed from the truth, and would not
hesitate to cross the line that separates those whose words are
their bonds from those whose words are scraps of paper.

This little flutter in the conversational field having had such
an unfortunate termination, Jack thought he would be seen and
not heard for the rest of the time; and he devoted himself in
consequence to watching the bust, mouth, and hips of the
ladies present and listening to their way of pronouncing words
with which he was not familiar, and their ways of reacting,
muscular and vocal, to unfamiliar stimuli. None came up to
Gillian; and he soon tired of this occupation.

113

'Oh, are you going?' Tristram drawled in great surprise; he had altogether forgotten about Jack being there. Gillian and he came to the door to show Jack the way: and the name of Hardcaster still echoed behind them as they passed out of the unhealthy vault – the 'studio' of his bawdy dreams. But his hostess had come right up to his expectations, and even started a new line of thought. Jill was a big fine dark girl with a skin like parchment (which was the result of bad cuisine but it somehow suited her) and when Jack first saw her he got a kind of shock but of a very nice sort, he said it was. It was such a shock as it's nice to have, if you get me. With some girls you seem to be matey right off, as if you couldn't help yourself! I believe Jack says – when the area door opened first and he saw Jill for the first time – he might have clapped his lip on her jaw and come away with a kiss in return, without thinking there was anything funny about his doing it, nor she either.

'Is Tristy here?' he might have said as he kissed her and walked in. 'Yes, Jack,' she might have answered. And he might have taken it in the ordinary course as what he'd expected. Now as he and they stopped at the door to say goodnight, Jill and he knew he would come back, because he couldn't refuse an invite where she would be; and Tristram had taken a fancy to him and asked him back at once, and he'd said 'Yes.' So that was settled. Jack didn't feel comfortable altogether in this company of young chaps at the first go-off, the Oxford Accent as they call it got him groggy. 'It makes my *own* accent feel sort of funny, I suppose,' he says. 'I catch myself wanting to imitate it too, it's catching, and when I catch myself at that I see red, a sort of butcher's-shop scarlet, believe me.'

Jack wasn't educated, he doesn't need anyone to tell him *that*.

There was another thing about Jack's going to Tristy and Jill's, all this crowd was youngish chaps. They used to say to him: 'Mr Cruze' – Cruze first, *Jack* afterwards – 'do you remember, Mr Cruze, the Dock Strike – you know when Ben Tillet was food-dictator?' Jack remembered the Dock Strike, yes, when this lot were scarcely out of their cradles, you might say. It made him feel he was getting on, though he wasn't so old. But I suppose I ought to have given more details about

Jack Cruze ('the widow's cruze' is the usual joke about old Jack's name – we had better get all the jokes over before we start). Well, Jack's round forty – you know, *round* it. That's the last of the jokes. No, it isn't. Jack's fat – as well as round forty, or on the fat side. But Jack's a handy man with his fists. And he's not afraid of using them. Is he any the worse for that? As an Englishman, is that to his discredit? It's the art of self-defence. Jack's a pretty handy man *on the defensive*. You can take it from me. I've seen him taking care of himself, I can testify that his defences are in good order.

Only the other day Jack defended himself against a man in his office for telling him he'd told him wrong about his income-tax. What this bird actually said was that Jack was 'a lousy Inland Revenue spy.' A man must know how to defend himself. This ruffian said he'd publish the fact, as he was pleased to call it, all over the neighbourhood, where they get a tidy bit of work amongst the tradespeople. So Jack knocked him down at the side of his desk, he only hit him once, and told a clerk to pull him out and put him under the lavatory-tap.

He called Jack *a thug* afterwards, outside in the streets. That's what you get, as Jack says, for helping people. He'd saved the man hundreds of pounds! Thug is an ugly word. For some people Jack's a thug – it's best to know the worst about people.

Chapter 4

WELL I've said it was *something* at first sight between Jill and Jack, and something came to pass very quickly. Jack soon found Gillian Phipps regarded him differently from the rest. This pleased him quite a lot at first. She'd say 'Jack, you're *different*,' when he'd say he couldn't stick the accountant's cor-roborees at Frascati's, or the Rotary Club beanfeasts Meopham and their bank manager went to and asked him to go along. And once he told her he shouldn't really come visiting so often, the others didn't. She said, 'But you're *different*, Jack.' So he began to think of himself as 'different.'

115

She meant, that was plain enough, that Jack was *better*. Feeling *different* gave him confidence, I suppose, about showing Jill how he felt about her on the quiet. One day he got there when Jill was by herself in the flat. This was two months after he'd first come to see the basement, and he'd dropped in more than once in the hope of catching Jill when Mr Phipps was absent, but he'd had no luck so far. If he caught her alone he had his plans laid; for he'd never yet got on fresh terms with a proper lady, and here was a highbrow lily that sprouted like a mushroom on a garbage-tin – her body sheathed in pink Kestos and a step as light as an antelope.

He knocked and waited, performing a devil's tattoo on his attaché case. But he was in luck's way. For, as he stood in the area, beating the charge, he saw her in the front room, between the gingham curtains. But he saw *more* of her than he'd ever expected to see just yet awhile. For she was coming out of the back of the flat with no clothes on, with a skating movement. The Aphrodite of the Sewers! As naked as God made her – as Jack said.

As Jack saw her body he caught his breath, as if he'd got smacked with a squall of wind in the mouth, stepping out on to a Channel jetty. She waved to him (he didn't move) and went back. Before Jack could say 'Jack Robinson' she was back. She came out of the inside door again properly dressed and let him in.

'Where's Mr Phipps?' said Jack.

'He's gone to buy some yellow ochre,' she said.

The place always stank of paints and Tristy was hard at it now for a great exhibition of his masterpieces, and worked double tides – off and on. Not steady. Trust an artist for that.

Jack didn't look at Gillian – he'd been ploughed up inside by seeing her body just now without any clothes on it. Jack knew his eyes would be telling and saying things they shouldn't. It's a fact that where the girls are concerned Jack's been a hot customer, there's no use denying that, I'm afraid. More than once this man has been called thug (entirely without reason); he's also been called *hog*. So put hog next to thug – a hard name or two's not going to bother Jack! A pretty lot of names this precious fellow of yours gets himself called or calls himself, I expect you'll be saying. But it isn't Jacko that does the calling. I'm telling you what he's called by others and I'll let you judge for yourself. But how about the beam in your eye, brother? How about all those shame-making 'undies' that gorge the shop-windows? But enough! Let's confess that our Jack's no little tin-saint and leave it at that.

If the plain truth has to be told, then, Jack wanted Gillian Phipps and he'd made up his mind to get her. She was a married woman? That can't be helped. Jack fell for her the first time he clapped his eyes on her and being what he was just had to plot how he could get her all for himself. She was a *lady* and that was a magical word for Jack. He had never been intimate with a real lady and the thought of a real lady sighing in his arms was what really settled it with Jack. But Gillian was one of the loveliest girls and maybe old Jack was not so wide of the normal mark when he felt that way about it, after all.

But Jack had to exercise caution, and at the moment his thoughts were not of a genteel enough cut, he reckoned, to show to a lady. So he kept his eyes down so that they shouldn't be seen. If he had looked up at her he knew he would be showing her how he was all steamed up. He kept his hands in his pockets – he did not trust himself to grasp her hand. Meanwhile he got red in the face, keeping the blood back and trying to carry on as natural as he could, as if it was business-as-usual between Jill and him.

'You don't look well, Jack,' said Gillian, and it's a fact he felt a little queer. It always went to his stomach – he had to push it back – and the repression made him feel as if he'd eaten something that didn't agree with him. His hands, as if he'd been afraid, shook in his pockets, and were damp with sweat. And he sort of blushed as if he'd been ashamed as well. Jack felt rotten just from having to damp down what he felt about Jill.

'Jack, are you sure you're all right?' she asked, throwing anxiety into her voice, and furrowing up her brow with a polite concern; and out of the corner of his eyes he could see her looking at him, though he kept his eyes down on the floor.

She had said he was *different*. Jack wanted to be different to her, from what he was with other girls. He was shamed, if it must be confessed, to show her the sort of man he was with

117

other girls. And he always hid Mr Thug as well when he was talking in front of her in company – he saw to it his voice shouldn't rise too high. He knew he was, take him by and large, as dirty a piece of work (the words are his) looked at from the objective (Jack's words again) as you could wish to meet. For afterwards he learnt to see 'the objective' from knowing Jill. Circumstances had made him as he was, the responsibility was not with him. What was he? He was just a hard-boiled man of business who went out after skirt after business hours, just as most of them do. He'd had to fight his way up where he had got pretty hard, and he had just formed the habit of paying himself for that with skirt – after office hours and sometimes in office hours as well. But he never let that interfere with his business and had a good name in his profession for selecting able and intelligent clerks, who knew their jobs, even if he didn't know it himself.

'Won't you take off your jacket? It's so hot down here. I've been sitting for Tristy for the nude and it's got terribly hot in here.'

'Yes, it is warm,' said Jack, and he passed a hand over his face which was as hot as if he'd been running to catch a train. But as to undressing he declined to do that, though he didn't reply.

Jill threw herself down on a butter-and-egg box – there was a great garden-bolster on it to stick in a hammock. It was where she posed for her picture. And out of the corner of his eye Jack couldn't help himself seeing as much legs – all white and unnatural, rubbed with flour as Tristy wanted them, it seems, for his sketching work – as he would have had to see if he'd been the artist and she posing for a 'white nude' – as Tristy called it, when he'd had her powder herself from head to foot. But there wouldn't have been such a power of painting done, thought Jack.

'Have a scotch, Jack?' she said.

'No thanks, Jill,' he replied. 'I don't fancy it. I'm on the water-wagon!'

And so as not to see anything more, as it was making him real bad inside, he turned and looked at a big photograph of a picture on the wall behind him that looked like a blooming air-

118

plane crash in the middle of a football scrum. An inch more of this girl's flour-whitened flesh and the game would be up! He would have to show her what he felt about it. And at that time he was none too sure that she wasn't after all laughing at him. She often had a queer sort of smile on her face. He had a hunch there was something underneath it and often when she'd say, 'Jack, are you sure you're well?' – well, he felt she was treating him as if he was *different* all right, but *different* not in the way that was altogether complimentary. Putting it without frills, Jack felt she was almost treating him sometimes as if he wasn't all there.

Not that that worried him much. He wasn't *entirely* all there, so why disguise the fact, and alongside of her anyway he felt just like a great big kid all the time, though maybe he was half as old again as she was – it would have been all the same if he'd been a hundred.

'You don't seem very sociable today, Jack,' she said, getting up from the butter-and-egg box they used as a settee. Jack pretended to be blinking away at the old picture as if he was a connoisseur, a thing he never pretended to do at ordinary times and she knew it.

'What's this, Jill?' he asked.

'That? You've seen it before, Jack. It's nothing, it's a picture of Albert's. It's not very good.'

He could hear her coming over towards him, scratching herself, he believed, as she often did.

'Come and look at what Tristy's been doing of me,' she said, 'if you want to look at pictures, Jack.'

She took his arm, it was the first time they'd touched like that. She ran her hand down to his where it was half in his pocket and leant against him. Then she pulled him off almost backwards, and old Jack keeping his eyes down all the time. It must have been a bit of a comic sight, he like a sulky youngster dragged off backwards. She towed him off at all events like that, his fists still stuck in his pantie pockets, into the back room, where a big picture stood on an easel, of her nude.

'What do you think of it, Jack? It's me. He's just done it.'

Jack raised his eyes, he had to, a little over towards it. Gillian lay all curled up in the picture like a hefty great serpent all

119

made out of lard – just like her skin was powdered, or it's as if he'd sculptured her in dough. And Jill was a big fine girl with a small head like a snake, too, with big green eyes that stared out at you and drew you into her vortex.

'You're not looking at it, Jack,' she objected. 'You're not looking. Have you got a stiff neck or what?'

'Yes, I have got a stiff neck,' Jack said, putting his hand up to his neck.

'It's the season p'raps,' she said.

'P'raps it is, it may be seasonable as you say, Jill. But I often get little stiff aches, it's inherited.'

'From your ancestors, Jack?' she shook up against him with a deep laugh like the big baying notes on a 'cello violin. 'You *are* grand today! You don't usually talk about your ancestors, Jack! You're on your high horse, Jack. Very stand-offish.'

I don't know how it was, but this somehow annoyed Jack a little – as if he'd never had any 'ancestors,' I suppose that was it. She was laughing at him as if he'd jumped up from nowhere (as he had) and to talk about a pedigree with the likes of Jack Cruze – even as much as is required to inherit a stiff neck – was a matter for laughing.

Jack turned his head, slow as if his neck had been properly stiff, a half-inch at a time, and looked at her full-on – it was the first straight look he'd given her since he had come in and seen her without her clothes through the curtains. Her eyes were laughing and his were grinning. They grinned and laughed with their eyes without speaking. They looked into each other deep down – as far as each went. And Jack pushed forward, as you might explain it for him, that disreputable Mr Porker he'd been hiding up all along, and the Old Thug too (where one went the other went). He stuck out his muzzle of cave-man indigo (for he was blue on the chin though blond on the crown and as sharp as a fretsaw) as if to say, 'Stand forth, you unmentionable member of the Cruze household and show the lady what a fine stout lad you are!' Thug speaking to his brother-brute, you see.

This eye-play went on for quite a while, he staring straight into hers, and giving her a wicked peep of all that he'd been keeping fastened down on the floor. He put his hand round

behind her body and drew it up against his, and she pressed
up against him, leaning her head back and looking down her
nose, as if she was measuring him a long way off, and trying to
get a view of him upside-down – her eyes with the lids dropped
with just room to see.

Her lips hung outside her face, in a scarlet pout, as if it was
the inside of something slit open with a scalpel like the sur-
geons use, and that had curled out on opposite sides where the
knife went in. Jack pulled her head down with his other hand
and pushed his mouth into the wet cut. And how long he
kissed her for he didn't know, when he heard the door open,
the one from the scullery in the area. It was Tristy back with
his yellow ochre.

Jack backed out and gave her a rather hard push, for she
didn't seem to take any notice of Tristy's coming in in the
other room. They would have been fixed there together still,
when he came in, it seemed to Jack, if it had rested with her.

'Didn't Jack come?' Tristy called out, as he could be heard
throwing his parcel down on the table and lighting a fag.

'Yes, he's here,' she said.

'Oh, is he?'

'At least I think he is – he's so *stand-offish* and has so little
to say for himself that I'm not sure yet whether it's our Jack at
all that's blown in or somebody else. Come and have a look
at him.'

That was pretty good, Jack thought, after what he'd just been
doing to her. 'So little to say for himself!' He grinned at her
and said so that Tristy couldn't hear:

'Jill, you're a corker!'

Tristy came in.

'Well, Mr Phipps, sir,' says Jack, taking him by the hand and
shaking it, very cordial indeed to be sure. Jill was smiling at
them, a little sad-like, Jack thought at the time, and Tristy
looked down on him from his six-foot something, smiling too –
but all friendly, as if he was reading his thoughts with good-
natured condescension: 'This is a very fine piece of work, sir!'

'You like it, do you?'

'I like it very much, Tristy, very much indeed.'

They all stood silent for a few minutes. Jack looked down

at the floor, and he felt his face getting red again. When he looked up Tristy was gazing at the floor, very grave and shut-off from Jack and her. And Jill had sat down, like an audience to watch them from the stalls.

'How much is that canvas, Mr Phipps?' he came out with it a little roughly. 'Just take it as if I am a rich city chap come to look at your pictures with a view to a purchase, see. Treat me as a stranger. I should like to buy it. What is the price?'

'When it's finished, thirty pounds,' said Tristy at once.

'Thirty pounds? Is that all? It's a snip! When will it be ready, Mr Phipps?' Jack asked him, very brisk, very much the buyer.

'It depends on the light. Next week, I should think.'

'Next week? That's settled then. Would you like my cheque at once, Mr Phipps?'

Jack was a swell art-patron, there he stood puffing himself up with importance, and his scowl swept round the room. He played it like a proper actor. 'I'm not the son of a cop for nothing!' Jack would say: and he took out his cheque-book to show he was as good as his word.

'Put that thing away, Jack Cruze! This has gone far enough!'

Jack believed that he started as she spoke. Jill was on her feet frowning in a comic cross way she had. She was pointing at his cheque-book which he had held open in his hand.

'I don't get that, Jill. I'm in earnest about it.'

'You're a friend, Jack. We don't want your money. Get that, Jack!'

'Of course we don't,' Tristy said. 'But's he's only *pretending* to be a purchaser, Gillian. Our Jack is play-acting for us. But it's nice of him all the same.'

'No, he's not,' Jack said. 'I want the thing, why shouldn't I pay for it? I've got the money – it's for sale, you say.'

'Because I tell you, Jack, it's *not* for sale – to you,' she said.

'Jack's not play-acting,' Tristy said. 'If Jack really wants it and can afford to pay as he says, I don't see for my part why he shouldn't. Skinner bought something the other day. He's a friend, just as Jack is.'

'But Jack is *different*.'

'Yes, I know Jack's different,' Tristy said.

'No, he's not!' Jack shouted a bit, shamming that he was getting tough. 'In what way am I different?'

She'd got his back up again with her *different*, that was the fact. He was going to know, Jack was – and have it out once and for all – in what *way* he was different!

They both joined in with each other in a sort of gentle laughing – *pitying* laughing, Jack felt it was. And you can just see how that put his back up a bit farther yet. He wasn't standing for any more of that.

'You're different in *every* way, Jack. Didn't you know?'

'I can't say I did, Jill.'

At this point for two pins he'd have walked out on them then and there, and never put his nose in their buggy flatlet again, he told Joe Manners. It would have been better for him if he had. But well, he sort of felt he hadn't got all he wanted yet. It was a bad business for all of them. He still felt so uncommonly sore about their laughing at him, and he was going to rub this cheque-business in a bit more before he left.

'Put up that book of food-and-rent tickets,' said Jill with a sneer and a laugh, 'and come away to the next room out of this nude-woman-market, for God's sake. You make me feel like an odalisque. I believe you have Turkish blood. Have you? Jack's been talking about his ancestors, Tristy.'

'Mayn't I buy Jill's body, Mr Phipps?' he asked with a sheepish grinning way he had when he'd got his back up, fingering his cheque-book.

'Ask Gillian,' Mr Phipps said. 'As far as I'm concerned –'

'Here, may I buy you over there, Jill, when Tristy's finished you?'

'*Buy me*, you old buyer-and-seller?'

'Yes, cheap. I like a bargain; it's my business mind!'

'Come back into the next room, you old simpleton!'

'We can't all be clever,' Jack said.

'And, Jack, if you don't put that thing back in your pocket soon, I shall take it away from you.'

She had really got his goat and the 'old simpleton' didn't improve matters. She went into the next room. Tristy kind of hesitated, Jack could see he wanted that cheque. He turned this

123

way and that once or twice and then followed her, and Jack came in after him and they sat down facing each other.

He put his cheque-book out of sight – *for the present*.

'Jack is being particularly tiresome today,' said Gillian. 'I don't know what's come over him all of a sudden.'

'Oh,' said Tristy, 'is he?'

'Ever since he came in he's been behaving in a most peculiar way.'

'Has he – have you, Jack?' said Tristy, and he stared at Jack a moment with his large hollowed-out eyes, under brows arched up to give him a blank and empty look as if on purpose, with a little of Mr Genius, you might have said it was.

Jack had noticed blind men with that look, and Tristy's eyelids were as a rule half-closed as you see with a blind person too, in the sunken pit of their eye sockets. When he was out in the street he would throw his head back often as if he didn't care if his neck snapped as he did it, and stared from way up as he walked along into the distance, clapping his hands behind his back as he started off. It was supercilious, you might have said, if you hadn't known him better.

But Tristy wasn't out of the way proud at all. Jack always made a great point of that, in discussing this business with his friends. If you asked *him*, Jack would say, he'd say Tristy was not all there – not all the time. He'd hop off into 'the abstract world,' as he called it. And then his head would go back crack on to his shoulder blades, like a cannon ball, just like a man might throw his head back as he said *Let me see!* who was about to turn something over in his mind.

To have Tristy staring at him, or *through* him would be better, like a blind beggar as I said, didn't please Jack any too well. Besides, at that time he didn't know them as well as he did afterwards, and he always felt this grand young man (a parson's son, and being country-bred he knew his parsons pretty well) was looking through him on purpose, as if to say he wasn't really there – as of course he *wasn't*, for Tristy, come to that. He took it for superciliousness, the more so as he could never figure out why Tristy and Gillian should cultivate his acquaintance, of all people's, who was not their stamp by any manner of means.

'Yes, Jack has behaved very oddly ever since he came in, haven't you, Jack?' she said.

'Have I?' said he, putting on the grin he gave her in the other room when he stopped hiding what was going on inside, looking into her face with the grin that went with his animal side – not his company-self.

'Well, don't you think you have? And then to crown everything you try to pull that cheque-book stuff! Explain yourself, Jack! We're curious to hear what you've been up to.'

'I? Nothing. I haven't been up to anything particular.'

'You must have been! Jack, you're *different* today!'

She laughed down in her throat, looking at him under her eyelashes as if playing peepbo with the poor simpleton Jackie. And he saw she was taking a rise out of him as she was before. He said, savaging his cigar a little as he will when his blood is up:

'I'm no different to what I always was, Jill, but I know you're fond of that word, so call me *different*, I don't mind. You must have your little bit of fun, Jill. We all must, come to that.'

Gillian was a real lady, Jack knew that, you could tell from her speaking voice and her looks too that she'd had all that money can buy in the way of schooling, and him as well. They treated Jack as if he'd been a child, as Jack saw it. He felt they were laughing whenever they spoke to him. To give you the feeling he really had, it was as if they had made a pet of Jack for a sport. 'I'll swear it,' Jack said in talking to Joe, 'I was no more than a dog to them!' Half the time they couldn't understand what he was saying. Then they'd both of them laugh and kind of pet him – he less than her. But Mr Phipps often laughed when there was no need to, Jack thought.

Sometimes they'd talk to each other as if he wasn't there at all. He might have been a bull pup for all the notice they took of him at such moments. At first poor Jack was as sore as hell as he sat there and felt he oughtn't to speak – as he wasn't supposed to be present! He'd take up a paper and read to give himself something to do.

By this time anyway he'd got his wits back. I mean he didn't feel any longer the way he did after he'd seen her naked inside,

125

as he stood in the area – waving her hand to him and not minding a bit if he saw her or not. He'd quieted down between whiles. But he was going to get his own way about that cheque. So he pulled out the old cheque-book once more and said, taking off the bloke visiting the artist in his studio:

'Now how about this cheque of mine, Mr Phipps? It was thirty guineas, sir, I think you said.'

At this they started one of those talks all of a sudden as if Jack hadn't been there. It was just as if he'd been a hundred miles away. They simply forgot about his being in the room and started arguing with each other about the cheque, for it was plain enough that they didn't see eye to eye about it, and he'd been doing some heavy thinking and looked upset, Jack thought.

'Gillian, are you sure you're right?' Tristy said. 'I don't see why we shouldn't let him buy it, if he wants to.'

'Don't you?' she said.

'No. He's got the money, I should imagine. It isn't as if he would miss it. He'd only spend it on something else.'

'On a woman probably!' she said, in a tone of the utmost contempt.

'It's quite likely.' He did not deny that that was what *might* happen – no.

'But consider *how he makes it*! We have to think of that.'

'I know, I've thought of that,' Tristy answered firmly. 'I've thought of that.'

'He doesn't know any better. I mean he's not responsible for his actions – but he *does* make it by means of all sorts of shabby tricks.'

'That doesn't worry me!' Tristy told her with a great deal of unnecessary emphasis, Jack thought – he was dying to accept the cheque. 'He gets his money out of people who are just as bad as he is.'

'But who do *they* grind it out of,' she cried: 'pound by pound and penny by penny?'

'Oh well, if you are going to argue on those lines,' Tristy exclaimed, throwing himself back and twisting one hand about the other, 'you would simply have to refuse payment for *anything* from *anybody*!'

126

'No! This man's money is *particularly* shabbily come by,' she asserted with as much sternness as a black-capped judge at the top of his hanging form. 'And we know it – the responsibility rests with us.'

'Not more than we know with all the people who pay me for my work.'

He stuck to his point like a limpet, did old Tristy.

'Oh yes, it is *practically certain* that he is hand in glove with every sort of business crook and shady little kerb merchant. I know it's not his fault, he's too stupid to have any responsibility in the matter. But have not *we*?'

Tristy shook his head.

'I frankly don't see it, Jill! These things are all six one and half a dozen the other.'

Then Gillian took a new line. Jack pricked up his ears.

'But why does he *want* to buy this picture? Have you considered that?'

'I suppose he's taken a fancy to it. Probably he likes nudes. One can't help that.'

'Well, if you're satisfied it is an honourable deal and all that –'

'As honourable as *anything* can be in such a world as we live in.'

*

They threw themselves back after this and there was a long silence. I need not say perhaps that Jack was not in too sweet a temper by this time – after having listened to these people discussing his business principles, but agreeing that he was too *stupid* anyhow to be held responsible for the crimes he committed in the name of *business*.

For some time Jack'd had an itching in his throat, and he'd wanted to cough like billyoh. But he'd had to stop himself because he wasn't supposed to be there. They both started when he cleared this throat and spoke at last. It was like as if Jack had got into the room on tiptoe and they had not known he was there till he opened his mouth.

'Well, ladies and gentlemen,' said he with the nastiest grin he could command to put round the words coming out of his

127

mouth, for Jack could be nasty at times, and letting them have it in the voice he uses in his office, when he feels a little under the weather and anyone tries to teach him his business or question his honesty: '*Well*, ladies and gentlemen, if you've quite finished discussing my character, and as I gather you have agreed to take my money, distasteful as you find it to do that, I will make out my cheque.'

'Why, Jack, if you feel sore –'

'Not at all, Mr Phipps.'

Jack always called him Mr Phipps, rather than Tristy, when he wasn't feeling amiable.

'No hard feelings – are you quite sure, Jack? We ought to have waited till you were gone, I know.'

'We should have gone into the next room,' sneered Jill, 'shouldn't we?'

'Don't mention it, Jill, please don't mind little *me*! What is the date, Jill?' Dates Jack can never remember. Time was not old Jack's long suit.

Jill looked sort of taken back.

'What is the date, Tristy?' she asked. 'I had forgotten this day had a date.'

'The date? I haven't the foggiest,' said Tristy.

He sprang up and going out into the area to where the trash-boxes stood, came back with a sodden copy of the *Daily Worker* with tea-leaves and fish-bones stuck to it.

'The sixth,' he said, or the seventh, or whatever it was.

Jack made out the cheque and handed it to Tristram Phipps. After that he left.

It was maybe a week later than this that a note signed 'Gillian' came to his private address. It was not scented – neither was it pale mauve, cantab blue, nor flushed with pink. But it did not require to possess these aphrodisiac properties. It simply said: 'Will you take me to a party tomorrow night, Jack? Come and fetch me – eightish. Love.' – and then the name Gillian. Under Gillian was a further remark. 'It's a party to celebrate the return of Percy Hardcaster. No white ties – nor yet black!' And Jack stepped briskly off, as if to the squealing of the pipes, to the Underground to go to his City office – after he had searched the *Daily Mirror* for pictures of bathing-girls, and found two rather skinny ones, and carefully studied the police-court reports of kisses in a tunnel and all the other little unexpected incidents of surburban travel, and his jaunty step as he passed her door provoked Mrs Clements (where he bought his half-weekly tin of Airman) to remark, as she bent over the column where she found out about the dogs: 'Dirty beast!' For Jack was as well known in this section of Paddington as he had been as a fresh youngster in the Wiltshire dales.

PART IV

SEAN O'HARA

Chapter 1

THE sparrows used their beaks as picks to break up the great spongy rocks of bread placed by Mrs O'Hara upon the Bayswater balcony. For much as she loved the common finch, Mrs O'Hara had not attacked, with her big loose trumpery intellect, the problems of passerine transport. She might have been providing for buzzards or for gulls.

These toy airplanes, from their hangars in the trees or roof-gutters, stormed the balcony, when the feast of bread began. Alighting, they considered Mr O'Hara with a certain measure of not irrational mistrust, while they took in hand the problems set them, or left unsolved, by Mrs O'Hara.

On the other hand, Sean O'Hara, sitting beneath the green awning, eyed the sparrows as if their problems had been his problems. An open letter was upon his knee. But like an absent-minded god, attracted by the traffic peculiar to other dimensions, he watched with staring, dispassionate eyes, the movements of these mechanical animals, the bustling protégés of his wife. He stared as if he were seeking to penetrate the secrets of their pathology, or their economy. But he was not. He did not see them. He was looking at another problem. He was weighing a pro against a con (a pro and a con of not much importance – much of the calibre of a spug, as a matter of fact). He was watching for the verdict of his judgment as it swung freely to and fro within his mind.

The die was cast, it seemed – or the pendulum had come to rest: and he closed his mouth with a snap and sat back and took the letter again between his thumb and finger. It was a typing quarto sheet, of lavatory-paper consistency and weight, that cockled and crackled: its violet script had been punched out offhand, at a one-finger gallop.

The name at the bottom of the sheet, penwritten, was P. Hardcaster. And in the typescript, in the midst of the third line above it, stood out, with its capitals, the name of Ellen Mulliner. 'I am bringing,' said the letter. O'Hara looked down at the names alone. Their neighbourhood upon the page was what he was studying.

The telephone bell rang upon the table at his side and the sparrows decamped as if at a take-cover fiat. Sean O'Hara lifted the receiver and said 'Yes!' He said it faintly and coldly, and listened to the voice bawling at him out of the *néant*, that had begun to clapper away in it, rather as an intelligent man picks up a newspaper and addresses himself to the absorption of the thick dope that is poured out, in the orderly ducts of its political columns · endeavouring, perhaps, to discover (if it is his business to understand such things) what motive the words conceal: not at all what facts, of course, it has been sought to convey, but what facts it has been intended to reduce to a deliquium.

An angry grin settled upon his face almost at once. With this contemptuous grimace he squared his impatient temper – it enabled him to answer this lousy old goose (cackling in the magic drum at the end of the talkative dumb-bell) levelly and civilly. And the leveller and civiller his voice became, the longer he listened, while the voice rattled and babbled in the ear-piece.

'But look – had he permission to do that? Or did he do it off his own bat?' he asked at last.

Upon this a great clappering and screeching broke out: it was as though his question had roused an expository storm that would never wear itself out till the crack of doom. The listening face underwent several changes of expression – from that of a scornful indifference to a painfully amused concentration. Brows knit and lips tightly leashed upon a frozen grin, he watched the sparrows returning, with an evil brilliance in his eyes.

'What did he mean by that?' he asked suddenly. 'I said, what did he mean by that?'

Only in the dull and heavy aspiration of the 'what' did any echo of the submerged Erse peep out, and a certain emphatic drum-tap in the concluding 'that' betrayed it.

The tinny roar in the receiver started up again.

'Stop!' he screamed. 'I see! Good egg!'

His hand crawled up helter-skelter upon the table, closed upon an indelible pencil, and scribbled 360 upon a memo-pad.

'Look, old man – leave it to me! No. *Leave it to me!* I'll see what I can do. No. Don't do that. Do nothing. I'll fix it. It doesn't really matter about the D.N.O.P. It was only to be expected. – Yes. – No, old man. The twenty-third, I think. – That's right. The twenty-third. Leave it to me, old man!'

A further burst of verbiage was to be expected – he rolled back in the deck-chair. He allowed it to expend itself. Then he said:

'All right – that's O.K. I see your point of view. Good-bye, old man. Don't get your rag out. Leave it to me. I'll ring you back when I've heard what he has to say. – Yes. Good-bye. – No, old man. I've seen nothing. What? No. Nothing!'

And he hung up the receiver. He scribbled a note upon the memo-pad, to accompany the figure reminiscent of geometric quantities, previously set down, and laid his spine back against the elastic canvas. His spine was not as straight as the spine of an honest man should be. A tell-tale crook made an arc at the top of it, on which his head hung – instead of standing up stoutly upon his shoulders, like a rooster upon a dunghill in the act of crowing.

There was nothing particularly Irish about O'Hara except his two names, or except for the fact that he was dwarfish and dark and of a dusky hairiness suggestive perhaps of something icelandic and mythological. For his darkness, and his shortness, was perhaps not of the sort that is customarily met with among the Saxon English – where even deformity is apt to be robbed of its compensating terrors and compelled to be commonplace. This stunted body came bang out of the repertory of a sagaman – where the physical assumes a symbolical importance. Had he been with Harold Hardrada in Sicily it would have been *his* brain that would have dispatched the Varangian fowlers to catch the small birds that flew out of the besieged town every day to the forests, and to attach smouldering wax vestas to their legs, that they might fire the thatches where they nested, and so smoke out the obstinate inhabitants. The malice of his bitterness against man – the ready access of his outcast mind to the planes upon which small creatures have their being – would have led him to this device, and given him the standing of a magician.

Mrs O'Hara came out upon the balcony.

'Sean,' she said; 'have you a cigarette?'

Mrs O'Hara was a big worried-looking girl of thirty, of the English middle-class. With a slightly exotic politeness he waved his hand towards a large silver box containing Craven A.

'I've only got Virgins,' he said. 'If you can bear to smoke them, Eileen.'

O'Hara was as fastidious as a Jew in his selection of the heartiest and most hackneyed idioms, in his fixed resolve to identify himself with John Bull at all costs – all the inflexions of whose homely voice he made his constant study. The last trace – he flattered himself – of the accents of Enniskillen had been stamped out of his speech. This might be said to be his weakness; he set too much store by detachment from the Anglo-Irish tradition. He overlooked its advantages. His hatred of the Irish gutter was too extreme – so that he forgot that the English did not understand the social status represented by those oily vowels, and the *divil-me-care* distrustfulness of that most disgraceful of Saxon slums, Ireland – as he thought of that 'little isle of green.' He forgot that John Bull did not know that he had made a slum of an entire country. And anyway O'Hara had turned his back beyond recall upon any Ireland except that important cell of the Third International known by that name, for purposes of identification. The whole idea of his 'native land' was, in common with many of the young Irish, distasteful to O'Hara – and he would have preferred it to be thought that his contact with it had been strictly ancestral: so that the *Sean O'Hara* upon his brass doorplate was in sort a paradox, and, if he could, he would have changed it into Sam Harris. Indeed, he might do so yet.

But Eileen, his wife, was Eileen because her good old Surrey and Surbiton father had always had a weakness for the Colleen Bawn, and when he heard *The Wearing of the Green* played by a good trombone at the street-corner he would hum to himself: 'They're shooting lads and lasses for the Wearing of the Green,' and would get quite moist-eyed about these

beautiful shootings, or rather about the fact that they should
have been so romantically provoked – by the wearing of such
a lovely and patriotic colour as green. And when he had to
christen his offspring he gave her an Irish name and would not
have been averse to her being mistaken perhaps one day for a
product of the Lakes of Killarney, or (had he known about it)
of the Lake of Innisfree; and sure his old mater once said she
had had an 'Irish ancestor' (so hot-blooded!) which accounted
for the violet tint of her eyes – though no one but herself could
ever see it, since her eyes were in fact a dirty grey.

Eileen had insisted upon O'Hara being 'the O'Hara.' And he
had grimly assented, for he was not much to look at and
there were two other men after her, one a gentleman. And
three hundred a year would make him as good as a gentleman
himself (although he found out afterwards that it was not,
even in a good year, a penny more than five pounds a week).

But many had been the altercations between himself and
Eileen over the old-fashioned nationalist fallacies. She had got
them in her blood, and especially as they applied to the Irish.
And that was where he mainly objected to them – for a spot of
Russian patriotism, or a dash of Negro-race-nonsense anent
Black Africa (and *anent* was the *mot juste* for this pedantic
immigrant Briton) was not amiss.

But Eileen was a great diehard where Irish patriotism was
concerned, it was no use. She was no stickler – very much the
reverse – where it came to Home and Beauty, when it was
England that was in question. Just as in her dear old dad's eyes
there had been something romantic even about Lord Roberts
(because of his Fenian compatriotism), so there *was a difference*
for her – as between any two small scrubby articled clerks, or
any couple of pink-cheeked, snub-faced saddlery factors – in
the case where one was known to be a Man of Kent, and the
other reputed to be a Man of Wexford. And it would have
taken more than the O'Hara to budge her out of this vice of
sentiment.

'I dislike the Irish,' he would say coldly. This was back in
the time when they were getting to know each other – though
he was getting to know her far better than she was getting to
know him. She did not guess in that pleasant ring-time how

relentlessly all romance would be stamped underfoot, until at last she would become positively ashamed at the name of Eileen, and feel a little queasy at the word 'Erin.'

'I have no use for them!' he added with brevity, after examining her for a moment, in those distant days, now five years off. But she would smile humorously, as if to say: 'There is your Irishman for you, every time! All paradox! As is to be expected!'

'No. I am serious,' he then would assure her as he saw how she was taking his remark. 'When last I was over there I hated the lot of them.'

She still would smile – for she saw in her watery mind's-eye a gemote of long-lipped bogtrotters, crouched over a peat-fire, engaged in a perfectly fascinating family quarrel, each with his shillalah tucked up his trouser leg.

'They are as impulsive in action as they are dull and pedestrian in thought,' he then would severely announce.

She laughed outright at such statements as this and their gaelic sententiousness won her heart and tipped the scales and finally made him her man.

'You don't know them as well as I do!' was the sort of thing he next found to say in his uphill demolition of this edifice of unreason. 'They are like the Spaniards – slovenly, pretentious, empty-headed. They are *hableurs*. And snobbish, dishonest, and extremely conceited. That is why they like that old bourgeois ranter of a Valera. Who is a Spanish grandee – didn't you know that? – it has been proved. Everyone knows it.'

'I read somewhere he was a Jew, Sean.'

'A *Chew* – who said that!' What a suggestion! 'He hasn't the brains! He hasn't the honesty! He's a grandee from Castille I tell you. You can take it from me on the evidence! I have seen his father's marriage-lines from a township in Spain. He is a count!'

But she would fight another round or two (since her family came from near Southampton) for Old Ireland and the Colleen Bawn.

'Oh, Sean!' she would exclaim, breaking into a slight brogue, and becoming a little 'hot-blooded.' 'And you call yourself an Irishman!'

'I don't, Eileen – I don't!' he would cry. 'It bores me, all this romantic flapdoodle about the Britisher – see how old Dev leads them all by the nose up the garden! Why, it is absurd. I'd rather have, any day of the week, a little English Cockney! I'd rather have an English yeoman than any of your Irishmen whatever – who have not a quarter of the guts that he has! He is a square shooter too. Which is more than you can say for –'

And he left unuttered the designation of the Fenian thieves and liars – who were a bunch of false-bottoms one and all if ever there were! But at the mere mention of an English yeoman Eileen felt a sinking at the heart. And as to a 'Cockney' – well! The O'Hara was perfectly at liberty to romance about Old Bill if he wanted to, but *she* could not follow him there. She knew too many Cockneys *personally* to be taken in by that line of argument. And it was of course only his essential Irishness that caused him to pursue it at all!

Upon such lines of radical readjustment – of romance to reality – did their relationship begin. And Eileen had by now travelled far upon the highroad of realism: she had found herself, too, upon some fairly sinister bypaths, besetting the particular highway which she had been called to tread. Her lot in fact had been that of a peregrine romantic, and she had wandered so far from her illusion that she might have been mistaken for a daughter of the grim universe of cause-and-effect, proper to the precise O'Hara. But she still had a something about the mouth and eye (a light that never was on land or sea flickered in the latter) that betrayed her.

*

'I've only got Virgins,' he said, then: 'If you can bear to smoke them, Eileen.'

She popped the 'virgin' she took out of the silver chestlet into her mouth, and Sean, drawing his lighter from his waistcoat pocket, held attentively the flame that shot up within a half-inch of her cigarette.

'We had better have a box of these for tonight,' she said.

'Yes,' said he, agreeable to her wishes, as always, but then going one better: 'Or two boxes perhaps. There will be quite thirty people.'

She considered for a moment, counting faces, or, where there were no faces (since she had never seen them) counting names.

'Yes, quite that. Nearer forty.'

'Then why not have three boxes?' Sean suggested. She rested her twilled rump upon the handrail of the balcony, and cast her eyes up into the great prongs of the public trees, of the square-gardens, on the look-out for absent sparrows. Only two now manoeuvred near a tall boulder of bread, not far from her feet. The blueness of the moist Indian summer atmosphere of London deadened the impact of the birds' cries, so that they sped from tree to tree as if in a tank, their voices deadened like the attempts at speech of the catfish in the watery medium.

Sean was looking at her as if she had been a long way off. He started speaking softly and with a preliminary purr in the throat, as if not wishing to disturb the sparrow-gazing but just to put in an aimless remark, for the sake of saying something, to this big idle woman, who had come out upon the balcony for a spot of company.

'Have you met Ellen Mulliner, Eileen?' he asked – not off-handedly, not at all, but as if making an effort to hit on some-topic that might rouse her interest.

'Ellen Mulliner?' she replied, with a discouraging lack of interest. 'I've heard of her. Isn't she a friend of Vivian's?'

'She may be. I don't know. You haven't met her?'

'No.'

'Hardcaster is bringing her tonight.'

'Oh yes. I did once hear they were friends, I think.'

Eileen heard the name of this prospective guest with complete composure. But she waited to hear what was to follow. For she realized that this was not all. Something dramatic was in the wind, she imagined: his approaches to dramatic situations being customarily developed upon such lines as these. There would be a marked slowing down of the voice as a rule. And his pronounced *sang froid* suggested that all was not well. The heart of man is a dark forest – but he was quite unaware that she possessed any woodcraft at all.

'Ellen Mulliner – and I have reason for saying it,' he began again, 'is a spy.'

'A spy! What sort of spy?'

138

This was undeniably, for him, a quite unusually dramatic opening. Still, it was not unheard of. It was not the first time she had heard of spies. Indeed, in one way and another, she heard a good deal about spies. She was quite used to the idea of a spy.

'Well, *that* I don't quite know,' he said, in reflective vein. 'I have my suspicions.'

'But how interesting! Will she be spying on us, Sean? I must lock everything up.'

'There's no occasion,' he said airily, but with an unruffled solemnity. 'She's not paid to do that.'

There was a longish interval of intent sparrow-watching and of sparring-without-speaking, between these two well-drilled life-partners. For there was much more to come. But Eileen was not disposed to show interest. She was not in fact interested. She did not on principle encourage Sean to be mysterious, and she felt that he might be about to ask her to remain concealed in a cupboard or a clothes-chest (as once had happened) when she wanted to be enjoying the party, or to remain for the best part of the evening maybe under a bed. He *was* such a born conspirator! She hated it. She would have liked him to give up politics altogether, and confine himself to a literary career.

But he now appeared unexpectedly inclined to hold back; so at last she said – getting up off the handrail and taking another nasty 'virgin' out of the silver box:

'I'm sure she's a perfectly nice girl and that I shall find her quite charming.'

'She is quite charming.'

'I'm quite sure she is paid by nobody – for anything.'

'You're wrong there. She's paid all right.'

'Well, we're all paid for something.'

'True. But she's a bit over the odds – where it comes to not being over-particular where she collects her cash.'

'She's paid by Hitler, I suppose – to shadow Jews!'

Sean shrugged his shoulders. Irony is indecent when employed by some people, and in Sean's view his wife was one of them. Before embarking upon irony, people should really ask themselves whether irony becomes them. It unquestionably made Eileen, for instance, look bigger and clumsier, more Saxon and more middle-class, than before.

'I once saw Miss Mulliner,' he said, with greater sedateness, 'when she least expected it. It was coming out of a certain restaurant. The fact that she was there could only mean one thing – she's a double-crosser. It was a restaurant not far from Vine Street.'

'I know the one you mean.'

Eileen was pleased to indulge in irony again. She accepted his owl-like procedure at its face value – as just another example of O'Hara importing the melodramatic politics of the Fenian into the humdrum surroundings of Piccadilly Circus. But she could not recall that he had ever given such a flagrant exhibition of atavism as he was doing at present. He showed no sign of stopping however: she sat down opposite to him in the second deck-chair and laughed. He did not respond, he did not so much as smile.

'Ellen's of no consequence,' he said slowly and with the most portentous deliberation.

'Then why are we talking about her, please?'

'Ah! Here is the reason. She has a very disagreeable habit. A very disagreeable habit indeed.'

'Most of us have.' Eileen persisted in her flippancy.

'She invents things about other people.'

'We all do. Really, Sean, she seems a very normal member of society.'

'To forestall criticism of herself, I suppose, she invents things about other people. She put about rather a disagreeable story about *me* as a matter of fact.'

Eileen looked a little startled at this; it was not what she had expected. But he did not glance in her direction. He looked almost smug, as he sat opposite her with his eyes lowered, his hands lying idle and motionless in his lap.

'What sort of story?' she asked, hesitating a little.

'Oh, nothing of any consequence.'

'Yes, but what was it about?'

'The usual thing. It's too absurd to repeat. I had it on the best authority – she spread the report that I had been employed –'

'Well?'

Suddenly Eileen became aware of an oddness about these hesitations of Sean's. This was definitely not what she was used to. It was almost as if he were being *coy*! The O'Hara coy! She looked at him again, focusing her attention upon this peculiar coyness, and there sure enough it was.

'Well?' she almost barked.

'I had been employed by a "certain government." ' He smiled coldly at his wife for a moment. 'She said I was involved – how I did not gather – in the arrest in Germany three months ago of Karl Rippe.'

Eileen's face fell. She stared at him as if she had not been sure that she had heard him aright.

'For smuggling money?' she asked.

'For organizing contraband of valuta, yes – and other things. Within Germany. Rippe will probably be beheaded. That régime does not do things by halves.'

'How absurd! Are you sure she said that?'

This put a different complexion on it. At first a little stupefied by hearing such a charge, Eileen became extremely indignant. She wanted to say something – exactly what, she did not know – and she stared at Sean, hesitating for words, expecting him to provide a suitable diatribe. At the moment she did not feel equal to coping with such a disgusting attack.

But Sean's restraint was uncanny: he remained quite impassible. He was even a little prim. Even *very* prim.

'She is an absurd woman,' he remarked, with weighty detachment. 'Quite absurd. There is no occasion to take any notice of what she may choose to say. But I thought I ought to tell you. Hardcaster is bringing her. It is unpleasant.'

'I feel very inclined myself,' said Eileen, her indignation increasing, the more the significance of this libel sank in and took substance in her consciousness, 'to tell Hardcaster *not* to bring her!'

He made a gesture of very forcible deprecation, dismissing with a sudden wave of the hand such a counsel of violence.

'But why should we have a woman of that sort in our place?' she asked indignantly. 'Really I don't see why we should entertain her.'

'We shall not. She shall entertain herself! Hardcaster will entertain her.'

'No, but I don't like the idea of her coming here at all. I'd rather not see her at all.'

Sean looked his most reasonable, the man-of-the-world gracefully uppermost. He took on an easy and rather benevolent air, and said with a lazy magnanimity:

'Do not let us take that too tragically. She is not the first woman who has been in Queer Street, poor girl, and resorted to peculiar methods of raising the wind.'

'It's not that. I shouldn't mind that. What I object to is her slandering other people.'

'Ah! That is tactless, and of course disagreeable.'

'Who told you this story anyway, Sean? Perhaps it isn't true. She may never have said it. You know what liars people are.'

'I'm afraid it's right. I heard about it from several people, at different times.'

'You should have told me, Sean.'

'It did not occur to me to do so.'

'I've never heard of such a monstrous thing. It's *monstrous*, Sean! Can't you stop her? Did you hear details of what she said?'

Sean stretched back in the deck-chair and yawned, to demonstrate a voluntary lowering of the psychic activity of the brain, and how small an effort anyway he would be prepared to expend upon tracking or checking such rumours.

'People *believe* such things – that is the worst of it!' Eileen remonstrated.

'People believe *anything*.'

'But they have been horrid about you before. You remember Eddie Hewin.'

His face was transformed by a brilliant light of recognition, that came dancing into it at the name Hewin: he opened his eyes in a wide, childlike stare of what looked like a naif pleasure.

'You mean the yarn about my decamping from Dublin with the communist funds – which were supposed to have paid my travelling expenses to London – and left me a bit over to start life with here?'

She nodded – a little doubtfully, for the 'start' he had made was getting the job at six pounds a week as her husband: and then she saw no real necessity for *repeating* this story, even in the domestic privacy of their balcony. Possessing as she did a full share of the British Reserve, she had even objected, on many occasions, to having the sort of politics in the midst of which she now had her being, bellowed out in this public tent. A hundred little would-be capitalists must be pricking their ears up all round them.

'Well, I don't like all this, Sean. I know it's bourgeois. I suppose I ought not to mind whether people say I'm married to a thief and an – to a –'

'To an informer.'

'To a thief and an informer,' she said – lowering her voice to utter these two evil-sounding epithets.

He laughed – it was a shrill and somewhat wild cachinnation. It was the signal for the ending of their talk, and he stood up, remaining, with his shoulders squared (as much as they could be), and his head thrown back – to make the most of such few inches as he'd got – gazing out into the gardens.

'I'll tell you what you can do,' he said.

'What?' she inquired.

She looked doubtfully over at him, for the last laugh he had given rang in a displeasing fashion in her ear. She had never entertained so much as a fraction of a suspicion that the man to whom she was married was capable of absconding with funds entrusted to him. That was unthinkable. Not the O'Hara! But she had once got so far as understanding that several *other* people of her acquaintance believed it. And the same people would, undoubtedly, believe and publish that he had sent this émigré to his death. They would believe *anything* about Sean if they would believe that he was a sneak-thief.

'It would do no harm to say to Hardcaster,' he said 'should you have the opportunity, that his young woman is a bit of a liar, and is not over-trustworthy. A good Partyman like himself should watch out. Show him that you feel pretty sore about her choosing your husband as a target for her impossible tittle-tattle.'

143

'I certainly shall say that, Sean.'

But he raised a finger of statesmanlike admonition.

'Old Percy lifts his elbow more than he should, remember. If he is canned, say nothing to him. Remember that.'

'Of course I shouldn't. I daresay I shan't have a chance of saying anything.'

'He wouldn't like it. He is rather unduly conscious of his own importance since he's been plugged. It's rather funny. As if it wasn't an uncommonly stupid thing to get one self shot in the leg.'

'Aren't you a little hard on Hardcaster?'

'A little, I agree. But he's in the first flight now – in the marxist circus I mean. He's a proper lion – and it's only cost him a calf. And he still has a calf to spare!'

Eileen was slowly relaxing, and the *détente* was very welcome to her. Sean was his old self again and she was able to shake off that perfectly sickening sensation that had taken hold of her just now. He had almost seemed *pleased* at being called a thief and an informer.

'Well, I'm going out,' she said, getting up.

Sean nodded.

'I must step in at Sainsbury's. I suppose we must be patriotic and provide caviar.'

He nodded and smiled.

'And two or three dozen hard-boiled Soviet eggs.'

He held the door open for her and she went into the house.

'Get a little good honest fascist ice for my Pilsener!' he called after her.

Chapter 2

'Oh damn!' said O'Hara, with a bottle between his legs. 'These corks are the bloody limit!'

His hairy wrist arched and bristled, as he gripped the corkscrew. But it was a stand-pat cork, mounting guard over much-too-expensive amontillado (a mistake of Eileen's) which doubtless would wish to be filtered through people of another kidney to those who were at present baying about him –

tongued with red ties and reddened with rich alcohol (Eileen's mistake – Eileen's middle-class mistake).

A snappily-dressed young woman, who was standing watching, laid hold of the neck of the bottle, and extracted it from between the legs of O'Hara with the bleak adroitness of a dentist, and thrust it down smartly between her own.

'Ooooh!' she cooed, as she heaved upon it, shaking her curls and making a series of attempts upon it, each of which threw into prominence some fundamental attribute of sex. She did this beneath the glittering and kestrel-like glances of Jack.

But it remained adamant to sex-appeal, as much as it had resisted the more orthodox practice of force. Jack, who had stepped smartly past his host, seized the neck of this difficult customer and with one bold wrench dislodged it from between the legs of the girl (who nearly fell backwards, so precipitately delivered of her bottle) and stuck it down between his own stout pins. It was the affair of a second for Jack to pluck out the cork from the bottle and hold it up in the air with a *How's that?* flourish – for he was no mean athlete, was old Jack, and his fist was as good at pulling out other people's sherry corks as it was at tapping their clarets.

'Who the devil is that Jackanapes?' O'Hara had muttered to his wife when he had first spotted old Jack.

'Who? That red-faced little bounder person over there talking to Gillian, do you mean?'

'The same.'

'That is Jack Cruze. That's all I know about him.'

'What's he here for?'

'I can't imagine. Except that he has just bought a picture of Tristy's. That's probably it.'

'Bought a picture of Tristy's!'

'So I understand.'

'A capitalist!' had hissed Sean; and with that he had rapidly moved off, in the opposite direction to Jack.

But although his aversion to Jack's class had been unmistakably indicated, it would have seemed, by this movement *away*, towards the opposite pole of the apartment from where Jack was stationed, the ultra-rugged implications of this gesture had not been carried out by his subsequent behaviour. For ten minutes later he might have been remarked circling round, until he was within hailing distance of Gillian, who accordingly hailed him.

'Sean darling! Come over here and meet *Jack*! This is our Jack, Sean!'

And Sean had bowed shortly, from his hollow, dapper waist, with a friendly smile, and grasped the 'capitalist' almost impulsively by the hand, and had received in return a hearty rotarian shake. Shortly after this auspicious encounter, and after a few clubmanesque commonplaces had been exchanged (in which the Irish Gentleman had outdone the British Capitalist in unctuously trite give-and-take) – and seeing that Gillian to all appearances proposed to monopolize the guest of the evening, and give Jack, if not the cold shoulder, only a minor part of her attention – Jack had accompanied his host to the *buffet froid*. And thereupon had in due course ensued the transactions, the salient points of which have been noted above.

Jack put down the sherry bottle in a very casual manner upon the buffet – its rôle had ended, and there were obviously other things that held more poignant interest for him than bottles and their corks. He turned with an alert and smiling face to the young woman, from whom he had taken it, and proceeded to overtures of a nature there was no mistaking, and in which there seemed little likelihood of his being repulsed. For she came up to him in the manner of iron-filings to a magnet, draggingly but clearly 'fascinated,' and stood smiling in a very friendly fashion, while he said:

'A long pull and a strong pull!'

'I suppose it was,' she replied with a ready demureness, spying out his scintillating eye with a benevolent inquisitiveness, reflecting perhaps that she might have done that trick before a dozen odd males, with many more archings and squirmings than that, and damn-all might have come of it – whereas here was an improbably ardent fan, lighted up like a jubilee beacon, such as she had not met for many a long day. It made her feel quite sentimental.

'The quickness of the hand deceives the eye!' said Jack, winking.

'*Your* hand is very quick!' she laughed with a succulent

abandon, to play up to the wink. 'You nearly knocked me down.'

'I'm full of those tricks!' he riposted.

'I shouldn't be surprised if you were! You look as though you might be!'

'I am!' cried Jack, at the top of his form. 'I am! – give me a number?'

'A number?'

'Yes. Any old number.'

She was about to give Jack a number, when she caught her host's eye, and it was bent upon her a little severely, she thought. It did not seem to relish the relaxation of the atmosphere of the party for which she was being responsible in this quarter of the room, it must be that; and so she did not say the number, after all, which was bobbing on the tip of her tongue.

O'Hara held a glass of sherry in his hand.

'Won't you have a glass of sherry, Mr Cruze?' he said. 'since your strong right arm has made it available!'

'Oh, ah. Why, I had forgotten – thank you, old man. I was just asking this young lady to give me a number.'

'Are you a superstitious man, Mr Cruze?'

'No. No! Not more than most.'

'But you believe in the power of numbers to affect our destinies?'

'There are numbers, I grant you, that I'm not so fond of as others.'

'It is as I thought.'

'I shouldn't take a house numbered thirteen!'

'You are one of those people for whom landlords change thirteen to 12a on their houses?' laughed O'Hara in very genial vein, emptying his sherry glass and putting it down by his side with the air of as good a bottle-companion as ever stepped.

'That's right!' Jack agreed.

O'Hara's eye had been soliciting Jack's attention, to the exclusion of the young woman, who did not go away at once. He had even moved round, in order to blot her out from Jack's field of vision, since he noticed that she was a disturbing element, and that Jack's glances had a tendency to wander off, to dally with a dimple or a curl, in the middle distance.

'I, because of my Irish descent, I suppose,' O'Hara said airily, 'am superstitious. About numbers, I find. They worry me quite a lot at times.'

'Yes,' said Jack, shifting uncomfortably from one foot to the other, and coughing; 'the Paddies are pretty hot boys where it comes to unlucky numbers. I had one in my office. If the thirteenth happened to fall on a Friday he wouldn't come to the office for fear of an accident. It's a fact!'

But O'Hara remarked that Jack's eye had not entirely quieted down. He now moved squarely round with his back up against the young woman. Then, dropping his cigarette down vertically beside his right foot, he trod it into the rug, and then with a quick backward movement (as if to withdraw himself from contact with the extinguished butt-end) he stepped as heavily as possible where he had noticed one of her toes. There was a muffled squeak of pain. He turned sharply round, with an expression of ill-favoured surprise, and drawled: 'I hope I didn't hurt you?' as if he had been totally unaware of the young woman's presence.

After that she thought it was time for her to move off, and he had the satisfaction, a moment later, of seeing this troublesome rival, out of the tail of his eye, in a distant quarter of the room.

*

A red patriarch, Percy Hardcaster reclined, propped by a plethora of red cushions, upon a wide reddish settee, in Red invalid magnificence. A red punkah should have been there to complete the picture. He was surrounded by men and women – by the Red men and Red women. There were four women beside him upon the settee; in the place of honour Gillian Phipps pressed up against his sick leg, which stuck straight out pointing at the assembly with all the declamatory force of Lord Kitchener's forefinger ('I want *you*') terminating in an ironshod stump, provided by the Lerroux administration.

In the place of lesser honour, because leg to leg with his more ordinary and less dramatic limb, was Ellen Mulliner. It

148

was further very marked indeed, the manner in which Percy Hardcaster displayed his preference for his new acquaintance, and was at no pains to conceal his desire to confirm his more recent success – rather than to advertise his triumph of long standing, which was already dating. It would have been impossible to find a more flagrant case of omission to be *off with the old* before being *on with the new*.

Before Percy Hardcaster, both upon the floor and upon chairs, was an impressive grouping of salon-Reds – of Oxford and Cambridge 'pinks'; a subdued socialist-leaguer; the usual marxist don; the pimpled son of a Privy Councillor (who had *tovarish* painted all over him); a refugee (an equinal headpiece, flanked by two monstrous red wings, which were the sails flung out by his eardrums, and which moved back against his head, as if he had been subjected to a hundred-mile-an-hour wind, in moments of agitation). And there were three sturdy 'independents' ('friends of Soviet Russia') from the headquarter-staff of the Book Racket. The roster contained other fish and fowl and more or less good red herrings. And Percy's protruding artificial limb pointed pointedly at one and all, and his eyes looked over the top of it steadily but not unkindly at the lot of them. But it was a cowed group round Percy – this man-of-action almost frightened them. A veteran of the *Ten Days that Shook the World* would have had less effect than this *grand blessé* of a month's standing. He was a *workman* – that, too, was calculated to provoke almost a panic, in the uninitiated; to whom a communist *workman* was distinctly an alarming notion. They soon got used to this, however. After all he had written pamphlets (and a Red playlet) which Collett's Bomb-Shop carried as a stock-in-trade : this made him much more human – almost a 'Leftie' P.E.N.man. And it was not long before they became aware that he possessed a Juan Gris (so a *possessive* man with a disarming 'culture') and was able to discuss Bracque as well as Trotsky.

Of course all the men thought constantly how exceedingly unpleasant it would be to have a wooden leg. An advertisement it was not, from that standpoint, of unsalonesque class-warfare. It made their own legs feel quite uncomfortable to look at it – and they couldn't help looking at it, Percy saw to that! But

149

of course such things only happened to workmen – no one but a workman would ever go where things of that order were likely to occur to his legs (just look how they fall off scaffoldings, or lose their arms in printing-presses or Lancashire looms, and think nothing of it). But one and all in their hearts determined that it was more necessary than ever to see to it that they should remain *the brains* of the Revolution. Never must they allow themselves to be inveigled into situations where such a drastic disfigurement awaited them, now or at any future time. So Percy's pointing had the opposite effect to Lord Kitchener's pointing. But all were anxious to hear how it happened.

'So what it boils down to, Percy,' said one who had known him before he went to Spain on this particular ill-fated job of work, 'was a rivalry between the two prison guards, wasn't it?'

'That's what it amounted to,' said Percy.

'And the head guard revenged himself true to fascist principles, when you turned down his blackmailing proposition?'

At the word 'fascist' a most ferocious growling grew in volume and was at once seen to be proceeding from a small and spectacled, pinkfaced and pinkminded, pugdog-like client of the Left from Brasenose – whose little father often shook his bald and toothy little head in his big London Club when the 'young generation' was mentioned (as it often was, especially after a study of Mr Haselden's morning cartoon), and allowed it to be understood that *his* ill-sprung little offspring was as proper a sample of really flaming-youth as could be met with between Half Moon Street and World's End, though there was no harm in the young devil (damn it, sir, he's too stupid!) and he could quite see that the young man should desire to kill his father – he had always wanted to kill *his* – and once his wild oats were sown like his father before him he would be sitting in that self-same club and writing a letter to *The Times* – insisting testily that our government should hand back at once Australia to the Blackboys, whom we had against every Christian principle dispossessed, but whom we had now quite sufficiently educated in the gentle ways of true democracy to enable them to take their place beside Mr Litvinov in the

Council Chamber of the League of Nations (without any un-
due embarrassment to Mr Litvinov – on the score of their
imperfect understanding of Freedom) and that the White Aus-
tralians should gracefully withdraw from the Island Continent
(just as the Anglo-Indians had left India – as they would have
by that time, bag and baggage, and have left it to the Baboos
to whom it belonged) and return to the Mother Country and
settle down on the dole – unless, indeed, this influx should be
found to bring down wages still further by the new threat of
unemployment and so ultimately 'benefit the country.'

Having stared steadily at the growler for a moment or two,
Percy inflated his chest and started dotting a few i's, and crossing a few t's.

'No, Geoffrey, you haven't quite got that right,' he said
frowning. 'Alvaro Morato was undoubtedly acting for the
governor of the prison. He was his factor, in the prison – for
all the matters of graft.'

'Ah!" breathed out deeply Geoffrey to indicate that the key
to the whole business was now in his hands, and there was a
murmur of understanding everywhere.

'Yes. The Governor worked through Alvaro – who naturally
had his rake-off. Alvaro named his figure to me – a stiff one he
said, but it was worth it.'

'Oh, he got as far as that, did he?'

'Yes. He wanted five thousand pesetas.'

'A king's ransom!'

'You're right – not a Communist's anyway! I told him so.
I asked him what he thought we were – bloody capitalists? –
and he said, *no*. But England was very rich, he said, and Spain
was poor. To which I replied that England wouldn't be rich
long if she paid dirty dogs like him five thousand pesetas for a
job that wasn't worth as many hundreds. He properly flew off
the handle at that, and said I ought to go back to England
where I came from – provided I could get out of the prison, of
course, which he would make it his business to see that I
didn't: and that they didn't want a lot of lousy Reds like me
in the land of Ferdinand and Isabella. Further, I had quoted
something from the Epistle to the Corinthians at him (I'd been
reading up about St Paul) – he said I was insulting a Catholic

saint and was an atheist. I said I *was* – but it was a great man
I had quoted and nothing so silly as a saint! When I was taken
to the hospital he told the sisters there I was an atheist. They
refused to give me bed-pans all the time I was there except
once in the morning – because, they said, I was anti-Christ.
My mosquito curtain was taken away and I was left at the
mercy of a colony of malarial mosquitoes, which sent my temperature up once or twice round a hundred and seven – so
much that I heard afterwards they were expecting me to die and
that a priest was standing by to offer me the sacrament!'

Don Percy paused, out of breath, and a babble of indignant
remarks churned up the smoky air all round him, while he
mopped his brow with a red-spotted handkerchief, very *pro-
letariado* and proud-of-it.

Ellen Mulliner, upon his left hand, ran her fingers over his
perspiring thatch of khaki-blond, with a possessive anxiety –
whispering to him some caution, evidently, not to overtax his
strength by holding forth at too great a length, or by reviving
these painful memories in too great detail. But Percy ducked
and with a touch of crossness reassured her shortly; then
silenced the officious young woman with a roguish push.

Upon the other side of him Gillian pressed his hand and a
tear stood in her eye, as she gazed sternly at this man who had
been broken upon the Spanish rack in the interests of *étâtisme*
and Dictatorship. Others would be broken after him – even
the State Triumphant, even Dictatorship itself might break men
too – but he had been broken, and he *was* for something else,
which had not *yet* broken as many men as the present system
(at least only in other quarters of the Globe).

'How perfectly beastly!' exclaimed the girl next to Gillian,
whom the old bed-pan yarn, heard for the first time, had impressed very deeply, as she suffered greatly from constipation.
'It's like hearing about the Inquisition, isn't it? They still live
in the age of Torquemada in that awful country. Spain is
terrible. I think it is worse than Germany.'

A 'Leftie' reporter had out his note-book, and he had noted
that Hardcaster, the English syndicalist, had been put in a cell
the window of which looked out upon a swamp, and there had
been left practically to his own devices for three days and three

nights, to be eaten up by malarial mosquitoes, so that to his wound (undressed) was superadded a pestilential fever, and that the nursing sisters – wrongly supposing him to be unconscious – had rubbed salt into his sores.

'It reminds me of Oranienburg,' said the refugee, his ears sinking back against his head, and his hair withdrawing from the front of his scalp – which involuntary muscular operation caused his eyes to assume a Chinese obliquity, in the blushing mask of a beaten hound.

'But did not the doctors do anything?' thundered Geoffrey sternly, self-appointed precentor.

'The *doctors*? They stood beside my bed with the *bonnes sœurs*, and laughed themselves sick at the sight of my face!'

Sensation. The reporter's pencil galloped in the suspense of utterance following upon these revelations.

'I was unrecognizable! They showed me my face in a glass. It was scarcely human. I don't mind owning that it frightened me when I saw it. In fact I went off in a faint.'

There was now a tense silence for some moments. Then the same girl, who sat beside Gillian, exclaimed:

'The brutes! The perfectly fiendish brutes!'

Gillian was dumb with a lofty horror of proud indignation, that made her bird-like beauty pass into a hawk's profile of almost malevolent passion of destruction directed towards the rank and file of the aviarium around it.

At that moment Jack – his trajectory made tortuous by the gossiping groups intervening – came over from the *buffet froid*. He stood upon the outskirts of the immediate audience of Hardcaster, grinning. Attempting to attract her attention by a cough or two, his irrepressible animal eyes were fixed upon Gillian, and were especially busy with her bust, which was thrust out at the saturnalian angle of a young *tricoteuse*. At length she became aware of him. But she immediately flashed over at him such an Oh-*you*-there! For-god's-sake-take-your-grin-away! sort of look out of her dry eye, that seeing himself so unmistakably *de trop*, the grin departing from his face, he hurriedly left the circle gathered about Hardcaster.

'But a report should be drawn up at once and sent to the Foreign Office!' exclaimed a Public School Boy.

'Haven't we got an ambassador in Madrid?' said the third girl upon the settee upon Gillian's side of Hardcaster.

'Or a consul in Barcelona!' called out the Public School boy, very red in the face.

Gillian turned upon the young woman, one place removed from herself, who had opened her mouth for the first time (and who was not quite out of the top drawer by a long way) and remarked, with a laugh of unpleasantly playful scorn:

'If you had been born in a legation, my dear, you wouldn't ask *that*!'

At this Percy Hardcaster turned his head, with a definite access of admiration in his eyes and laughed in hearty approval over this sally of hers, which had afforded a glimpse of Gillian Communist in a highly-placed cradle, enjoying infantile extra-territoriality, and her first lispings enshrined in affairs of state: while the young woman definitely not of top-drawer status looked suitably crushed, but certainly gave Gillian rather a spiteful look.

'You said that the other guard, Percy,' Geoffrey said, 'was, if anything, a dirtier piece of work than the – than who is he –?'

'Alvaro Morato,' said Percy. 'Did I give you that impression, Geoffrey? No, that's not quite right.'

Percy frowned gravely – it was obvious that in a matter of such international moment he was anxious that nothing should be said to distort, or to weigh unduly, upon one side or the other, the evidence (direct or indirect, substantive or contingent, intrinsic or extrinsic, parole or under seal) – seeing that he was the principal, and indeed the sole, witness: no *plena probatio* existed. It was Percy first, and Percy last, and Percy all the time who would testify. Or if Percy was to be a party to the action, then Percy was prepared to march forward through Rejoinder, Surrejoinder, Rebutter, and Surrebutter, holding aloft, with steady hand, the exact image of the truth, and nothing but the truth, so help me Lenin!

'Serafín – that is what he was called,' said Percy, when he had sufficiently paused and collected himself and focused his mind on the facts, 'and I can assure you he was some seraph and all! – he was not a bad type in his way. That he got behind

154

me when the firing began is true, and that I shouldn't be in the mess I'm in if he'd acted like a man, that is true too. He was shot on the ground where he was shamming he'd been hit. Though of course *I* had got what was meant for *him* and he was never hit at all. He just fell down and shammed dead. But old Alvaro had it in for him, because he'd taken the job on at a tenth the figure fixed by the governor, so he plugged the poor devil for muscling in on his racket!'

'These police gangsters are unthinkably awful,' said one of the men from the headquarters of Propaganda Limited, or Red Dope for Leftie School-teachers.

'The police-terror gets worse in Spain every day,' said Geoffrey: 'it is really a bit too much over the odds at present. The Germans have nothing on them in the matter of sheer beastliness.'

'And the Jesuits are behind it!' hissed the girl-neighbour of Gillian, still thinking of nuns and torture by bed-pan.

*

Victor Stamp stood with his back against the wall and his hands in his trouser-pockets and talked to Peter Wallace (*né* Reuben Wallach) and Tristram Phipps. Upon the wall at the side of his head hung a colour-print of a painting by Picasso. It was one of the 'blue period.' Two emaciated itinerant guitarists or acrobats stood forlornly in the very wan moonlight of the 'blue period' of that artist's work.

'It is bourgeois art all the same. Its values are capitalist!'

Tristy stood like an early Christian, with whom it was an article of faith and a matter of fixed belief that the world would come to an end in a hundred and forty years at the outside, and the graves give up their dead. But it might – according to prophecy – terminate considerably sooner than that. In the meanwhile he was prepared to confabulate with men of similar beliefs to pass the time away, when off duty – for the Communist Party disk was in his buttonhole. At present he was off duty. His head was thrown back and his eyes were silvered with the otherworldly sheen that discussion was accustomed to provoke – discussion of a religious nature, of course.

'I don't quite agree with you, Peter, I am afraid,' he said.

155

There was a quaver in his voice, an effect of nervous strain, for Tristy did not like to have to disagree with this friend, so much of the elect, whom he recognized as a Levite, and who always made him feel small. In the words of the poet: 'Why, when we see a Communist, do we feel small!' – and here was the genuine article, beyond a peradventure and merely to see him he 'felt small.' Whereas, was he himself the sort of man to make other ordinary men feel small – was he, in other words, 'a Communist'? He could not decide! He wished he knew! He could not succeed in making *himself* feel small, when he contemplated himself, that was all he could say. In matters of high doctrine, such as Pete made him feel *very* callow and half-baked, unquestionably. He knew the highest when he saw it!

'Surely without Picasso, Bracque could have done nothing. No, perhaps not *nothing*, but he might not have done so much – what do you think?' he asked, smiling nervously. 'I can't help feeling that Carl Einstein is a little mistaken. About *that*, I mean,' he hastened to add.

While Tristy was speaking Peter had stood quite still, as if he had been listening to the recitation of a lesson – say, over the telephone, for his eye was fixed upon a distant point, while a slight smile played upon his lips. When Tristy had finished and was standing a little guiltily, to hear his fate from the lips of the great fountain of pure doctrine, Peter began gently, as if he had been patiently waiting to take up the argument:

'There's something in what you say, Tristy. But Picasso got it all from Bracque, you know. Bracque taught Picasso everything. The father of Bracque was a house-painter.'

'Like old Hitler!' said Victor Stamp, guffawing a little, lazily.

Pete's manner changed at once. He had two quite separate responses, one for Tristy (a sheep out of his own fold) and one for this wild goat of the places of the wilderness, for whom he was nothing but 'Pete' – a little guy who scribbled pretentiously about pictures and sculpture.

'No. *Not* like Hitler!' Pete archly retorted, in a soft low growl, his hair retreating from his forehead, and his cat-shaped eyes flirting, reproachfully sportive, with the big rough boy before him; who did not like him, and regarded him as a pretentious 'word-slinger.'

156

'Hitler's a Böcklin fan, I believe. Isn't he?' asked Stamp. 'I seem to have heard so.'

'I don't know what Hitler is, and I don't care,' said Pete at that – putting his foot down firmly and brushing Hitler aside.

'I've heard so,' said Victor, rubbing his head.

Tristy had looked distressed at the mention of a certain political personage, whose name had just been introduced jokingly by Victor – whose long suit was decidedly not his sense of humour.

'Was Bracque's father a house-painter, Pete? I never heard that,' said Tristy, anxious to purify the air by agitating the thurible of Marxist discussion – for a *house-painter* mentioned by Tristy because as it were a *marxian object* on the spot.

Pete nodded.

'It was he taught Bracque the wood-graining racket. And he taught Picasso.'

'So all the surface-business comes from Bracque?' blustered Victor.

'All the surface-business comes from Bracque,' repeated Pete looking at Victor from under his eyelashes while he removed a speck of tobacco from his lip.

'So now you know, Victor, where your surface-business originated!' Tristy laughed.

'I hear what Pete says,' Victor replied.

'I don't see all the same, Pete.' Tristy painfully reopened the subject (Pete grinning as he did so and watching his spasms with open amusement), '*quite* how you can say that Picasso's reality is that of capitalist society. It isn't, as I see it. Would you say it was altogether?'

'Altogether!' snapped Pete a little severely, becoming bored: just as a visiting vicar might become bored after too protracted a pumping by an elderly *dévoté* upon matters of doctrine. 'Picasso does his best to get away from that reality: so much is true.'

'And succeeds!' Tristy pleaded.

'Does he? I can't see that he does, I'm bound to say. His "periods" are so many struggles *away* from decadence – or back to it! To me Picasso is just like a portentous moth, *flinging* itself against an electric light. He beats himself up against

157

a new ethos (there's no question about his being *attracted* by it): but he always flies back again into the shadows. Into the shadows – where he belongs!'

Tristy looked very miserable. He could not deny the justness of the description. The *orthodoxy* of the picture was not to be questioned. And yet he was compelled to sustain an opposite opinion to all that he *knew* to be true, for the reason that there was another conscience, namely that of that pitiable thing, the artist. And conscientious at all costs he had to be!

'I know Carl Einstein says that.' Tristy knew that Carl Einstein said it – and he looked deeply distressed, for this made things very difficult, and poor Tristy realized that he *must* be in the wrong.

'Carl Einstein's talking through his hat when he says that, Pete. What's he know about painting anyway?' blurted out Victor roughly, with a somewhat aggressive smile at Pete. 'He's one of those Jewish smart-alicks from Paris.'

'Well, let's leave Carl Einstein out of it, Vic!' Pete said smoothly.

'Yes, why not?' said Victor. 'Why not? Let's leave everyone out except Picasso.'

Pete smiled indulgently.

'Let's get back to the fundamental thesis of the Marxian dialectic,' he proposed genially.

'Why drag old Marx in? What's Marx got to do with it?' objected Victor. 'Marx wasn't a painter.'

Tristy smiled brightly. *This* proposal caused him a certain chilly amusement – that Marx should be left out of anything!

'All right, Vic! Let's leave Marx out!' Pete grinned. 'But that won't help you! That's not going to help you, Vic!'

'Nor would Marx help me to understand a Picasso,' Victor retorted.

'He *might*,' said Pete.

Tristy laughed brightly and fiercely, staring away, up into the air.

'You see, Vic, it's no good,' Pete said kindly. 'You *can't* regard painting as suspended in the ether, attached to nothing in heaven or on earth. That's art for art's sake. You can't do that.'

'No. I don't want to do that.'

'Well, you talk as if you did. Look, Vic – will you admit that Picasso is, outside of his cubism – we won't count that in – a classical sensualist?'

'A classical what?'

'He hots up all the old stuff, doesn't he? It's a *réchauffé*.'

'He belongs to the *sensual* world. That is what Pete means,' Tristy looked down to say. 'You said that once yourself, Victor. And I didn't agree with you!'

'No, I never said that!' Victor rolled about against the wall, as if he were a hobo dealing with his parasites. 'I never said anything about his being sensual.'

'You may not have used the word. But that was what you meant.'

'No.' As Victor rolled about, his head came into contact with the Picasso on the wall. 'Look at that! You can't call that sensual!' he said.

Pete and Tristy looked at the 'blue period' colour print.

'Oh, that!' said Pete, turning his head away. 'Yes, what's Sean got that up on his wall for?'

'But is it *sensual*?' insisted Victor.

They were now a foursome. For Old Jack had joined them: and with an inquiring grin he was contemplating the Picasso, with his head on one side, formulating the question *Is it sensual?* in the sensual depths of his intellect, and supposing the question referred to the semi-naked condition of one of the beggars in the picture. But there must be something more in it than met the eye, Old Jack concluded, since its sensuality did not exactly hit you in the stomach.

*

Margot Stamp – melting away before large human obstacles, stealthily and swiftly occupying any vacant space that suddenly gaped open before her in the wall, darting around the corners of clangorous groups, allowing herself to be carried along with the current when it was setting away from the buffet – was making her way across the room. She held in her hand a plate, upon which was a piece of cold salmon. There was also a hard-boiled egg, and a neatly packed cube of miscellaneous sandwiches with a lobster claw in one. She was taking food to

159

Victor. She had observed his departure from the group of Pete, Tristy and Jack. Then she had lost sight of him. But she thought he had vanished through a crevice in the panelling – as it had seemed. He would be found behind it somewhere – she imagined him alone in the dark behind the panelling, waiting for her, perhaps. She thought she knew just where he was. She would follow him through the crevice, with the piece of cold salmon. She knew he must be desperately hungry. He might have mistaken the direction of the buffet – he supposed perhaps that it was outside the room, probably downstairs.

When Victor and Margot Stamp had arrived they had at once unfortunately encountered Pete, and with him was Tristram. After a desultory talk they had of course fallen into one of those chop-logic séances which Margot so disliked – with Tristram wringing his hands, or pulling at a lock of his hair, and Pete baring his teeth in a self-confident and self-satisfied grin as he withered the air with his tongue.

Within a few minutes, led by Pete, they got into the thick of a jeremiad and were discussing those things that made her blood run cold. Everything they said bore upon the fact that in the modern world – that meant this tragic scene upon which she and Victor lived and suffered – there was no place for the artist, no place at all. Everyone they knew was in the same boat, it seemed, all robbed by dealers and cold-shouldered or hated by the public. And Pete, you would have said to listen to him, had been employed to disseminate terror and despair amongst all those who wielded brushes and held palettes on their thumbs. (He himself never seemed to be in want of money – he must have received it for the predication of death.) He seemed to experience a diabolical satisfaction in this picture of apocalypse (as it concerned the artist): of starving craftsmen, unsold statues, and unwanted masterpieces in oils and chalks – *avantgarde* or strictly of the beauty-doctor-class, it made no difference. All was a fat grist to his multure. Even, he would positively fall into a rage like some nasty spoilt-child she thought, if anyone so much as demurred, or brought forward so much as a single fact to spoil this hangman's-holiday, or detract from the blackness of the gloom. The hair would hurry back from his yellow forehead and a most vixenish and vindictive look come into his eyes. She had often heard him at it, in pubs and studio-rooms, and of all the people they knew she disliked him most and had what amounted to a dread of him. For she felt that almost *physically* he was forcing Victor's head into the gas-oven. She would have walked a mile to avoid him. And after Victor had been seeing him, she always knew with whom he had been, by the dark set look upon his poor lovely brave brown face. It had taken her many an hour to put right what this Pete had put all at sixes and sevens. To drive the sounds of this destructive tongue out of the head of her darling – who responded to Pete only too actively, although she knew that he hated the man as much as she did herself – had cost her many an evening, in which they otherwise might have had some peace. Yet of course *hatred* was not the word with her, since Margot was incapable of that, but perhaps *aversion* might be used; and it anyway amounted to disgust and dread.

On this occasion she had stood listlessly at Victor's side, overhearing, as it were, this terrible conversation – as it went from bad to worse. And then, unable to stand it any longer, she had left them silently, hoping that perhaps Victor would follow her before long to the buffet.

From her place at the extreme end of the buffet she had watched him with anxiety. For a great store of food was collected there. And she felt that, as the evening wore on, it would inevitably disappear, she could do nothing to stop it; and instead of finding its way into Victor's inside, it would disappear into the better-fed and merely greedy innards of the persons beside her, carelessly devouring it. Every mouthful, especially of that great delicacy, the salmon, which was consumed by one guest after another, who came up and looked round to see what he could find to devour (simply for the sake of eating, not because they were hungry), filled her with an anxious concern. For she wished so much that Victor would come and cut himself a large slice of this delicious fish – with a good big helping of Intourist salad *à la russe*, and a cordial lashing of fruit-cup out of an earthenware pitcher – which looked very good with the pieces of apple and cherry floating in it.

She pecked and nibbled herself at a small sandwich or two

and drank two cups of strong coffee with *Slag*. And always her eyes returned to the spot – now hidden by bodies, and now partially exposed by the erratic movements and displacements of same – where Victor rolled against the wall, chatting with Pete and Tristy about the heartlessness and stupidity, the stony misery of the world.

While taking a sharp turn, in her haste, around the corner of a biggish party of Red gossips, Margot collided head on with another hurrying form, and the plate of salmon flew down to the floor, where it was broken, the food scattering to left and right. The hard-boiled egg shot away like a squash-racket ball, to disappear among the legs of the debating society she had been negotiating.

'Can't you look where you're going?' she heard an imperious voice exclaiming, as she was bowed down towards the shattered plate. She raised her eyes and as she did so observed that a portion of the salmon had marked with its oily pink pigment the surface of a party-frock, worn by the girl who had cannoned into her. And then the next moment she realized that this was none other than Gillian Phipps. She smiled in apologetic recognition.

The face of Gillian Phipps still wore the mask of a moody hawk, that it had acquired while she had listened to the account of Hardcaster's ordeal by bed-pan. And now it was as a hawk – which has surprised perhaps a peewit in the act of carrying a worm to its young – that she stared down angrily at Margot Stamp.

'Good gracious, is it you, Margot? I'm sorry.'

With an ill grace Gillian changed her tune – altered it from the menacing clamour of the stronger vessel into the patronizing drawl with which those of drawing-room class address those of kitchen status.

'But what possesses you to go scuttling about with your head down?' she scolded. 'We might have injured each other! Are you hurt?'

'Not at all!' Margot said, in her rather unearthly, hollow voice. 'Are you?'

Gillian collected, with an expression of impatient disgust, a pair of cress sandwiches from the floor, and placed them in

Margot's open hand. In her other hand Margot now held the fragments of the plate and the slice of salmon, recovered from the floor.

'Have you seen Mr Phipps?' asked Gillian. 'I have to be off. I wanted to find him.'

'He's over there,' said Margot nodding to her left, a slight flush of humiliation upon her face.

'Where? Oh, I see him! It's a good party isn't it? I'm going to take Percy Hardcaster home. He oughtn't to be out really. Give my love to Vic!'

And Gillian proceeded across the room, while Margot made her way back to the buffet. There she immediately cut another slice – not quite so large a piece – of the luxurious salmon, collected another cube of the little sandwiches, and started off again without delay.

Gillian Phipps was yet another person whom Margot could not find it in her heart to feel over-charitable about, though certainly she felt no animosity against her. She was painfully aware that Tristy's lady did not like her. She was conscious that her treatment at Gillian's hands very often slipped down on to the plane of patronage. Because Margot was not a 'lady' and because she had to speak slowly, and with a stately brittleness of intonation, not to betray the fact. And she guessed that there was something else – although to that she was unable to give a name. However, the only way to keep this big proud girl in her place would have been to speak in the accents of Shoreditch to Notting Dale; to speak 'in character' – to allow that to be fastened on her, like the placards hung round the necks of offending Jews in the Reich. And even then Gillian would have merely mocked her openly, instead of in the veiled way she was accustomed to do at present. Margot understood that no bridge existed across which she could pass to commune as an equal with this Communist 'lady' – living in a rat-infested cellar out of swank (as it appeared to her) from her painfully constructed gimcrack pagoda of gentility. Nor did she wish to very much because – for Victor's sake – she dreaded and disliked all these false politics, of the sham underdogs (as she felt them to be), politics which made such a lavish use of the poor and the unfortunate, of the 'proletariat' – as they called her

163

class – to advertise injustice to the profit of a predatory Party, of sham-underdogs athirst for power: whose doctrine was a universal Sicilian Vespers, and which yet treated the real poor, when they were encountered, with such overweening contempt, and even derision. She could not fathom the essence of this insolent contradiction: but association with such inhuman sectaries could be of no profit to any pukka underdog whatever, she saw that, and her concern was always for one whom she felt to be utterly helpless. For that Victor was a pukka underdog she saw quite well: though pukka had not yet been incorporated in her vocabulary, and all that has to be presented as what she thought, was, in fact, transacted upon the plane of emotion, where words were all mixed up with images.

When Margot reached the further extremity of the room she searched for the crevice, as it had looked to her, in the panelling. She followed the wall for some distance, back and forth, dimly searching for this opening which had swallowed up her Victor.

The house in which the O'Hara's lived and of which they occupied the two topmost stories, was large. And this room, in which their guests were mainly assembled, comprised the whole of the top of the building. Large studio-windows had at some period been built into one side of it. Throughout it was panelled, in an unbroken plane, up to the ceiling, with three-ply, of a deep tawny buff. And the walls were honeycombed with cupboards, of which only the locks were visible (except for one which stood open two feet from the floor and provided a three-sided chamber reminiscent of the shops in an Eastern bazaar). But narrow doors likewise, here and there, announced the presence of larger recesses. And there were certainly cubicles behind the panelling upon the side opposite to the massive windows.

As she became accustomed to this very large empty apartment, Margot had felt that she was moving about the inside of an immense box. It was a box that had false sides to it and possibly a false bottom: for she was not at all sure that she was not treading upon trapdoors and the masked heads of shafts, as well as leaning against a hollow wall, in a deceptive security. She speculated as to what this dark and dwarfish little Irish fellow kept hidden in the recesses of his walls. With a finger concealed behind her back, lest she should appear 'nosey,' she tapped the panelling and everywhere she found that it was an artificial limit, and not in fact the real wall – as it would have been in a straightforward room – with which she was in contact.

The intense uneasiness that all these people aroused in her was as it were perfectly expressed by the sort of place in which they were at present congregated. As she listened to their voices – big, baying, upper-class voices, with top-dog notes, both high and low – shouting out loudly in haughty brazen privileged tones what they thought, as only the Freeman is allowed to – the subject of their discourse invariably the commonplaces of open conspiracy and unabashed sedition – *coups d'état* and gun-powder plots – she felt a sinking of the heart. It seemed to spell, for her private existence, that of Victor and her, nothing but a sort of lunatic menace of arrogant futility. They were not so much 'human persons,' as she described it to herself, as big portentious wax-dolls, mysteriously doped with some impenetrable nonsense, out of a Caligari's drug-cabinet, and wound up with wicked fingers to jerk about in a threatening way – their mouths backfiring every other second, to spit out a manufactured hatred, as their eyeballs moved.

Her mind strained, in an inward tension, to seize exactly what it all might mean, or might portend. But it was no use at all. It all seemed to register *nothing* – or just nonsense. They recited to each other, with the foolish conceit of children, lessons out of textbooks – out of textbooks concocted for them by professors with thick tongues in their treacherous cheeks, with a homicidal pedantry, in the jargon of a false science – such as might have been established by a defrocked priest of International Finance, for the amusement of an insane orphanage.

She could not reach out, to express her misgivings, into the difficult realms of speech, where all these disparities of thinking and acting would fall into place and be plausibly explained: but she was conscious nevertheless of a prodigious *non-sequitur*, at the centre of everything that she saw going on around her – of an immense *false-bottom* underlying every seemingly solid surface, upon which it was her lot to tread.

She now perceived a slit in the wall, where a sliding panel had been partly opened. Plate first, cautiously, she entered. Probably Victor was inside!

Over a table, upon which stood a reading-lamp, two men were leaning. One of them was writing something, was writing something upside-down, upon a large sheet of paper. What was this? But he turned the paper round, and she saw it was a signature, or rather three signatures, one above the other. All were the same. When the paper had been turned round, what she saw, in a large flourishing hand, was:

'Not at all bad!' said one.

'The pen is too thick,' said the other.

The two men then looked up and found her standing behind them, with a plate in her hand, upon which was a piece of cold fish. Both had been so absorbed by the upside-down penmanship of the taller of the two, that neither had remarked her entrance. The man holding the pen Margot recognized as a friend of her husband's, called Abershaw. The other man was Sean O'Hara.

Margot was too astonished for it to occur to her to account for her presence: she stood with her mouth open, her eyes fixed with a bewildered scrutiny upon her husband's handwriting – as if she had been summoned to witness a signature, and had then suddenly observed that the signature to be witnessed was in her own handwriting, and then lastly, with a start of horror, that the name was *her own*!

Abershaw quickly reached across the sheet of paper and collected, just outside the radius of the light of the lamp, another sheet, much smaller in size, which she had noticed lying there. This he thrust into his pocket. The retrieval of this subsidiary sheet, from the outer darkness, had been effected by Abershaw with a suggestion of the manipulative deftness of the conjurer,

166

pokerfaced and lightning-fingered. He might have been one of the members of that profession in the middle of a trick, who suddenly had remarked that an object that should have been secreted in his sleeve was in fact lying in full view upon his property-table.

Abershaw drew himself up – a good way, as he was a six-foot-three-er – with a series of deep mocking clucks in the back parts of his throat.

'We've just been trying our hand,' he said, with a great deal of cheerful *fauxbonhommie*, 'at forging your husband's signature, Mrs Stamp! What do you think of it?'

'It's very good, I think,' she said.

'Not bad. The V is a little too feminine. That V would give it away at once.

'I should have known the difference,' she said faintly.

She could not say why this scene should have affected her so much: but extreme alarm for Victor prevented her from returning to her normal self and she remained pale and her arms trembled.

'Were you coming in here to get out of the maddening crowd, Mrs Stamp? Going to have a little quiet supper, I daresay, what?' O'Hara with great affability inquired. 'I don't blame you.'

'No,' she said. 'I was looking for my husband.'

'I saw him a moment ago. He's downstairs, I think,' said Abershaw.

'I think I'll go and look for him.'

She retired backwards through the slit in the panelling, pressing her elbows into her sides in order to pass, and holding the plate stiffly in front of her.

*

An hour after Margot's exit from the small closet-in-the-wall in which Abershaw had been discovered playing at handwritings, three people entered it together – one the mystery 'capitalist' of the party, the other two the young genius of whom he had become the patron and their host. The latter pushed his 'capitalist' guest, even a little roughly, inside – he almost bundled him in, as if he had been angry with him, and

167

a slight stagger as the 'capitalist' came to a halt resulted. Then he slid to the door.

'Let's keep that row out!' O'Hara said.

Jack looked over his shoulder at O'Hara with the rustic craftiness of Hodge in the booth at the Fair, who has been requested by the conjurer to hold the silk hat and keep his eye skinned, that nothing should escape from the performer's rolled-up sleeve undetected. He perceived by this time that it was some sort of charlatan with whom he had to deal – though what sort he was at a loss to imagine.

Tristy flung himself into a chair. The demands of this party had exhausted his reserves of social energy. He was asking himself: *What should a socialist fellow do when the parties of his socialist friends prove too much for him!* Should he leave, as would any ordinary man? Or should he stay to the bitter end? But Tristy was a die-hard. There was a brightness, almost a humorous brightness, in his eye, which seemed to say: Try me and see if I can't take it! *Bore* me a little more! I am ready for you! I am your man! I am your true Communist man!

'Try one of these, Mr Cruze.' O'Hara took a box of cigars out of a drawer – it bore the label, a little battered, *Flor de Mercedes*. 'They are the real thing. They are not made for export. It is what the Cubans themselves smoke. They are called *Flor de Mercedes*. Try one.'

Jack was silent – in the way that a man condemned to play the part of a fool before an audience out to enjoy itself, and on the look out for a public butt, will hold his peace and bide his time. With a slight smile, he helped himself to a cigar.

'Try one, Tristy,' said O'Hara. 'No, do take one. I should like to know what you think of them.'

'Oh,' said Tristy. 'But I really know nothing about cigars.'

'No? Try one all the same. – Take a pew!' O'Hara said heartily, turning to Jack, and dropped himself in his best club-man style into a slum-purchased basket chair, waving his hand towards one from a second-hand leather suite, to be occupied by Jack. When they were all seated, O'Hara said:

'Well, let me see. I was telling you, Mr Cruze, wasn't I? I was telling you?' Excellent as was his ear, there were some things subtly British that O'Hara had either not noticed, or else had omitted to acquire. One of these was the quick dropping of the 'mister.' He retained the habit of a provincial formality and he *mistered* away without intermission. 'I said to this inspector-fellow: "Because I write books you think I am unpractical. But you are mistaken."'

'They're all right if you know how to talk to them,' said Jack.

'I count myself a practical man!' declared O'Hara. He protruded his chest a little in the direction of Tristy.

'I believe you are, Sean!' Tristy agreed, nodding at him – stamping him, with his nods, *practical*.

'I'm sure of it!' said O'Hara. 'Only the other day I put through a deal for a friend of mine. A sum of a hundred thousand francs was concerned.'

'How much is that?' asked Tristy.

'It isn't the amount involved – that was nothing. I had to play the capitalist for the time being – I imitated a capitalist to the life! I should have liked you to have seen me, Mr Shandy! I even began to *feel* the capitalist! You would have turned from me in scorn and loathing! You would really.'

'What fun!' said Tristy, who laughed heartily at the idea of this imposture on the part of a Partyman. 'Did they find you out, Sean?'

'Not them! I carried it off famously.'

'Good man!' said Tristy.

'But I was down on the deal.'

'Too bad!'

'A thousand odd.' O'Hara laughed at himself and encouraged Jack to do so, but old Jack wouldn't.

'What I need's a spot more practice. It's not difficult to be a capitalist. I've proved that.'

'Capitalists are often down more than *that* on their deals,' Jack told him, speaking as one who knew a good deal about capitalists, since he audited their books.

'Ah, but in this case I ought *not* to have been, you see! That's where it is.' And O'Hara looked 'rueful,' as it is called in the vocabulary of the bookstall, and he frowned, with a certain vexation, at the thought of the profits he had allowed to slip through his fingers, because of his lack of practice.

'Better luck next time!' suggested Jack.

'There *is* going to be a next time!' O'Hara told them impressively at that. 'And this child is going to be in on it on the ground floor.'

But at that he drew up, almost with a jerk, as if he feared he had said too much, and had realized, just in the nick of time, that the *nature* of the transaction in another moment would transpire should he go on gossiping about it. There was a long pause, during which he continued to look owlishly and steadily at Jack. It was a little contemplatively, too, maybe – as if he were weighing his guest's capitalistic capacities in the balance, and perhaps finding them a little bit wanting.

'The capitalist is stupid. That is what principally impresses one about him,' said Tristy, breaking the silence.

'Oh, not always,' said O'Hara. 'Besides, we all need the capitalist, whether we like him or not. Take the manufacture of arms. The people who manufacture arms are capitalists, are they not?'

'Undoubtedly,' sneered Tristy faintly. 'Yes!'

'Undoubtedly they are. Well, supposing you are an Irish patriot – which Heaven forbid! Or a Catalan same. You are consumed with the pure flame of patriotism. You desire to "shake off the yoke of the oppressor"! Good! You have to go to the capitalist, don't you – for the mere physical means to do so.'

'Would that be of any use?' asked Tristy, very astonished at the notion of Capitalism combining with or assisting rebellion in any form, even Sinn Fein.

'Any use?' cried O'Hara. 'How should it not be of use, pray?' He leant forward and spoke with deliberation. 'If I go to a capitalist and say to him: "Will you sell me a Lewis gun?" what does he answer? He says, does he not, "Certainly," he says, "as many as you like, old man, if you can pay for them." That is the beauty of the capitalist system. The capitalist will sell you bombs to blow up other capitalists. Or to blow *himself* up with, for that matter! That is the great beauty of the capitalist system. You can do anything you like in it. Even destroy it – if you can only get money enough, to do it with.'

'If you become a bigger capitalist yourself, Mr O'Hara!' laughed Jack, who saw the point immediately.

'Exactly. I see that you understand the system, Mr Cruze.'

'Well, Mr Phipps here always calls *me* a capitalist. So I suppose I ought to.'

'That does not follow, Mr Cruze. But anyhow the capitalist will sell you anything. He is a functional creature – a buyer and seller. Why, he would sell you his own daughter, if you paid him enough.'

A bright light shone in Jack's eye, like a window lighting up upon a foggy English evening; and, watching him with extreme attention, O'Hara saw the illumination, and noted it with interest. Old Jack was looking at a rich girl in his mind's eye, standing naked in a slave market, with her hair one lovely cataract of gold, or raven black, that tumbled about her dainty ears, and that sprang out of her eyelids, or which arched beautifully above her eyes. All promise and provocation. Crouching forward in his chair, O'Hara watched his guest with a lacklustre grinning.

'If,' said O'Hara, 'he had *a dozen* daughters to sell, he would sell them all to the highest bidder,' and he watched the effect. 'He would not worry about their age. A fourteen-year-old flapper would go the same way as the Lewis gun, if the purchaser had the dough – and she would be delivered in a plain van, all nicely packed in silk and lavender.'

At this Jack laughed outright – it was a peal the simple-heartedness of which astonished and impressed O'Hara.

'In plain vans – so as the neighbours shouldn't know what was inside!' old Jack chuckled, to encourage him. But he looked round at Tristy as if to tell him with his ribald eye-play that Mr Phipps could send Gillian round any day he chose and he'd foot the bill. And Tristy, smiling with lofty embarrassment, turned his head away and taking the ceiling into his confidence, beamed quietly away at that – for there was nothing else in the room that could any longer be considered intelligent enough to share a little quiet mirth with.

'Exactly!' cried O'Hara, now at the top of his form. 'And good luck to them, I say, capitalists or no capitalists. I don't blame them. If it's guns or girls you want, you *have* to go to

the capitalists. And what the patriot wants is *guns*, that is all.
It is as simple as that.'

'I'd rather have a girl!' joked back old Jack.

'There's no accounting for taste!' said O'Hara, with the most
accommodating cynicism. 'What's one man's meat is another
man's poison.'

'I prefer the former,' said Jack.

'You would be more interested in the White Slave Traffic
than in the traffic in arms, I gather, Mr Cruze!'

'It is more in my line,' Jack answered, 'that's a fact.'

'I am a married man, like Mr Phipps here,' said O'Hara.
'I'm a father as well. So the White Slave Traffic from a strictly
business angle, yes. But for me the White Slaves themselves are
out of bounds.'

'We once audited the books of a White Slaver,' said Jack.
'He got pinched though.'

'A clumsy fellow!' O'Hara said. 'If I were a capitalist now!'

'Oh, ah!' Jack began going over in his mind the quality, as
sheer skirt, of some of the girls in the other room, one by one,
and his mind stopped affectionately in the neighbourhood of
the corkpuller.

'A friend was telling me the other day about the traffic in
small arms, by the way. That is some racket! He gave me the
figures. A good deal of money changes fists in the course of
the year, believe me.'

'It must.' Jack yawned, tapping his long upper lip.

'The Chinese War Lords, as they are called in the Press,
want boatloads of rifles and ammunition. And they pay
through the nose for it. The profits are fabulous.'

But the word *profits* seemed to leave Jack's mind stone cold.
O'Hara did not fail to remark this.

'Suppose for argument's sake,' he said, 'an Armament King
wants a pretty girl. Such things are of daily occurrence. He
gets her shipped to him, all ready for use. And he pays through
the nose for her. *And* he gets the money to pay for her by
making a War Lord in Canton pay *him* through the nose for a
consignment of dud rifles or a few rickety tanks! That is the
way of it, Mr Cruze.'

'That's the way of it!' Jack a little absently agreed – for this

172

account of the budgeting for skirt sounded to him of an excellent accountancy. And he considered the steps that he took himself, in his capacity of chartered accountant, auditor and actuary – auditing the books for shops or for corporations, calculating life interests, annuities and insurance policies – so that he might obtain money to buy all the Ediths, Violets and Pearls he could lay his hands on.

'I am in a position,' said O'Hara, lightly flourishing his Flor de Dindigul, 'as it happens, to put anyone on to a good thing at this very minute – I heard it over the telephone only this afternoon. It's a snip – from the word Go!'

Jack listened with his mouth open, an unfeigned look of pleased anticipation upon his ruddy face – for he was now persuaded that – by devious roads and tortuous methods – this man was about to try and sell him a *girl*.

'She's not been returned from Hollywood *Not Wanted*?' inquired Jack, with a cautious grin. 'There's lots of that sort going about.'

O'Hara, divining the nature of the misunderstanding that had supervened, laughed with a touch almost of disinterested gaiety.

'No, no. This is the goods! But I will keep this under my hat, if you don't mind, for the present.'

He jumped up and fell into a paroxysm of stretching, his joints cracking and the basket chair upon which he had sat cracking as it expanded, like a fire of dry twigs, at his back.

'I think that's rather mean of you, Sean!' said Tristy, who had risen too. 'Won't you tell us?'

'Not now. I wouldn't tell you anyway, Trist. You're too young, old man. You don't understand the ways of capitalism, you poor mutt.'

'On the contrary. I understand them only too well.'

'No, you don't,' O'Hara turned upon him suddenly, aiming a blow up at his shoulder but slapping his arm instead. 'You think you do. Let's go and have another drink – what do you say, Mr Cruze? There's a girl I want you to meet.'

Jack came to his feet with alacrity.

O'Hara was even rougher with Jack at the going out t'

the coming in. He stood so little upon ceremony – he was so pedantically hearty – that he practically flung Jack through the narrow opening. He was projected out into the midst of a sheepish group that had got up near to the door – unaware that such a thing existed in the smooth face of the panelling. Even the rumble of voices had been very faint, owing to the sound-proofing of seaweed from the Sargasso Sea with which the panelling was lined.

*

'Sean is a twister!'

Victor Stamp, spoon in hand, swept his arm out horizontally to cut down all those *twisters* liable to infest his neighbour-hood.

'Sean is an old twister!' he repeated – as Margaret with glazed glances seemed not to have registered this, and he wanted *somebody* to know it. Australian, Victor, becoming drunk, was finding his nation returning to him out of the thick mists of the alcohol – a Victor that he always playacted a little now when he encountered him; but one of those down under, nevertheless, it was – who felt the call of the quarrelsome blood. As heavy as a malt horse, built and bred to carry a ballast of malt liquor, Sean's porter had effected a change, of the back-to-nature order preached in *Emile*: gin-slings and a shot or two of schnapps in the host's particular closet, was getting him where he wanted to get, where one was out of reach of the mad money-sharks and the gombeenmen, and where a man speaks a mouthful straight out of his stomach, as a man of guts should, and tells a twister where he gets off. – So his voice had grown thick and reckless. 'The Graces' were rapidly departing from Margot's god, from her manitou.

He sat upon a cushion, leoninely slumped back against the panelling, as if luxuriating in a technical knockout. And Mar-got sat beside him. He was eating a *kouskous* out of a por-ringer, brought him by Margot steaming hot, from where it was being prepared by the hostess. When she had first smelt it in the air and realized that public cooking was afoot, as a mid-night one-course supper, considering how she could contrive

174

to get a double-helping for her 'man o' mine,' wrestling with her bashfulness, Margot had started off upon as uncomplex an errand as a bird that quits the nest at an unexpected promise of fresh worms.

'That's what Sean is!' Victor growled thickly at her, gulping a spoonful of hot rice.

'Not so loud, Victor!' Margot entreated him, in her hollow piping delivery.

'How do you mean?' and Victor glared at his pallid mate, but she looked with apprehension upwards at the big drawling group of upper-class Reds, straddling dogmatically above them, and threatening to tread on their feet as they trampled about in their talk.

'I don't give a hoot for this crowd, Margot!' he said, with a violent earnestness. 'I tell you he's a twister, everyone here knows that. I'm not telling them anything they don't know, if they want to listen!'

'Perhaps so, darling.'

'There's a poor devil who trusted him who's going to have his head chopped off. In the Fatherland.'

'Hush! You mustn't, Victor. You're eating his food.'

'Eating his food! What of it?'

'The laws of hospitality,' she suggested, with the shame-faced simulacrum of a smirk.

'Laws of my –!' and he named what they were the laws of, as he saw the matter, through his bloodshot eyes, at that moment.

But she looked at all these big untidy gentlemen, of Public School type – moth-eaten from the standpoint of the charlady, but somehow all the more alarming because of that – and at the sprinkling of imperfectly-powdered ladies, their grinning, donnish highbrow Molls – oh, so much more snobbish than any duchess! She shrank against her penniless young protector, who had little standing here. He was not their sort in politics, or even in nationality – he only had the status of a stranger. Everyone, when they gave him a thought, wondered how Victor lived, but supposed that he lived on her. And then she wore his ring, but everyone knew it was not a serious ring, and that she was not a proper wife. She had never had the

175

heart to coax him to the Registry Office, against which he had an unaccountable prejudice. But Margaret knew that these women's class of Communism would hold this against her, because they were cats, who were giving away nothing – especially to humble girls, who had not had rich business fathers or foxy little doctors as dads, to send them to schools for ladies, and have them taught to talk in these grand voices that oppressed one like the helmet of a policeman.

'Victor darling!' she said in a very low voice. 'Please don't speak like that!'

Should his vulgar expressions be overheard, they would think that he did not respect her, because of her birth.

'Not say what I think? Why? Do you suppose that these people are *real*? Do you think they exist?' he bellowed darkly in her ear.

'Aren't they real, Victor? I wish I could believe they were not real!'

Sending her eye out upon a secret journey of inspection, she asked herself, shuddering at the question, *were* they real? If they were not, again, did that make it better or did it make it worse? Of course, if she *really* came to believe that they were not, she would feel afraid. Who would not?

Was this after all a great complicated dream she had got into against her volition, where all these vivid likenesses of life only existed in her dreaming mind? Were these tweed trousers and cotton shirts, buttons and fingernails a few feet away, imaginary, as she had been told so often by Victor that they were? Of all the conversations Victor was apt to hold with such young men as Pete, she perhaps disliked more than any others those that bore upon this topic, namely of the appearance and the reality.

Apart from anything else, this sort of talk had caused her to regard everything, herself, as more shadowy and floating than before. But she had the strongest feeling, whenever she was listening to them, that their intentions were *not* charitable, as *they* argued upon those lines with Victor – for it was *they* who had made Victor believe that he was not 'real,' of that she was positive. He always had thought he was real until he met Pete, to that she could swear. The malice would flash out of Pete's

176

eye. It was *their* reality, that of Victor and herself, that was
marked down to be discouraged and abolished, and it was *they*
that the others were trying to turn into phantoms and so to
suppress. It was a mad notion, but it was just as if they had
engaged in a battle of wills, to decide who should possess most
reality – just as men fought each other for money, or fought
each other for food.

But if this assembly of supposed people was an effect of
delirium, in the 'fever called living,' then in that case Victor,
too, *he* might only be another ghost-person, in very fact. They
were all ghost-persons together! Her love would be a passion
of her brain; with no more stuff to it than the rest of the rig-
marole – if nothing in time *could* be real, as Victor so often
would say, when he put on his thinking cap, and started ex-
plaining to her all about *Time* – about 'becoming' which was
not *being*: and she could quite follow that of course – for your
self of last week or of next month did not really exist in the
way you existed at the moment you were thinking. And yet it
had existence, and in so far as it *had*, it took away from what
you possessed of reality at any selected moment. *That* it did
not take a great philosopher to see.

But the mere notion of Victor as a shadow-person distressed
her so much that she grappled him to herself, so that he, at
least, should not be outside herself among *the unreals*, resolved
to fortify herself against scepticism in this capital matter, and
as a munition against Pete-ishness to use violence if necessary.
Slipping her hand in beneath Victor's arm, she hugged it to her
body. As his muscles played about like fishes under his skin,
she tried to catch them with her ever-timid fingers, like little
apologetic pincers – as if to arrest life, and its reality as well, if
she could only catch one and hold it still *in her hand*, ex-
tracting it from its bloody element.

Even in her physically lowly position, she had her head
lowered; and, without looking up, or leaning her head back
against the wall – which would have smacked of defiance,
since it would have been publicly to *loll* – she could see little
more than footwear and legs moving capriciously inside
squirming or wavering pantaloons or 'bags,' or the more secretive movements of the lower sections of women inside their

skirts. All these strangers looked bigger than ever because of her position on the floor.

As she clung to Victor she felt that what he had said was true, and that they were not in fact very real at all, the people with which this room was packed. They were a dangerous crowd of shadows, of course, that hovered over them. But if you stood up to them, if you called their noisy shadow-bluff, as Victor would be able to do if he so desired – if it came to a showdown, between a shadow and a man of flesh and blood – they would give way. She could see that they would move off, chattering, but admitting their ineffectiveness. They could not really bear you down. They could only browbeat you like a gramophone, or impose on you like the projections on the screen of the cinema. Spring up and face them, and they would give way before you. For they had no will. Their will to life was extinct, even if they were technically real.

But she saw in her mind's eye the two silent figures in the darkened cabinet, where she had passed through the slit in the wall of the room, imitating a signature. Why should those two shadow-persons be practising the signature of a real man? What would the purposes of those evil-looking shadows be? What would they do with the name they had been caught in the art of stealing, in their peculiar world? To what was Victor to be supposed to affix his name? Or were they in fact, as they had pretended, just engaged in an insignificant pastime, in a quiet corner, such as one would expect shadow-persons to indulge in if left to themselves – as objectless as children, mimicking the handwriting of their betters, in a preposterous but harmless sport?

'But what were those two men doing, Victor, imitating your signature?' she could not help asking him, with a shudder of anxiety at the sound of her anxious voice, framing the question.

'God knows!' Victor replied. 'Playing the fool, I suppose. If I had more in my bank than I have, I should want to know maybe. But as it is!'

'It isn't only about money that people can use a signature, Victor.'

'I don't see what else they can use it for.'

She did not argue with him about this. She could not off-

178

hand think of any particular use (though she felt there must be one) to which Victor's signature could be put that would matter a great deal, so at that she left it.

'I don't like that man Abershaw!' she said.

'Don't you, Mrs Stamp?' said Abershaw – the astonished and somewhat indignant voice reaching her from far overhead. She saw the flap of a familiar greenish trouser-leg, and knew that it was he. Where had he sprung from? Like Jack-in-the-box, he might at this moment have shot up from a trap at her feet, and be talking to her there up in the air, all in one movement.

Abershaw sat down beside Margaret, with a duck-like clucking in the back-part of his throat – rather as if he had been a goose that had just laid a golden egg, and was quietly congratulating itself on the fact.

'Why don't you like me, Mrs Stamp?' asked Abershaw, smiling. 'I should have thought you would – I appeal to most women of your type, I have found.'

'My wife doesn't like you, Abb, because of your face. She says it's the face of a crook.'

At this Abershaw gave a hearty laugh.

'That, I think, is putting the cart before the horse, Vic.'

'You mean I ought to push your face in first and say why I did it afterwards?'

'No. I mean that most people call others crooks because they don't like their faces, not the other way round.'

'I daresay you've got it right, Abb!'

'But I believe that in fact Mrs Stamp was merely informing you that she didn't like me, lest you should suspect her of liking me too much! Has that occurred to you, Vic? I make the suggestion for what it is worth.'

Margot saw the big slack muscles, of an indiarubber consistency, working about in the face of this highly bogus personage who had sat down beside them. His face was of a dark yellow tan, almost of the colour of mustard, and his hair of the same shade, only darker. He sported a small and what seemed a peculiarly postiche moustache. He smiled and then went back, with a sudden collapse of the countenance, to his watchful owlishness, in a manner that positively advertised its automatism, and shouted at you that it was *unreal* – boasting, as it were, that you could not hurt it, because it was all a gutta-percha pretence. This more than life-size discursive tallow-catch, dropped down from the sky, was so poker-faced as to be the obvious answer to her metaphysical speculations, or rather sensations. For here was a mask of such transparent *fauxbonhommie* – a presence which displaced so many meaningless square inches of the ether, as to pose the whole problem of *the real* and its various mixtures and miscegenations with its opposite, right up to the negative pole of absolute imposture.

So here this negation of a person sat and conversed with them, as if nothing in the world were amiss, or certainly not with *him*, and she could observe Victor taking him (or, should she say, it?) seriously, and proposing to quarrel with it. And she felt that whatever happened she ought to prevent a clash between these two worlds, that of sham (in no derogatory sense), and that other one of hall-marked fact, as repesented by her Victor – passed out of the Assay Office fully-carated if ever a man was! For she recognized, as she thought, that this figure was the bearer of a challenge from the underlying unreality: she must not allow Victor to take it up. So she attempted demurely to ogle the questionable intruder.

'Have you and Mr O'Hara been studying any more handwritings, Mr Abershaw?' she asked, with a ghastly attempt at the roguish.

'Not any more,' said Abershaw, politely and matter-of-factly. 'Did you tell Vic about our little experiment?'

'Yes, she told me,' Victor answered sourly. 'Here, Abb, what were you and Sean doing, anyway, with my signature?'

'That is easily answered,' said Abershaw, with a pleasant laugh. 'We knew you were a man who always kept rather a large fluid cash balance in his bank, for his day-to-day operations, and so we thought if we could imitate your signature satisfactorily, we might make a scoop!'

He looked round at Victor like a giant Puck, puckered and peeping, with two big twinkles for eyes.

'Well, I should be glad if you'd let my signature alone another time. Do you get that, Abb? I'm rather particular who uses my signature.'

'You are perfectly right, Vic, as a matter of fact. You should be. You're perfectly right.'

'Thank you.'

'Will you tell me something, Victor? Is it true that at the present moment you're hard up?'

'It is. What of it?'

'Well.' Abershaw drew an unusally large pipe out of a large side pocket, placed it in his mouth, and drew on it with his indiarubber lips, studying Sean's parquet with a reflective eye. 'Why don't you go in for a little mild forging yourself?' he asked with absent-minded sedateness.

'Forging? What are you getting at now? Forging?'

'Merely this. If Victor Stamp's pictures don't sell quite so quickly as they should, why not do a few Van Goghs, say, for the time being?'

'Because I don't want to. I'm not a forger.'

'That, of course, is another matter. But I have a friend who runs a sort of Van Gogh factory, out in the suburbs. He has just lost – in a motor accident – one of his best hands. I was telling Tristy just now about it. He mentioned you.'

Victor shook his head.

'Forgery's not in my line.'

'You could start on Monday,' said Abershaw.

'Thanks awfully. Nothing doing. I should make a bum forger.'

'You wouldn't have to forge *the signatures*!' cried Abershaw, in a sudden explosion of almost frenzied roguishness. 'Only *the pictures*!'

'Thanks, old man. I prefer to go on the dole,' said Victor.

'Love on the dole!' Abershaw embalmed in a guttural chuckle the title of the play, and rolled his eyes merrily at Margot, who responded with a sickly smiling to his pleasantry. There was no question but what the underworld of the half-real was getting out-of-hand. The creatures who had crept out of that False-bottom beneath all things were taking an interest in Victor. They were commencing to sniff around her precarious nest.

Here was a strange and disturbing proposal! And she believed that for a moment Victor had hesitated. He had seemed reluctant to say *No*. That was the Australian coming out (and she was conscious of the distant shadow of Botany Bay – there was no use blinking the facts of history!). But what a temptation, all the same, to be put in the way of a hungry man, living on cheap tea and unable to find his rent!

This horrid Abershaw had been despatched to entrap Victor into some criminal scheme. They lay in wait, of course, for a man of Victor's stamp, until he was up against it. Then they came and tried to persuade him to become a criminal, in order to keep body and soul together.

Help him to work honestly they *would* not. That was a fixed principle of theirs. But they would give him a leg-up on the ladder of *fraud*, with the greatest pleasure. They said no one could make an honest living today. And they saw to it that he shouldn't. Indeed it was dishonest to make an honest living today. How often had she not heard that! It was not their game, the devils, to have men hard at work, in honest occupations. Where would they be if men *were*? To make criminals of everybody, that was their settled policy – to get men in their power. A genius like Victor was not allowed to make an honest living. They hated his honesty. They hated all honesty so bitterly, because it countered all their plans.

So they did everything to depress and discourage you to work and pay your way. They would rather get you lent money (and put you in their power by debt), than get you a sale of pictures, so that you could honourably own money of your own, as Victor had said to her more times than once, in his bitterness against them. Oh yes, to work was 'bourgeois' – and they disseminated the belief that because society was rotten, work was out of the question: for they wanted the whole world slowly to strike, to go into chronic unemployment and to be idle, that they might take it over and rule the roost, with a hand of iron. But you could *start on Monday* if you would agree to forge pictures, to be sold as other people's – which would sooner or later get you into jail. And then they would raise a universal shout that you did not have private showers, and muffins for tea, in the lockup, and were in short a martyr to the vindictiveness of society! But jail is jail. And she did not want her Victor to get in there if she could help it.

182

To indicate her distaste, ever so discreetly, for this insult on the part of an insolent shadow-person, she withdrew a little bit away from Abershaw. With an expression of self-absorbed and indifferent fatigue upon her face, she gazed in the opposite direction. It was then that she caught sight of a pair of hungry little eyes fastened, yes, upon *her* – there was no doubt about it. She had aroused a guilty passion! And she noted, with dismay, that these boldly tell-tale eyes belonged to a diminutive individual, not much bigger than herself, whose appearance was anything but improved by an angry crop of pustules on his cheeks. He was by himself, it seemed: and he had been keeping her under observation from the rear of the big group that rocked immediately above them. She pushed down her skirt to convey her reprobation, and her look of weary isolationism deepened by a good shade or two, to show him she was not that sort of girl.

Abershaw got up, a low-pitched mocking cachinnation dropping from his mouth as he rose to his feet, an obscene and lazy succession of reports.

'Well, don't turn down my friend's offer without thinking it over, Vic,' he said.

'I shan't need to think it over, Abb.'

'Van Gogh himself forged Rembrandt to start with, remember.'

'Is that so, Abb?'

'So my artist friends tell me. It's only poetic justice really that he should be forged himself a little too! Think it over. And let me know.'

He was gone. And Victor remained sprawled back against the panelling.

*

Dancing had been going forward and there was a pause, while they hunted for a record. Meantime the tone of the party had deteriorated. 'Sex had reared up its ugly head' in the words of Ballyhoo. Here and there couples were melting into each other, and were to be seen establishing relations of unbelievable intimacy. The host and hostess had disappeared. The guests had the bit between their teeth, and having talked

183

themselves hoarse, and drunk a good deal, were turning to Cytherea.

Victor slept. In sleep he was heroic, with the balance of the High Renaissance in the proud dispersal of his limbs. He slumbered upon Sean's cushions as if upon iron clouds, in a Michelangelesque abandon. Margot watched him, with the maternal patience of a tiny bird mounting guard over a giant cuckoo foistered upon it, which she loved more than the child of her own humble egg.

Abruptly the room was plunged into darkness. Someone had turned off the lights. A match was struck and blown out again, Margot saw the slight opacity of figures passing her in the darkness. They were spluttering to each other as they moved. There were bursts of laughter upon her left, of people stridently announcing their identity in the midst of a blackout, in masterly good humour, as if showing off *sang froid* in an emergency.

An electric torch punctured the blackness, and its ray was directed hither and thither revealing to Margot's disgusted eyes glimpses of involved figures and vignettes of violent disorder upon the floor, as when a boulder is suddenly lifted up at the seaside and a world of marine creatures revealed, scuttling to safety.

'Put out that bloody light!' shouted somebody. The light of the torch was snapped off, its owner exclaiming 'Sorry!'

The darkness would have been much preferred by Margot if she had not felt uneasy at the bottom of this immense box in the dark, with so many lewd shadow-persons at play, who she felt were crawling about and might at any moment attack her. She saw visions. For supposing all the lights in the world began going out, and they all had to live with each other in darkness forever, whispering to people one could not see? Her little hollow voice would be begging the pardon of this shadow and that, with whom she had collided. Would she and Victor subsist more happily in an unlighted world? They would find their way about, no doubt. They would gather in parties just the same and grope their way into public houses. People if they could not see you would be more civil, but you would never be certain what they were going to do.

Out of the darkness an arm materialized and hooked her round the waist. It came from the opposite direction to Victor. And she felt somebody pressing up against her, upon the side where Victor was not. Her heart stood still. She was being attacked by one of them! A hot and alcoholic breath was on her cheek, a hand was on her knee. A faint scream escaped her lips. She fell forward upon the floor in front of her, locked in a suffocating embrace. A mouth was fastened upon hers, acting as a most effective gag.

But wrenching her head free for a moment, she piped, shrill and terror-stricken, 'Victor!' several times. And she heard the thick bellow of her mate, *Margot!* as he woke, behind her, asking her *what was the matter*, and then *where was she*? Her next sensation was that the shadowy aggressor – whose enterprise was forcing from her gasp upon gasp, in quick succession – relaxed his grip. There was a convulsive vibration, a choking expostulation, and then he seemed to be lifted up in the air from off her shrinking body. At all events all contact with him abruptly ceased. There was a sound of dull smacking blows upon flesh and awful hollow thumps that were accompanied by the emission of stifled squeaks, there was a breathless gasp or two, and then, as she lay panting on her back, looking straight up in a dazed stare, she saw a shadow fly through the air above her head, or so she thought. Following immediately upon this came a dull crash, like several people falling downstairs, and several voices shouting together; and she received the impression that a lot of people were struggling on the floor some distance away. She drew in her feet and crawled back to the cushions. Then suddenly the lights were switched on.

As, without warning, her sight was given back to her in this way, she heard Sean O'Hara's voice, pitched in so angry a key as made her recoil (as if the question had been addressed to *her*) shouting:

'Who turned these lights off?'

Guiltily turning her head, she saw their Irish host standing in the doorway, with a lowering and indignant countenance; but his eyes were not directed at her, but glared over into the far corner of the room. Following the direction of this basilisk gaze, she observed a girl she had met once or twice, Ellen

Mulliner, in so compromising a position that she hastily turned her eyes away again.

'Who turned these lights out?' Sean shouted again. 'You can cut that out! If you want to do that, you can get to hell out of this! Do you hear me? Let the lights alone!'

There was an embarrassed silence for a moment.

'Sorry Sean, I did it!' a young man called out. 'Ellen said it would be cosier. She felt shy with the lights on.'

'If Miss Mulliner wants to make love she'd better go home,' Sean replied. 'This is not the place for that.'

Sean's face bespoke with the greatest plainness his icy ruffled dignity and the hot uprush of those Irish snobberies that had made him feel that these people had sought to convert his establishment into a brothel, or a cheap saturnalia of nobodies. It was all he could do to stop himself from turning the lot of them out into the street. A guilty hush succeeded his outburst.

In the middle of the floor three people were sitting as if they had just been flung down there, in an awkward group. One of them was Margot's late assailant, who was none other than the small pustular amorist whom she had remarked spying her out earlier in the evening, but whose face was now smeared with blood. The other two were slowly picking themselves up. They began shaking themselves and dusting their trousers, one laughing and one scowling.

'I say, Victor, old fruit!' called out the former, 'I wish you wouldn't throw people at me in the dark!'

'I'll ring his neck for him if he comes over here again!' Victor answered, very angry still. He took a step in the direction of the still prostrate figure, but Margot seized the bottom of his jacket and pulled him back, in great alarm.

'Victor darling! Please come and sit down!' she said.

He flung himself down on the cushions beside her, staring darkly at the bleeding object on the floor, with a look of puzzled outrage, as if he had been stung by some affront of so peculiar an order, one without any known precedent, one so little amenable to any accepted response that he did not know exactly how to act, as much baffled as indignant. He did not look at her at all.

Slowly gathering in volume, from the neighbourhood of the

buffet, a roar of laughter grew to homeric proportions, until the whole room was laughing, except Victor and herself. She turned her head, in obedience to the orientation of all these delighted faces, and discovered the cause of their satisfaction beneath the buffet table. The spectacle that met her eyes caused her to turn her head quickly away again. For it was Jack — just Jack, with all that went with that, for there was a female form as well.

Hastily crossing the room, a grin now on his face, and seizing as he went a low screen that stood at the head of a settee, Sean made for the centre of disturbance. Amid ribald cheers and more laughter, he placed the screen around the spot upon which his capitalist friend, in company with the corkpulling young woman, was giving his exhibition of faunish light-heartedness. And the action of the host reconciled him with his guests, the restraint removed, and all was once more moving on the plane of pleasantness.

There was one guest, however, between whom and Sean, her host, the guffaws built no bridge: and a few minutes later, as Margot stared in front of her — as puzzled as Victor by what had happened to them — Ellen Mulliner passed, evidently in the worst of humours.

'Are you going, Ellen?' someone asked her.

'Yes — since my presence is not desired by our host!'

'Yes, he did tell you off, didn't he, darling?'

'Tell me off! He could do with a bit of telling off himself, the poisonous little rat! Nothing if not the gentleman Misther O'Hara! Living on his blood-money pretty comfortably, what! I'm ashamed of myself for having come to his party — no decent person should come inside his door.'

'You came with Percy Hardcaster?'

'Yes. But I should have known better. Percy would go anywhere if they made a fuss of him. He's as vain as a peacock. Good night.'

'Let's get out of this!' said Victor to Margot. 'I have seen enough of these people for one evening.'

He stood up and held out his hand to help Margot up.

'Won't you have a sandwich, Victor, before you go?' she asked.

187

'No, Sean can keep his victuals. As that girl said, he pays for them with blood-money.'

'That was only because she was cross, Victor.'.

'Anyway, I've eaten enough!' he laughed.

PART V

GILLIAN COMMUNIST

Chapter 1

JACK was pretty sore about the party. Not that the party
wasn't a good party: he'd worked off some of his feelings
under the table anyway. He had made the very best of a bad
job. But Gillian had led him up the garden – asking him to
take her to a party and getting him all steamed up in the hope
of what might happen between them, and then as soon as they
got inside palling up with another man and leaving him to his
own devices amongst all those rotten freaks.

But Jack was not a boy to bear a grudge. And a few days
later he went round to Gillian's on the off-chance of finding
Tristy not at home. This first visit was ill-timed, however, as
it turned out. For he arrived at the head of the area steps
almost at the same moment that a taxicab drew up and out of
it stepped, or rather was helped by the courteous cabman, a
corpulent fellow with a large flushed face, holding in his hand
an enormous bouquet of flowers, as bashful as a youngster
with his big fussy present. Jack descended the steps, and his
man with the flowers followed on his heels, stumping down
one step at a time. They stood at the door together. They
were much of a sort and much of a colour and much of a size
– though the other had not Jack's merry-andrew glances, or
long upper lip, and was of a grosser build as well. Jack eyed his
fellow-visitor with the most eloquent dislike – and the other
did not seem to take to him. For this was the guest of the evening from the night of the party.

It was Percy Hardcaster – Jack had recognized him as soon
as he put his full moon countenance, with a frown like a fretful
pram-pushed protagonist of the nursery, out of the taxi-win-
dow. So Jack and Percy waited together, grim and silent, and
it was pretty close quarters, at the basement door until Gillian
came to open it.

Immediately taking Percy's hand she exclaimed in a very

caressing and understanding fashion, and dropping her voice as if to keep Jack out of it:

'*Hallo*, Percy!'

'Hullo, Jill!' Percy answered, flushing pink like a slum nipper who had just been made a fuss of by a member of the governing classes – also in a *low* voice, as if he quite understood that their affectionate greeting should not be overheard by this stranger, whom he too had spied. And very firmly, not waiting to be asked, he passed into the flat, leaving Gillian face to face with Jack.

'Hallo, Jack!' said Gillian, wrinkling up her face as if to say: '*Well, you see – this is a little awkward, isn't it?*'

'Hallo, Jill!' he said, taking her hand.

'I'm terribly sorry, Jack, but Percy Hardcaster' – and she uttered the name in the same important way that he had noticed before when she was referring to someone way up the ladder in the Red racket – 'Percy Hardcaster and I have something rather important to talk about.'

Jack scowled.

'It's quite all right, Jill,' he said. 'I thought I'd pop round, that was all.'

'It was very good of you, Jack. Let's make a date. Let me see!'

'I'll take pot luck,' said Jack, moving off. 'I'll come round some time when you're not busy, Jill.'

'Yes, do, Jack. Don't forget!'

After a few days Jack was all right again. He never could bear a grudge against a woman for long, any more than with a piece of furniture that dropped on his toe. And at his next visit there was no painful encounter with Percy Hardcaster to make matters difficult. Tristy was there.

'Old Jack was very ruffled,' Gillian said, 'when he met my new young man on the doorstep.'

'Which one was that?' asked Tristy.

'Percy,' she said. 'Jack's as possessive as a peke. Jack is really an old nabob.'

They talked about him for a while. Jack bit his nails, and at length picked up the evening paper and read about the Big

Fight at Madison Square Gardens that night, and how the big Jewish gladiator said to a reporter: 'I'd never forgive myself if I hurt Dan!' whom he was matched with.

It was a new experience to Jack then, though I think he got quite used to it a little later on, for people to think aloud about him to each other, and talk before his face as people always do behind our backs. Jack quite got to like it in time. Later on Gillian explained to him how narrow-minded this was, to object to it, and he saw it in a sense, though he never got quite used to it.

'Why after all, Jack,' she said, 'should Tristy and me have gone into the back room and closed the door? Isn't that rather silly?'

'I don't see that,' he said, nor did he.

'Look, if we *think* something, is that any better than *saying* it?'

'A lot better, I should say.'

'But everyone knows that other people criticize them when they're not here. So what does it matter if they *hear* it now and again? – when it would be inconvenient if one didn't speak in front of them?'

'It matters to them.'

'It oughtn't to, Jack. It's not civilized to prefer *concealment*, Jack. Why hide up everything? It's a compliment to a man to tell him what you think of him!'

'He may not look at it that way, may he?'

'But we shouldn't mind you telling *us*, Jack, what you thought of us. Indeed we know – we can't help knowing it, Jack! Your thoughts are so easy to read!'

When first he had all this explained to him properly, it took a long time – and Jill stroking his hair, or such of it as had been left over and collected together by him on the top (Jack could *never* have been a genius at any time, he never had hair enough for that). He was pretty much impressed, he agreed. Because the way she put it *did* only sound common sense – that we didn't gain any by people just waiting till our backs were turned before starting saying what they wanted to say on our account. They might just as well – that sounded like reason after all – fire away while we were still there; and the same with us, sort of tit for tat. At least everyone by so doing would know where they stood.

But in *practice* Jack found this precious method did not answer so well as you might expect. He tried it out in his office. There was the devil to pay, it seems. The sergeant, their commissionaire, behaved like 'a thug' on the spot to start off with. He laid out one of the best clerks who wasn't waiting till he got outside to say what he thought of the sergeant. And Jack noticed too, he couldn't help it, that Tristy and Jill reserved for *him* most of these exercises in mental communism. That's what Jack didn't like. He never heard them but once speaking out their mind to each other about somebody who was there all the time (bar Jack). Then it didn't come off properly, because the man got up and left half-way through. And he never came back for any more.

Well, Jack went away too, without stopping to hear any more about himself, when it first happened. But Jack, *he* came back. He wanted Jill as much as ever if not more. And the disappointment at the party, and the presence of Percy with his flowers in the background, only whetted his appetite. He brought a bouquet twice the size of Percy's. Whatever happened. Jack was not going back till he'd got her. It did sort of pass through his mind that maybe Tristy had guessed something, and that might have something to do with their insulting him. But he wasn't going to be scared off so easily as all that, if that was the case.

Two or three times after that Jack went there and had drinks with them. Mostly a pal or two of theirs were present. No reference was ever made to the picture of Jill by either of them, and he wasn't asked to go into the other room to look at the canvases. He thought it occurred to them he might take out his cheque-book again, or rather it did to Jill, perhaps.

Then one night Jack dropped round and Gillian Phipps was there alone. Tristy had just gone out with a young painting acquaintance to his studio to see some canvases and wouldn't be back just yet. O.K., thought Jack. He said in that case he'd wait. She laughed and he sat down. It was then they got talking about what had happened when Jack bought the picture. She explained how it was that Jack had been dumb, as they say on the films, to feel sore because they'd discussed the problem about taking his money in front of him.

'Don't you see, Jack,' she said, 'we couldn't possibly regard you any differently to that?'

'I suppose not,' Jack replied.

'Jack, you are the natural man. You are in fact *a natural*, as it's called. Why object to that – if you *are*, after all?'

'Thank you,' said he. 'I don't object, Jill. I didn't say I did, did I?'

And Jack got on to the butter-and-egg box beside her and did a lot of his 'natural man' stuff until she wriggled out of his clutches and sat on the other side of the table.

'Yes, I know you're a natural man, Jack,' she said. 'I said it and I stick to it. But please remember I'm only *half* a natural woman. You go too far.'

'I go too far?' he grinned over the table-edge; he was breathing a little heavily for Jill had had to struggle a bit with him on this occasion and she was a strong girl with muscles like a blacksmith's bubbling all over her back, though as straight and supple as you could wish.

'Yes, much too far, in some respects. You make love like a man of property.'

'I don't get that, Jill.'

'No, I don't suppose you do.'

'All right, keep it to yourself! *Man of property*. All right.'

'I meant, Jack, you march in and take vacant possession a little too much.'

'I intend to take possession of you, Gillian, before long, girl!'

'There you are! That's what I meant. You feel to me as though you were staking out a claim. You do a bit too much *prospecting* to my way of thinking, Jack.'

'I'm sorry if I was rough, Jill! I apologize.'

'It's not *that*. It's your attitude, Jack, that's all wrong. You treat my body as if it was a tract of unknown country on which you were planting the Union Jack!'

'I'm sorry, Jill – what's bred in the bone, you know!'

'I can almost hear you crow cockadoodledoo when you think you've struck oil.'

'Well, I've been called a swine by lots of girls but never a rooster!'

'You make me feel like a "native." You are terribly English, Jack – in other days you'd have given your name, I am sure, to a stretch of new earth, like Ellesmere or Van Diemen.'

'Go on! I shall get conceited in a minute.'

'Yes, I can see you may. But I don't want to be a sort of *terra incognita* for you, Jack. Understand me, Jack! No prospecting on *me*, please.'

'I get you, Jill.'

'I'm not the "mysterious woman" or any old thing of that sort I'd have you understand, Jack.'

'No,' he said.

'I'm as well mapped as Pimlico, fresh rain-proofing and plumbing, I have no need of officious inspectors, thank you. I have nothing hidden on my person either. I'm all square and above-board. So, please, Jack darling, no rummaging around! I don't care for that.'

That's what Gillian was like. 'She was so goddam sensible that she was a proper spoilsport,' old Jack said, 'though when I kissed her on her mouth she didn't run away; she was as keen as I was, I could see that. But she wouldn't let herself go because of her bunch of notions.' Jack was nearly given the hysterics once or twice, he confessed. She'd jump out of his arms just as things were shaping nicely after a spell of all-in and no-quarter, and left him panting there with his tongue out like a dog in a drought.

This time, when she gave him her lecture on the pros and cons of *prospecting*, as she called it, they fell to talking, for the time was getting on and Jack thought Tristy might be back earlier than he was expected. So he threw in his hand for that evening. It was then she explained why they talked before him about the money, for instance, instead of going into the back room. He heard all about the *backbite direct* as you might call it, or *mental communism* were Gillian's words. No thoughts hidden away from your brother-biped but all laid naked to inspection, share and share alike: so that no one could say that

anyone was keeping anything away from anyone else, or claim-
ing they had *a self*, as she put it. Properly considered, she said,
aren't we all just one Big Self? So nothing must be *kept back*
and *locked up*, like a private possession, which is all that the
self is,' she said.

'Jack,' she called suddenly, 'oh, Jack, you are an old goose!'

'Am I?' said he – she was laughing a great deal and he knew
she was getting ready to give him a broadside about himself,
so he dug himself in and waited.

'When you came in that night you were terribly funny –
when you saw me undressed through the window. Do you remember how you went on? You stood there as red as a turkey-
cock and wouldn't look at me – do you remember? You were
so funny, darling Jack!'

'It's a good thing to see the funny side,' he said – he knew of
course she had been making a fool of him but he didn't quite
savvy how. 'I see lots of funny things, too!'

'Nothing so funny as yourself, Jack – nothing half as funny
as you are. *Especially*, Jack, when you were standing over
by that photograph with your hands in your pockets!'

'Ha ha ha!' he joined in with her making a laugh of it too.
But he was getting fed up with his comicality and wished
they could have a laugh at somebody else for a change. Well,
anyhow, he who laughs last laughs best, they say, thought
Jack.

'Anyone would think, Jack, you'd never seen a woman with
her clothes off before. And you must have seen hundreds,
haven't you?'

'Two or three hundred,' he said. 'What of it?'

'Nothing – but why did you hold your head down and all
on one side, darling, as if you had a stiff neck? I've never seen
in all my life anything half as good as that.'

'Ha ha ha!' he laughed neck and neck with her, only louder.

'How was your mind working, Jack?'

'I don't know, Gillian.'

'Let's hear your explanation of the phenomenon.'

'What phenomenon?'

'Your behaviour – it's a great curiosity if you only knew it!'

'I suppose it is, Jill, it must be.'

'It is. You are a phenomenon from top to toe, Jack. One's never dull a minute with you.'

'That's something,' he said.

'*No one* but you could possibly have screwed his head down in just that way and looked at me out of the corner of his eye. You're as comic as the ostrich! What's your account of yourself, Jack? Let's hear what it feels like to be *you*!'

He had had about enough of this, as I daresay you can fancy; he felt he'd better shut her up if he didn't want to get really mad with her and perhaps do something he would regret.

'What it felt like, Jill, is that it?' he said, in a stupid thick drawl he puts on when he's angry.

'Yes, Jack. Come over with it, make a clean breast to me.'

'There's no occasion, Jill, for me to go confessing, there's nothing to confess. I just felt all funny inside when I saw you, as you were –'

'Yes, *undressed*, Jack! Don't be afraid to say it. Undressed.'

'I wanted badly – oh, something *funny*, I suppose.'

'Yes, I see.'

'I didn't want to look at you because I thought you might see how I was feeling.'

Gillian laughed – hers was a hardboiled laugh sure enough, and he always preferred it when she didn't laugh too much at a time. It was throwing cold water on his kind of affectionate feelings for her, laughing like that, and he didn't like her doing it, and always wished she'd stop.

'But can't you see how stupid that was, Jack? Why take so much trouble to *hide* that, if you felt it, Jack? What's it matter?'

'I don't know why. Looked at in that way, it doesn't, I agree, Jill. But I didn't know then, did I, that you wouldn't mind if I felt like that?'

Alongside of his feeling in a rage as he did – being as he was the *natural man* – he saw that this constituted an invitation. Everything was to be strictly *informal*. Very well! Nothing was to be hidden up, that was the idea. Well, that suited his book if it suited hers! And he made up his mind on the spot that at the next opportunity he'd make as plain as words could make it, and actions too, what it just was he was after. And he felt pretty sure he should get it.

Jill was a dead cert, he reckoned now. And he allowed his *prospector's* eye to rove across the table. She seemed to ask to be looked at that way, Jack thought. She threw out her bust in a great sobbering sigh – a love-sick sigh it sounded to *him* such as girls give when they feel worked-up. He'd heard it more times than he could count – not being a first-rate man with his figures. She stretched herself this way and that as if she felt as he did (which was still pretty well steamed up) shooting up a big white arm to show him where to bite, as if to give his eye a run for its money – for its thirty pounds, to quote the figure. For Jack hadn't forgotten he paid cash down, in advance! He hadn't forgotten the picture.

He had to wait another week or two for his next chance, a long two weeks for him. Then – it was a Saturday – he called round between two and three. She waved her hand from inside as if pleased to see him at once, and he waved back as pleased as her. He felt from the look in her eye she was all by herself. She let him in saying Mr Phipps was out: 'But come in, Jack,' she said, 'all the same.' It appeared old Tristy had gone off to the Zoo to do a sketch of a humming-bird he wanted to paint in a tropical picture. He wouldn't be back till tea-time when the Zoo closes, or after. So Jack had only himself to blame, as he saw it, if he didn't pull it off. He got ready to make a quick job of it this time.

He went right over to her at once and got hold of her against the table as she was standing as if expecting him, with a funny smile on her face.

'You know, Jill, what I want?' he said. 'I needn't tell you this time what I want to do.'

He had a funny thought at the time – it was like a detective making an arrest, what he'd just said. But he'd got now to feel as if anything he said was a bit comic.

'I don't at all know, Jack,' she said. 'How should I?'

'Yes, you do.'

'Tell me what it is, Jack,' she said.

He told her what he wanted as he'd been invited to do – he kept nothing back! – and she shook her head, more in sorrow than in anger like.

'I can't do that, Jack. I don't love you, you see.'

197

This hadn't been what Jack had expected. It took him aback, he couldn't say why, but it did. He then saw how it might make things *more* awkward instead of less, everything being so blooming easy. On this sort of outspoken basis things *should* have been plain sailing. But they weren't when you came to the point. She was a lady, and the fact didn't make things any easier. He felt he'd been caught out a little, and I suppose he showed it in his face – being a *natural* of course, and showing everything he thought like a two-year-old, whether he wanted to or not!

'I didn't say whether you loved me, Gillian.'

'It does really matter whether one is in love or not, Jack. Can't you see how it might?'

'But I *am* in love, Jill.'

'Yes, *you* are, or you say you are – that's the word you use. But I'm not! I'm sorry but there it is, Jack.'

Jack could not help wondering if all this went on with Percy. He put his face down on her neck and kissed her hard, doing a good bit of pressure too with one paw and the other – she had no clothes on but her dress, he found. Then he said to her still holding this big wasp of a girl in the small of her waist:

'Why do you let me do this, Jill, at all?'

'What, kiss me? I can't keep pushing you off. You do it without asking me.'

'I don't see why you couldn't stop me, if you wanted to, Jill.'

'But I like you, Jack. I said I didn't love you. That's another thing.'

'What's the difference?'

'There's a great difference.'

'Shan't we ever be lovers, Jill, then?'

'How do I know?'

'Is it because of Tristy?' he asked her.

'Oh no,' she said, 'it's not Tristy. We are quite free to do what we like. I just don't feel that way about you, Jack.'

'Why didn't you tell me that before, Gillian, instead of leading me on?'

'Leading you on? What do you mean by that? You've been leading *yourself* on, as you call it. You've been leading yourself on at a great pace.'

'All right, Jill, why did you let me lead myself on then?'

'Really, Jack, you're asking rather a lot of me, aren't you?'

'Why did you come out undressed where I could see you? You're a married woman. You know how men feel about that.'

She threw up her head in a sort of contemptuous way and gave a snort in the air for a laugh, which cut him like a whip, he says. He couldn't stand laughs, that was Jack's weakness.

'In order not to inflame your passions, Jack, must I be so careful not to show bare flesh to our male acquaintances? You'd make a poor woman's life difficult, wouldn't you, Jack, with your rules about what they may show and what they mayn't show?'

'Why do most women keep their bodies covered up?'

'Don't ask me, Jack. My grandmother wears twice as many clothes as I do. If you want to know about these things you'd better go and ask her. I'll give you her address.'

'Thank you and all that, Jill.'

'Why do men as a rule respect the law of hospitality – why didn't you ask me that instead? Why do most men behave like gentlemen, as they put it, and respect – as they call it – their friends' wives?'

How all this might be a bit of a damper is plain enough. I daresay old Jack may have had a sort of scowl on his face in place of the smile to start off with by this time.

'Very well, Mrs Phipps!' Jack said, separating from her in a rather sudden way, calculated to hurt her woman's pride, so that she found herself a few feet away from Jack, and he turning his back on her. 'I'm only a policeman's son, I know.'

'That's nothing to be proud of! I shouldn't boast of that.'

'Where would you be without the police?'

Jill looked round the dark basement room, all the contents of which no rag-and-bone man would have given more than a couple of half-crowns for, if that.

'We don't need any policeman to protect *our* property, Jack. It's where would *you* be – that's what you meant, isn't it?'

'You're a professional man-teaser, Mrs Phipps,' he said, taking his hat. 'But you keep it. I don't want it.'

'Keep what?' she asked, opening her eyes in a sort of childish way, and making her lips hang open in surprise, like a little innocent girl.

'You know what.'

'Myself, do you mean, Jack? Surely not me?'

'Yes. There are plenty of girls in the world.'

'But you talk about me as *a girl* as I were an object – to which a mind had been attached to make it walk about and talk prettily to you while you were preparing to eat it! You must see how absurd it is, Jack! And on that view you are trying to steal me from Tristy: and it is my duty, as an honourable object, to summon a police constable and have you arrested for the attempted theft! – That is no doubt why Nature has provided me with *a squeal*! So that no man should take me in the absence of my master!'

But Jack's feelings were changing again – the baby-face she had put on had done it. When as a diminutive ruffian he had burst out of a hedge upon a startled little village virgin, dreaming of ever bigger and better wax-dolls, in his Wiltshire birthplace, these were the sort of looks that had stamped themselves upon his senses. And as a veteran satyr he always fell for the pouting mouth, and the blank rounded eye, of pseudo ten-year-olds. A child's voice in a woman's throat had the same effect. The little flute sounding out of the big instrument, that wrung out of him the blissfullest wishes, with its insidious paradox. If women had got gruff voices when they grew up, *then* old Jack might have become a respectable member of society. But nature kept squeaking at him out of the massive breasts of full-grown people!

A slow grin crept over his face and he restored his hat to the chair, and, a little shamefaced (for he had called her Mrs Phipps), he sat down again.

'That's right, Jack!' she said. 'Don't go off in a pet because we don't see eye to eye about it.'

'All right, Jill,' he said. 'I'm stopping.'

'That's right, Jack.'

Though he stayed, his initiative had been slowed down. Something had been deadened by her words and was unable to get going again. Try as he would, he could not shake off a feeling that, though this beautiful girl had It all right, it must be in some way *different* to anything he had met. *Jill was different*. Just as he was (as she had always told him). He feared her rational tongue – any move on his part to renew the assault would be the signal for a deadly argument, he knew, which would hold up his impulsive advance. Once having been beaten, he would be beaten again, or so he felt. He couldn't stand up against common sense. Thank God all girls didn't spout this way!

She had started him *looking at himself*. As yet in a dim way, old Jack had begun to look at 'Jack' from the outside as *an object* – just as Jill had said that *he* looked at *her*. There was a little crack, in short, in the impulsive make-up of the love-machine (an ill-bred British Casanova). From head to foot *one thing*, compact of pure desire – had disintegration set in? The pale cast of something abstract had fallen upon this pagan soul and no mistake. Though as yet it was just enough to keep him on his chair, and stop him from rushing like a setter upon the scent dilating his nostril.

'How did you get like this, Jack?' she asked him in a minute, with commiseration, having frowned and blowing cigarette smoke through her nose.

'Like what?' he asked.

'The way you are. Or have you always been like that?'

He shifted uneasily upon his egg-box.

'Do you mean I'm funny, Jill? Aren't all men like me, Jill – with you?'

She laughed, poking the fire, as if intending to keep her thoughts to herself.

'No, you're in a class apart, I'm glad to say. I should have to wear armour if that were not the case, shouldn't I? But go on – tell me when you started in as Don Juan. Have you ever been in love?'

'I am in love,' he retorted, with his crafty country grin, eyeing her as a sturdy English yeoman would eye a stranger, come to look over his live-stock with a view to purchase, and re-solved not to part with his best cow for anything under a tidy figure.

'Yes, I know. Tristy tells me that you have a sort of harem at your office. He says he's never seen so many pretty girls.'

'There are two or three who are not so bad. That's Manners. He thinks it's good for business.'

'Oh!' very doubtfully she said, smiling and shaking her head a little at Jack. 'How about Doris, Jack? Does she see eye to eye with you?'

'Doris? Oh, did Tristy tell you about Doris?'

Gillian nodded.

'Tristy tells me everything. And I tell him everything, as a good little wife should.'

'I never mess about in office hours. I have too much sense.'

'That I don't believe, I'm afraid. I think Doris would tell me another story.'

'Do you think so?'

'You should set up shop as a Mohammedan – it would be great fun visiting your harem, and sipping Turkish coffee with your favourite, or smoking a chilbouk.'

'What's that?'

'A water-pipe. My father was at the embassy at the Sublime Porte – I was born in Turkey. So I'm not talking through my hat – you have a *Turkish* eye!'

'Have I? What's it like?'

'Rather like a rooster's.'

Jack thrust out his neck and suddenly gave forth a tremendous and deafening crow.

'The escaped cock!' Gillian laughed pointing at him. 'The escaped cock – well, I'm damned! Have you read Lawrence? What a good sound that is! Do it again!'

Seeing that this accomplishment was well received, Jack crowed again, two or three times.

Much refreshed by his performance, his eye bright again, he prepared to leave her. Later on he knew that, before leaving, he would have been well-advised to have forced his advances on her whatever the consequences, and not to have left her until he had had his way; and his empty crowing appeared symbolic. As it was, all that passed between them was a perfunctory caress, and he kissed her at the door. She kissed him back.

Chapter 2

PERCY was perspiring. He lay back on the rotten couch in the Phipps's flat and mopped his massive pink forehead. He had been kissing Gillian and was hot and short of breath.

'What is the time?' he asked in matter-of-fact manner. He had implanted the tissue of his lips upon a real lady's drawling mouth for a quarter of an hour without stopping, and his desire to sip the nectar of social success, without being satiated, was in a mood to take some heed of time, especially in view of his overtaxed bodily condition: the sense of time being in the blood of the workman. But Gillian put this unlovely clocking-in and clocking-out obsession in its place at once.

'Half past kissing time – time to kiss again!' she remarked tartly and firmly.

'Well, what about it?' exclaimed the gallant Percy, scrambling to his feet, compelled to play up to such an invitation to the waltz as *that*, on the part of his aristocratic conquest.

But feeling rather weak and dizzy, Percy sat down again, shaking his head, ostensibly at himself, as if there were a Percy who was a reckless amorist, inclined to ignore the elementary distastes of health.

'I ought to be in bed,' he said, in the tone of an embittered invalid.

'In bed?' Gillian opened her eyes – she had got so used to talking to Jack that she was apt mechanically to drop into the responses proper to a Jackish dialogue. And the word bed was decidedly a cue that could not be ignored. It was up to her to parody the part of the sporting girl.

Percy had a feeling that something was wrong, not for the first time, and looked up quickly. But he could not guess that he was taking part (at times) in a Jackish dialogue! And so he remained with his sensation that all was not quite as he would have expected it to be, as between himself and this Communist girl born in the ambassadorial purple.

'Yes, in bed,' he said however, but not smiling. Then he

added, in a flat voice of no conviction, as though he had
turned it over dubiously in his mind, and now released the
remark for what it was worth: 'But not with you, I'm afraid,
Gillian!'

It had a 'fresh' sound he did not like – he had been drawn
into the Jack-business in spite of himself. And, with an awkward flush, he shook his head once more, very mawkishly, over
his lonely occupancy of a celibate fourposter.

'Not with me?' she said, still herself beneath the spell of
Jack, and his irrepressible *joie de vivre.*

Percy shook his head.

'Not with you, Jill. All on my lonely-oh.'

'On your whaty-oh!' she involuntarily persisted, Jacking
away without restraint.

'He-manning it, Jill!' he exclaimed. 'I left hospital too soon,
that's the fact of the matter.'

'I don't think you *did.* Not a day too soon, I should have
said.'

'A month too soon,' he retorted gloomily, with another
mournful elephantine head-waggle.

'You'd have passed out if you'd stopped there. It makes my
blood boil when I think of those nuns!'

Percy mopped his brow.

'How do you mean?' he asked in a surprised voice.

'Why, those monstrous nuns. They'd have been the death
of you.'

'They might have killed me with kindness, that's a fact.' And
Percy laughed – the laugh of a popular man, overwhelmed a
little with spoilings and marked feminine favours.

'Killed with *kindness.* I like that! If rubbing salt into a man's
wounds is *kindness*!'

Percy hesitated a moment. Then he said, with a contemptuous shortness almost, as if to brush something quickly out of
the way:

'Yes, but that was only propaganda.'

'What! What was propaganda?'

'They didn't do that, of course.'

'They didn't refuse to give you a bed-pan?' Her voice had
a stern note.

204

Percy looked puzzled and astonished, and also a little annoyed.

'You didn't believe that bed-pan stuff, did you, Jill?' he asked, a little severely, in his turn.

'Of course. Why, wasn't it true?'

Percy scratched his head violently, throwing into disarray the pale cornland of his scalp.

'Of course not,' he said. 'That's a stock story. We always tell that story – on the Spanish Front! I thought you understood.'

'I'm afraid I didn't.'

Gillian looked crestfallen and even a little indignant, rather like a much-petted star-pupil who has been caught out by some quite simple problem of grammar – even of A B C.

'That's atrocity propaganda – a most important branch of our work,' he said, swelling very slightly with importance.

'I see.'

'I thought you understood. We have to get the last drop of emotional appeal out of any situation that arises – that stands to reason. It's just the same as in war. Propaganda plays a big part.'

'Oh.'

'No. There were no inhuman fiends of nursing sisters – such things only exist in the imagination of the public. It was worse than that, if anything! They wait on you hand and foot.'

'They don't torture you?'

'Why should they? Everyone is a potential convert of course, as they see it. It's far worse sometimes, believe me, than if they did the opposite. They hover round you like a pack of sanctimonious moths until you could scream the place down. But that wouldn't make a good story. *Percy Hardcaster killed by kindness*. That wouldn't go down at all well!'

'I'm afraid it wouldn't.'

'I'm afraid not. People are such crazy fools – they want something to make their flesh creep. They like feeling good and indignant. It's our business, as revolutionaries, to supply that want.'

'Do you suppose the other people you were talking to at the party understood all that?'

'I suppose so.'

'Then I must have been the only person –!'

'Some didn't, perhaps. As far as I can remember them, they were a bunch of sentimental intellectuals. I didn't pay much attention. Yes, they *might* have taken all that as gospel. It never occurred to me.'

Gillian was attempting swiftly to adjust her feelings to these new revolutionary truths. Here was the *ultra-professional* point of view, in all its unattractive starkness. She saw that at once. She was unquestionably in the presence of the real thing – which was of course thrilling. Or it should be so. She saw before her a communist, and (in the words of the poet) *she felt small*. It was perfectly clear that she should glory in this misanthropic cynicism. But, very ashamed of herself indeed for having been such an amateur fool, she could not help experiencing the prickings of mortified vanity, to the detriment of the cause of it, Percy Hardcaster – it was no use.

'If that was all bluff from start to finish –' she began.

'Not *bluff*,' he interrupted her. 'Not bluff. There is no chivalry in the class-war. There's only one way of fighting a lie, and that's with a lie.'

'I see that, of course. Everyone knows that.'

'It's like, well, call it Machiavelli – if you have read his *Prince*! Have you ever read it? One of the most truthful books ever written.'

'I have.'

'Well. You understand then. *There* is the principle. It's not *bluff*, that's not the word. There's no room for George Washington in this sinful world.'

'Who "never told a lie," do you mean?'

'Who never told a lie! If you don't use *the lie* it is as if you made war upon a nation armed with bombs and gas with flintlocks or just with fists.'

'But how far can you take that principle?'

'As far as it will go! To any length you think necessary.'

'But communism *itself*. The theory of Communism is founded on what you label "atrocities." I mean you must be sincere about what you start from!'

Percy laughed good-temperedly.

'You mean is Communism itself just a fairy story too? Is that what you mean?'

'I mean if you are such a diplomat – with façade behind façade, of deliberate bluff.'

'If you'll allow me to say so, Jill, you shy at a verbal "falsehood" like a thoroughbred – as you are.' He swelled and flushed at the idea of his proximity to a 'thoroughbred.' 'It does not say that because a man invents something that he is incapable of truthfulness. Look at it this way. Lies are the manure in which truth grows.'

'Still, even in the matter of *evidence*. Wasn't it the warder you spoke about who shot you, for instance?'

Percy laughed with condescending indulgence. 'Yes, he did that,' he said. 'I *have* lost my leg all right!'

'I thought you must have done!'

(Leg was her cue upon the Jackish plane – she responded to it without knowing that she had done so.)

'But I made all that up,' he said, 'about his asking for a bribe. That was expected of me. As a matter of fact, I don't believe old Morato would have taken a bribe, no matter how big. There are such people. He was an ex-Civil Guard. The fellow just plugged me because he found out I was going to make a get-away and he probably fancied it was his duty to stop it. The honour of the service demanded it.'

'The stupid brute!'

'Morato was rather a fine man in his way,' Percy said, fixing her with a reflective eye.

Gillian frowned at him heavily upon this. She could not follow him in *that* sort of attitude. This was too much of a good thing! She went on frowning. A civil Guard – *a fine man in his way*! No! There was something wrong here – amateur or no amateur she knew better than that!

Was she not perhaps right after all? For what manner of man was this, who spoke about a Civil Guard after that highly unorthodox, that unconventional fashion. He was taking too much on himself, on the strength of his wound. There were limits even to *professional* paradoxicality. And this was taking professionalism too far. Even if it had been said to *épater* the amateur. A Civil Guard! No. That was the last straw. She would not stand for that.

She looked narrowly at Percy. Was this hero of the barricades after all a heretic? Was there a streak of treachery in this moon-faced child of the people? The proletariat were the weak-spot in the communist scheme of things, ultimately. Like all his class, had he a *bourgeois* streak? A workman, after all, must always be suspect to the revolutionary. This fellow had suffered in the cause, certainly. One must allow him that. But that after all might have been an accident. Filled with new and peculiar suspicions, she addressed herself to a fresh cross-examination.

'Did you expect to be shot, Percy? I mean did you know the risk you were running?'

'Expect to *be shot*! Good God, no!'

'You didn't!'

'It was the last thing I expected to happen to me. I was never so surprised in my life as when I found myself on the ground with a bullet in my leg!'

'Oh!' She no longer cared to disguise the fact that he was lowering himself in her estimation.

'It was a damned silly thing to let myself in for, that was obvious, I should have thought!' he exclaimed, with a touch of asperity.

'Such things do happen – when one is at war,' she remarked with coldness and a glitter of the female eye of the *We don't want to lose you* order.

He laughed, with undisguised impatience.

'Do they?' he sneered. 'No, it was inexcusably foolish! I was turning myself into a first-class propaganda-piece, I grant you. But at what cost to myself! It was the silliest thing I've ever done in my life. I'm under no illusions about that, Jill! Here I am a cripple for the rest of my days. Isn't that so? Very nice! What use am I as a cripple? I'm a show-piece. And that is all! I'm only fit for a museum now. *A museum of class-war atrocities.* I have no excuses to make. I've just been a fool.'

She gazed at him in amazement. He was turning into something else definitely – beneath her eyes. Into a stupid fat little man, of the working-class (treacherous and full of self-pity, as

208

the working-class always were – ready to turn round and bite the hand that feeds them!), who had not had the intelligence to keep out of the way of a bullet: and now he'd not the good taste to accept it, but must snarl and complain about it (in true working-class fashion): and probably blamed Communism for his misfortune! Percy Hardcaster was a *show-piece* all right – by which *she*, Gillian Communist, had been taken in! Well!

She laughed. Her laugh was distinctly unmusical, and weighted (in its snort at the end) with animal insult.

'Yes,' she said; 'I suppose you have got yourself into a pretty mess. You should have known better, at your time of life. But I should make the best of it, if I were you. Why not accept it with a good grace?'

'I think I do. I was talking to you privately. To a friend!' said Percy, gazing back at her steadily: for *she* was changing a bit, too, beneath his eyes, though he took it in more slowly.

'I took you for a hero!' she said, with a laugh.

'A hero? A *hero*!'

'Yes; a notion I had. I see I was mistaken. You have explained the true position with commendable clearness, I'll say that for you. I didn't know you were an intellectual!'

'But do you get worked up about heroes!' he protested, in a tone of heavy mock-astonishment. 'I thought you were a Communist.'

'In your sense I must be a bad Communist. A street accident is after all rather dull, isn't it?'

'It certainly is. Dull is just the word. Damn dull.'

'You make Communism seem very dull.' Gillian yawned. 'Perhaps you do so on purpose.'

Shortly and loftily Percy laughed, with the pride of the man of common sense at bay. For he now saw that he was in fact at bay.

'We don't want frills on things. We Communists prefer to see things *as they are*, Jill. If you don't mind my saying so, there are still some bourgeois prejudices you have to get rid of. *Heroes* is one. We of the working-class, who've always been up against it, have the advantage over you there. What's showy and cheap we've always *had* to despise because all that's been denied us. We are given a raw deal and a *plain* deal. You still feel lost without your little bit of sentiment.'

Gillian's face registered anger so unmistakably that Percy halted a little abruptly in his class-harangue, for he was not prepared to encounter anger.

'P'raps I do,' she answered. 'I can't be cold-blooded about some things. As to that being *cheap*, isn't it cheap to be cynical?'

Percy permitted himself an impatient gesture. 'Those of us who have to *do* the job —'

'Yes – you *men-of-action*!'

'Exactly! We have to be workmanlike and do our stuff in a workmanlike way. There is a *technique* of the general strike, of agitation, of the *coup d'état*. Those are technical problems. Once you begin *acting*, instead of merely talking, you become a technician. I was speaking to you as a technician speaks. That's what I *am*. I am an agitator. Remember, I am the man who pulls the trigger!'

Gillian laughed suddenly, and so offensively that Percy flushed a mantling pink, frowning sternly to counteract the tell-tale coloration.

'A trigger-man! A hero after all!' she sneered at him almost with a maenad fierceness.

'No, not a hero,' he retorted, with some energy. 'You'll have to overhaul your vocabulary, madam! What I took for granted you understood, was that the last thing I wanted to be was a *hero*. That is capitalist dope. It is a war-word. It means nothing to us.'

'But who are *you*? You say *us*. To what do you belong?'

'To the working-class, to start with.'

'Excuse me for telling you so, but you no longer belong to the working-class – since you no longer do any *work*. You are, as you say, a paid agitator.'

Percy looked at her fixedly, through a long, constipated and angry silence. Always collected and cool, however flushed his volatile cuticle, this shell of the rational man had a considerable strain put upon it, as Percy gazed as if interrogating a well-connected sphinx – the rough side of whose tongue it had been his lot to attract to himself.

210

'Yes, I am, as I said, an agitator,' he answered at last, very evenly and with irresistible deliberation. 'You prefer to say a *paid* agitator, don't you? That is quite correct. I *am* paid. I am a workman who is paid to stir up other workmen. But I am not paid by the working-class.'

'Who *are* you paid by?'

'We won't go into that. But I don't just float round on air.'

'Obviously not. That is why I said *paid* agitator.'

'I am not paid *much*. Our work is not overpaid.'

'I am very sorry to hear that. You should ask for a rise. I should.'

'Yes, and you might get it. But I shouldn't. I'm only a workman.'

Gillian sprang up impatiently.

'Oh shucks! – do stop whining about only being a workman, for God's sake. I'm sick of this! You thought your skin was as safe as houses, it seems, and it *wasn't* – because you made a stupid miscalculation, and your dear friend the ex-Civil Guard wasn't so civil as you'd naïvely supposed and shot you down when you least expected it – as *naturally* a Civil Guard *would*: that was too bad! *Et tu, Brute* – what? It was too bad of the treacherous Civil Guard to shoot down the confiding Percy Hardcaster, it was and all! But you're so *damned* sorry for yourself that really I don't see why anyone else should be sorry for you! I'm not, anyway! Sympathy is *cheap* – it doesn't cost anything. So I won't indulge in it. Now that you have explained your sad case to me, you must find some other woman to make a political pet of you, for I've had enough.'

'Very well. I will advertise *a political pet* to be disposed of!'

'Do. I think I've *done my bit* – to employ my capitalist vocabulary, invented for nationalist war!'

'I see that rankles! I'm sorry, Gillian.'

'Not at all, Percy! And now I know more about them, I don't like your politics either. I think you'd be more at home in a fascist organization than in ours.'

'*Ours!*'

'Yes. I don't believe you are a true Communist at all. Like all your class, you expect to be paid through the nose for everything you do, and then you grumble all the time because you aren't paid enough.'

Percy rose to his feet, or rather rose on to his stump, with a maladroit scuffle. For the first time in his life, he was really pale. In his placidly frowning, fleshy earnestness there was a nervous tightening that sharpened his expression, almost refined it.

'Thank you – thank you, milady, for those kind words!' he exclaimed, with a slight tremble in his voice. 'You have just demonstrated how important it is never to tell the truth – except to a very few people. Very few! Also you should now be able to see for yourself why I am very vexed at losing my leg. You must see why I feel it was such a silly thing to do.'

'It's no use, I'm afraid. You'll get no more pity out of *me*.'

'I wasn't asking you for a kiss, if that's what you mean – I've had as many of them as I want.'

'I was kissing an idea. Not a fat little bricklayer fellow.'

'Well, take my advice and stop kissing *ideas*,' he said with detachment, an expression of carefully controlled distaste on his face. 'That's not the way to treat an idea. Keep your kisses for your boy-friends, like Mr Cruze.'

'Jack Cruze is a better man than you are!'

Percy tossed up a thick laugh over his head with masculine superiority, and moved towards his hat and stick. Then he turned back towards her and spoke as follows, with an almost pedantic composure:

'I'm sorry, Gillian, I haven't been able to live up to your pretty picture of a Communist. I did my best. But I miscalculated in the matter of my audience. Again, I was not quite clever enough. I supposed you were, well, more *intelligent* than you are.'

'No. I'm stupid enough to rather dislike people who get embittered when they have to *pay for* their principles, instead of being *paid for* them.'

'All right,' he said, with a maddening airiness, looking over her head: 'all right. You didn't understand what I was saying, but you couldn't have, of course. You're in this game for the fun of it, like most people of the moneyed classes, and you want it to be *all* fun and excitement. The little peep behind the scenes you got from me debunked your little romance of revolution. An error of judgment on my part.' And he wagged his head gravely at himself. 'No. Let me finish what I have to say, please. For us of the working-classes this is an ugly and hazardous business – we know if we go in with you that it's not *our* revolution but *yours* that we're working for. That is self-evident. We have no illusions about that. We know that it is not for our beautiful eyes that you run about with little red flags and play at Bastilles and Jacobin Clubs, or put your hands in your pockets to finance strikes and insurrections. We know all that only too well. We know that as much money is being spent in fomenting revolution as is being spent in resisting it, and we know that those fabulous sums of money do not come from the working-class – on whose behalf *all* revolution is *supposed* to be set in motion. For it is *me*, as a member of the working-class, that *you*, as an enlightened member of the owning-class (you have no money yourself, you say, that's neither here nor there) are *supposed* to be getting so excited about – though, as I am not entirely incapable of putting two and two together, I see quite well that is what you would call *bluff*. Why then – you are about to ask me – do I throw in my lot with proletarian revolution; or continue in it, once my eyes are opened to the true meaning of all this disturbance – this *class-war* as the greatest middle-class theorist called it? Because, *in spite of yourself*, you cannot help benefiting us. You are tearing each other to pieces in any case. That is all to the good. When thieves fall out, they say, the honest man always stands to gain. But – I am going to be very indiscreet now, Mrs Phipps, and I hope you will be lady enough to let this go no farther and respect my confidence. *But*, if it ever comes to a showdown and if there's a bit of a shoot-up, it will be a matter of complete indifference to me *which* of you – whether you "Communist" intellectuals, you fancy *salon*-revolutionaries, you old-school-tie pinks, or on the other hand your fascist first-cousins – are wiped out.' He raised his hand and almost lazily directed his forefinger at her, perspiration, however, bathing his forehead and neck. 'I'd as soon see *your* sort hanging from the nearest lamp-post – to put this matter plainly to you, since you asked for it, and we are telling each other

213

home truths – as I would see your uncle on the gibbet, if you've got one, who is, I expect, some purse-proud old boss! It's all one to *me*. I'll leave you to think this all over now at your leisure and form your own conclusions. There are the facts. Regard this speech of mine as part of your Communist education! All my working-class friends think the same about your lot as I do. Remember that. Forget that it's *me* that gave you the lesson. You might have gone through life without ever guessing what I've just told you. You'll be a sounder Communist by far, believe me, if you take this to heart. If you hadn't slobbered over this wounded *hero* of a little bricklayer-fellow, you'd have been living in a fool's paradise, wouldn't you? So your kisses have come home to roost, but they have not been in vain. You've learnt something through kissing the workman that could be learnt in no other way!'

With arms coiled horizontally under her breast, Gillian, her eyes fastened upon the face of her schoolmaster, had listened. Words seethed behind her compressed lips but none burst their way out, because none recommended themselves to her as sufficiently barbed and fanged to meet the situation. She preferred to brood darkly *en marge* of this bitter and heavy-footed exordium. But indeed she was no proof entirely against the hypnotic quality of this ponderous apotheosis of the matter-of-fact, delivered in the insidious singsong of something laboriously pondered, and rolled out slowly from the dark places where it had been piled up for possible future use. She was impressed, even, in spite of herself. For here certainly *was* a Communist, such as she had not encountered before, and (to employ the striking phrase of the poet – not for the first time) Gillian *felt small*. For when the sham Communist beholds the real Communist, in all his authentic reality, the former must of necessity feel small – as all other counterfeits must feel diminished under similar circumstances. Even without the poet we could imagine *that*. She shrank. But her irritability, too, was stimulated almost beyond endurance, and the sensation of *smallness* superadded did not help matters.

As he bent down from the waist, perched upon his artificial limb, to pick up his hat, she sprang to her feet, shouting:

'I suppose you think to insult a woman is excellent Communism, do you? You've been enjoying yourself hugely, haven't you? It seems pretty *cheap* to me to insult a woman!'

'I have not insulted you.'

'Oh, you *haven't* been insulting me?'

'You have *tried* to insult me – and to fling my class in my face. Which is a cheap thing to do, isn't it?'

'*After* you had flung my sex in mine!'

'No. *Before* there had been any question of your sex. You have forgotten the order of this slanging-match – which *you* started, didn't you? I didn't ask for it.'

They both started slightly – a repeated rat-tat upon the basement door broke like a rain of bombs in the tense atmosphere of this tête-à-tête. From where she stood, Gillian could see into the area. Her eyes flashing with destructive purpose she passed with the crispness of an electrical discharge into the scullery and flung open the flat door, to admit the person who was waiting there. Re-entering the room at once, she exclaimed in loud, hard tones of high excitement:

'I'm glad you've come, Jack! You're just the man I want. There's a fellow here who has taken advantage of the fact that I am a woman to abuse me like a pickpocket. I wish you'd throw him out for me. I'd have done it long ago if I could.'

Old Jack came quickly in, his springing, faunlike woodland gait changing into a quick march-step – his froggy-would-awooing-go smile altering to a stern zero-hour alertness, wound-up to go over-the-top. But as he caught sight of Percy, Jack halted, in disgusted astonishment. An expression of the crudest displeasure made itself seen: for at first he firmly believed that Percy had, characteristically, forestalled him as chucker-out. But Percy stood still, looking at him in so odd a fashion, as if to say *No – it's me*: and he saw at last that Percy it *was*. That *he* was the man. And he noted that but for Percy there was nobody else in the room. As he realized this, a slight smile tipped his lips, it made his nostrils bulge, and put a stormy fleck in his wide-open eye.

'Ho ho!' said Jack. 'It's him, is it? What's this bird been up to, Jill?'

'Oh, only calling me *cheap* – informing me that I vamp the working-classes because men of my own class won't have me, I suppose, and such-like. Because I didn't make fuss enough of him as a wounded frontfighter!'

'Oh, he did, did he?'

And Jack looked Percy up and down, as if measuring him roughly for a suit.

'That's what he said, was it?'

Taking up his two sticks, Percty started to walk towards the door. His way was barred by Jack, however, head high and legs a little straddled.

'Let me pass, please!' said Percy politely.

But with the flat of his hand used as a tampon, Jack pushed him roughly back. Percy reeled, a little theatrically, propping himself on his sticks.

'Not so fast, Mr Percy!' Jack cried. 'Not so fast! Before you go, my fine fellow, you're going to apologize to this lady here!'

'Don't talk nonsense!' Percy said. 'I have done nothing for which to apologize. Get out of my way and don't make a fool of yourself.'

The two stock figures, of such a Saxon sameness, of breadth and of pigment, Old Percy and Old Jack, confronted one another, pausing to measure the five foot eight of proletarian massiveness opposite each, a dull thick match, tissue for tissue, in a sort of Box and Cox melodrama. Both had their hats on, Jack's a high-crowned black bowler, Percy's a fawn trilby. The big lymphatic eye of the intellect, and brilliant glassy one of the five senses, signalled defiance across the few feet that separated them.

Turning to Gillian, Percy said, with a breathless and perspiring stateliness:

'Will you please ask this gentleman to allow me to leave your flat? I have nothing more to stay here for.'

'Oh, yes you have – quite a lot!' snapped out Jack. 'You won't get off so easy as you think! First apologize to this lady here as I told you – and pretty quick too! When I say a thing I mean it! So look sharp!'

Old Jack's fighting glands were all in good order, thank you, there was never any question about that. What that had to do with Jack's *other* glands, it's difficult to say. But they matched each other in a remarkable fashion. Gland for gland he was more irritable than most men, and he was in no mood now to miss an opportunity. Chance had delivered his worst sex-foe into his clutches. The interest of *all* his glands was engaged in this transaction. Here was the bearer of offensively large bouquets to ladies. Here was the celebrated Red beau, back from the battle, who had scored off him in the skirt-hunt. Jack was a-tingle with what he felt had dropped into his mouth, in the way of revenge that would be sweet. Very sweet indeed.

Grasping his crutch-sticks firmly at his sides, Percy again advanced. When he reached Jack, he attempted to force his way past him. Old Jack was as handy a man with his fist for his size as it would be possible to find, as natural a boxer as a flea is a jumper; and before Gillian could see what had come to pass between them there had been a sickening smack that walloped the damp air, in the dimness of the flat-room, and as if struck by a hammer, the body of Percy crashed at full length on the floor.

'Well done!' called out Gillian, clapping her hands, in imitation, it seemed, of the pugilistic report of flesh upon flesh. 'It serves him jolly well right! He's got what was coming to him!'

Jack was jumping about like a Jack-in-the-box, unable to keep still.

'*Now* apologize to this lady here, you ugly swine, before I throw you out on your head!' he shrieked.

Percy sat up, wiping blood from his nose. His weakness caused him to perspire excessively, and his eyes were watering from the effect of the blow. He made no reply as he scrambled to his feet, holding on to the table and wrenching himself up upon his rigid leg. The other two watched him do so in silence.

Percy turned his head this way and that as if dazed. Then with extreme suddenness he whirled one of his walking-sticks in the air and brought it down upon Jack's head, at the same time flinging himself at the door. Before he could open it, Jack was upon him, his fists springing out from his sides, returning, and darting forward again, like deadly hammers of gum-elastic. And each time they tapped their target, with a wet smack, Percy's head crashed against the door; there were half a dozen crashes in quick succession in the time it would take a church clock to strike three. As Percy sank to the floor he clutched at Jack's leg.

'Let go of that!' shouted Jack, as he shook his leg free. 'Let go of my leg!'

He sprang back as Percy rolled on the floor, and delivered a pile-driving kick at his fallen rival's weak spot, the mutilated stump. As the boot struck him, where the Spanish surgeon's knife had cut in, Percy Hardcaster turned over, with a bellowing groan, against the wall, and Jack sent in another one, after the first, to the same spot, with a surgical precision in the violent application of his shoe leather. And then he followed it with a third, for luck.

Then Jack stepped back. He surveyed his handiwork with gleaming eyes, which feasted upon the writhing human body beneath him.

'Don't!' bawled out the dumbfounded Jill, whose eyes were now starting out of her head. 'Come away! Don't do that again! Jack! Come here at once!'

She was just in time, for Jack was gathering himself together for a knock-out kidney-kick. But the spell had been broken, and his rage began to leave him. He passed his hand over his face, massaging it from left to right. His bowler hat had been on all the while, bobbing about, and giving him the air of a puppet as he struck out and leapt back, and now he removed it, placing it on the table. He did not look at Jill.

The room was filled with Percy's groans. They were hollow, bovine, deep-fetched expressions of pain. Stepping over his legs, Gillian went into the scullery, and fetched a glass of water.

'It looks as if you'd injured him. Here, take this!' she said to Jack, her face gone sallow, and her eyes almost as much scared as angry, for she saw only too plainly the possibilities of this situation. 'Give him this. Don't stand there goggling at the floor!'

'He'll be all right in a minute,' said Jack in a sulk.

'No, he won't. What did you want to kick the man for? You knew he'd just had his leg amputated.'

'No, had he?'

'You knew quite well he had, you stupid brute. Do you

218

usually kick people when they're down? Give him that water.'

'He doesn't want any water, he's all right. The devil's only shamming.'

Gillian took the glass roughly from his hand, and bent down beside the martyred pedagogue, who was quite unconscious of their presence, his eyes closing in tumefied lumps, his mouth fixed open, as if he were singing some fruity patriotic song, which required the fetching up of deep notes from the pit of his abdomen.

'Here, take this,' she said unpleasantly, offering him the tumbler. Percy's head rolled back slackly. He had fainted. She frowned. He had fainted on her, the old devil! She dashed water from the tumbler savagely into his face, and sprang up, watching the effect with a brooding concentration – spell-bound, as it seemed, by the compulsions of this distasteful task, suddenly imposed on her by the irresponsible fury of this mad Jack-in-the-box. She had had thrust on her, somewhat sardonically, from one moment to the next, the rôle of those beastly Madonnas of the Bed-pan, blackened by propaganda, for the salvation of the working-class. How would she fare, according to the machiavellian rules of Communist policy, it flashed through her mind? Would she subsequently be described as splitting her sides with laughter, in the company of Jack – after rubbing vinegar in the wounds inflicted upon a defenceless man?

But the groaning started again, a strident booming of immense self-pity – the dark oxlike bellowing, beneath the shadow of the slaughterhouse, of the eternal working-class – *her* doing! She gave a gesture of vindictive impatience, and went into the scullery again, from which she fetched a towel wetted under the tap, and wiped the blood off the swollen face of this hateful casualty. More blood took its place. He was determined to bleed like a pig. This great fat pig was just going to bleed, and bleed, and bleed! This sickening full-blooded man-of-the-people, as he called himself, was going to bleed her flat full of proletarian blood, which he was going then to lay at her door! She could see that well enough.

'Here, fetch a taxi – don't stand there picking your teeth!' she shouted violently at Jack. 'Quick! Can't you do *anything*? We can't go on like this. We must get him home, or to a hospital.'

'A hospital?' said Jack quickly, looking at her sideways.

'Yes! A hospital. If you will *kick* people when they're on the floor like some demented jackass you must take them to a hospital, unless you want to find yourself in the dock for homicide, you half-witted yokel! Do as I tell you! Go and fetch a taxi at once!'

Jack put on his bowler hat and went out of the door without making any remark. He was followed by Gillian, who stood at the top of the area steps. Jack, swinging his arms, went off down the street. At the corner he disappeared, and Gillian leant against the railings, with folded arms.

She was only half aware of where she was and why she was there. It was raining steadily; her hair was soon dripping and the skin of her shoulders and arms wet. It was a hot rain. She took no notice, except for a shake of the head, as the water guttered down between her bobbed locks. The deep organ-notes of Percy Hardcaster, baritone, reached her, through the open door beneath, like the voice of a person coming out of an anaesthetic. It was the sorrowful bellows of the pneumatic house of clay, deserted by the mind, pumping its wind in and out in burdensome fashion, in the absence of its rational house-holder – just fetching sigh after sigh out of its resonant basement, at the thought of all the tribulations of this unhappy contraption. She loathed this automatic voice out of the deeps, even more than the offensive discourses that had so recently issued from the same lips, that were now only a mechanical mouthpiece. It never occurred to her to doubt its bona fides.

Meanwhile images of every variety of unpleasantness stalked through her mind. This sick man, just come out of one hospital and just about to go into another, who had been brutalized on her orders, upon her premises (and Tristy's), might quite well have received some serious internal injury, who was to say? He might even die in her flat. Or he might be taken home and die there. Of course he might die on the way. There might quite well be a charge of manslaughter standing against her and against Jack, as she had said. They might even say that she and her 'lover' – the lovely Jack – had done him in. She might be in Madame Tussaud's yet, in the company of Charlie Peace.

She was probably disgraced, at the least. She wished Tristy had not been away. He would not be back till midnight. And what was she to say to him after all?

The taxi arrived, and at the window was the face of Jack, beneath the bowler hat, looking out at her – a framed picture for you if you wanted it! – looking in a way that she had come to know only too well. For his eyes, from the moving vehicle, were directed at her breasts. He was back once more in the fields of asphodel, and had forgotten already that he had made a charnel-house of her flat.

Gillian helped Jack carry the body of the still groaning Percy up the steps. At the sight of this dishevelled, heavy man, covered with blood, the driver of the taxi looked at them both a little oddly.

' 'E ain't 'arf in a pretty mess!' he said. 'That's a blighty one, I reckon.'

'You're right, mate!' said Jack. 'He pitched down these steps on his head.'

'Ah, he must 'ave done,' said the driver, squinting at the tumefied face, the swollen and blackened eyes and lips, of his third passenger.

'He doesn't want to go to hospital!' said Jack to her, as she turned away from the driver after directing him where to go.

'I'm not going to have anything happen!' she replied, getting into the cab. 'I shall have to pay for this if anything goes wrong. He'll probably have to have his other leg off now! I shall have to keep him for the rest of his life!'

'You're crazy, Jill. Half that's shamming!'

'I don't care. If he's shamming there's no harm done, anyway.'

'Why shouldn't we take him where he lives?'

'Because I say so. He's going to the hospital.'

Bickering, Jack and Jill crouched side by side upon the flap-seats of the taxicab. Percy, upon his back, occupied, in pasha-like abandon, the main accommodation in front of them, sprawled across the whole width of the vehicle. He had practically stopped groaning, revived by the air and rain and, instead, was breathing in a laboured way, coughing once or twice.

Suddenly he remarked, without opening his eyes – indeed he could not:

221

'Where are we going?'

'To the hospital, old man,' said Jack, in an ingratiating voice, of proletarian complicity.

There was a silence, during which Percy groaned a little, as he rolled about in the belly of the cab.

'Gillian!' he said thickly, moving his lips with difficulty.

'Yes.' She bent forward. 'Do you want to say something to me?'

'Tell them,' he said, 'that I fell down –'

'Yes, old man,' sang out the jolly voice of Jack.

'I fell down,' said Percy, 'into the basement.'

'We'll tell them that, old man,' said Jack. 'You leave it to us!'

'Very well,' said Gillian.

Percy lay unexpectedly still and limp.

'I hope we make it before he goes off again,' Jack muttered to her behind his hand. 'It'll look better coming from him.'

As Gillian gazed at the battered body – refused a bed-pan by the nuns (she had believed only an hour since by the clock), into whose wounds salt had been supposed to have been rubbed, and as she heard the hoarse, conspiratorial whisper at her ears, still with a trace of dialect in its chastened but excited rattle – she said to herself with dramatic irony: 'This is your first lesson in Communism, my girl! See that you make it your last!'

Percy was carried into the hall, from the casualty entrance; and, propelled by a male attendant and a couple of sisters, passed in to the operating theatre almost at once upon a rubber-wheeled trolley.

'We don't want to stop here. Let's beat it,' said Jack all of a sudden, as they sat side by side, upon a bench for visitors.

'I shall wait to hear the result,' Gillian said.

'I don't see why you want to do that, Jill. What can we do? We can come back later on, can't we?'

'You go if you want to,' she said to him with a look he did not like.

'Why don't you come?' Jack asked, getting up.

'I will wait. But you can go. In fact I wish you would.'

'Well, I think I'll go and have a brush-up,' Jack said, tossing

222

some money about in his trouser-pocket, and following a passing nurse with his automatic eye. 'When will Tristy be back?'

'Not till late, unfortunately,' she said, with considerable coldness.

'Well, I'll come round an hour from now and we can go and have a bite.' He turned back as he was going, and said to her behind his hand, with a wink; 'Stick to that dope about his falling down the steps. Never mind what *he* says!'

She watched Jack's jaunty back as he breasted the swing door, nodding a cheery good night to the porter. The working-class man again! The dregs – the majority! The backboneless, mindless mob. Well!

Back in the flat, Gillian flung herself down and, with the deliberation of a person turning on a bathroom tap, wept into her hands. A couple of ounces of water, perhaps, were discharged by her tear-ducts, and flowed down between her fingers. She felt better.

'A great idea, this water-business!' she reflected. 'Poor dry-eyed he-men, they must be lost without that gadget.'

She remained in the flat for half an hour after that. Jack had not put in an appearance by seven. He will keep out of the way! she commented to herself upon this typical absenteeism with disgust – until the risk, as he supposes, has passed. A charming class! These sons of police constables, and working-class agitators, broken on the Lancashire looms and then in the class-war, they are six one and half a dozen the other! She did not know which she despised most. But, as that insolent old beast of a Percy had said, thumping himself on the chest, it was all for *their* sake that the Gillians and Tristrams of this world were going to make a revolution! And those who were *not* of the class for whom all this was being done had to be a sort of saint, as far as she could see, to stomach all that they had to stomach – in the way of ingratitude, recrimination, and general brutality. She left the flat on her way to go and seek consolation from a girl friend, also a Communist – feeling a very angry martyr, and seething with *noblesse oblige*. She was at the moment full of class-hatred of the class it was her hard lot to have to save.

223

Chapter 3

RETURNING about midnight, she was met at the door by Tristy, who evidently had heard her on the steps from the front room. His manner indicated an extreme anxiety on her behalf.

'You *are* all right, are you, Jill?' he exclaimed, as she came in at the door.

'Of course! Aren't you?'

'Whatever has been happening here?' he asked, as she followed him in.

The bloodstained towel with which she had attempted to tidy up her guest's battered face was hanging over the back of a chair. Tristy picked it up.

'This is the first thing I saw when I came in,' he explained. 'And then I caught sight of *those*.'

He pointed to the floor, where, near the door, large tell-tale bloodstains were still intact. Gillian had intended to eliminate these traces of what had occurred, but at the last moment it had escaped her memory.

She laughed, and putting her hand behind his shoulder, kissed him on the cheek.

'Did you think I'd been murdered?' she asked.

'I didn't know what to think.'

'Well, no one's been murdered. There was a sort of accident.'

'Oh. What are these?' he asked, picking up the two walking sticks belonging to Percy.

'What have you found now? Oh, those. They must be the sticks Percy Hardcaster uses.'

'Has he been here?'

'He certainly has! Has he not! He came in head first!'

'Head first!' Tristy looked at her in amazement, with a new type of concern supplanting the first.

'Yes. He fell down the area steps.'

'What! Did he hurt himself?'

'Quite a lot.'

224

'Where is he now?'

'In hospital.'

'In hospital? Is he badly hurt then?'

'He was naturally rather badly shaken up. He is not in danger, if that's what you mean.'

Tristy stood staring at her as if he had not quite understood what she had said. Announced by her in this way, it seemed like a joke in incredibly bad taste, not certainly *a fact*. He was twisting and weaving the lock of his hair to which he always resorted in moments of excitement or perplexity. As she looked at him, she thought how like a handsome young sheep he looked. And this profound concern, on his part, for Percy Hardcaster, filled her with resentment and at the same time with alarm.

'I must go to him at once!' he said, looking round for his hat.

'To whom?'

'To Percy Hardcaster, of course.'

And he uttered the name upon the same privileged tone of almost snobbish satisfaction which formerly she had been guilty of herself, she recognized – as she heard, after the slightest ceremonious pause, the pomp of those compelling words, *Percy Hardcaster*, issue from his lips.

'What, go and wake the hospital up and say "I want to see Percy Hardcaster?"' she exclaimed scornfully. 'Besides, they've probably given him a shot of morphia. He's in a blissful sleep, I expect – dreaming that he's escaping from prison in the company of a beautiful Spanish nun!'

Tristy was very much disturbed. He began to pace up and down the room, in a high state of nervous excitement.

'I think I ought to go, Gillian!' he said, stopping in front of her, still with that same look of overmastering astonishment in his eyes, as if it were quite inconceivable that Percy Hardcaster should fall down his area steps in his absence, or any area steps, for that matter.

Gillian had lighted a cigarette, and was inhaling it slowly and sombrely, watching the behaviour of her husband with a circumspect displeasure.

'Of course you can't go there now!' she said. 'Do sit down

and don't get so worked up about it because a fat little man has fallen down into your area.'

At this he looked up at her definitely shocked as well as startled. It was his turn now to wear a frown.

'I don't understand you, Gillian!' he said, almost angrily. 'It sounds a queer business. Why should he fall down? I don't understand.'

'Don't ask me! He's naturally not very steady on his pins, after his – after his accident.'

'His *accident*?' There was literal horror in his voice at this word *accident*.

'You know what I mean. After having his leg off. Nobody would be. He probably tripped.'

More mystified than ever, especially at something persistently odd in the manner of referring to Percy he could not help observing in his wife's replies – and indeed at two or three expressions that to him appeared quite unprecedentedly coarse and uncalled-for – and incredibly inappropriate, in speaking of such a man as Percy Hardcaster – he threw himself down violently upon their wrecked settee, and went on gazing at her in growing amazement.

'I just can't make head or tail of all this!' he said, hugging one hand with the other, a painful embarrassment settling down upon his face. 'He seems to have bled pretty badly. On the floor over there there's quite a lot. ... He must have been very badly hurt.'

Gillian impatiently flicked her cigarette with her little finger into the fireplace.

'My darling simpleton, if *you* had pitched head first into a person's area, wouldn't you be feeling a bit under the weather?'

'What did you do?'

'I naturally bathed the brow of the injured hero, as any woman would, put him in a passing taxi, and took him round to the hospital. That's all.'

There was now a longish silence. Gillian's exasperation with this Communist-worshipping mate of hers was so great that for two pins she would have told him that his little god – the great Percy Hardcaster – happened to have been *kicked*, as he thoroughly deserved, by that equally preposterous pet, Jack

226

Cruze; and so had been transported to the nearest hospital. But she mastered her desire to do this, and scowled at him instead.

On his side, Tristy sat in deep perplexity, plaiting and re-plaiting his much-fingered drooping silent lock. He could not disguise from himself that it was Gillian's attitude that was perhaps the most mysterious thing about the whole affair. Why should she adopt this attitude to an event of this order, where all her sympathy should have been enlisted, and where, if any-thing, he would have expected her to be more distressed even than he was – instead of just unconcerned? For the great man's flowery visits had not passed unnoticed by the deeply-apprecia-tive and highly-honoured Tristy. And Jill's attitude to this great Partyman had if anything been more marked by a de-monstrative respect than his own.

'You don't think I should go,' he said, at last, 'and at least inquire about him?'

'I have told you several times. Of course not. Go in the morning if you want to. We can go together.'

'When did you last see him?'

'Oh, I don't know. About six, I should think.'

'About six? And how was he then?'

'Really, darling! You are uncommonly stupid tonight! At six he was not feeling over well. He had just had a tumble down our *area*!'

'Was his head badly injured? You said he hit his head.'

'No, I don't think so. It was his leg he seemed to be suffering with most.'

Tristy looked relieved. He looked almost happy.

'I'll go there first thing,' he said.

Gillian bent over towards him, snorting two plumes of smoke at him out of her nostrils, and said:

'You are a good little Partyman, *aren't* you, darling? I feel we should both have good-conduct stripes, but you should have *two*.'

He stared at her.

'If Jill, your wife,' she said, 'if poor Gillian Communist had fallen downstairs, and broken her neck, you wouldn't have been half so upset, would you, as you are because you hear

227

that the great Mr Percy Hardcaster has had an accident? Anyone would think you were in love with him!'

'He is a man for whom I have great respect,' said Tristy,
formally, and coldly, throwing up his head, as if he were about
to snort, too, and looking away from her. 'And I was under
the impression that you had, too.'

'No, I haven't,' she exclaimed defiantly. 'I haven't at all. I
have come to disagree with you on the subject of that gentleman, I am afraid.'

'Indeed! Since when?'

Tristy was looking at her with quite new astonishment and
extraordinary displeasure.

'Oh, since today.'

'How is that?'

'Well, if you want to know, I had a conversation with him –
about a great many things. It shattered a few of my illusions.
And if you had been there I think even some of yours might
not have survived.'

Tristy raised his eyebrows in a supercilious arc, and Gillian
saw that she was now in the presence of a highly incensed
fanatic, not encountered before; with whom she would have to
watch her step, if she set store by the issue. He looked at her
as if he might have addressed her sternly as *Woman*! His party
badge gleamed upon the lapel of his jacket, or at all events it
forced itself upon her notice, like the star of the film-sheriff,
out to get the bad man dead or alive. And an angry smile
came and went upon her lips as she observed all this. She
leant over and took another cigarette from the box on the
table.

'I do not think that anything would change my opinion of
Percy Hardcaster,' he announced, after a truly painful and
disturbing pause, in a voice that left no room for doubt that
if you were going to weigh something in the scales against such
a one as Percy Hardcaster, it would have been something compared with which gold as to its specific gravity would be gos-
samer, and those personal and family ties which Saint Augus-
tine so fanatically belittled would be of utterly no effect.

'All I can say is that you should have been there,' she said,
'to judge for yourself.'

228

'But when did you have this illuminating conversation? After Percy Hardcaster had fallen down the area?' Tristy inquired.

Gillian flushed and replied impatiently:

'No. He came back – I suppose he had forgotten something. This was before.'

'Oh, I see,' Tristy said, doubtfully.

'To my mind we've all been taken in by Percy Hardcaster,' she said. 'He is not a true Communist at all.'

'No?'

'Don't say *No* like that! No, he isn't! He's nothing but a sort of unconscious fascist, like so many of the working-class.'

'Why are the working-classes unconscious fascists? If you had said unconscious Communists I should have understood you.'

'That's where you're so naïve, Tristy! You are much more truly a Communist than any working-man *could* be! It is we so called "intellectuals" of the upper-classes, who are the only real Communists. Don't you see? When a workman becomes a Communist he only does so for what he can *get*! He regards it just as another *job* – a jolly sight better paid than any he can get out of the bosses. And when he makes himself into a Communist he brings with him all his working-class cynicism, all his underdog cowardice and disbelief in everything and everybody. All his tinpot calculations regarding his precious *value*. That is why Marx insisted on the necessity of his *hatred* being exploited. It's the only pure passion he is capable of! As a Communist he has mixed with his Communism the animal characteristics of his class. All that cheap sentiment and moral squalor. At the best he is a mercenary. And a mercenary is always a potential traitor!'

Tristy listened to these unheard-of heresies proceeding from his wife's excited lips with stern stupefaction. He opened his mouth several times to interrupt her, but closed it firmly again, his eyes glowing with doctrinal fire. As she seemed to have ended, he made up his mind to speak, to take the floor: but in such a manner as to stamp out forever these poisonous growths that had lifted up their heads, as it were, overnight, in the mind of his wife. His voice was no longer his own, but resembled his father's as when that organ was employed in deafening his flock, from his pulpit in the Lincolnshire fens, after some particularly pernicious village scandal.

'Gillian,' said Tristram, but beginning quietly, with her name, 'it is to free the working-class that we have dedicated our lives. Without them we are *nothing*. They are our *raison d'être*. To speak as you have of the poor suffering masses is a crime! It is as if you yourself were trampling on the faces of the poor and rubbing salt into their wounds, out of sheer wantonness. It is as if you were siding with the enemies of civilized man, the kites and vultures of the underworlds of High Finance. It is *you* who are in danger of falling into fascism. I will go so far as to assert that what you have just said makes me wonder if you have ever been a Communist at heart at all!'

Gillian leapt to her feet, and the expression that she directed down upon Tristy was a good imitation of one of the looks she had levelled at Percy Hardcaster earlier in the day, when he had gone so far as to call her Communism in question.

'What sickening blah!' she screamed. 'Quasch! Nonsense! *Nonsense!* You are as simple as a sheep – anyone can fool you! Why don't you *think*, instead of just mooning around! Is my *raison d'être* some drunken stupid slum woman? Have you so poor an opinion of yourself that you believe you exist only by permission of some fat little impostor of an ex-boiler-maker, gone Red to feather his nest, who would sell you every time to anybody who bid a couple of tanners for you? Haven't you the rudiments of an eye in your head, to help you to see what the working-class really and truly *are*! Or don't you ever see anything – except *abstractions*? Like your pictures! It's all right as pictures. But you are dealing with men and women of flesh and blood. A mob of treacherous idiots! That's what you're doing! – who snigger up their sleeves at you for the sucker you are; yes, and would string you up to the nearest lamp-post as soon as look at you! It is with *that* that you have to make your Communism rhyme!'

Tristy rose, like one of the Zoo's most stately, gauche, and inhuman animals, a frosty smile culled among the chilliest fields of theoretic romance playing about his lips, which had been visibly paling as she proceeded.

'I'm afraid we disagree, Gillian,' he said, 'in a way I had not supposed it possible we should. It is you who show no sense of reality, however. If you felt like that about the general run of men, then Communism would be the most *unreal* thing it is possible to conceive. If you were so self-centred that you held it up against people that they were not perfectly rational and virtuous beings, then to be a Communist would be to class yourself as a lunatic sectarian, crying out for a strait-jacket. I don't know what Percy Hardcaster has been saying to you. But you have evidently misunderstood him, and allowed your personal feelings to run away with you.'

'Thank you! The words of wisdom of the infallible Percy Hardcaster have fallen upon barren soil! My intelligence has been insufficiently developed, and so I have been unable to understand what that sage meant. Thank you, Tristy! I am much obliged for your version of this *lesson*, as he called it, which I have received upside down, putting of course the cart before the horse. That is what comes of being a woman!'

'As you have not told me what he said –'

'I will tell you word for word, if I can remember it.'

'I would prefer not to hear. Let us drop the subject.'

'Yes, let us drop it. I shall lose all patience in a minute.'

Tristy put his hat on and went towards the door.

'I'm going out for a walk. I may not come back at once. Don't wait up for me.'

'I certainly shall not. I'm for bed, after such a day as I've had.'

PART VI

THE FAKERS

Chapter 1

WHAT colossal presence, these trees near whose summits she sat – to be shut up there like that, in a London garden-lagoon! Who would have supposed, on the pavements of the streets not fifty feet away, that these great bodies stood behind the house-fronts like giraffes at bay! Five-floored ramparts of blackened brick, the late Victorian terraces – irrelevantly vast, and of course sepulchrally-basemented, for staffs of vanished domestics – secured the secret of the continued existence of this fragment of park. The weakening rays of the sun of this particularly feeble autumn found their journey's-end upon the hecatombs of leaves – a shimmer of melancholy rust – of these towering creatures of the forest.

A well of beautiful loneliness – at the bottom of what the horrid Americans would call a 'block'! No one ever appeared to have time to stroll in it. To lie down under a tree would be considered, probably, unsuitable in a householder, and of the last tactlessness in a guest. Yet to lie down at the foot of an elm – these must be elms, with their great stature – as a sentimental guest of this estate – at the bottom of this sylvan well – with the steep plumes of verdure ascending into the sky above her, was what Margot desired to do. With a book! Yes, with an appropriate book.

And as she idly considered what book she should take down with her, if this were *her* room, to read in the exquisite seclusion of this heaven-sent deep bit of park (thrown away upon barbarians like Agnes), she thought that *A Room of One's Own* would exactly suit the requirements of the case – would beautifully abet the lonely occasion. Though, of course, that slender peacock-wrappered volume – which had been for her a *livre de chevet* at the time when she still had *a bed of her own* – during that period of her life when Margot (as she had now come to be, complete with voice, coiffure, and carriage), was painfully in the making – the pages of that militant little treatise she knew so much by heart, she would take down into the garden only for dipping-in. But it would not be her intention, in any event, to read, only to lie in listless contemplation – a fragile figure, alone, in an abandoned scrap of park.

Here indeed was a very *Park of One's Own* for a solitary woman; and that was distinctly a luxury, to have attached to the regulation *room of one's own*, if one had one – if, like Agnes Irons, one had lived by oneself in a posh little service-flatlet! Margot almost wished she could sail forth from this spotlessly tidy bachelor cell to go to dinner with Victor in Soho, as in the days before she was 'Mrs Stamp,' and experience the romantic courtship of 'the hermit girl,' as she had nicknamed herself, all over again. Victor was so happy then! It was for Victor's sake that she desired to go back and retrace her steps; to sacrifice once more, upon the altar of Australian passion, 'the hermit girl' of her a little enervated fabrication – the clever picture of a lonely girl, to whose immaculate conception Virginia Woolf had so decisively contributed.

Musing at the open window, as if already under the greenwood tree with her favourite author, she fancied herself back in Oxford (where she had never set foot) at the don's lunch, by the side of her goddess, Virginia (unseen, but there all the same). Or there they both drooped discreetly, side by side, perhaps, two feminine *outsiders*, as it were, in a masculine universe of one-sided learning. And how delicious to be *an outsider* with such an one as the stately Virginia, thought she, and blushed with a little wistful happiness. As onlookers, then, in this sense, they found themselves at the post-war academic banquet – remarking upon the masculine wealth locked up in these colleges, announcing itself in the pomp of the table, in vintage wines and in great vainglorious cigars: and they would be comparing together (if Virginia and she had really *gone* there in each other's company and as two girl-friends) the quality of those present with what the pre-war had had to offer in the way of luncheon-parties – the talk, the ambitious, almost naïf effervescence. But the pre-war, it went without saying, was to be vastly preferred (though, of course, Margot had

234

been in a humble tradesman's cradle at the time, in a factory-city, and *pre-war* was for her – like everything else that was elegant and socially beautiful – a name, no more).

And (delicately dipping-in, hovering above the delicious pages, in her imagination) she came upon the verses of Tennyson – the literary lord, the Arthurian poetry-baron – as she had done with a thrill of romantic surprise, when first she had entered this 'highbrow' feminist fairyland – purchased for five shillings at the local Smith's: and very softly indeed, and with a mincing distinctness, she spoke to herself, she said to herself the lines, as she imagined that great queen among women (that great weary queen, as she romantically pictured her), her adored Virginia, would have spoken them –

> From a passion flower at the gate
> Has fallen a splendid tear.

She heard the deep rich baying voice, of such a great weary queen among women as her fancy suggested, underlying her own whispering: she *saw* the gate, she *saw* the passion flower – which was of an imposing size and of a bold heart-blood red. And a superb dew-drop had detached itself from the dew-gland at its perfumed centre, revolved proudly along the slight declivity of one of its velvet petals, and plunged towards the ground, like a falling world!

> I am coming, my own, my sweet!
> I am coming, my love, my dear!

Her lips uttered, with scarcely more than a phantom of sound, the romantic declaration. And the words, so diaphanously winged, passed out into the haunted air of the unexpected park – where, at any moment, the solitude might be invaded, and heightened, by two figures who, at a likely guess, if you followed them to discover their habitat, would reintegrate the pages of Framley Parsonage, but *never* derive from anything more grossly twentieth-century or anything privy to internal-combustion – to name the arch-serpent of the pre-war Eden. '*What poets they were!*' she repeated to herself, in the very words of Virginia Woolf. 'What poets they were!' *They* being those splendid Victorian monogamists – flowering, as great-hearted passion flowers, hyperpetalous and crimson red, upon the spoils of the Anglo-Indies and of the Dark Continent.

But this seductive train of images – which had contrived, by the medium of Margot, to quicken themselves to quite a respectable degree, if not exactly to achieve the status of protoplasm – these were all rudely dissolved. All the dreamy rout of them were sent smartly about their business, at the brazen entrance of Agnes Irons, the clamour of whose voice broke out almost immediately behind the small thaumaturgic head of her friend, this self-consecrated Bloomsbury priestess.

Margot stiffened, but at first did not move at all, so that Agnes supposed she had fallen asleep. Indeed, like one of the Trollopian figures now brutally expelled from the landscape, Margot almost felt that she herself, as well, had been forcibly liquidated, and had followed her day-dreams into their limbo. For the moment she allowed herself to wonder if in fact she was still there at all, visible and in the flesh.

An appreciable fraction of time did, indeed, elapse, during which she *was* not present – during which she had done a precipitate fade-out. She sat quite motionless, in her pale taffeta dress, with the effect of a crinoline – with at the throat the hint of a locket – with a fashionable felt female helmet arranged to counterfeit a bonnet. Her head rested upon her slender hand, her elbow upon the window-sill. Literally she had been *suppressed* by this dynamic intrusion, so much was she involved in the things that she was prone to imagine.

Then she recovered. She became sorted out from all those shapes which were susceptible to extinction at the mere vibration of a human voice, and resumed the narrower mould which was contingent upon the mortal give and take of objective experience. The colour flowed back into her cheeks. A painful light of welcome came into her eyes. She turned her head upon her shoulders; and her eye twinkled feebly, as the image of a starched-collared and jacketed, a scotch-tweeded amazon, equipped for the sex-war with an alarming chin and jet-black eye – Agnes! – impressed itself upon her senses.

Margot rose there, straight up from the seat of the chair, as if dreamily to defend herself – with the movement, rather, of an entranced medium. She met the blast with a brave breath-

lessness, as Agnes seized her to be kissed. For the striding
woman, who had put down a collection of small parcels upon
the table, was now upon her, grabbing the frail wax-work
to her wizened, muscular bosom, in a spasm of masterful
girlishness.

'Darling! How are you?' she hailed her, at very close range.
'Have you been here long?' Why didn't you make yourself
some tea? You look a little cheap.'

A doctor had once told her she looked *cheap*, and at the
doctor's word Margot now recoiled instinctively, as then: for
however the word was intended, it was not nice to have it used
about one. And Agnes smelled of peat, which always made her
feel a little sick.

'Do I?' she said, smiling with tired composure at the big
dark energetic face of her best girl-friend. '*You* look very well,
Agnes! Did you enjoy your holiday?'

'My dear, I had the most perfectly topping time.' (For it is
'topping time' still in distant Malaya.) 'Perfect weather!
Oceans of golf! Awfully decent people! In the water half the
day! Look at me!' She displayed her sun-blackened chest, and
her biceps ditto. 'I was jolly sorry to come back!'

'I expect you were.'

'If I could only live on my golf. Or if daddy weren't so
poor!'

Margot looked round the room.

'Isn't there something different about your room?" she
asked.

'Nothing except this!' Agnes pointed, grinning broadly, at
a large writing-desk. 'How do you like it?'

'Yes, of course! That's what it is. It's very nice indeed,
Agnes, isn't it? And very useful too. For you. Was it a
present?'

'It's a present from Agnes Irons!' For five or ten minutes
after her entrance Agnes made no remark whatever without an
obbligato of deafening laughter, which lasted for a longer
or shorter period upon some principle of jolly-good-sortish-
ness, of seeing the humorous-side-of-things, admitting no
visible relation to the ratio of comic matter in its verbal
counterpart.

She stood rocking with laughter now, as if shaken by hiccups, her legs wide apart in golfing attitude. Her merry eyes were bent upon her self-present, screwed up as if to spy out a distant bunker: all her teeth were uncovered, and anyone would have thought that the most side-splitting object on earth had now been given house-room in her flatlet, and that there it stood, a constant provocation to the humorist every true Briton conceals – if *conceal* is indeed the word. And Agnes Irons would probably not have stopped laughing for a long time yet if Margot had not said:

'It must have cost a great deal of money, Agnes darling.'

'Do you like it?'

'I think it's a beauty.'

'Guess what it cost!'

'I couldn't, I'm afraid.'

'I paid six pounds ten for it.' She exploded. The room reeled with clap upon clap of laughter. 'Not bad, is it?'

'It's lovely.'

'I bought it out of my golf prizes. I had over five pounds in vouchers.'

'Really! It do wish you would go in for it professionally, darling. You would get so rich.'

Agnes shook her head.

'Yes, I made quite a lot. In a small way – the local club is not very large. There was an open meeting. I made five pounds five in vouchers, and fifty-three shillings in the sweep. Not too bad, was it? About eight pounds. That's better than a spit in the eye!'

'It is indeed.'

'So this child thought to herself: *How about buying a desk?* And there it is as large as life. I've wanted one for a long time. I really do need something of the sort.'

'Of course you do. It's made of beautiful wood,' said Margot, stroking it.

'Rather nice, isn't it? It's supposed to be antique!'

A ghastly clap of laughter shook her from head to foot, at the notion of the absurd pretensions of this *per se* so humorous object – won on the playing fields of Stoke Poges, or Witton le Zouche, with her strong right arm.

'Weren't the local people very impressed with your playing, Agnes? I wonder if they knew you were a champion?'

'They *were* a bit impressed, I think, when they saw my handi-cap certificate!' Agnes answered – always a little more sober when referring to what was her long suit – for *a golf champion,* although not exempt from drollery, did not knock you back, exactly, so much as cause you to just fall slackly half-recumbent into a simmering smiling reverie.

'They must have been!' said Margot faintly. 'When they saw your handicap. Of course, you have to show it, haven't you?'

Agnes sat down, and began to untie the little parcels. One was a Brooke Bond packet, another a box of Kensitas. Margot likewise sat down, lightly touching her neck, her hand afterwards drifting into her lap.

'Daddy *is* such an old lamb!' Agnes exclaimed. 'He's so proud of his little girl.'

'I'm not surprised,' said Margot, still more faintly than before.

'Came out on the links every day, poor old darling, and insisted upon following his little girl around, bless him. He was tremendously bucked when I won!'

Winning anything, naturally, requires a great deal of demo-cratizing and must *always* be treated with a big dose of dis-infectant British mirth. Which Agnes promptly administered.

'I expect he was,' said Margot, almost inaudibly. 'He must have been, darling.'

'You do look jolly well fagged out, Margot! I'll make us a cup of nice tea, shall us? Let's! Yes – what?'

Margot nodded.

And watched by the visitor, the broad square shoulders of the open golf champion of the Straits Settlement – *mem-sahib* and white wage-slave – squared up to the domestic cupboard – routing out of their hiding-places the jolly old tea things, drat them, and chucking them down on the jolly old table in open order – the gallant teapot at the head of his men, of course, and the commissariat – biscuits and bath buns – bringing up the jolly old rear, with a segment of obsolete chocolate cake ab-solutely at the fag-end, hiding behind the caddy – the *tea* same, not the golfing variety, not the niblick-wallah.

Still swimming in a homeric ocean of thunderous laughter, of course, out of which she incessantly flung up some hearty remark, outwards at Margot, Agnes moved hither and thither, in massive attitudes of overwhelming competence. And to see her prepare the tea was something like witnessing Jove's thunder-bolt brought down from heaven to brain a gnat.

But with great suddenness a fearful obstreperous piercing shriek shattered the last vestige of such peace as Agnes had left intact in the poor little room. Margot put her fingers in her ears and closed her eyes. But, as it turned out, it was only the whistling kettle, announcing the climax of its activities; where, discreetly out of sight behind a screen, it had for some minutes been subjected to a relatively intense heat. Agnes laughed ruggedly, and swung over to the centre of the disturbance. It was a kettle with a sense of humour, such as Agnes approved of, that's why she had bought it. It sang out, with a good hearty shriek, when it was approaching the boiling point, and, like the pukka sport that it was, kept down the gas bill.

As the slice of old chocolate cake was the least desirable thing on the table, it was the chocolate cake that Margot selected. She could not be prevailed upon to 'sample' a bath bun, or 'try her luck' with a moka biscuit.

'I wish I hadn't put out that stale bit of cake now,' Agnes complained of herself, driving her artificial fangs into a bun.

'Why? It's lovely. It's all the better for being a little seasoned.'

'*Seasoned* is right!' roared Agnes 'ruefully,' furrowing up her batrachian skin – seasoned, that, in the sunshine of the tropical colonies – and displaying the entire expanse of her dentures, which had to be pretty large not to be shattered by her laughs.

'You *have* got brown, Agnes! You are almost the colour of a dago, if you don't mind my saying so. I should take you for a Spanish girl if I saw you anywhere without knowing you.'

'Yes, it's pretty bad, isn't it. I *could* pass for a Philippino, I believe! I get sunburnt very quickly. I'm like this all over!'

She roared with laughter at what she must look like *nude*! How the jolly old sun can turn a *mem-sahib* into a mulatto in

240

time! Liked doing it! Just to take the White Man down a peg
or two! – and show her – *Misses* White Man, that is – that the
Colonel's Lady and the shadiest of the shady are sisters under
their skins!

'I *am* very dark,' she confessed. 'Always have been. Don't
know where I *get* it from!' – this rather roguish. As she
drawled out these things she seemed to be transferring a hot
vegetable, or a big juicy brandy-ball, from one side of her
mouth to the other. And she gave another hearty roar at the
absurd idea of being *dark*. Nature is a topping old sportsman!
And all nature's little jokes are worth a guffaw or two – even if
some are in questionable taste (for, of course, we know that
nature is, well, not exactly *white*! – but a jolly old sportsman
nevertheless – a sort of sporting nabob, don't you know, res-
plendent at gymk'anas!). And then a good laugh against oneself is always more of a pukka laugh, isn't it, than one at the
expense of another person – especially if they are a social
equal. To possess a saving sense of humour *eases* the White
Man's Burden just a little. It is indeed what the White Man has
had bestowed upon him, especially the Englishman, to make it
possible for him to go on carrying it at all – the too vast orb of
his globe-trotting fate!

There was an interval during which Agnes expatiated upon
the topping character of her uncle, whose jolly old Rolls was
always looming up at the psychological moment, and rolling
the jolly laughing person of his sporting niece away in
this direction or that. And then *other* persons, who were
beastly rich, also *would* keep breaking into the narrative.
'Rolls Royces – butlers and footmen – pots of money!' was a
wistful incantation never for long off her chuckling lips. The
magic words were drawled out in a tone of comic commiseration at the absurdity of the 'pots of money' these same sahibs
had and which, of course, one could not help noticing – though
between one sahib who *had* the shekels and another who
hadn't, the beastly things would be only one more joke, and, of
course, not such a bad one as all that. These fleshpots *had*
their uses.

When Agnes had drawled 'Rolls Royces – butlers and footmen – pots of money!' for the third time, Margot said:

'Have the Bulkeleys – did you say Bulkeleys –?'

'Yes, Bulkeleys,' Agnes confirmed her, with an indulgent smile, as if *she* were 'a Bulkeley' herself (or the next thing to it) and understood that it must be a struggle for those not 'a Bulkeley' to get the name right without a good deal of privileged practice – which obviously Margot could not be expected to have had.

'Have the Bulkeleys a lot of pictures?'

'Oh yes, swarms of them!' said Agnes with a great careless confident heartiness. 'Gold frames – Old Masters –'

And she was *just* about to add 'pots of money.' But she remembered that she had said that already. So she stopped, and smiled opulently and misty-eyed instead – a whole picture-gallery of priceless masterpieces reflected in the mirthful glimmer of her far-away gaze.

'Have they any pictures by living people?' Margot asked.

'Pictures by living people?' That the living were rather common for the Bulkeleys to have anything to do with, in the matter of artists (who were only made respectable by death), obviously was the first thing that occurred to Agnes.

'Oh yes, some of them must be *alive*. Though, of course, most of them died long ago. They are the Old Masters.'

'Oh.'

'Family portraits, you know! Dear old gentlemen in periwigs and breastplates. Awfully quaint.'

'No modern pictures – really modern?' Margot gently persisted.

'You don't mean those *cubist* horrors, do you?' Agnes exclaimed – as the trend of these questions became plain to her suddenly. 'No, I don't think they have anything like that, in fact I'm sure they haven't. I should have noticed. But then, they wouldn't have anything like that.'

'I only wondered – as you said they had so many pictures.'

'Another cup, darling? And *do* have one of these bikkies, they're not bad at all.'

It was at this point that the laughing stopped. Agnes seemed to admit that even *her* sense of humour required a rest sometimes. Beyond a certain age – and Margot judged that thirty-nine summers was about the correct mark in the case of Agnes, sometimes she looked very creased and stained out in the street – once you had passed whatever the age might be, a quarter of an hour at a stretch was about all that could be managed, in the way of *really* hearty and incessant laughter. Then one must rest on one's oars for a bit – discharging an occasional guffaw for the say-so.

But the cue for a spell of quiet in this instance was the mention of the art of the Cube. For the humorous mind that subject would normally be irresistible. It would be the signal for an orgy of jokes. But having regard to Margot's feelings, this unfortunately must be nipped in the bud and sternly repressed. So Agnes became rather suddenly deflated. A somewhat careworn shell a little alarmingly took the place of the 'dynamic' personality. The young veteran of the links – whose nickel-plated trophies stood in a row upon the mantelpiece – showed for a moment the strain of the White Man's Burden and of ten thousand rounds of golf.

'And how is Victor?' she inquired dutifully and soberly, at this, as if asking after a sick person. 'Going strong, as usual?'

'He is working,' said Margot, bashfully.

Agnes sat up. She looked very grave, almost alarmed.

'Working? You don't mean he's got a job?' she asked.

'A sort of job,' said Margot, with docility, and in a tone of some deprecation.

'Not in an office?'

'No.'

'Gone on the screen?' This was facetious. Her massive scarlet lips flowered lazily to show the naughty intention.

Margot shook her head, smiling a little reproachfully at Agnes.

'But still, he's got a pukka job?' crashed Agnes Irons, prepared to leave it at that. 'I'm glad to hear Victor's got a job, it's sporting of him. It makes things easier, doesn't it? You won't have to work now, darling, I suppose. Or will you all the same?'

'I'm afraid Victor's job is not very satisfactory.' Margot looked over with her direct, expressionless, filmy gaze. 'He's faking pictures for a living.'

'Doing *what*?'

'He goes every day and fakes pictures in a sort of factory. It's not a *factory*. It's a studio.'

'Fakes pictures!' repeated Agnes – as if Margot had said that her husband had been faking horses or cats. 'What's that! I've never heard of people faking pictures.' Agnes stared back at her mistily-staring companion – attempting to picture to herself, evidently, an artist-fellow, a sketcher, in the act of *faking* a sketch, instead of *sketching* it, or whatever it was the fellow did.

'He hates it!' Margot faintly intoned, with devotional intensity.

'Why does he do it then?' came back from Agnes, in her rugged drawl.

'I didn't want him to do it. I tried hard to dissuade him. But Victor said he might as well be doing that as anything else.'

'It depends what he was doing. What did he mean?'

'It's not bad money. But I don't like his doing it at all.'

Agnes lit a cigarette. The brains of Agnes Irons were now called upon to engage in paths where, to say the truth, they were not exactly at home. So she was cudgelling her brains, as it is called, that was painfully evident.

'But what *is* this faking exactly, Margot?' she asked, as one person soliciting the confidential low-down upon something from another.

'Oh, didn't you know how people faked pictures? It's often done.'

'I know old furniture is faked!'

And Agnes looked hard at her new desk, a self-confessed fake – a rather noble possession, but with, as it were, a big bar-sinister.

'Yes, except that's easier.'

'Which?' asked Agnes sharply.

'Well, I meant the furniture.'

'Are they sold as genuine antiques?' Agnes asked, hesitating, to show that it was not her wish to in any way suggest that there was anything *dishonourable* in what Margot's eccentric bread-winner was doing.

'They aren't antiques,' Margot told her, hesitating, too. 'Victor was faking a picture by a living artist all day yesterday, for instance.'

'One who's still living!' This was very peculiar. 'Why did he fake that?'

'Picasso, the artist is called. Have you heard of him?'

'I can't say I have – what an odd name! It sounds dago.'

'It *is* dago,' said Margot, smiling with the mildest of mild mischief. 'He's Spanish.'

'Foreigners are, of course, always good at that sort of thing, aren't they?' said Agnes a little defiantly, sleepily half-closing her eyes – lying back in her chair, in monumental ease, one arm flung over the back, her short hard legs sturdily crossed. 'They're very clever, I suppose, as artists.'

'Victor says they have it in their blood.'

'I suppose it's the blood,' Agnes agreed, yawning, and tapping her mouth – for the by-products of tainted and un-English blood was a subject after all that could not be described as thrilling.

'*We* haven't, Victor thinks,' Margot timidly continued, for the sake of talking about Victor. 'He doesn't mean *everybody* of course.' (He didn't mean *Victor*!)

'I'm bound to say I think Victor's right there,' the golf champion of Malaya drawled, giving herself two or three smart raps on the lips, out of the farded tissues of which yawn after yawn was attempting to expel itself.

'I think he is.' Margot made no difficulty about assenting to that.

'I suppose I'm an out-and-out Philistine. Don't say *Oh no!* darling – it's not necessary, really! But we can't *all* be artists, can we? The Britisher's got a good deal to be said for him, one way and another. Patriotic – what! Yes, I know. A proper jingo – that's Agnes Irons! But the Britisher can leave art to the foreigners, since they seem to be cut out for it. Why not? Or so say I! – I *know* you want to *chuck* something at me for talking like that – why don't you?' And Agnes shook in a storm of lazy chuckles as she lay back in her chair, offering herself as a bombastic target to this outraged partisan of the Muses.

Margot looked away, confused by the aggressive diversion, her mind full of Victor and Victor only.

'I've never pretended though, have I, darling? – give me credit for that!' pleaded Agnes, fiercely arch – 'to be anything but a hardened old Philistine!' And she laughed full-chestedly, an unrepentant hardened old Philistine cackle.

Margot blushed a little.

'I'll be damned if I know, darling,' Agnes drawled on, 'how you can put up with me! I've often wondered. We are an ill-assorted couple – as they say!'

A further crash of bonhomie from the more humorous member of the ill-assorted couplement. Margot flinched – she almost *ducked*.

Margot recovered. She smiled with difficulty, a sickly smile in truth, and gave Agnes a weak caress with her a little haggard, red-rimmed eyes of liquid blue: for at these times she did certainly find Agnes a handful and she never left her without a bad headache and usually a troublesome singing in the ears.

'I'm not very patriotic,' Margot said, in a washed-out voice to start with, though it got stronger afterwards. 'I don't think it matters, Agnes, really who are artists or who are not.'

'No, I don't think it does. You're quite right.'

'But as to my putting up with you, I don't know, darling, how you manage to put up with *me*.'

'Darling – how sweet you are!'

'I'm not an Empire girl, I'm afraid. I think I must be a cosmopolitan.'

'Empire girl! Oh Margot! I think that's meant to be unkind!'

'No, why? No, it wasn't really. But I'm not for the Red, White and Blue,' she gulped, 'quite as much as you are, darling.'

A stern British bulldog-bark of grim mirth greeted this statement.

'Well, I'll let that pass!' said Agnes. 'We'll say no more about it. But there is something that's worrying me, darling.'

'What is that, Agnes?'

'Well. Is it *honest* – you know what I mean, could one get

into trouble? – to fake these pictures? Especially by *living persons*, Margot – even if they *are* foreigners!'

Margot nodded, a painful frown upon the tightly-drawn skin of her forehead – as tightly-drawn as the straight old-gold panels of her centre-parted hair.

'Of course it isn't,' she said. 'That's just it. Victor hates doing it.'

'But couldn't he get into trouble, Margot darling, if he was found out?'

'Victor says not.'

'I should say he *could*.'

'Victor says he wouldn't care if he did.'

'A nice young man, I must say! What would happen to you?'

'But I don't think he *will* be found out, Agnes. It's not that.'

'Why shouldn't he?'

'But so many people are doing it, you see. As a matter of fact Tristram Phipps has just gone there too.'

Agnes betrayed a reawakening of interest – the name Tristram seemed to stimulate her slightly.

'Tristram's rather a lamb, isn't he?' she said.

'I like him,' said Margot.

'He's doing it too, is he?' Agnes drawled in reflective fashion. 'It all sounds very *irregular* to me – very *irregular* – it's the business woman speaking!' (A crash of sportive gaiety for the business woman.) 'But artists are a funny lot – you don't mind my saying! They're quite irresponsible!'

'The business woman again, Agnes!' Margot smiled.

'All the same, *irresponsible* is what they are!'

'Some of them are. Victor is very unhappy about having to do this. He threatens to throw up the job. I shouldn't mind if he did. I should be glad.'

'Well, I suppose it *is* regular work, which is something.'

'If Tristram hadn't gone there, Victor would have left, I think – I wish he hadn't! Tristram and he work together.'

'That must be rather fun.'

Agnes was softening towards this illicit nest of 'fakers.'

'It amuses Victor in a way – it is after all *painting*.'

247

'I suppose the work is *light*,' Agnes said. 'He just does the sketching I mean.'

'That depends on what they're doing. Van Gogh is easy to do, he says. The other day they turned out a Derain. He's French. *He's* alive, now, still.'

'Is he?' Agnes looked startled again. It was 'faking' a *live* sketcher that seemed to her to smack of the risky.

'Oh yes. But Victor said it was too good for Derain, what they did.'

'Then why not sell it as his own picture?'

'There's the name.'

'I see. Yes, I suppose the name is everything.'

'Victor says it bores him to tears imitating all the *mistakes* of the artist he's faking.'

Agnes scratched her head with a red-dyed finger-nail. This remark was practically meaningless, she decided: as you would not, it was obvious, take the trouble to fake a *bad* picture, one that was full of *mistakes*.

'Have you seen Gillian lately?' Agnes asked. 'That is her name, isn't it? Tristram's *wife*, I mean. She was an awfully sweet kid, I thought.'

Margot shook her head.

'She's gone away. She and Tristram are not together now.'

'What, has she left Tristram?'

'No. I think Tristram left her.'

'Whatever for?'

Margot thought a moment, as if the terms of this question had assailed her with doubt.

'I don't quite know what it was all about,' she said. 'I think it was politics.'

'Politics!'

'So I understood,' Margot nodded, with a special phantom-smile she reserved for Agnes. 'That's what Victor says. There must be something else, I think. But I don't know what it is. Victor says it was because they didn't agree about politics.'

Agnes stood up and stretched, looking at a large photograph of a girl-child of about ten years old, with a large determined chin and an unmistakable *mem-sahbish* expression already peeping through the puerile accessories of the tender years.

'Politics!' she drawled. 'You are absurd really, all of your crowd. Who ever heard of a young man and young woman separating because they didn't agree about *politics*?'

'I said I didn't believe it was that altogether, Agnes.'

Agnes began putting away the tea things, and Margot got up and joined her without speaking.

'Oh, thank you, darling. But don't you trouble.'

'Victor suggested we should meet him at the Swan,' Margot said.

'What, that pub in Shepherd's Bush?'

'Yes. It's near where he works. Tristram will be there. Shall we go? What do you say?'

'Yes, let's!' said Agnes Irons.

'Tristram lives down that way now. We might have supper there.'

'A jolly good idea!'

And Agnes straddled in front of the window, her hands in her skirt pockets.

'These mangy old trees give me the hump,' she said.

'The hump?'

'Yes. The hump. Don't they you, when you're dopy I mean? Give me the tropics every time!'

And she released a pukka laugh, to salute the ridiculous tropics.

Chapter 2

IN the fake-masterpiece factory at Shepherd's Bush, Stamp sat his workstool easily, with a limber grace – erect in the saddle. A frowning eye was fixed upon his image in the glass. He was disguised in the fur cap of a Canadian trapper. A heavy white bandage, descending under the chin, covered his right ear. He was supposed to be Van Gogh. He was engaged in the manufacture of a Van Gogh 'self-portrait.'

Stamp's face did not exactly lend itself to this device. The face of the imitator was high-cheekboned, certainly, and that was as it should be. But it was far too swarthy; cooked, as it had been, in the Pacific sun. Its tan would have been better suited for the faking of the self-portrait of a brown-skinned Venetian than for counterfeiting this sentimental pink rat from the hysterical North. Still, Stamp could distort himself, he found, after a fashion. That the man was a beastly blond could not be helped, could it? So allowing for the bleak albino look of the Dutchman's face, Stamp had decided to use his own face in a looking-glass as best he could. And now he sat scowling into this looking-glass as nearly as possible as Van G. had sat scowling into *his* looking-glass.

Stamp had come heartily to dislike these red-rimmed ferret-eyes that watched him from a dozen examples – photogravures, half-tones, and photographs – pinned-up for reference. His own big calmly hostile eyes surveyed with disgust this affected prison-crop (as he considered it). He had never liked him much as a painter. And as a man – now that he had been compelled to climb into his skin for the purposes of this portrait – he liked him even less.

In consultation with Tristy, Stamp had got his palette about right. The Van Gogh palette was a gay palette, of pure colours. A child's-paintbox palette it would look like to the layman. The complementary colours, of course, must be kept at arm's length from each other. *Red* and *green*, being 'complementaries,' must never meet, much less mix – to conform to the practice of this purist.

For a number of weeks now Stamp had been at work on these counterfeit pictures. He had formulas, by this time, for everything. The pupils of the eyes, for instance, in a typical Van Gogh, were painted – it was Tristy had pointed this out – as a nest of concentric wedges of greens, reds, blues and yellows, with their apex inwards. He had got the trick of that. And he had mastered the bald look of the pale eyebrows, which marked the base of the bony swellings. Then more wedges stuck on end, a miniature hedge of them, for the tissue of the lips. He could do a Van Gogh self-mouth pretty well by this time. And he had got the collarless neck, like a halter. An old pilot-jacket had been obtained for him by his employer, which, in combination with a seaman's shirt, produced the weighty yoke that was required.

Why Stamp had a bandage on his ear was because, when they first talked the matter over, they had decided to do a *bandaged* portrait of the mad master. That would make identification easier. Half the likeness was there, ready-made, once you had the famous bandage over the famous ear. Everyone seeing the familiar square woodenness of these gauche likenesses, and then the famous bandage, would say 'Van Gogh!' as soon as ever they clapped eyes on it. 'Look,' they would cry, 'where he has cut off his ear!'

Here is the story of the ear. All artists have heard the story of Van Gogh's ear – Stamp had read his letters too. But Vincent Van Gogh lost his ear somewhat as follows. Vincent Van Gogh was a Dutchman, as his name would suggest. He was the mystic and naturalist painter: he was a great friend of Paul Gauguin, the exotic faker of South Sea scenes (who pretended to be a half-caste to account for this Pacific sensibility). Van Gogh was very jealous of his friend's astonishing skill as an oil-painter; for he admired skilfulness very much. And as his intellect clouded, as it did about that time, this jealousy of the skilful French painter made him quite dangerous at last.

He and Paul Gauguin were in the South of France together, and they occupied the same bedroom – since they were neither of them rich, though the latter had started as a stockbroker. And at last one night Gauguin was woken up by hearing his room mate – this Dutchman of the unquiet mind and abhorrence of his clumsy fist – prowling about in the dark without good cause. He called out to him, and immediately the other scuttled back to his bed. But later on he was again woken up, and he found Van Gogh in a crouching position, not a yard away from him, with his eyes fixed upon his face.

'What is it, Vincent?' he shouted out angrily, as he did not move. 'Go back to your bed, Vincent!' And Vincent obeyed him at once and returned to his bed without speaking. A third time however he was disturbed. And on this occasion he saw Vincent approaching with an open razor. He drove him off with a few massive French curses. But this was enough for Monsieur Paul Gauguin, and next morning he changed his hotel. A few days later he received a small postal packet, and discovered inside, carefully wrapped up, a human ear. It was a present from his friend. For Vincent had cut it off and sent it to him as a little surprise. He was a simple man, and now was become a little over-simple maybe. And it occurred to him, thinking the matter over, that having intended to cut his friend's ear off, and driven him away, by advertising too crudely the intention, the least he could do was to mutilate himself, and sort of give his friend his revenge, but without his being put to the trouble of *taking* it!

But this made Paul Gauguin think, as he looked at the ear lying in the palm of his hand, that he had been wise in a way to move when he did, from the bedroom where he had slept with the unbalanced impressionist, struggling so dourly with his medium. And I think we must agree that beyond question he had shown his good judgment.

*

The place that had been selected by Freddie Salmon for his factory of counterfeiting pictures was a large studio in the yard of a private house converted into flats, within sight of the White City. It was entered *via* the front hall.

Tristy was established in the opposite corner to Stamp. He, like Stamp, was busy increasing the number of pictures by Van Gogh in the world. At present he was engaged in solemnly faking, with the utmost dignity, a largish picture, which was a cunning variation upon a well-known Provençal sunset: the idea being that Van Gogh painted two sunsets instead of one, and that this was the best, although it had never been heard of before.

Tristram conferred a peculiar respectability upon the whole proceedings: his mere presence made faking almost an august occupation. He lifted it upon a plane where Public Spirit reigned supreme, in a disinterested lustre – as, obviously from the very highest motives, he applied himself to deceive the public as to the authorship of this remarkable masterpiece, whose very existence had up till then been unsuspected.

Salmon had several experts in his pocket who could be relied on, the moment the piece was completed, to cover it with their authority in the market. Indeed, it was destined for the collection of a specific American, who already had absorbed half

252

a dozen spurious canvases signed 'Vincent,' which would almost certainly be joined by Tristy's little contraption. Three thousand bucks was as good as added to Salmon's bank balance, for what he planned he planned well, and generally was found to execute. It was a pretty foxy collector who slipped through Salmon's fingers, once that gentleman had marked him down for a deal.

Stamp's self-portrait was another matter. If Stamp was not a dud – and Salmon was not entirely satisfied that Stamp was the goods, for he had made a mess of one self-portrait, which had to be thrown upon the market for what it was worth, without an expensive O.K. from a world-famous 'expert,' and take its chance in the sale-room – if Stamp earned his four quid a week and had the stuff in him to pull it off – this wounded hero of the art-racket (the romance of the missing ear playing its lucrative part) should represent a really worth-while profit.

Salmon had all the dope ready. This self-portrait was a little surprise of Vincent's for his brother, the Amsterdam dealer, that was the idea. But, as usual, the cantankerous Vincent was dissatisfied with his work. That was why it had been left at one of his favourite brothels, to discharge a food-debt. And Salmon was so exercised about this little nest-egg that it was all he could do to leave Stamp alone, and not paint the picture for him, or at least interfere, at every step.

For Salmon had his doubts about Stamp, and he had not concealed them from Stamp either – he could not, for he felt too strongly on the subject. He wished he had put somebody else on this job now. And between Stamp and himself no love was lost, by and large, and he knew it. And a quite good West-End dinner he had given Stamp, with wine *ad lib*, if not of the best, made no difference. It made no difference at all. He could not get Stamp to like him and regard him as a jolly good sort. So he chafed continually as he recognized that Stamp's heart was not in his work.

Without Stamp's perhaps being conscious of it Salmon knew that Stamp might as likely as not play him up. He knew that Stamp's limitations as an artist were not the only drawbacks an employer had to reckon with. The man was a surly mule, no doubt with a kick ready, too, for his benefactor. (For Salmon

253

was of course a benefactor in all this, as, seeing what his suffer-
ings were, most people would agree.) This human mule, as
vicious as they make 'em, might quite well bitch the picture
just out of cussedness! One could never establish with any
exactitude, in dealing with such a *crétin*, where incompetence
left off and cussedness began. Ah, these idjot-roughnecks that
one was compelled to employ for one's sins! hissed to himself
the unhappy Freddie Salmon; and young Isaac Wohl, who
turned out with exemplary neatness forgery after forgery
almost for the love of the thing, in the respectable shadow of
Tristram, sympathized with poor Freddie on the quiet – everything about Isaac was on the quiet, for he was a quietist (who
worked quietly, walked quietly, and thought quietly, even).

What differences there were in the human material! This
deft young Jew, now, was a perfect, reliable machine – for
turning out Marie Laurencins, be it understood. Marie Laurencin herself could not have told the difference between one of
his and one of *her* Marie Laurencins. And what a comfort,
too, on the personal side! There was no damned nonsense
about *him*, none. He did not mind whether he did a Marie
Laurencin or an Isaac Wohl – unless it might be that it amused
him slightly more, intellectually (or, if you like, it bored him
less) to be somebody else than to 'be himself,' and he relished
sleight-of-hand for its own sake.

But Isaac could only be used on certain stuff. Here was the
ever-recurring difficulty in this business. Isaac Wohl was a
better artist than Stamp, yes. But he was not man enough, as it
were, to be put on to the big rough stuff of a Van Gogh portrait. This Salmon understood quite well.

You had to pick a roughneck for that work. You had to
pick him big – yes, even physically sizeable. But, at the end of
it all, was Stamp *artist* enough? For you had to pick an *artist*,
somehow, too! Here was the major problem in employing
this type of labour. Among the heavyweights there were so few
who could be trusted even to understudy the 'giants.' And it
was in the 'giant' class – and especially in their figure-work –
that the big money lay. An agonizing problem for a poor
business man!

*

Van Gogh, in effigy, got up from his work-stool, stretched with a mighty abandon, and, with a slow buttock-waggle, swaggered over to where Tristy was at work.

Tristy was in the thick of the sunset. He gave a smile to Stamp, and went on with his painting. The sunset piece was a great rain of opaque particles of light – each particle dipped in a bath of a reddish, or brazen, solution. Gnarled figures of peasants, with the striations of tree trunks, gathered in the foreground like hobos in a hailstorm. But this hailstorm was the sunset. And the hailstones were the opaque particles showering down from the conflagration of the romantic solar disk, about to set, like a bloated firework.

There was a big clumsy cartwheel system, ordering the distribution of the particles. The nave of the cartwheel was the body of the crimson sun. The usual woolwork effect proper to Van Gogh obsessed everything that was terra firma – the rocks, the olives, the farms, the churches. There was a small town half submerged in the welter of incendiary particles.

More mannered than any Van Gogh, except for his pictures after he got into the asylum, it was a most successful specimen of the forger's art. Tristy had turned out a commercial article of a high order – quite in the diamond-pendant class. He had earned his fortnight's keep. Stamp considered the result in silence, as Tristy peppered a corner with a minor vortex of atoms.

'Why don't you put in a dog, to account for that little disturbance there, Trist?' he asked at last.

Tristy laughed.

'There are no dogs in the South of France,' he said.

'That doesn't matter. Put in a jackal.'

'There are no jackals in Van Gogh's pictures,' Mr Phipps told him demurely.

'Then let this be "the Van Gogh with the jackal,"' Stamp insisted.

Tristy shook his head. He refused to have anything to do with a jackal.

'No, that would be risky. I don't think Freddie would like it.'

'To hell with Freddie!' Stamp exclaimed with robust conviction.

Isaac Wohl looked up from his Marie Laurencin and smiled. He had a sly appetite for massive disrespect, when he encountered it. Such outbursts on the part of the stupid side of creation should be encouraged. Stagnation could not occur where such breezy expressiveness obtained. So he flashed out a quiet smile, a discreet salute for rebellion, and quietly returned to his *bleuâtre* and pallid *Jeune fille en fleur*.

Victor Stamp sat down, and took out of Van Gogh's pocket a packet of cigarettes.

'Have you finished the right eye?' asked Tristy. He picked up a large magnifying glass, and approached it to a photogravure of a late Van Gogh, which was pinned upon a drawing-board, resting against the back of a chair. 'These late things of his always fall away to the left,' he said. 'His right hand must have been losing its priority.'

'How do you mean, Trist?'

'Like a man would always hold up a falling wall with his *right* hand, I mean. A right-handed man.' Tristy looked round at him, and then away again.

'He may have been a left-handed man,' said Stamp.

'No. In his self-portraits it's his right hand he's using.'

'You're right,' said Stamp.

'Have you finished the right eye?' Tristy asked once more, dreamily but deliberately, as he mixed colour on his palette with a clean brush.

'Yes,' Stamp said.

And as he said *yes*, a little sullenly, the door of the studio opened, admitting a nervous burst of jocular voices, an aroma of cigars, and the elegant person of Freddie Salmon followed by Abershaw, towering behind him with a broad sardonic grin.

Freddie Salmon had a really enormous false bottom to his face. The face proper obviously terminated a short distance below the line of the lower lip: and what was palpably a bogus jaw had been superadded, for some not very evident purpose, by inscrutable nature; unless, of course, he had grown it himself, in the progress of his mortal career, for ends which, again, were none too clear. It caused him to have a somewhat stupid look, however, at times. And he may of course have desired to look stupid. And it perhaps imparted, observed from immediately in front, a somewhat *soft* apearance to the face. It was not impossible that he may have desired to appear 'soft.' But it was so patently *postiche* that it could only have deceived a very inattentive man.

'Hallo, Tristy – how is the sunset? All set?' he called out heartily as he came in, swinging a lunch edition of the *Evening Standard* in his hand.

'When a sunset is *all set*,' in a gigantic purr Abershaw put it to his hearty pal, 'what remains should be a *nocturne*, shouldn't it?'

It was four o'clock. These two impresarios were dressed like twins in city suits that exactly matched, of braided black, with striped whipcord trousers – the black wings and the white wings of their neckties and collars discovering the spacious laundry, beneath the neckline, of an immaculate chest, which passed down out of sight – if not out of mind – behind the perfectly jiggered panels of the double-breasted waistcoats.

They had lunched well at their club, the Sackville, in Grosvenor Street, or rather the drinks and cigars had been upon a prosperous scale, even if Ye Olde English Clubbe had lived up to the traditions stipulated by ye members (determined at all costs to be of *la vieille roche* or nothing) and provided a stolid British brisket succeeded by a bald apple tart and custard. There these two immaculate macaronis, in this White's *de nos jours*, had met other gentlemen like themselves – agents, publishers, touts, critics (both of art and of letters), shilling-a-liners, experts, museum-officials and moneylenders. And they had become loudly, if mildly, intoxicated, exchanging tips and gratulatory jokes and messages, and cocky topdog gibes – re such matters as the spot price of American 'mystery' bestsellers, or the heavy backwardation on forward pieces of the early Umbrian school.

How could they, therefore, as they entered the dirty workshop together, avoid appearing like two Olympian personages a little, visiting some unsavoury underdog sweat-shop – paradoxically and amusingly enough belonging to one of them, run as a profitable joke as a society lady may run a steam-laundry – and they were at no pains at all to tone themselves down, that was

257

not their way, or to affect *not* to be flushed with insolence and liqueur-brandies.

Stamp eyed this brace of prancing sharpshooters, who had burst in so blandly, with aloof disfavour. Abershaw snapped him a naughty wink above his wholetime grin, and Stamp nodded back with lazy condescension. They came up and stood behind Tristy, inspecting the sunset. Salmon looked at Abershaw.

'It's the best Van Gogh I've seen,' said Abershaw, playing the outsider. 'Most impressive – I can't believe he didn't do it himself! How much?'

'Ask Van Gogh!' Salmon answered, looking at Tristy.

Abershaw turned to Victor Stamp – who, *for him*, was the master, he would have it understood.

'I admire your picture very much, Mr Gogh. May I acquire it? I should like to. What will you part with it for?'

'I'm not Van Gogh, sir!' Stamp answered with a surly smile. 'You've made a mistake.'

'You look remarkably like him, sir!' Abershaw insisted, in an energetic Johnsonian boom, fixing upon the other's fancy dress an eye big with doubt and sturdy conviction.

But Stamp began divesting himself of his disguise: he pulled off his trapper's fur-bonnet and removed the dressing from his operatic ear.

'I don't know what I've got this stuff on for,' he said, with distaste, as he did so.

Freddie looked greatly alarmed.

'You haven't finished, have you, Vic?' he clamoured suddenly, expostulation, or not far from it, dramatically tinging his voice – turning towards the self-portrait, his chin seeming to swell inordinately with dumb protest.

'Yes, that's finished,' said Stamp. 'That's finished, Freddie. How do you like it?'

And the tone could leave no doubt in anyone's mind as to his consciousness of Freddie's secret feelings about the portrait, nor his degree of concern regarding the feelings of Freddie.

Abershaw and Freddie Salmon moved over with stately deliberation – Freddie with almost menacing absence of haste – · to Stamp's corner of the workshop, and stood before Stamp's work. Stamp did not follow them. He sat with his back towards them, smoking.

'Have you ever done a portrait of a fashionable woman, or a fashionable man?' he asked Tristy.

'I did once. A woman.' Tristy smiled. 'Never again!'

'If you're getting a big sum for it,' Stamp said, 'it's a hell of a moment when the time comes to tell them that the thing is finished. To watch their faces gives me a pain in the stomach, I always turn my back.'

'The best thing to do!' Tristy agreed. 'I'd sooner not have the job. Once was enough for me.'

A discouraging silence now reigned in the studio. The over flesh-coloured face (as if violently pretending to be flesh and blood at all costs) with the preposterous false bottom to it gazed at the portrait. It gazed and gazed with a cowlike, cud-chewing concentration. All the irritability of the last fortnight or more of suspense smouldered in the capacious false bottom of this fauxbonhomme's headpiece – with its leaden secretions it weighed down this impossibly innocent chin. For it could be a receptacle on occasion for dissatisfaction, as well as for bluff 'kindliness.' The complete gamut of hatred felt by its owner for this disaffected craftsman expressed itself in the ex-pressionless eyes, as their vacuity deepened from blankness to abysses of utter blankness, from a bland blankness to a brutish blankness, from Pickwick or Pecksniff to the orang-outang: till nature's dark abhorrence of a vacuum – of such a vacuum! – became so intolerable as to be really malignant.

Interpreting this painful silence of his colleague without difficulty, Abershaw considered it advisable to cough; and at the same time he turned affably to Stamp and addressed Stamp's unresponsive back.

'The only criticism I have to make, Vic,' he said, in his smoothest conversational clubman vein, very much the uncon-cerned outsider, come into an atmosphere that he recognized as being somewhat strained, 'is that you've given our Dutch friend such an intelligent look in the right eye!'

'He had some intelligence,' said Stamp with sarcasm.

'How can you say that?' Abershaw objected. 'A man who was in the habit of chopping off his ears and sending them to his friends couldn't have an eye like that! Or had he? I ask in ignorance.'

'It's about as intelligent to cut off one's ears,' retorted the handsome profile from the Australian hinterland, coming into view above the uncompromising, immovable back, 'as to fake pictures for a living.'

'There I cannot agree with you at all, Vic!' Abershaw exclaimed heartily.

'Can't you, Abb?'

'I can't. But in any case your victim was always faking pictures himself, that's how he started – as I told you, do you remember, when we first discussed the matter?'

'You've got that mixed up, Abb,' Stamp replied indifferently, rising from his stool, taking down his jacket from a peg near the door, and putting it on, having first removed the garments that had provided his neck with a ponderous canonical yoke.

'I never heard that,' Tristy remarked at this, displaying interest. 'Did Van Gogh fake? Was he one of us?'

'Yes,' said Isaac Wohl, looking up.

'Indeed.' Tristy tossed up his head, as if about to neigh. Thereupon he became engaged, it was plain to see, in self-communion. For with him, when he took counsel with himself, the thing was done in public, as it were; and upon his face, as upon a screen, was reflected what was going on within. He did not pull down the blinds, so to speak, in order to think. He would have regarded it as improper to possess a *self* that had any secrets, from other selves. So as a consequence of this information he withdrew within himself – but leaving the door wide open – to examine the evidences at his disposal. Even he could be seen within, communing with his great revolutionary precursor. Vincent and Mr Phipps were tackling the subject of the laws of property together, as it were: the laws of property as exemplified in the work of man's hand (of his *own* hand, if 'own' is a word that still can convey anything).

Patent rights, Mr Phipps argued, were at the very heart of the problem of property. Individualism stands or falls upon that issue, it is clear enough. What in capitalist jargon was described as 'faking' was understood, if what Wohl said was true, by this far-seeing iconoclast (plain 'Vincent' for all the world) to be merely a 'share-the-wealth' proceeding – performed, of course, at the expense of the capitalist enemy.

Tristy was predisposed to believe that Van Gogh must have been a determined and inveterate 'faker' – a confirmed muscler-in, coin and cribber, of other people's art, and most prone to help himself to all he could lay his hands on – since Rembrandt does not belong to Rembrandt, but to mankind: and the extremely disgusting money values – inflated by the picture-racket until they reach proportions retrospectively compromising even to Rembrandt himself – put upon his major works under the capitalist system, are so many invitations to trickery and theft – all in the Cause, of course. And if you can beat the criminal exploiter at his own game, good luck to you! And of course such a far-seeing man as Van Gogh would understand that. And doubtless why so many of Van Gogh's pen-drawings are almost indistinguishable from a Rembrandt pen-drawing is because Van Gogh had so often faked the lucrative scratchings of the older master: and perhaps because, in consequence, many Rembrandt pen-drawings *are* actually Van Gogh pen-drawings!

Tristy was dreamily elated at the thought that Van Gogh had burgled the capitalist art-citadel way back in the bourgeois eighties of the last century, and had spat upon the notion of property that resides in that unregenerate principle that only Rembrandt should paint Rembrandts, and only Van Gogh a Van Gogh. *La propriété c'est un vol* – and how, except by counter-theft, can that balance be restored? He who evolves *property* out of his own guts (if 'own' possess any significance) should be shot or pillaged as a matter of course.

But, with a keener sense of property than Tristy, and possessed of the most full-blooded instinct for the many-sided capitalist advantages – though in hearty agreement that every description of theft was justified up to the hilt – Salmon darkly contemplated the small square of painted canvas which might be worth one pound, or which might represent a four-figure return against a paltry outlay of fifteen quid. Anguish and rage, in a light-lipped embrace, continued to heave uncomfortably beneath the shell of that carefully faked exterior called 'Freddie.' This surly brute *must* be held to his bargain! reflected Freddie. Freddie did not know enough about painting off-hand to say what was wrong. But his nose was a sharp one, and it told him unmistakably that this was not the goods. It had not come off. Or simply it was not finished. And so he gazed and gazed not in fault-finding but in a homeric attempt to detect the essence of the flaw, and when he should have detected it, to find the words that would not be too offensive to express his findings, and indicate what he considered should be done.

But meanwhile the villain of this piece, the unaccommodating Stamp, did not share, by any means, these unorthodox views of property. As he saw it, a poor devil of an artist had been engaged in a petty larceny. And the work of his hand, even left-handed work, was a property belonging inalienably to Stamp. And Stamp, he was being sweated in exchange for the work of his hand – and for this illegitimate dirty work he should, according to the human canon, have been paid not less, but more, than for legitimate work. Furthermore, or so would run his simple argument, Stamp would have preferred, on the part of Freddie Salmon, a bit more of the 'share-the-wealth' spirit, if Communism was to be the order of the day (and Tristy had not failed to urge upon him the doctrine of the high morality of their present undertakings). He was, in fine, congenitally incapable of understanding. And he sat there, an obtuse lump that *could* not be digested into his select universe, marked off by these four walls, and to which each of the others, in his peculiar way, belonged – as much Tristy as Freddie, as much Abershaw as Wohl.

So, an animal amongst men, this young giant crouched, doubled up where he sat, his back eloquently presented to Freddie Salmon should he turn about to address him. A striking picture of the Odd Man Out. For better or for worse these broad and hostile shoulders belonged to Nature, with her big impulsive responses, with her violent freedom, with her animal directness: unconservative, illogical, and true to her elemental self. He subscribed therefore to the larger scheme: the smaller, the watertight, the theoretic, the planning of man's logic, he repudiated. Like the camel, he must remain a creature of the wild, and never, like the horse, wholly submit to discipline.

So Stamp crouched and waited, attending the blow he knew would descend, and which, fatally, he would resist. For *self-preservation* was still his law. Indeed the lightest rap, and he would have sprung into action. No words that Freddie could have found would have been insinuating enough to prevent an outburst. And Abershaw considered this expressive back with a broader grin than usual; then he turned and glanced at the now positively immense chin of his exasperated colleague, and his eyes twinkled merrily; and back went his gaze, heavy with mischief, to the expectant rebel, doubled up dourly in his corner, and spoiling for the fight.

But there was not a moment to be lost. Even Salmon's silence was of such a quality that if it continued but a very little longer, spontaneous combustion must occur in response to it, on the part of Stamp.

Abershaw's face went solemn in a flash. He put away childish things as if by magic. At one moment there was the heavy mischief of his grin; next moment there was the big owl-like mask upon which the grinning was done, hollow and grinless.

Abershaw stepped quickly over to Freddie's side, and muttered for a moment in his ear. Freddie did not answer but thrust out his bogus jaw. His eyes flashed, to show the stuff he was made of – the fiery business stuff. Abershaw knew as well as he did what sort of sum was at stake – and how he must feel about it, and how he must be able to give any animal defending its young points in ferocity. One of *his* eyes flashed too, and the effect was far more sinister than anything Freddie could compass. But time was short. He muttered rapidly once more to his mettlesome colleague.

Wohl looked up for a moment from his palette. Not a word of this colloquy could be overheard by any one – *except* Wohl; who, of course, read lip-language with perfect ease, and who looked down again with the strangled flash of a pale smile of secretive appreciation.

Stamp moved. The workshop was shocked with the impatient revolution of a heavy body, ominously flung over from the left haunch to the right haunch, and the guttural rasping of the suddenly shifted legs of a stool. Abershaw felt that he had not

263

been a second too soon. He now stood back, without further parley.

'Well, Freddie, we had better go at once – if you can bear to drag yourself away from Vic's masterpiece!' he shouted, with overpowering roguish vivacity, holding down and paralysing opposition from whatever quarter.

Freddie wheeled round, and without looking to left or right, went towards the door, followed by his big hypnotic pal, wreathed in grins (who had now visibly taken command) and by whom he was being removed from the danger zone in the most masterly manner.

'We shall be back shortly – we shan't be long!' Abershaw announced gaily, as they were passing out of the door, and after he had seen Freddie safely through it. Then, half of a grinning head only inside, he beckoned to Tristy with a big magnetic finger.

Tristy got up, limp but obedient, and put down his palette and brushes carefully upon a chair.

'Me?' he asked.

'Yes!' Abershaw cooed roguishly. 'Yes, *you*!'

Tristy went towards the door with an undergraduate smirk upon his face that seemed to say: 'How odd that you should want *me*! Am I dreaming? What mystery is this? Have I done something wrong? Am I to be rusticated?' But of course *he* knew he had done nothing wrong. All of his demeanour, at all times, unconsciously advertised the fact that he was confident of being far above any suspicion of wrongdoing, as that would be interpreted by those with whom he consorted.

Five minutes elapsed, Stamp and the indefatigable Isaac, one as uncommunicative as the other, between them contrived to promote an atmosphere of the utmost gloom, the London fog dankly collaborating. Then Tristy returned: and it cannot be said that that brightened things up. On the contrary. If, on the principle of *to fade out*, you could say *to fade in*, then that would describe tolerably well Tristy's manner of introducing himself into a room, where other people were present, and sinking among them with the opposite of a resounding splash. Had he taken a leaf out of Salmon and Abershaw's book, and attended to his entrances, his two colleagues would now have

264

felt themselves taken by storm: whereas Stamp, at least, did not notice, for a moment, that he was once more present – so much had he come in like a gentle draught under the door!

If Tristy's entrance was silent and self-effacing, his expression too was accentless and non-committal. But it was noticed by Stamp that Mr Phipps had lost his undergraduate smile, and he gathered that it was not his intention to volunteer any statement regarding the nature of the business upon which he had been called out. Also, to Stamp's surprise, he did not return to his easel. He strolled over instead to Stamp's self-portrait, at which he started to gaze, still without uttering a word. They were a silent lot in the studio, at the best of times. They now had the air of having definitely been struck dumb. The sleek and almost noiseless manufacture of Marie Laurencins was the only thing that impinged, however stealthily, upon the deathly silence of the place.

Stamp rose sluggishly from his careened position, where he had been slumped half bottom-up, and went over to where Tristy sat.

'What did those two birds want you for?' he asked straight out.

'Oh, nothing. It was about a brooch for Abershaw's wife – Elizabeth.'

Stamp snuffled sceptically – for why go into hiding to discuss a brooch? There was an interval, during which Tristy continued to contemplate the picture. Then he spoke – and what he said struck most disagreeably upon the ear of the expectant Stamp.

'Is it really finished, Vic, do you think?' he asked. He was the good little schoolboy, saying his lesson. But it seemed to be an effort, and this fact he scarcely cared to disguise.

'What do you mean?' said Stamp.

'Is that as far as you propose to take it, I meant.'

'Yes, that's finished. How much further do you expect me to take it?' Stamp inquired, with muffled indignation.

'I don't know. I suppose it's really a question of how far you suppose Van Gogh would have taken it, isn't it?' Tristy answered him, in a tired voice.

'What's your opinion, Tristy? Have I left off before Van Gogh would?'

Tristy hesitated. *Esprit de corps* and friendship were at war within him, but the *corps* won the day, and he said:

'It could, I think, with advantage, Vic – what do you think? – be worked on perhaps a little more. I don't know. It's difficult to say. How do you feel about it, Vic?'

'How do I feel about it? I feel that it has been worked on quite enough.'

'You do?'

'That's why I told Freddie the thing was *finished*. For me, it is finished. It's finished and done with.'

Tristy was silent. He went on looking at it (as if he had been sent there to mount guard over it and he could not evade his trust), blinking and convulsively wringing his hands.

'Did those two lousy business tykes call you out, Tristy, to get you to ask me to go on working on my picture?' Stamp asked him with disgust. 'Was that the game?'

'No, I do really feel about it that you might improve it if you worked on it for another day or two. Don't you?'

'No, I don't,' said Stamp, in a little less cordial tone. 'And what's more I'm certain Freddie asked you to say what he funked saying himself. He wanted to say that himself in here. I could see that well enough. He hadn't the nerve. I wish he had. There was a thing or two I wanted to say as well! And I'd have said it good and hot!'

Tristy did not answer. He remained gazing down upon the ground, embarrassed.

'Not that I think the thing is a prize-fake or anything of that sort,' Stamp said. 'But I'll soon put old Freddie's mind at rest. He shan't spend sleepless nights on my account.'

He caught up the picture, lifting it off the easel.

'What are you going to do?' Tristy inquired in alarm.

'Put my foot through it!' Stamp laughed. 'That will settle it, won't it? No more need for palaver!'

And throwing the picture down against the wall, he trod into the centre of it, putting all his weight upon his foot, which tore through the canvas, the ragged edges of the gap gripping him about the calf. He shook the thing off his leg, and, as it lay on the floor now, trod his heel down into an undamaged corner.

'That's a pity. Why did you do that?' was all that Tristy said. He sat twirling his thinking-lock, and staring at the mutilated picture.

'Because this is a lousy job, that's why, and that just about expresses my feelings about it. I thought I'd give my feelings a break too. They've earned it.' And Stamp planted his heel upon Van Gogh's 'intelligent' eye, and ground it round and round with gusto, and then indolently, here and there, applied the sharp edges of the shoeleather to the bumpy pigment where the work was still intact, and went on defacing it intermittently while they talked.

'So ends my career as a faker!' he laughed.

'I'm sorry,' Tristy said.

'I've had a square bellyful of old Freddie lately, anyway. I couldn't have carried on with him nosing round the whole time and asking why one didn't do that and why one didn't do this.'

'Did he make himself a nuisance?'

'Oh, I don't know. Yes, he did! He couldn't help it, I suppose. That's what he's like – he can't help it.'

'Freddie is a bundle of nerves sometimes,' Tristy agreed. 'It's his asthma.'

'Yes, it's his asthma! Call it asthma. I'd rather do anything else, anyway. To sit here doing my stuff, day in, day out, under a blasted dealer's eye, is more than I can stomach. I'm through! The *gentleman* dealer too! God – these high-hatting money-spinners! That's what gets me down most, about these nasty birds! They are sent by their Mitropan pappas, with their names changed, to Oxford or Cambridge to be polished up – to learn how to cheat people better! To get themselves a nasty little sham polish on their lowbred hides, to trick with, in shady trade! And that they get away with it shows the world's an outsize sucker, that deserves all it gets and more!'

Tristy bowed his head before the storm, as it were, in mournful assent to the co-existence of modes of feeling so widely at variance with his own, with which it was impossible for him to sympathize – since to him Freddie was a harmless fellow and in fact, yes, rather nice. But this undeniably was Stamp's manner of experiencing life, and he could do nothing about it.

They walked back towards Tristy's picture. Isaac Wohl looked up and smiled.

'I thought you'd do that!' Isaac said suddenly.

'Why did you, Isaac?' Stamp asked genially.

'I don't know. I suppose I must be psychic!' he spluttered, in a guttural chuckle, choking with mirth over the word 'psychic.'

Stamp laughed easily (for he was pleased with himself, if nobody else was) at the facetiousness of this little spectacled East-ender.

'Well, I shouldn't have done it,' he said, 'if that guy hadn't set Trist on to nag me about it!'

'Oh!' exclaimed Tristy faintly reproachful.

'That was the last straw,' Stamp assured his Jewish colleague. 'Well, there's nothing more for me to do here. I'm out of the cast now. Good luck!'

'Good luck!' said Wohl.

'Will you be at the pub at five-thirty, Trist? That's fine! Margot will be along. Look, Trist, can you loan me ten shillings?'

Tristy pulled a bundle of tattered documents out of his breast pocket, and searched among them. Then he handed Stamp a ten-shilling note.

As Tristy was in the act of effecting this exchange – Stamp's hand and his both had hold of the note still. Tristy had not quite parted with it, and Stamp had not quite taken possession – the door flew open. Abershaw, followed by Salmon, had returned. The former beamed darkly as he observed the passage of the note, and subsequent disappearance of same into the Australian's pocket.

'Here we are again,' he croaked, as he stalked in. 'We've turned up like a couple of bad pennies.'

'Well, I'll beat it!' said Stamp to Tristy.

'Ah ha!' sang out Abershaw, in arresting accents, as he caught sight of the wreck of the self-portrait. 'Well, well, well!'

He beamed yet more darkly – indeed it was a very overclouded effulgence – from his protégé's latest handiwork back to his protégé.

'What on earth have you been doing, Vic?' Freddie burst out, in thrilling complaint. 'What is this, may we ask?'

'I'm sorry, Freddie! Tristy sort of hinted – no, he didn't, I guessed it – that you were grumbling about my work, so I kicked a hole in it! I thought that would cut a long, long story short! I'm sorry.'

'You shouldn't have done that!' said Abershaw, expressionless, significantly omitting to grin. 'That was somewhat hasty, Mr Stamp!'

'All right, Abb. I'm sorry I didn't stop to consider your feelings, Abb.'

'What you should have stopped to consider,' Abershaw corrected him, a threatening eye playing about him a little coldly, like comic black lightning, 'what you should have stopped to consider was your *pocket*, I should have thought! But if in that direction everything is as it should be, then of course –!'

'How about *my* pocket?' broke in, now an apoplectic turkey-red, the outraged Freddie. 'I'm ten pounds out of pocket. I don't mind. Still, it *is* ten pounds. I do think it's a little casual, under the circumstances, to just go and put your foot through a canvas that after all doesn't belong to you, and then march off – as pleased as Punch, apparently!'

And he stared indignantly at Stamp's good-natured face.

'I can't help being pleased.' Stamp smiled, and continued to smile to testify to his pleasure.

'Yes, I know! It's all very well.' The false bottom to Salmon's face almost became *real*.

'Look, Freddie, old man – sue me for ten pounds!' Stamp suggested pleasantly, as he started to swagger away towards the door.

'Thank you! All the same, these gangster methods won't exactly encourage people to help you, if you think they will. You'll do it once too often, let me tell you!'

Stamp stopped to listen, frowning and smiling at once – patronizingly ready to listen, yes, yet unable to pretend that he could take anything seriously that might be said by his aggrieved employer.

269

'Cut it out, Freddie!' he replied good-temperedly. 'As a philanthropist, old man, I don't somehow see you. P'raps I haven't enough imagination.'

'I'm glad you don't!' in a wounded bellow Freddie retorted. 'That I am bound to say is *one* satisfaction! Please stop thinking of me as that, if you *do* feel tempted to do so by any chance – to avoid disappointments, you know!'

'Don't worry, Freddie! Each can pay for his own drinks when we meet!'

But it was Abershaw who returned the ball on this occasion.

'I couldn't help noticing, Vic,' he answered, in an icily-crashing delivery, 'when I came in just now, that you were occupied in providing yourself with the necessary capital to that end!'

This was so palpably below the belt that Tristy looked a little pained.

'If I ever drink with *you*, Abb,' Stamp called back, as bland as ever, 'it will always be *on you*, I'm afraid – as in the past, Abb. As in the past! There *are* some people who have to *pay one* to drink with them! You must know that by this time.'

Nodding to the company, Stamp left the workshop, passing through the door at a brisk swagger, his hat at a bushranging angle.

This particular underworld of art – this particular false-bottom to the dream of Beauty – having rid itself of this discordant particle, settled down to unruffle itself and get down to business as usual.

Gravely grinning – weighing upon his heavy lips, as if in a subtle scale, the most portentous mirth yet, Abershaw, looking wryly at the self-portrait upon the floor of the workshop (savaged, while his back was turned, by his intractable pet), stood for a few seconds in silence.

'Well, that's that!' he said, summing up the situation with precision; and all felt, if they did not define it, that a violent purge had been effected, and something had been cast forth that was hopelessly incompatible – and that, after all, if it had not been today it would have been tomorrow. 'I have a great affection for Victor. But I have never pretended that he was not one of the most tiresome young men of my acquaintance.'

'Your sentiments do you great credit,' Freddie told him, 'great credit. But I must say that I – perhaps not unnaturally – fell less warmly towards him than you do.'

'I can understand that,' Abb assented, stroking his chin as if it needed a shave.

'I have *never* been attracted by him, I'm afraid,' said Fred. 'I have been quite impervious to his charms from the first. So for me your Victor (a most appropriate name!) is just a tiresome brute. "By their works ye shall know them." There is his!' Freddie indicated with his finger what first had been the work of Stamp's hand and had ended by becoming the work of Stamp's foot. *Victor Stamp – his mark!*

They all looked at the badly battered oil painting upon the floor. No one left in the workshop after Stamp had withdrawn would have been capable of such a piece of work as that – such a piece of footwork in contradistinction to handiwork. And all gazed upon this damning evidence of a lawless disregard for others – for the human concert – with differing expressions of disapprobation. Tristy was just *triste*, moodily inert. Abershaw adapted his sardonic façade to express a negation even of amusement. Isaac Wohl peered intently at the debris, as if it might be expected to burst into poisonous flower. Freddie's baldish temples and forehead were a uniform stormy red.

The stupid side of creation had taken itself off. It had left behind it the sort of unintelligent mess that was to be expected of it. As if any fool could not put his foot through a piece of canvas! Oh dunce, where is thy sting? Oh fool, thy victory? The dog cannot be prevented from messing on the sidewalk, nor such as Stamp from dirtying in any place where a big-hearted benefactor should ill-advisedly invite him to come and spend his time with profit to himself, instead of just loafing round or cadging bitter beer in public houses.

'And when one considers that that fool hasn't two pennies to tinkle together in his trouser-pocket and hadn't had a square meal for a twelvemonth when I offered him this job!' Freddie bayed. 'What's he going to do now?'

He looked at Tristy. Tristy shrugged his shoulders and turned away.

'I like Stamp – I can't help it!' Abershaw with resounding sturdiness announced. 'I'm sorry for the beggar. I don't know why. I couldn't tell you *why* if you asked me. But there it is.'

As this was said for the benefit of Tristy, he looked pugnaciously at Isaac Wohl, who shrank a little in his place.

'I am rather sorry for Margot,' said Tristy. 'She seems to mind so much being hard-up. I'm sure Victor doesn't – except for Margot's sake.'

'I'm with you there – I'm damned sorry for his wife!' boomed out Freddie, his eyes flashing blankly, as if with artificial rage – as though with the false fireworks of some bogus passion. 'She's very much to be pitied, there's no doubt about *that*. How any woman can live with such a senseless blackguard defeats me! She must be a bit mad too. Is she mad?'

'I don't think so,' replied Tristy smiling. 'She's a very nice girl. I like her.'

'Well, I pity her if she's not mad, that's all I can say,' Freddie shouted defiantly, walking to and fro as he spoke: 'though I can't believe she's quite all there – to elect to spend her time with such an ill-natured, stupid lunatic.'

Abershaw, who had now recovered his equanimity, performed, in the background, a cross between a chortle and a yodel.

'I think that is a reflection upon *me*,' he remarked archly. 'For I have said that I find Vic *attractive* – although I confess I should not care to be married to him.'

'Does he treat everybody like this?' Freddie inquired abruptly of Tristy, touching the gashed self-portrait with the polished toecap of his Phiteezi.

Tristy found it necessary to consider this question for a moment.

'Victor is very obstinate,' he said.

'Obstinate you call it!'

'Well,' Tristy smiled, at the passionate Freddie: 'his is the religion of will.'

'That's too deep for me,' Freddie Lowbrow sniffed, disdainful.

'Is it?' Tristy tossed his head, laughing. 'Well then, how shall we express it? His attitude towards the world is what, if

272

he were a Great Power, would be called typically that of the *Have-not* – I use the current jargon of the Press.'

'Yes, I understand. The *Haves* and *Have-nots* – my paper tells me about *them* – that *is* more within reach of my understanding.'

'Victor, I think, suffers from an inferiority-complex.'

'I must say I haven't noticed it!' burst out Freddie.

'Oh, yes. Victor is very like Germany!' Tristy smiled at himself at his simile. Victor as *Germany* appeared to him a particularly good joke – both against Victor and against Germany.

'He is a brute, and the Germans are brutes!' Freddie agreed.

'Can a man be like a country?' inquired Abershaw.

'I wonder what I'm like?' asked Wohl.

'Brave little Belgium!' said Abershaw.

But Tristy was somewhat pleased with his simile for Victor. He could not have his exposition curtailed.

'Victor really *is* like the Third Reich!' he repeated. 'He is very nationalist. His nation is Victor! And he suffers from a permanent sense of injury. He really does believe that *you* are very unjust!'

The three 'Allies' present scowled at Tristy, whose face confessed to his childish pleasure at having the formula for Victor Stamp.

'I shouldn't like to be a Jew – *inside Victor*,' Isaac Wohl remarked with conviction, smiling at the inventor of the formula for Victor.

'If Victor were a Great Power, as you expressed it,' said Abershaw, 'that would be all very well. But he isn't.'

'He's a small and barren island the size of a pocket handkerchief, with one mouldy little coconut palm!' said Freddie.

'With tortoises lumbering all over it!' Abershaw suggested. 'I see what you mean, Freddie. Not a nice place to be cast up on!'

'He *feels* like a Great Power,' Tristy assured them. 'A rather impoverished, mutilated, but extremely chauvinistic Great Power!' Tristy insisted.

'Yes, yes! Naziland. We heard you the first time,' Abershaw said.

'But he is quite convinced – he really does genuinely believe

273

it – that you are all a lot of hypocritical crooks, between whom and himself there can be no common ground of understanding. If you can see what I mean!'

'Yes, we can see what you mean!' Abershaw told him hurriedly and a little crossly. 'I must say, according to you, Mr Stamp has a pretty low opinion of us. However. What's his opinion of you? Less extreme, I hope?'

'Oh, I am too poor for him to consider *me* capable of injustice.'

'That is fortunate for you.'

'I get on very well with Victor, and like him very much,' said Tristy in conclusion; he was not taking a leaf out of Abershaw's book, but the latter, recognizing the similarity between this declaration of Tristy's and an earlier one of his own, perforce refrained from comment.

'Well, there's no accounting for taste,' was all Freddie Salmon troubled to say. He turned and moved towards the door in pursuit of Abershaw, who had suddenly referred to his wrist-watch, and put himself rapidly under way.

Upon the steps leading down into the street Abershaw stopped for a moment, after he had signalled to a passing taxi. 'I'm sorry you've been let down, Freddie,' he said, 'by my – protégé.'

Freddie smiled but said nothing.

'Mr Stamp, however, will come to regret his day's work,' Abershaw said, as if as an afterthought. 'I think I can find him a type of work that he will like even less in the end than what he has been doing here. We shall see. Good-bye.'

'Good-bye,' said Freddie, turning back into the house, as Abershaw went quickly over to the waiting taxicab.

Chapter 3

'WHERE is Gillian now? I forgot to ask you,' Percy Hardcaster inquired.

He lay upon a sofa, in a shabby dressing-gown, his shoulders engaged in pillows, not overclean, which shored him up behind. A peon-rug of a flaunting Mexican pattern was drawn up to his waist. Carpet slippers protruded from the rug where the sofa ended.

Tristram Phipps sat beside the sofa. Tristram's expression was almost lowering.

'She has gone to live with Jack Cruze,' he told Percy, staring hard at the wall behind the invalid.

'Ah!'

There was something scornful and perhaps offensive, to somebody or other, in this uncompromising 'ah.'

Percy Hardcaster was considerably altered. The alteration was of two sorts. As to his body, he was a fat man no longer. He was a thin man now. His cheeks were wasted: his mouth was shrouded by a heavy flaxen moustache which seemed to grow there as weeds appear in a disused garden: his eyes were unnaturally large. He wore no spectacles.

Then permanently his eyes had a look in them that decidedly had not been there before. It was a somewhat unpleasant look. At present to look Percy too squarely in the face was no longer an agreeable experience. He was well aware of this. And he went out of his way a little to compel people to do so. He would not let them off! Lest they should pretend not to notice, he insisted upon this alteration for the worse in his appearance, but especially upon this alteration in the Percy that was inside. A far *worse* Percy than before was inside – and he liked being noticed, about that there was no question.

At the present moment Percy, in fact, appeared to be engaged in just this occupation. He seemed to be coercing his visitor to *look him in the face*, before going any further. His eyes, with a new rudeness, addressed themselves to the forcible seeking out and pinning down of the far politer eyes of Gillian's ex-husband. But the rudeness was not so altogether one-sided – though Tristy's rudeness was of another order, and at least not deliberate.

But when Tristy spoke again he certainly sounded – if sound went for anything, and if the unceremonious wording of his remarks were any indication of his attitude – deliberately rude. If Percy Hardcaster had changed, it would have seemed that the world's attitude (of which Tristy was, as a rule, so faithful a reflection) had changed as well.

'So they beat you up, did they, and then dumped you down in a hospital?' This from Tristy – and to Percy Hardcaster! Times had changed, one would have said! But it was not quite like that either. Tristy was questioning him almost fiercely, coming, as he had, out of his abstraction in a passionate rush of indignant discovery. He had forgotten Percy, in his indignation about Percy. He was looking his wife's victim full and fairly in the face of his own accord.

So for a moment they both stared each other out of countenance; or they would have done so, had they not been changed men. He who was the more changed of the two glared; he who was the less just stared. But both, however, were changed men.

'They have brought you to this,' said Tristy, 'the stupid brutes – one as much brute as the other!'

'They have brought me to this,' Percy echoed him ironically – 'as you put it!'

'Why, you are a different person! What for? What was it for?'

Percy shrugged his shoulders.

'For nothing.'

Serafín himself could not have said *nothing* with more feeling for the false bottom underlying the spectacle of this universe, and making a derision of the top – for the nothingness at the heart of the most plausible and pretentious of affirmatives, either as man or as thing. And that his 'nothing' meant nothing, just that, not more and not less, but a calm and considered negation, caused Tristy to stop abruptly and look away.

'Of course,' he said, after an interval, 'I was in ignorance of all this until yesterday. I was staggered when I heard the true story of your illness. I could not believe my ears!'

'Excuse me! Why not? What was there incredible in what you heard?' Percy asked him this question in so aggressive a tone that Tristy was again pulled up and compelled to direct his mind outside its personal orbit, and to recognize the existence of an alien standpoint, incarnated in this wrecked man upon the lodging-house sofa.

'What was there incredible?' he asked with a frown. 'It was, of course, because I would not have believed it possible – oh,

I don't know – I still can scarcely credit it, although you tell me it is true.'

With an expression of bitter contempt on his face, and as if his lips had been called upon to react to some pungent taste, Percy lifted a hand to arrest him.

'Listen!' he said. 'The sooner you leave off dividing up events in your mind into those which are *possible* and those which are *impossible*, the sooner you will be in a position to understand a few of the capital facts of life. You are, if you will forgive me for saying so, like some pampered young schoolmiss who averts her head when brought into contact with certain violent matters, which she regards as "unpleasant" or "too horrible to be true," and refuses to admit their existence.'

He paused, a little short of breath.

'There was *nothing* at all out of the way,' he continued violently to lecture his visitor, 'in what happened to me in your flat. You understand me? There was nothing in it that one would not have expected, or that was *exceptional*, or not in accordance with the everyday pattern of events. You are talking nonsense when you suggest that there was! It was a perfectly rational occurrence. If you go into a flat where a woman lives who takes on men and who has a sort of bully hanging round her, to have a little talk and perhaps something more, you must expect to be kicked in the mouth. Nine times out of ten you are not. But that proves nothing.'

His voice had grown angry as he proceeded with his exordium. His rebuke was administered with a heavy arrogance, lying back in his pillows, only his head moving. As he ended he continued to gaze haughtily at his visitor.

'I am sorry,' Tristy said. 'But, although my view of Gillian has changed a great deal of late, I still am unable to regard her behaviour as normal.'

'It was perfectly normal. It was so normal I don't know what we're talking about it for.'

'I cannot – whatever you may say – not be horrified!'

Percy shrugged his shoulders.

'Horrified! If that gives you any pleasure you must go on feeling that. I'm only telling you that it is silly.'

'No, I am *horrified*. When I consider what, I understand, took place in my flat, I am disgusted, and *horrified*. I can't help it.'

Percy looked at him in silence, at long range. A really ugly smile settled upon his lip, and was quite at home there, it was but too clear.

'Well, what *did* happen in your flat?' he asked. 'What was this extraordinary thing that happened there? Let's have it out!'

Tristy indulged in a gesture which seemed to indicate his great distaste for what happened in the flat, and his desire not to return to the subject.

'No, but that is important,' insisted Percy. 'I was sweet on your wife. She took me for the usual sort of fancy Communist, and she was sweet on me. Like calling to like! But in your flat, on the last occasion I called there, when I went to make love to her, I disillusioned feu Mrs Phipps, and told her what I thought of her sort of Communism. As a matter of fact I gave her a damn good lesson in the gentle art of Communism – one that she'll never forget as long as she lives! Communism, you understand, from the working-class angle – not the Communism of the Chelsea party, or of the young Foreign Office or Air Ministry clerk. Not *Intourist* Communism. The Communism of the *Barrikadenfodder*!'

A little of Tristy's old self returned: and almost with the old deference, he put forth a polite plea.

'May I hear what you said?' he asked.

Directing a very quizzical glance at his young visitor of a Communist recruit – the expert eye travelling from the boastful party-badge down to the attenuated hands, which were foregathering in anguished jiu-jitsu – Percy shook his head.

'No. Better not! It was rather a stiff lesson. It was meat for men, what I handed out to her! You might think the worse of me, just as your wife did. I might lose caste with you. And I don't want to do that!'

Tristy blinked. He was being pushed back rather brutally into his customary self. He had not changed enough. This was after all a frontfighter he had in front of him, and he 'felt small', in the words of the poet.

278

'Well, I gave her a free lesson in Communism,' Percy continued. 'A good stiff lesson. And the lady didn't like it. She
reminded me I was only a boilermaker. But most people don't
like Communism when it's naked, with the frills off.'

He was speaking with great fluency, with the ferocious restraint he had employed in administering the fateful lesson
which was the subject of his present discourse.

'Your ex-wife,' he went on, 'is an offensive little snob when
she's worked up and off her guard and we had words. We had
words! I was still too sick a man to be of much use as a lover,
and anyway these little intellectuals put me off somehow. I told
her I'd had enough kiss-stuff, and that, on top of my exposure
of her Communism pose, put her in a nasty little rage. I went
to pick up my hat and to take myself off and at that juncture
her present soul-mate strutted in. She set him on me, as you
set on a dog. As I was helpless he had no difficulty in pushing
me over and jumping on me. Seeing I was in a bad way, after
I'd been kicked about, on the floor, they taxied me round to
the nearest hospital and left me there to stew in my own juice.
And I stewed in it. In all that I fail to see anything abnormal.
One shouldn't talk so much, that's the fact of the matter, as I
was in the habit of doing. One should keep a civil tongue in
one's head too, when one is conversing with members of the
class in power, whether calling themselves Communists or
possessed of some other fad, and whether penniless or bloated
with dividends. And one shouldn't kiss what one can't respect,
except in a brothel – that is a golden rule I think. In Spain,
where they have brothels, they understand that. We, not having
brothels, get into erotic difficulties all the time. I got into a bad
mess, in this case. That was my luck. The whole transaction
was on the same footing exactly as a brothel row, in fact –
your ex-wife being a tart without a ticket, that is her status,
who drivels about Communism and puts a poor devil off his
stroke. I got kicked by the bully kept on the premises – and
serve me right, for going to such a place, while I was still on
crutches. What more is there to say? Nothing. As cause and
effect the whole episode is perfectly logical. You take up what
I consider a rather offensive and unreal attitude about the whole
business. Anyone would think, to hear you talk, that I had

279

been assaulted and robbed by the sidesmen in a church, while I was at my devotions!'

Tristy's face had taken on the bleak look which was his protective mask when confronted with a dilemma, or when first finding himself between its horns. As he found himself being tossed by Percy, he withdrew into his shell — if that figure of speech does not too violently conjure up a crustacean strayed into a *corrida*. Gradually he had come to understand that he, in his turn, and in his capacity of husband of Gillian, was being given a lesson in Communism, and not the sort he liked. And he had not come here for that. But since it had been sprung on him and was in full blast, he submitted with an excellent grace. He even perhaps displayed too much gracefulness.

He had heard from one quarter and another that there had been some trouble with Percy. A good Partyman had told him that Hardcaster had become rather cantankerous of late. He had not gathered what it was all about, but his informant had implied that Percy might leave the Party. He and Communism might part company. He had distinctly got the impression that they were a little disappointed in Percy; or rather that they did not rate him quite so highly as before. At all events (for yet another Partyman had shown incredulity at the idea of his leaving the Party) he had thought that he had detected the fact that Percy had lost caste as a militant. And when Percy himself had just now referred to his 'losing caste' with him, Tristy, these matters had recurred to his mind.

But Tristy saw that what was at work in Percy Hardcaster's mind just now, and which prompted him to adopt this attitude, so foreign to a fraternal Partyman, was some purely personal reaction of Percy's where his accident (if Jack and Jill and their misdeeds could be catalogued under accident) was concerned. This broken man was full of resentment, it seemed. This was perhaps natural, when one came to think of it; though it had not occurred to Tristy that he would mind so much. And it was fairly evident that he identified him, the inoffensive Tristy, in some way with what had happened to him, and did not dissociate him from Gillian and her 'bully' as completely as he would have expected. He sighed: for this was rather a petty point of view to encounter in the breast of an outstanding Partyman. Perhaps it was *because* he was a militant, however. He was not a thinker – perhaps that was it; and suffered from the limitations proper to all men of action.

'Have you been very ill?' he asked him softly and soothingly.

'Yes, very ill!' savagely the now glaring Percy replied.

'You have had a serious illness,' Tristy said, as if to himself. 'What sort of illness was it? Was it a haemorrhage?'

'What *sort* of illness! If you want to know its scientific name, it was what is called osteomyelitis of the stump.' Percy Hardcaster delivered himself with a fluent unction of the Latin name, contrived by medical science for his misfortune.

'What is that?' asked Tristy mildly.

'Abscess of the bone! Of the bone of the stump.' Percy tapped the rug, beneath which the stump lay. 'If you get badly kicked there shortly after you have had your leg amputated that is what you are liable to get. I got it. And I got it pretty badly.'

'So it seems. I am sorry, Hardcaster,' said Tristy, with sympathy. 'You must have gone through it. And all for *nothing* – as you have expressed it.'

Percy looked at him sharply. But, seeing nothing offensive in his expression, he shrugged his shoulders with contempt.

'All for nothing, as you say,' he consented to make answer. 'All for love!'

There was a loud knocking: Percy called out roughly, 'Come in!' Sean O'Hara and Abershaw entered – in that order.

'Ah, Mr Hardcaster!' O'Hara exclaimed. 'How's the old stumpy? Got your wooden leg fitted yet, old man?'

'No. Have you?' Percy rejoined, without modifying either his position or expression, greeting the newcomers with an anything but friendly eye.

'Ah ah – that is good!' laughed O'Hara, fixing his brilliant eyes upon the wasted features of the man he had come to visit. 'Not yet. Not until I have "my accident," as they say in *Back to Methuselah*. We are not all going to stump about on wooden legs, just because *you* are, old man! Did you think we were?'

Both he and Abershaw unceremoniously laid hold of chairs and sat themselves beside Tristy, facing the sofa.

'How are you, in fact?' asked Abershaw, with grave politeness. 'You will be getting about again soon now, I expect? You have had a long spell of illness. You must be getting pretty sick of it!'

'Not much more sick than I was of health,' said Percy.

'No, you did enjoy the most depressing of rude health, didn't you?' O'Hara agreed heartily.

'Still you have had a packet of it,' Abershaw remarked.

'Yes, he's had a spot of bother all right, hasn't he?' O'Hara eagerly seconded this, turning to Abershaw, who nodded his head gravely.

'He has,' said he. 'And I'm very glad to see him looking so fit.'

'Yes, he does look well. You feel well, do you?' O'Hara asked, bending forward, grinning with his eyes alone.

'I am convalescent,' Percy answered him, surveying the couple with undisguised aversion.

Abershaw now addressed himself to Tristy.

'I have just seen your friend, Victor Stamp,' he said.

'Oh, how is he? I haven't seen Victor for a month or two. I live so far away from him now.'

'He seems very well. A little thin.'

'Did you see Margot?' Tristy asked.

'Yes. Unfortunately.'

'Why unfortunately?' Tristy smiled.

'I don't know. I just feel that it's a pity Victor should have her on his back. It's as much as he can do to look after himself.'

'Margot is not very expensive, I should have said.'

Abershaw drew a long, gravely judicious breath.

'Two mouths are always more difficult to feed than one,' he said. 'And then she tries to stop him from doing anything to make money. It's a curious point of view. You'd think she'd be glad.'

'But *does* she do that?' Tristy objected.

282

'She always *seems* to,' Abershaw returned gruffly. 'She's one of those women who would like to see her husband selling matches in the street, to be able to show what a good wife she is. I am positive that given half a chance she would pop his head in the gas-oven, and put her own in after it.'

O'Hara laughed with relish.

'No, I am serious. The woman welcomes misfortune – she bares her breast and invites it. She'll be the death of the poor chap yet! That's how it strikes me, anyway.'

'Who is this?' asked Percy.

'We're talking about Victor Stamp, and Mrs Stamp,' Abershaw told him.

'That young Australian painter?'

'Yes. We were saying what a very tiresome woman Mrs Stamp is.'

'Yes, she's all that,' O'Hara endorsed him.

'You seem to have a vendetta with Mrs Stamp,' said Percy.

'No, I have no personal feelings one way or the other. I just feel she stands in the way of Stamp doing any lucrative work, that is all. I suppose she thinks he's a genius!'

Sean O'Hara took out a large silver cigarette-case.

'Do you mind if I smoke, old man?' he asked the invalid. 'Does it matter?'

Percy shook his head.

'I smoke myself,' he said.

'I don't think you're right about Margot,' Tristy began.

'No?' said Abershaw.

'She's a thoroughly good sort, is Margot. I happen to know that, if it hadn't been for her, before now Victor would have gone hungry. Victor of course is hopeless about money.'

'You may be right.' Abershaw was very dubious indeed. 'You may be right. But it always seems to me a tragedy when a woman has too high an opinion of her husband. It's worse than the other way round. Far worse. It is a tradition that the "genius" should starve in a garret, and such a woman as Margot encourages the garret situation.'

'I've never noticed it,' Tristy said.

'Oh yes. Little Margot would like to immolate herself beside the great "genius" in the domestic gas-oven. You take my word for it.'

'What's she been doing to you?' asked Percy, breaking into the conversation again; but, without waiting for a reply, returning to converse with O'Hara.

'To me? Nothing. It's what she's doing to Stamp I was talking about. It was she put him up to walking out on Freddie Salmon six months ago.'

'Not a bit of it! She thought a great genius oughtn't to fake pictures for a living. So she influenced him against the job, with the result that he threw it up, and has suffered for it ever since. They're down to their last sixpence now. It's all her doing.'

'Are they really so hard-up?' Tristy gave an anxious frown. 'I must go and see them.'

'Yes, do. And try and persuade that wretched woman to let her husband do something that will, anyway, keep the pot boiling for a bit. I have just made him an offer of a job.'

'I'm glad of that,' Tristy said. 'What did he say to it?'

'He rather likes the idea, I think. He'll do it – that is if *she* doesn't come along and prevent him.'

'But why should she?' Tristy asked. 'What sort of job is it, Abb?' he added a little doubtfully, looking over, not with suspicion, certainly, but with a preoccupied gaze of respectful speculation, at the face of the worthy Abershaw – the peculiar nature of whose activities was apparent even to the dreamy Tristy.

'What sort of a job is it?' Abershaw turned to O'Hara, who had been talking with animation to the unresponsive Percy. 'How should I describe it, Sean?'

'Describe what?' O'Hara inquired.

'I've been telling Tristy here about the proposition I was making to Victor Stamp.'

'I have been starting to tell Percy Hardcaster about it, too,' O'Hara replied. 'Only in outline, of course.'

'And what does he say to it?'

'Well, I hadn't arrived at the point yet.'

'I think I see the point!' said Percy, with his grimmest smile sardonically etched upon his sunken face.

284

'Oh, do you? I hoped you would!' exclaimed O'Hara.

'And what is your reaction – if, in fact, you have guessed our intention?' Abershaw asked him, with grave affability.

'You want me to go to the Spanish frontier and supervise the smuggling operations you have in mind. Is that it?'

'That indeed is it – if we could persuade you to do so,' Abershaw said. 'We know that it is an affair that would not adequately engage your energies. It is, as it were, a holiday job. But, as it happens, you are in need of a holiday. You would be going away soon to pick up after your illness in any case, I imagine. So why not go to the Pyrenees while you are about it, gratis, as it were, and occupy yourself in a congenial way, in the fine mountain air, at this attractive season of the year?'

'Just to keep your hand in!' cried O'Hara. 'Have a busman's holiday, old boy!'

'This would be big-scale smuggling,' Abershaw took up the tale again. 'It is machine-guns, not mere pistols. It will not be an operation that any fool could handle. It would be child's play for you; but a less able man might bungle it badly.'

'And, especially, it must be someone conversant with conditions in Spain, and who knows the lingo,' O'Hara in his turn pointed out.

'You are the man, Hardcaster, that we want. You are our man – if we can get you to take it on. If it fits in with your plans.'

They both had been watching Percy's face while, by turns, unfolding their scheme to him; and they were compelled to recognize that the face before them was indicative of nothing but derision; it was a stormy barometer they had before them, it was set hard at 'Foul.'

'Where, might I ask,' Percy inquired of them, 'does young Stamp come into this picture?'

'Well,' said Abershaw, 'that is a very natural question. Where indeed does he come in? I admit that my personal interest in Stamp has resulted in my rather pitchforking him into it.'

'What do you propose should be his function?' Percy asked.

Abershaw scratched his head, to convey the perplexing problem involved in devising any use whatever for Stamp.

'Well, he could, up to a point, and in a minor way, make himself useful. You could find *some* use for him, I suppose. He might just manage to earn his keep. What do you think?'

'What are his qualifications?'

'None!' Abershaw agreed with great finality. 'Absolutely none. But he is used to roughing it. There might be some rough work you could find for him, once you go there.'

'He might carry heavy things about,' O'Hara put it to Percy. 'It's always useful to have a strong man on the spot.'

'You would be sending him out, I gather, then, as a sort of pack-animal,' Percy looked at them inquiringly. 'A beast of burden if I have understood you. What is your idea – that he should be the smuggler proper, heave a case of contraband arms up on to his muscular shoulders and carry it over the passes into Spain? Or do you mean he should be the handy man about the base, who would unload the goods as they arrive?'

'You put it humorously,' said Abershaw drily, rising and walking over to the mantelpiece, against which he leaned in an eighteenth-century pose – there is nothing like a mantelpiece for emphasizing the possession of the *bel air*, and Abershaw was fond of mantelpieces. 'I like Victor.'

'You like him quite a lot – more than I do, I confess,' O'Hara joined in.

'I don't believe Victor's much of a painter. I'm sorry for the beggar. He can't be allowed to go on starving here! We must try and do something for him. He could carry out your orders and he would like the work, I believe, once he was out there. He would be in his element in the mountains. He's an out-of-door man!'

'Besides,' O'Hara said, 'if he loafed round the hotel and did a spot of sketching that would serve as an alibi. It would distract attention. You might do a little sketching your-self!'

'Thanks,' said Percy.

Tristy laughed, fell silent, and became very grave again.

'His wife would go with him,' Abershaw explained.

'What for?' Percy asked.

'Oh, I don't know,' O'Hara answered – it was his cue. 'She

could darn the socks of the expedition. Besides, she would be in the nature of a hostage. In case Stamp ratted on you.'

'Ratted on me? What do you mean by that?' Percy inquired, in polite astonishment, raising sarcastically his eyebrows, and charging his eyes with an insulting childish candour.

'I understand he is rather liable to walk off at the critical moment. If, for instance, you had had occasion to send him into Spain. You would have to supply him with funds. He might never come back.'

'I see,' Percy laughed, as unpleasantly as possible. 'I see. I would just lock up Mrs Stamp in her room until the runaway came back to fetch her.'

'You present it in a facetious light,' Abershaw intervened, with a severe urbanity, strolling over from the fireplace, and sitting down, just a little as Patience would have sat down again on her monument, should she have had occasion to leave it for a few minutes. 'But of course you see what we mean. Nothing is worked out yet. How do you feel about it? Does our proposal appeal to you? – that is the main thing. Or do you consider that we have been presumptuous in asking you at all?'

'Do you turn it down out of hand? We hope very much you do not do that! Or will you give it your consideration – will you?' O'Hara carried on – looking straight over Percy's head with an expression of complete indifference as to the issue, but on the other hand leaning forwards in an attitude of eager expectancy.

Percy heaved up his shoulders in a savage shrug, and looked at the two of them without speaking, for a moment. Abershaw turned his head away at this, as if desiring not to influence Percy's decision. O'Hara continued to stare over Percy's head with an absolute lack of concern.

'I turn down nothing,' Percy said at last. 'Why should I?'

Both Abershaw and O'Hara rose quickly to their feet, before the words were properly out of his mouth. It was as though he had been a criminal and they two detectives, who had been waiting for him to make up his mind to confess – and now the confession had come. They did not speak – they both drew back a step or two.

287

'I need a holiday,' Percy said, 'as you say.'

'Yes, there is that, isn't there?' said Abershaw.

'I should have to know the terms.'

'Of course,' O'Hara agreed. 'Of course you would.'

'May I ask you a question?' Percy was not looking at them.

'Certainly. Fire away.' It was O'Hara who answered, upon a sign from his colleague.

'Is this politics, or business?'

'Business!" O'Hara replied at once.

'There is no organization behind you?'

'None.'

'We should have to go into that rather carefully.'

'By all means,' O'Hara assented. 'Of course.'

Abershaw stepped forward, holding out his hand to Hardcaster.

'I think we have to congratulate ourselves, Hardcaster, that you have consented at least to consider our proposition. I am very glad indeed. I feel sure we shall be able to come to an agreement satisfactory to both parties. We shall meet your wishes in every way.'

'You may depend on that,' O'Hara said, in his turn holding out his hand.

It had grown rather dark in the room while they had been talking. Turning to O'Hara, Abershaw remarked:

'We ought to be getting along, Sean. It is late. Supposing we leave it this way, Hardcaster: you will think it over. And when you have decided one way or the other, we can have a further meeting, and go into the matter in greater detail?'

'In the course of the next few days,' O'Hara added. 'Will that be O.K.? The sooner the better. We want to get on with the good work,'

'Very well,' said Percy.

With the crackling of Abershaw's parting jokes, as they passed through the doorway, and the high-pitched sharp laughter of Sean O'Hara, this light-hearted couple vanished. And Tristram Phipps decamped – a little hastily perhaps – with them. They seemed to suck him out in their wake. He, too, at all events, was gone. Percy was left exhausted on the sofa, scowling into the twilight. In a few minutes he was sleeping soundly, the frown still on his face. Then, after an interval, the frown disappeared. A gratified smile flowered upon the lips of the dreaming Percy. Something had pleased him.

PART VII

HONEY-ANGEL

Chapter 1

AT five o'clock Victor Stamp and his wife had crossed the
frontier for the first time. They had walked up the hill to Puigmoro, the first Spanish town. Thus they had penetrated for a
mile and a half into Spain – into an enemy country, as it were,
seeing what they had come there to do, just out of reach of its
arbitrary, dressed-up constabulary.

But they had entered it as tourists. They had strolled in
merely to have a drink, in the cool of the evening, and then
return, in the course of an hour or two, the way they had come
– into the safety of France. Nothing more.

Margot was silent, as they ascended the hill. She was uneasy,
for none the less she did not *feel* in the least like a tourist. She
and Victor two harmless tourists! That pretence did not deceive her, and it would deceive no one else! Such was her overmastering sensation, as she stepped, gingerly, as if picking her
way upon the dusty soil (which seemed quite different to the
equally dusty soil they had just left). This under her feet was
that of a State they were busy undermining from the outside.
Might it not blow up under them, if with too confident an air
they trespassed on it? To have been treading the solid earth of
the French Republic, against which they had done nothing,
would have been a much more agreeable experience to her unwilling feet – they would have borne her forward without that
slight faintness of the limbs above them. France was quite
unfamiliar enough, she was never at ease. But its northern
edges rubbed up against England. Its lighthouses winked at the
couples on the holiday cliffs of British watering-places. And at
least they had not been arming its malcontents with Czecho-
slavakian machine-guns!

Bona-fide tourists they were, *upon this occasion*, yes. But it
was in vain that Margot attempted to take a Cookly or a Lun-

nish interest in the vaguely African flatness, the stuccoed rose and apricot, of this little Catalan city they were approaching. There was no thrill at all at being in Spain, discernible in her cowed senses – except the wrong sort of thrill, that is. Though often she had dreamed away an idle moment in front of a travel poster in an English railway station; of a minaret, a matador, a posada, and a palm.

No, all the globe-trotting vibrations in her spine were decidedly extinct. Instead there was established there a numb and convulsive alarm. And then Spain, as you entered it, was not reassuring. It was certainly 'foreign parts.' It was as alien as any two inoffensive sightseers could have wished. Even in its dust, kicked up by its mules and its donkeys, there was a pinch of something hot and harsh, which was absent from the regulation poster, of the posada and the palm. Was not this the native soil of the Inquisitor? It was: and they, who now passed themselves off as peaceable tourists, feeling as safe as houses in the sublime innocence of their hearts, had offended against it beyond forgiveness – whatever Mr Hardcaster might say, for he had seen no objection to their making this little promenade. Criminals in the argus-eyes of this cruel Jesuitical commonalty were what they were. And they were *worse*, not better, for being English!

The Union Jack had grown to be no better than a red rag to a bull to these bitter Dons, even Mr Hardcaster admitted that! For half Europe, he had said, it called down hatred on your head. To be English was no longer honourable and important.

So with growing apprehension she had trod this sullen soil. Here was nothing fast but a false and deceptive surface. Even its touristic blandishments savoured of deceit. She felt that she had engaged upon the crust of something that concealed a bottomless pit, which bristled with uniformed demons, engaged in the rehearsal of a gala Third Degree, to be followed by a slap-up autodafé, for the relaxation of Lucifer.

'Shall we turn back?' she had asked, half-way up the empty hill, though she still walked on beside Victor. There was no one in sight. This emptiness had alarmed her at first, as if it had spelt an ambush. But so far at least the road was clear.

Whereas, if they went forward, they would get farther and farther into this threatening geographical abstraction, which would of course become more and more irretrievably Spanish. And the further back they would have to walk, at every moment beset with uncertainty. Even now, a man might be in hiding behind that wall, noting their unconcerned advance with satisfaction.

'Turn back! What for?' asked Victor. 'Are you tired, Margot?'

'No, not tired, darling.' She walked on beside him steadily. 'I feel afraid,' she said.

He looked sideways at her with stolid astonishment. He was enjoying Spain. He had been squinting professionally at Puigmoro. He liked its pinks and apricots.

'Afraid?' he asked. 'What of, darling? There's nothing to feel afraid about. There are no savage dogs here. All the bulls are in the south. There's nothing I can see.'

'I suppose not,' she said. 'My nerves must be bad.'

'We have as much right to be here as anybody else, if that's what you're thinking.'

'Have we, Victor?'

'Of course we have. We're doing no harm.' He peered round at the landscape – he *was* after all a bona-fide artist, and artists did no harm to anybody, except themselves.

'Not at the moment!' Margot attempted to pop a cheerful flash into the tamest of tired smiles.

'Well?'

'After all we are not in this part of the world, Victor, for our *health*! I wish we were. How I wish we were!'

'No, but no one knows that. No one knows we're desperados.'

'I wonder!'

'Everybody back there thinks we're a bunch of Anglais come to enjoy the scenery.'

Margot sighed; it was hard that she should have to undeceive him and make him uncomfortable!

'Except old Percy,' Victor said. 'They think he's a bit queer perhaps. No one takes *me* for anything but just an artist. I'm certain of that.'

293

Margot sighed. Certainly at the hotel the pretty maids and waitresses smiled upon 'Monsieur Victor' whenever he appeared, and for them Monsieur Victor was all that a Monsieur should be; they did not look beyond the prepossessing *pensionnaire* to the hired conspirator – how could they, as mere women?

She looked up at his face. She saw nothing but easy confidence in his handsome face. To be so handsome as Victor, she reflected, was to have that sort of easy confidence. These proud Apollos had it to a man. Handsome men had to be put on their guard! They took risks that plain men would never run! They were really unteachable fellows! Oh, this unfortunate optimism of good looks – as if good looks could do anything against circumstances! She hated to have to bring Victor down to earth. Such a dangerous earth, no respecter of handsome persons. But it must be done.

'Why, Victor, did that Civil Guard at the police post just now,' she put it to him as gently as she could, wishing to let down softly all this manly beauty, without an unmannerly bump, 'why did that Civil Guard at the frontier ask you twice if your name was Stamp? I didn't like that at all. He said Stamp *twice*,' she said timidly, looking away.

'He wanted to know how to pronounce it, I expect. P'raps it means something fresh in Spanish,' he suggested, with a rugged grin – the grin of an attractive six-footer.

Margot shook her head to herself. This was *just like a* handsome man! There was your handsome man all over!

'No, but he went into the hut, Victor, with your passport, do you remember? When he came out he had a rather disagreeable smile on his face, I thought, as he handed it back to you.'

'He'd been having a little joke in the hut maybe. He had a most lousy countenance in any case. He couldn't help looking *disagreeable*.'

How, without seeming alarmist and tiresome, could she awaken him to the reality of these unsatisfactory symptoms? These police, with their capes and carbines, did not see things at all as Victor did. They took their capes and carbines seriously. Godlike antipodean beauty meant just nothing to them – they thought that all the manly beauty in the world was to be found beneath their own helmets and cloaks.

She was *positive* that the disagreeable smile had something to do with the passport, or rather with the identity of its user. Victor had been recognized at the police post. The police there knew all about them. Something had passed inside the official hut – it was *not* a joke. But where was the use of insisting upon this with Victor? He would not listen to her, he would only laugh. She must joke too, that was all about it. She must enter into the joke that was not there. She hadn't got the heart, it was no use, to put the wind up her beautiful private Apollo! – or rather to try to, for she could scarcely succeed, he was quite fearless.

So she put on, with a sinking of the heart, the invulnerability of the goddess, too. She summoned to her lips a gay and confident smile. Even, she began to *trip* a little – in her voice there was a trill.

'We mustn't come *again*, Victor,' she said, scolding, but relenting, as it were. 'But I suppose as they haven't put us under lock and key immediately they will let us have our drink this time in peace.'

And in saying it she found she came to half believe it. It would probably be all right. She was only a nervous girl!

'It looks as if they might!' he said.

'Let's step on it!' said she, with a bloodcurdling brightness. 'Is that the right expression?' She strode along, with a hiking gait. 'I am longing to see what that town is like *inside*. It looks lovely from here! It's like the Arabian Nights, isn't it?' And it did look to her like a fragment of fairyland but probably the headquarters of some evil magician.

The Plaza Cabrinetty is on an inclined plane. A person looks down it, not across it if he is sitting outside the most considerable café to be met with in Puigmoro. Margot Stamp looked down the plaza. She strained her eyes in an intent stare – a fanatical sightseer, indeed, a most determined tourist, a native might have thought. For it looked as if she were resolved that nothing should escape her. But this was not in fact on account of her greater curiosity about the people in the distance, in contrast to those near at hand. It was in order to avoid looking at the dwarf – at this terrible little figure of fun!

The dwarf had now begun to fill the plaza with the horrible sound of his sobbing and wailing, in imitation of a child. With a pocket handkerchief, in expressive pantomime, he patted his bloated eyes, with their mastiff-droop. He ogled the company from behind it. Then he burst into an ear-splitting howl.

If Margot's spine had been the string of a violin, and had this howl of his been its vibration, she could not have suffered more. But it was not only the sound. There was something worse. She had a motive for more legitimate dismay. For the fearful little creature was addressing its mock complaints *to her*. He had picked on her to be his dramatic mother.

With his spoilt-child status, enjoyed among the Spaniards by all dwarfs and midgets – but more especially achondro-plastic monsters of his sort – it was permissible for him to do this. The really true-blue stump-of-a-man, in full and flourishing health, suffering only from swelled head, in every sense of the word – with a swagger as if they owned the entire earth – that sort of citizen has the freedom of Spain. But how could Margot have guessed this? These prescriptive codes are closed books, till they are found out, to the members of other nations. She was a mere excursionist. Yet by this oddly backward public accepted as a mysterious charge, her persecutor was quite within his rights. He could impress Margot or anybody into his preposterous exhibition; none could object. Whatever his age, his status was that of a tiny tot: he was in the nature of *a public orphan*, that was it. So as a certified *desgraciado* he was free to insult or to hector, having paid the price of extreme deformity – it was his quid pro quo.

The dwarf's privilege was on the model in fact of all female privilege, which takes with it the counter-injustice to make good the handicap. Must we not be prepared to suffer at the hands of *incarnate* suffering? the Catholic spirit asks. But, as an English girl, Margot would have supposed herself, had she been in the secret, exempt. She would have thought that this hideous comic-cut should have picked on some Spanish person,

296

for preference a ponderous señora, such as might in fact have lent herself (without stretching of the imagination) to the belief that this big-headed adult brat had been the fruit of her out-size loins. But as it was, Margot was amazed and confused. All this dark and outlandish crowd were acting at cross purposes with her – with one who saw only something deformed, where *they* saw someone to whom everything must be pardoned.

Stamping up and down now as if in the crisis of an infantile incontinence, this howling little monster attempted to catch her eye.

Oh, what was she to do? She had been marked down by it for make-believe motherhood, in this impromptu pantomime, beyond the shadow of a doubt – though Victor had suspected nothing, so far, thank goodness! At all costs *he* must not be embroiled in this ghastly comedy. It was of the first importance that he should not get a hint of her wretched discomfort, for if he did so, there was no knowing what action he might not take. She knew her Victor! He would certainly go over and attack the dwarf, if he realized what was going on. Perhaps he might kill him. Victor did not know how strong he was, and a pat from him might be enough. They might find themselves in the lock-up before you could say knife (was it *knife* you were supposed to say?).

So she must pull herself together and make an effort to be natural. Margot cast about for something, to make conversation, that she might distract Victor and confirm him in the belief that all was as usual. Her eye fell upon an exotic shawl. That would do. They were in Spain. He would expect her to be on the lookout for shawls.

'Oh, look, Victor, at that lovely shawl!' she exclaimed – in a tone so preternaturally bright that she made him start and look up in deep astonishment. 'I do think that's a nice one, don't you? No, Victor. Not over there. That dark girl – where I'm looking now, darling!' she hastened to add. For he started looking in the direction of the dwarf, where, as luck would have it, there was *another* woman in an exotic shawl.

'That girl's got a better one – look, Margot,' he said, however. 'No – over there.'

And Margot was compelled to turn her eyes to just that quarter of the compass which she was most anxious to shun. She quickly turned her head away again, and the subject of the shawl was pursued no further. Victor began laughing, however, at the antics of her enemy. But that was better, after all, than if he had seized him by the throat! Far better! She even smiled wryly a little, to encourage him.

No matter how fixedly she examined some distant object – which, in any case, she could not properly see, she was so near-sighted – she could not abstract herself from her immediate surroundings. With their mischievous Spanish smiles the neighbours at the café tables turned towards them. They gloated upon her discomfort. They looked from the dwarf to Margot, and back again. It belonged to her, that was the idea, this 'little man.' She – the childless 'hermit girl' – had given birth to this joke. And very naturally, perhaps (as the smiles of the onlookers were by way of suggesting), she was ashamed of it. Ha, ha! He, he! This foreign girl repudiated her own offspring – because of its unorthodox anatomy! Consequently it cried in vain to her to be consoled. But she would take no notice – hard-hearted mamma that she was! Such was the plot of the comedy in which she had become suddenly entangled.

The more passionate the mimicry of its ear-splitting complaint, the more fixedly Margot stared straight ahead, till her eyes started to water. *Tears!* went up the guttural whisper from the Spanish crowd. The dwarf had, as it were, drawn blood.

But everyone was amused, Victor smiling with the rest. The Spanish officers, especially, who sat all day long having their shoes polished, threw coppers to the amateur mountebank.

The affair had started with the arrival of the dwarf – he was just a passer-by, like any other passer-by. But his appearance was the signal for a broadside of chaffing. The dwarf had stopped in the street before the café, in the first instance, merely in order to answer back. He had entered into a comic word-warfare with the indolent officers. He would affect to waddle off in a great huff at all the rude things they said. But then he would turn back again, and in his high-pitched fluting voice denounce the company for interfering with a citizen on

298

his way to do a little shopping, and visit his tailor to have his trousers fitted.

His trousers fitted! bellowed the officers. *Yes, to have his trousers fitted – why not?* retorted the dwarf – *It was not only they who had legs!* And at this point the comedy degenerated into the obscene horseplay of mediaeval farce: though Margot, who up till then had been watching what was going on, could only guess at the allusions. It was then that she had turned away her head, with a sick feeling that she could not help. She supposed she was a prude, where dwarfs were concerned. Victor, on the other hand, had laughed heartily. Later he had taken out his sketch-book. Margot could see that he was making notes. He had the artist's passion for the grotesque – he had the he-man's appetite for the obscene. This was as it should be. He was drawing the dwarf, and laughing at the dwarf. She felt still more sick at that.

Finally the dwarf had stopped, and had begun to give a series of impromptu performances. From the particular hysterical timbre of the response, and even more from the indecent noises that came from the direction of this conceited little monstrosity, Margot knew that he was recommending himself by an animal obscenity. And her painful sensations increased tenfold when suddenly Victor shook beside her, tickled, it was evident, by some savage horribleness. She shrank, even from Victor. What beasts all humans were! She too – for she would not let herself out. Where Victor was, she would always be found.

But all that horrible horseplay, horrible as it had been, was in a different class of things from what was transpiring now. This uncanny parasite upon the normal world, which it took off and insulted to everyone's extreme delight, had singled her out. There was no escape, she must play her part. There was no use pretending she did not belong to this system of roaring and spluttering bestial life of flesh and blood. And this sub-human creature had been sent there expressly to humiliate her – as a punishment for something, perhaps!

The terribly lifelike pretence of inconsolable anguish rang out, in crisis after crisis of deafening grief. Nothing in the world could compel it to stop, she felt! It affected her far more than any real grief she had ever encountered. Was it not perhaps real, though, after all? Perhaps these mimic explosions were, for him, *real* explosions. And the louder the dwarf howled and bellowed, the greater was the glee of the childish officers, who flung themselves about upon their chairs, vociferating *Camarero!* and clapping their hands for more drinks.

This clamour of misfortune (at the source of which she must not even look – which made it more difficult by far, since then it was just *the sound* which assailed her, and it was a magnified replica of life), this insane uproar had administered a crazy stimulus to her uncertain nerves. To her horror, she found herself *responding*! Margot even – out of sheer aversion, out of mechanical sympathy, or because of both together – felt that she was actually holding this implacable infant in her arms. She was attempting to subdue its cries. And she could not master this horrible hallucination, try as she would.

Fancy if she had a baby of that sort – one which bellowed incessantly – one which had Victor's eyes – one which she loved – one which she adored! Out of their misery – should they give birth to something – might it not turn out to be some crooked monstrosity? Its hideous outcry would snap her heart-strings. Would she love it? Yes, she could answer for that all right. She knew she would love it; just as she had not revolted from the spectacle of their ill-begotten distress. She had not shrunk from the squalor of their circumstances – the fireless room, even some days no food but tea – after all the effort she earlier had expended to escape from squalor. She would love the crooked offspring *more* because it was obscenely ugly. It would indeed *have* to be only half-human to be true. That would be the way that it would please her best!

The somewhat glazed, the a-little-prominent normal aspect of her eyes, was at present terribly enhanced. An idiot fixity was the result. And to the eyes was now superadded a grinning of her parted lips. To such purpose did she grin and stare that the women at the table in front suffered a change as well. All the mischief went out of their jocular faces, its place taken by the vulgar relish of aversion and of fear.

Margot grinned straight into their faces without a blink, but

300

totally unaware of their presence. The eldest of them looked away with sullen offence; for Margot's countenance had acquired a malignant look, and the woman took it to herself. She supposed that it must be directed at the conspicuous absence of feminine It, to which she knew she must plead guilty. She huffily scratched her black moustache; and slightly withdrawing the straw from the cloudy bottom of her *refresco de Solar*, and squinting down its stem, she sucked a few frozen drops.

'*Está loca!*' she muttered to her younger companion, whose moustache was in its infancy. 'The woman is not all there!'

'*Claro!*' answered the pompous hill-town midinette, with a scowl of aggressive dismay.

And the two others, of the same bearded ilk – all lady shoppers who had sat down for a mild tipple and gossip – rolled their heads, in instinctive mimicry of the potty, to convey that the unreason in the grinning mask of the *extranjera* had not been lost on them, and that she must be pretty far gone and in a pretty bad way!

Looking up from his lazy scratching in his sketch-book, Victor caught sight, as well, of what had disturbed their nearest neighbours. The sardonic profile of Mrs Stamp was as unconscious of him as of the rest of the company. He put down his chalk abruptly on the table.

'What is it, my honey-duck?' he asked in a Clark Gable growl. 'Aren't you well, peachie?'

But the honey-duck only nodded in answer, and continued to grin, like a honey-duck exposed to the effect of a non-stop wisecrack – like a Walt Disney honey-duck, cut out for life in dumbshow, upon a more expressive plane than that of humdrum spacetime.

Victor Stamp looked at her out of a lazily narrowed eye, in almost as much alarm as the others, although his concern was masked in the manly reserve of the stockman, coupled with the furtive impassability of the swagman.

He perceived that her grimace was deeply grafted, and directed outward at nothing in particular – or at the nothingness which is all that is there, unless you conjure things up for yourself, and furnish this white screen with your private pic-

301

tures. His poor angel-bird, with all her hieratic Persian feathers, her stiff and cautious repertory of response, had been shot down by the shaft that flies by night, from the fingers of the dark Bowman! She had passed out, poor darling, and just pushed down – or had had pushed down for her – her rational self, and allowed this evil madonna to come up grinning to the surface of things, where we are all on our best behaviour, and go about to smile and to be polite. His poor Margot had gone to pieces at his side, without his guessing what was in progress. As he had sat sketching the dwarf something sinister had happened to his darling companion.

Ever since their arrival in France, Margot had been jumpy and full of moods. She hated these towering landscapes. She had said that she felt oppressed as if she were surrounded by unfriendly giants: and now she had got a seizure, if this *was* a seizure. She seemed to have stuck this way, at all events. It must be something of that sort. And he shot a further glance at the face at his side, and it was the same as before. Dropping the sketch-book back into his pocket, he beckoned to the waiter and stood up to go.

'Bezahlen!' he barked.

'Jawohl!' sung the waiter immediately.

They smiled at each other, these two linguists.

'Español?' he asked. 'Spanisch.'

'Jawohl! Spanish,' the grinning *camarero* answered.

'Good!' grunted the lordly Victor.

'Yes pleece!' this polygot person retorted, putting down the change on the table, upon which Victor left it. He had the *bel air*! He knew how to leave money untouched on a table and walk away.

'Honey-angel, look!' said Victor softly in Margot's ear, as he bent down. 'Let us be getting back.'

He took her by the arm. He was compelled to half-lift her out of the chair. Grinning to herself with a secretive malice, she staggered to her feet. There was a sensation among the café-guests as Margot and he stood there a moment – he with a somewhat ill-humoured frown as he glanced round, she grinning with great knowingness, as if sharing the joke with the spectators – a joke against her fussy cavalier.

To a rolling and nodding of heads, to a muffled muttering of dozens of tongues, he led his angel-bird away, directing her like a tractable automaton along the top of the Plaza and into a hilly street of little shops.

As they walked on, in a sort of goose-step time, as if her limbs, like her features, had been inflexible at first, she continued to peer forward and to enjoy the joke. He supported her with his hand beneath her arm. They had not gone far when tears started to slide down her cheeks, out of her staring eyes. With that the lips relaxed, and the bitter grinning mask showed signs of breaking up. Then her lips commenced to tremble and to work painfully, as though she were attempting to speak. Finally a savage wail broke from them, and the joke was at an end.

Flinging herself against a great panelled door, like something out of a Hollywood set, which offered itself, she pressed her streaming face into the hollow of her lifted arm. She was convulsed from head to foot. Great cries came from her. Settling in against a sculpted jamb, Victor drew her round, and supported her head against the big twin-pillow of his chest. There he gripped the agitated body of her skull, stroking the wings of her soft hair, as he might have secured a wild bird that had come to some harm, and have attempted to reassure it. Her head was no bigger than the body of a sea-gull, she was extraordinarily small and light.

Then he began to whisper to her in the tone employed by men to a frightened horse, in a very low and penetrating voice, to show that they are speaking only for its ear, in private messages. 'Honey-angel!' was the most frequent name he used. And 'honey-angel' was the name this sub-self answered to.

As he called softly and coaxingly to the irrational soul that had usurped, in broad daylight, the personality of the 'hermit-girl' he stared away from her with a straining and abstracted eye, in a listening attitude. He was waiting to get a message up from the submerged tenth of Margot Stamp, which was now in action, to the exclusion of the rest of her. And at last sure enough came a hoarse whisper, and he looked down at the top of her head.

In place of the brittle, hollow voice, picking its words, of his ostensible 'Margot,' there was an unintelligent muttering speech. This was the 'honey-angel' he had got in touch with, where it had been beating itself against the walls of some dark pit out of sight. It said 'The dwarf! The dwarf!' He said 'The dwarf, peachie?' in considerable surprise, for he had never connected the dwarf with Margot's sudden distress. And then he understood what it was all about. In the fairy-tale life of his fragile little honey-angel *of course* a dwarf would have another meaning to what such a figure would have in the adult world. He would be either a 'wicked dwarf' or a 'good dwarf'! So now all was plain sailing and Victor knew where he was. A look of great kindness came into his rugged face. As the bene-volent giant he could now play his part. And his big dirty hand, with its blackened thumb – where he had been using it to stump his drawing – made a padded shell for the back part of her head.

'Tell him to make less noise!' came her soft muttering from underneath. 'His crying frightens me!'

'He's stopped,' said Victor. 'He's gone away, my love.'

'I know it's true – he saw us when he started, he had tracked us down : it's more than I can bear though, darling! Make him stop – I can't stand it much longer, dear!'

At which the soothing, syrupy whisper rolled gutturally down, from the kind giant above into the little waxen, mid-Victorian ear :

'Honey-angel mustn't get upset at the noisy dwarf! He's *gone*! Your Vic's holding you now, darling, and telling you to forget the noisy little dwarf. He's not here any more, my honey-duck!'

But the honey-duck croaked sweetly back :

'Take me away, Victor my darling – take me away from this horrible country!'

These fairy lands forlorn, that was but too plain, had scared his baby, and he supposed he would have to do something about it. He frowned as he replied :

'We shan't be here for long, my pet. There is no danger, and the dwarf's gone. He has really.'

'I want to be in London again, with my Victor!' she began

to cry, her voice growing stronger, and coming to sound more like his Margot's now. 'Then I will die, my love – I will gladly die!'

'Why die?' he asked matter-of-factly and mawkishly at the same time. 'There's no need to die.'

'This place, Victor, is more than I can bear! You must come away with me too and leave it now before it is too late! *Too late*,' she whimpered, very sensationally, as if to herself. 'Victor, my darling. Oh please, before anything happens.'

'Happens! What can happen, Mar?' he asked, almost venturing upon a little sceptical laughter.

'I don't know, Victor. Listen to your Margot this once though, Victor. There's something wrong. I can't just tell you what it is.'

While Margot and Victor stood close up against one another, Victor coaxing away scientifically the terrors of fairyland, with its dwarfs and Cinderellas, and getting his wife into shape for the walk back, two men, with heavy walking sticks, passed them on the other side of the street, coming up from the Plaza Cabrinetty. One said to the other, out of the corner of his mouth:

'That is Stamp!'

'Is that him?' muttered back the second, cocking a wary eye from its ambush under an ideal eyebrow for a detective.

'Yes. That's his moll he has with him. It is Stamp.'

'What a neck to be up here! Are you sure you're not wrong, Blasco boy?'

'No, sir! That is Stamp. A dangerous man – there is no foreigner on the frontier so dangerous as Stamp! He is the leader.'

'Why is he here?'

'Who can say? Orders are to leave him alone. He will keep! He won't go far away. Emilio has him under observation.'

They snarled darkly as they pounded their hooked cudgels on the stones. They seemed to conform to the looking-glass or wonderland dimension of the honey-angel, as if they had been crooked creatures of her brain.

'Does he speak Castilian?' asked the second.

'Perfectly! He pretends not to. Stamp is one of these English

305

blackguards who has the gift of tongues – he speaks Castilian better than you or me.'

The second man tossed his head, to express disgust.

'The beetle! In my opinion it would be better to catch him while we can lay him by the heels.'

'I think so too. But such are the orders. He must not be touched.'

The couple withdrew into an archway, that led to a dark yard, and waited. As Stamp and his wife moved up the street towards them, they affected to be engaged in a brisk argument, and wagged their heads at each other – two *aficionados* falling out over a controversial bull.

'Those two men are watching us,' said Margot, as she and Victor drew level with them.

'Are they?' Victor laughed, looking at them good-humouredly. 'They appear to me to be having a difference of opinion.'

'They are more interested in us than in each other.' For all reply, Victor put his strong right arm about his wife's shoulder, and gave her an apologetic protective hug, as they walked along. His physical patronage did not offend her, she even squeezed his hand before it left her shoulder. But she sighed. It was *these handsome men* again, with her, now the normal Margot. Ah, these reckless Apollos!

'Supposing they *were* watching us, Margot,' he said, 'what could they do? Even if they suspected me of being engaged in the contraband of arms, they can prove nothing. My passport's all in order. I'm an innocent painter-fellow. Don't you see?'

'All the same, they are watching us.'

They had reached a street which crossed at right angles. Taking him by the arm, Margot led Victor across to the other side, and they left the street they had been following. A yard or two down the new thoroughfare she stopped him.

'Let us stand here, Victor, for a moment.'

'Why?'

'I will demonstrate something to you.'

'What?' he laughed.

'Wait a moment and you will see,' she said prim-lipped, with her bloodless, faded, roguishness. And sure enough not twenty seconds had passed before the two men sailed round the corner, stamping with their heavy sticks, hot on the trail. As they found themselves face to face with Stamp, they both started back and stood stock-still, measuring the sinister Stamp with a professional eye, plainly disconcerted. Then the elder of the two, Blasco, a scowl descending upon his face, recovered himself. He waved Victor and Margot aside with his stick, as if they had been obstructing his path, without warrant, and in defiance of the unwritten rule of the road, for law-abiding foot-passengers. Stamp laughed at this, with insulting good-humour, and said (in his offensive mother-tongue):

'Not at all, old fruit! It's *you* who must leave the sidewalk, isn't it? Don't you see I'm with a lady? *I'm* sorry. *Toujours la politesse!*'

But Margot took Victor's arm and drew him out of the path of the detectives.

'Come, Victor,' she said. 'We'll go the other way. It's time we were getting back.'

As they walked off, the two men stood watching them in silence. Then, at a sign from the senior, they started to follow the Stamps.

'Stamp is playing a comedy!' said the veteran, between his teeth. 'Stamp is up to his old tricks!'

The other nodded.

'Very plainly he is up to no good! He wants to give us the slip.'

They stamped down their cudgels fiercely as they followed in the wake of the lackadaisical stride of the Australian con-trabandista.

Chapter 2

MARGOT lay upon the bank of a mountain stream, and gazed with a look of uneasy surprise at the playfulness of its waters. Power, elasticity, brightness: she could not have believed that the high spirits of these liquids and the grandeur of these stones could disturb a casual visitor, who had brought herself up on

The Excursion; for whom nature was an open book. And yet she observed the incessant sport of the waters, as they poured in and out of the rocks, in their delicious obstacle race, with a mild aversion. At this placid health of sunlit nature she peered with a puzzled attention, her look suggestive, at once, of blank astonishment and involuntary reproach. To so bound and to so plunge, and to make such a jolly noise, as you went, struck her, one would have said, as peculiar and vaguely not *comme il faut*. There was a definite relish of wide-eyed, breath-taking scandal in her gaze – which mildly and sportively demanded enlightenment; but, more than that, which seemed pressing nature to give an immediate account of herself.

With nature in the flesh, as it were, Margot had not much acquaintance. In the pages of Wordsworth, on the other hand, she had had considerable commerce with it. She had attended lectures on 'the discovery of nature.' In London bed-sitting-rooms she had trod the untrodden ways – surprised a violet by a mossy stone, half-hidden from the eye. But this was, in fact, the first occasion on which Margot had lain upon the banks of a pukka torrent, like a character in a book – in the mountain air, among the uncivilized birds and bustling insects, some of alarming dimensions. She had encountered two or three in the course of her walk that morning which were objectionably large. At these manifestations of nature she had looked frankly askance, especially the beetles.

And this was such a perfect stream! This was such perfect sunlight! – *So this is nature*: this small bird-woman appeared to be remarking to herself. And she had not been prepared for this, it was pretty plain: without feeling a fish out of water, she nevertheless would not have wished to be a trout in this particular watercourse. She reserved her right to remain *outside* of nature, now it came to the point; not to participate in its sunny dream. It was *too* sunny altogether! It was too artless; it was too empty; it was too much a senseless agitation of unfeeling things.

Under different circumstances, however, the behaviour of these jolly liquids, the phlegmatic grandeur of these chaotic stones, would have called forth other responses; all would have passed off quite differently had her mind not been obsessed with the actors, for whom these pastoral sets were the incongruous backgrounds, and if she had not been part of this agony of men. It was Victor who was her *nature* now; and 'wild nature' too, at that. So the company of nature – all the blatant bustle of these liquids and gasses, and the chilly festivity of organic bodies attached to them, propelled upon wing, foot, fin – did not recommend itself to her, greatly to her surprise. Though was that to be wondered at, seeing that it jazzed around her breaking heart, so that she was astonished, if not almost scandalized.

Slowly she brought her eyes back to her book, which lay open in the grass. Here was a more subjective and obedient medium. She was glad to shut out all that unsympathetic beauty, and listen once more to the sad voice of man, recording his disharmony with the universe of things. And yet it was Ruskin of all people she had beneath her hand – that high priest of the natural order, and of those panoramas by which she was now beset and from which she felt the need to cut herself off, against which she must put herself on her guard.

As she began reading once more – pages which she had often perused before, and from which she had drawn more than her fair share of nourishment – she started to scrutinize, with unexpected independence, the propositions of which this particular piece of special pleading was composed. Was this treatise going to follow 'nature,' into that limbo into which all her life was falling? Was she about to cast away even *Sesame and Lilies*? Did her quarrel with nature involve everything upon which her personality had been grounded? It looked as if it might.

'Queens' Gardens!' What did the master wish one to understand by that? He was telling you that all women were *queens* – how lovely! and that they all had *gardens* – how comforting and how apart! And the little fairy queen, that Margot, had first learnt in these eloquent pages the secret of her exalted birth. What special kind of royal authority, 'arising out of noble education,' was possessed by women, she had first discovered here. Tears came to her eyes, however: her heart registered a regretful pang.

The Larkspur listens – I hear! I hear!
And the Lily whispers – I wait.

The spell of these lovely words could still command her
tears. For these lilies and these larkspurs were not the sort that
grew in common earth. *What poets they were!* obediently as
ever she whispered to herself, in the thrilling words of that (for
her) incomparable 'queen', Virginia. But when she tried to
visualize *the garden*, she experienced a slight disillusionment in
realizing that it was merely Maud's. 'Oh you queens – you
queens!' vociferated Ruskin in his final transport – after he
had substituted Jesus for Lord Tennyson as the figure at 'the
gate,' and Magdalen for Maud. And since there was a flaw in
that, maybe there was a flaw also in the figure of the 'queen'
which she had been so eager to adopt? To be consistent she
must face up to that.

'I would take Chaucer, and show you why he wrote a Legend
of Good Women; but no Legend of Good Men.' All Spenser's
fairy knights were faulty: only his women were perfect and
unassailable. All Shakespeare's men were ghastly failures: only
his women were admirable and without fault. 'Shakespeare has
no heroes: he has only heroines. There is not one entirely
heroic figure in all his plays. ... In his laboured and perfect
plays you have no hero. ... Whereas there is hardly a play that
has not a perfect woman in it.'

For some reason, Margot was unable to say why, these ob-
servations depressed her. This sweeping belittlement of the
male she had never even noticed before, in the course of her
dreamy reading of this particular chapter. She had only had
eyes for the chivalrous flattery of women, who were described
throughout as 'queens.' And of course this account of things
excluded Victor. She smiled with a wistful melancholy at all
the handsome things that this too emotional master out of the
old days had found to say about her sex: as she reflected how
much stimulation she must have required to overcome her in-
feriority complex (horrid expression!). She had overcome it almost at the expense of Victor; for Victor was a man, and
Ruskin would have it that no great writer who had ever lived
had shown a man as a hero. 'Are all these great men mistaken,
or are we?' she read, with dubious eyes. 'Are Shakespeare and

Aeschylus, Dante and Homer merely dressing dolls for us?'

And her small voice asked, inside her head, 'Were they?' and she wondered? Was *she* a doll? If she had been in the book of a great man would she have been a doll, 'dressed' by him out of contempt for all that she was, or could ever be? And why were these great men such pessimists (if the great Ruskin was right about them), and why did they find it impossible to portray a man as a 'hero'? Were *she* one of these authors she would have no difficulty about the hero side of the business, she was sure of that. *She* would not fill her books with 'queens'! But she was afraid that her heroes would all have a certain family likeness! She smiled to herself at the thought of the different versions of Victor which would flower beneath her pen.

She turned over a page or two and her eye fell upon the names of Dandie Dinmont, of Rob Roy, and of Claverhouse – great resounding and heroic names. 'Men who reach the heroic type,' these were: though they were not *heroes*. But these were older men. Whereas 'his younger men,' she read, 'are the gentlemanly playthings of fantastic fortune' – was Victor a gentlemanly plaything of fantastic fortune? – 'and only by aid (or accident) of that fortune, survive, not vanquish, the trials they involuntarily sustain.' She shuddered at that word *survive*. A dark shadow of foreboding fell upon this sunlit page, and wrung all the glitter out of the torrent, too, till it was of a grey and neutral tint, and they were leaden waves, of washed-out quicksilver, that dashed between the rocks.

But she stubbornly addressed herself again to the unravelling of Queens' Gardens. *Was* her Victor, she asked herself, like these young men of Walter Scott's who *just* scraped through, in spite of themselves, with the contemptuous assistance of their fate? Was he a contemptible 'plaything' of fortune? She had to confess that at present fate seemed to have the whip-hand of Victor; and that *had* he been a hero in a book, he would have answered to the requirements of Ruskin's generalization. But Victor *was* not a hero in a book – she only wished that he were! They were hemmed in by a chaotic reality, against which 'heroism' (book-heroism) would be of little avail.

As to the women coming off better, in Chaucer, or in

311

Homer, or what not, she saw that their rôle, as understood by this heavy Christian, was a much easier one in which to acquit oneself with competence. You were in league with Nature in a sense, as Victor explained it (though she was not sure that *she* was exactly that). The 'playful kindness and simple princess life of happy Nausicaa; the housewifely calm of that of Penelope' – yes, yes! almost with impatience she dismissed the threadbare arguments of this chivalrous patronage. Without saying it in so many words, and far more in sorrow than in anger, Margot guessed that she had been taken in. The word 'queen' had done the trick! She had found out both the Sesame and the Lilies – she had parted from Ruskin on this issue, too! He and 'nature' were no longer at her side. She was in the camp of the defeated Victors!

But there was one passage upon which she fastened with a brooding dismay. For here was a different sort of woman – Ophelia: one singled out to be an example of all that a woman ought not to be. Of this she took far more notice than of all the rest. It was, as it were, the parting gift of her discarded master; as if he had said: 'You do not any longer believe in my "Queens"? Very well. Here is something for you to put in their place, to remember me by.' For herself, she never felt anything but a very *weak* woman; she had supposed that weakness was of the essence of the thing. Yet – 'Among all the principal figures in Shakespeare's plays there is only one weak woman – Ophelia; and it is because she fails Hamlet at the critical moment, and is not, and cannot in her nature be, a guide to him when he needs her most, that all the bitter catastrophe follows.' And then, after the *weak* woman – the one weak woman – follow the evil women. But of those Margot took little account. She took no interest in evil women.

If she was not in the mood to swallow the 'queen,' and if she had turned wearily from his 'garden,' she was only too ready to examine that unworthy exception to the queenly rule. *The incompetent mate!* That was what was being held up to her scorn. This type of all weakness began to impose itself upon her with as much force as had formerly the figure of the 'queen.'

Closing the book abruptly, even a little brutally, she threw

312

up her head and stared past, or quite through, the present scene. She discerned the figures of herself and Victor stopped at the frontier by the military police, as if in a diorama: their two passports were changing hands. She ought not to have allowed Victor to undertake that excursion: she scolded herself. She had been criminally weak. Indeed, they ought not to be here in France at all; and that was that. What was she doing lying by the side of this pretty stream, too, while Rome was burning? What sort of figure would she cut in Chaucer, or in Homer? She asked herself that with a half-hearted, one-sided smile. Was this a moment to be flirting with 'nature' – with a guide-book to its charms, to make it worse, and more ridiculous?

The rattle of the water sounded empty and menacing in her ear. The luscious sunbath, if she could have enjoyed it, she would have been enjoying at the expense of *her* Prince of Denmark. But she could not enjoy it. Which was as it should be! The powers of the earth and air had read her a sharp lesson, a very sharp lesson. They had rattled their empty box of tricks in her face.

She rose to her feet, as if she had suddenly called to mind a pressing engagement. In her haste she left the book lying on the grass. Without looking to left or right she started back, at a rapid walk, in the direction of the village.

Chapter 3

THE main street of Bourg-le-Comte ended in a small bridge, in the centre of which Spain started. Spanish excise officers and picturesque bristling constabulary were stationed beyond it, at the mouthpiece of a deep tunnel of verdure, formed by an avenue of planes. As they chatted together in the middle of the road, these watchdogs stared over into a French village street. There sat Percy. Or sometimes, rather, their eyes would fall upon him, indeed quite often, and he would stare back at them from his solitary orchestra stall outside the front door of the Hotel Internationale. This happened especially in the evening. For Percy was fond of gazing over into the Forbidden Land, as if this tunnel of leaves had been a sort of telescope enabling him to pick out well-known *politicos* at the heart of the distant capital, though he took good care never to cross the bridge. That would have been to invite a snub.

The Hotel Internationale was a very small hotel, of six or eight beds; and it allowed itself two metal tables, no more, outside for stray travellers, or a guest or two. There was very little optimism about any of its arrangements. It expected little of human society, about which it held rather forcible opinions.

The proprietor of the Hotel Internationale was Catalan, from the suburb of Perpignan. He was a hot Socialist. Percy and he were on capital terms – on Das Kapital terms, call it that: Karl Marx was a tolerable cement. Illicit *palomas* supplied an effective moistening agent. When Don Mateu – Mat – appeared in the doorway, having heard that Don Percy was there, and when he had given the handshake across the table, these two old *moscoutaires* passed inside in solemn silence and moistened their Red whistles within with that pearly decoction described as a 'dove.'

Mat and Percy worked together. He brought a letter putting him in touch with Mat. Far more than Victor, Mat was in his confidence. Also Mat was Percy's best bet, or his first selection, if any of his party wanted anything; from him he bought bad honey, of suspiciously sugary bees; he used his dilapidated saloon, in which he rattled over the mountain *pistes*. And his saloon was used for other purposes besides picnics. Just how much Mat was in on their racket Victor did not know. Mat's standing remained undefined. For Victor he was a 'mystery man,' somewhat.

Mateu was the only Red in the place acceptable to the rather particular Percy. He certainly trusted none of the others. And here this Red man of confidence squatted upon the very lip of the Spanish Republic, running this small stagnant business, defying the slovenly might of Tradition incarnated in the glistening black-winged helmets of the crack police of the peninsula.

There was a heavy snag in Mat's tentative half-hearted contemptuous hotel-keeping. They would not give him a licence,

314

not for love or money. But that was because they would give no one a licence. They thought one institution in a village to enable the workman to squander his money on beer was enough. Mateu petitioned in vain. As a good Red he stood as good a chance as any in the Third Republic, too.

So nothing but coffee or Evian could be drunk outside at the tin tables. That was why there were only two, and it was two too many. No headway could be made at all without alcohol in the commerce of hospitality. And Victor would rarely follow his colleague up the street to this austere observation post – literally upon the lip of the front-line trench of one of the bitterest class-wars in the West. He turned his back when the Hotel Internationale was mentioned. To stare over into Spain was not one of his pastimes. He felt no interest in things Spanish. And Margot, in any case, kept him headed away from that country as far as possible.

Percy of course put down his aversion to refreshment at the *terrasse* of Mat's hotel to his lack of enthusiasm for Mat. He would give a veiled smile, in consequence, when Victor excused himself, when a bit of watercarting at Mateu's was proposed. And so generally Percy Hardcaster took up his position just short of the bridge alone, except for Mat, when Mat was *en casa* or disposed for an idle chat.

But Mat, as also Victor, was seated with Percy Hardcaster as Margot Stamp came up the street. With quite unprecedented speed she drew near, the ribbons of her Kate Greenaway hat aflutter, her muslins showing the lean outlines of her striding understandings. As she passed the gap in the houses beside the principal café, midway between their hotel and Mat's Internationale, she saw the uninhabited snow-covered mountains to the south, where Mat wished his mechanic to take them tomorrow to paint a snow-scene. That must be tactfully countermanded! Those were Spanish mountains. Henceforth she would draw the line at hostile ice-caps. No more playing with fire: just what was necessary, no more! She would see to it that if Victor must move about, he should only in future move *backwards*, deeper into France, not nearer to this nasty danger-line, much less *over* it – whether concealed in snow and ice, or exposed to the precocious eye of the Mediterranean sun.

These Pyrenees, where Africa began, were just a stupendous rocky man-trap, thrown up by nature in some ice-age, to catch Victor and to crush him. And the hermit-girl had changed her tactics. She had become an amazon, beside her mountain stream! She would shout warnings in Victor's ear. She marched almost, she well-nigh goose-stepped, up the village street, with a quasi-obstreperous eye. It darted upon the bulging back of Percy Hardcaster – his face, as ever, towards Spain – as if it meant business. Ruskin had armed it with Victorian pugnacity and will-to-live, even in the moment when she had cast him out for ever as a queen-maker.

The three men were unconscious of Mrs Stamp's approach. Something commanded their undivided attention. In his hand Percy held a typewritten letter, and Victor was saying, in his deepest digger-drawl, with its odd cockney smack:

'Use my name! Why not? It's all one to me. What's in a name?'

'That's not it, Vic,' answered the frowning Percy, a little crossly. 'You *must* have signed this, old man – you must.'

'Not at all. It doesn't follow.'

'This is your signature. Can't you remember?'

'I can – and I didn't sign it. I've never seen it till now.' Victor laughed, with one eyebrow ironically elevated, looking lazily down at the letter in question. Percy had placed it on the table, and pointed to the foot of it, where, with a bold flourish, were certainly the words

'How can we account for it then? It has no meaning if it's not your signature, Vic!'

'It's my signature right enough,' said Victor. 'But all the same, it was not my hand that did it. What's the matter? It seems to make me out to be the boss of the outfit. But as I only draw the salary of a bell-hop, what does that signify?'

'It's not that, Vic. What I want to get at is how your fist's found it's way on to this bit of paper.' Percy looked at Stamp, and then at the letter, as if he'd found one of his friend's molars in the marmalade, and insisted on knowing how it got there, as a mere matter of discipline. 'I want to get to the bottom of it,' he added, in pigheaded apology, blinking at the troublesome document. 'We ought to get to the bottom of it.'

'You'll never get to the bottom of it, old scout!' It *has* no bottom!' Victor gave his somnolent cachinnation, picked up in his native stockyards and steppes – the vegetative bonhomie of the big easy horseman drugged with the sun. 'It's not got a bottom, boy! – it has neither head nor tail, nor rhyme nor reason, as far as I can see, signing somebody's name who's of no consequence, so why worry?'

'It must have *a cause*.'

'Not necessarily.'

'Don't be silly, Vic. We're not talking philosophy.'

'It's you who are being loopy, Perce!'

'Do you want me to believe that the spirits sign your name sometimes by mistake?'

'No, old man – *as a joke*! Just as a joke. Someone's having a joke, that's all. That's what I should say it is.'

'Yes, but *who* is having a joke?' asked Margot, matter-of-fact, in her faint, exhausted voice, as she sank down upon the vacant chair between Victor and Percy, commencing to powder her nose, which had been burnished by the sun.

The three men's eyes abruptly withdrew from the letter, and fastened, in fascinated astonishment, upon Margot's nose. No word was uttered, and except for the sudden readjustment of the three pairs of eyes, switched over from the letter to the nose, no change in their attitudes occurred. They were all three men-of-action, and had she dropped down from the skies, on purpose to ask this question – dispatched, by supernatural interference, to put that particular question, at that particular point of the debate – they would have all three behaved in precisely this manner. There would have been no unseemly panic. And of course her sitting there among them and collectedly powdering her nose – just as though she had been

317

there all the time in fact – had the appearance of a trick, and helped to intensify the impression of magical interloping on her part.

Percy Hardcaster was nonplussed: the arrival of Mistress Margot as far as he was concerned put an end to the conversation. Displeased, he was at no pains to conceal it, he collected his letter, once he had mastered his surprise, a little hurriedly. This was to signify that the discussion was closed, or to remove out of this unexpected newcomer's reach the mystery document.

'Who is having a joke, Victor?' Margot inquired again, still jabbing away with the puff wherever she caught sight of a tell-tale glow. 'Is Percy having a joke?'

'No. Percy's not having a joke.'

'I didn't think he was. Who is?'

'Oh, nobody really.'

'I thought you said somebody was, Vic.'

'Somebody forged my signature, Marg.'

'Just like that? Was that a joke, Vic?'

'I suppose it was. What else could it be? Yes, that was a joke.'

'Where was it forged?'

'Back in England, I imagine.'

'What for?'

'God knows.'

'But you think someone is being funny?' Margot was looking down in her lap and returning the compact to her bag.

'Of course it must have been a bit of fun. Percy's a little worried about it. But it's nothing. Don't *you* begin to worry!'

Margot looked up. She regarded doubtfully first Victor then Percy, with polite expostulation at the reluctance displayed by everyone to enlighten her. Rather as an old lady might gaze in turn at two angry small boys, whom she had just separated, she gazed ironically from one to the other. Percy turned away his head.

'It's nothing?' she repeated.

'No,' Victor shook his head. 'It's just a joke.'

'But why should anyone want to forge your signature, Victor? Was it about money, darling?'

Victor slowly shook his head, meeting the word *money* with a Clark Gable smile, wistful and reproachful.

'No, I don't get any more money for the use of my signature. No fee goes with it as far as I know!'

'That is funny.'

'It *is* funny. I said it was just a joke, Marg.'

'It's funny without being a joke, perhaps.'

'Should I put in for a rise in salary, Percy?'

'I think, Victor, I must be very dense today,' said Margot. 'If it isn't a cheque –'

'Or a last will and testament,' suggested Percy, turning his head away as he made the remark, and staring at a Civil Guard, at whom he often stared, and who often contemplated him.

'Is it a will, Victor – have you made your will, or has somebody else forged one? Is that it?'

'No, it's about machine-guns,' Victor said.

'Oh.'

'I'm supposed to have signed a business letter, if you want to know, describing myself as "director," acquainting someone in Barcelona with the arrival of a consignment of "typewriters." That's how they refer to machine-guns, when they have occasion to write letters to each other about them.'

'I see.'

'It's a joke of Sean's, I expect. Old Sean must have his little joke. It's called blarney where he comes from.'

'Why Sean?' drawled Percy, still looking away at the frontier of the land of his adoption.

'Who else could it be? Perhaps I'm going to be made a director. Sean may be going to promote me over your head, Percy!'

Simultaneously the heads of Victor and Percy pivoted in the direction of Margot, who was sitting between them but a little back from the table, and their eyes met, as it were, upon her face. A faint chuckle had attracted the attention of both of them at the same time, and both for a moment blinked uncomfortably as their glances crossed, and recrossed, as they did for a second or two, for neither was quite satisfied at first that what he saw was not a trick of vision, in the rapidly fading light.

319

Margot's eyes were staring more than natural for a person in a brown study, and her lips had got a smile on them that no joke, however much of a scream, would entirely account for. In fact, it was the identical grimace that Victor first had encountered at the café invested by the performing drawf. But while he was still looking at her in dismay, she turned towards him in so rational a manner as to prove that she was in full possession of her senses, at least.

'Abershaw perhaps has been at his monkey-tricks again!' she suggested, with diabolical pleasantness. But the pleasantness put Percy more at ease, though it caused Victor to sit up with a still more anxious look, if the intensification of his humorous gravity could be described as anxious.

'Maybe,' Victor replied hastily.

'He can do your signature beautifully, Victor. I wondered at the time why he wanted to forge your signature, Victor.'

'Did Abb do that?' Percy inquired quickly, turning from his saturnine inspection of Spain.

'Oh yes,' said Margot, savagely smiling without mirth. 'I found Mr Abershaw practising. He forges Victor's signature very well indeed. Beautifully.'

Percy Hardcaster laughed, definitely, relaxing his watch-on-the-Rhine, and looking towards Stamp good-humouredly.

'Perhaps Marg's right,' he said. 'But this Spanish gentleman has evidently been in correspondence with you, Vic, before.'

'One would say so.'

'In his eyes, Vic, you're a man of international reputation. You're the cat's best pants. The king of filibusters. You're the Stanley of the Pyrénées Orientales!'

'I'm all that, Perce! I shall have a lot to live up to!' answered Victor, but his eye scouted round gloomily towards Margot, to keep him informed of what was going forward there since he last looked. No change was the message.

'Quite.' Percy's mind appeared easier, for some reason, he was almost light-hearted at last.

'Well, as I said, it doesn't matter a row of pins to me,' Victor declared.

'Why should it?' agreed Percy.

'I'll carry out what I signed on for. Beyond that, anybody's at liberty to make me out anything they like. If the comrades across the frontier like to think I'm Trotsky's pyjamas it's all one to me! It won't mean I'm any more on velvet than I was before. But if it gives them a dandy feeling to be in touch with the Grand Mogul – then of course ... !'

'Of course, Vic!'

'They are *not* at liberty to make you out anything they like!' Margot almost wailed suddenly.

'Why not?' Victor stood out sulkily for their rights.

'What right has anyone to forge your signature?' The grin still transfixed Margot's face, but there was no mistaking the sound of the voice. It broke out upon the sleepy air with a raw vehemence which was far more disturbing than her soft and sinister smiling.

Percy's good-natured expression went out at once; Victor's brow furrowed, like the surfaces of a lake attacked by a thundersquall; as for Mat, he squinted hard at the centre of his stomach. A stern silence fell upon the company. Percy glanced across the table at the taciturn Red. The latter understood, evidently, that something was not going so smoothly as it should with the social revolution, on the British Front: he rose and went back into the house, with a surly slouch, as though to register his displeasure – as a helpless, necessarily deaf and dumb, outsider. The English Miss was making trouble. She had a bourgeois look about her for which he had never cared. Her ribbons gave him the Spanish jitters; and her waxen face was suggestive of gilded cots at luxury bazaars. Why did they not shut her up, her two male companions? It was always the same with the English!

Percy Hardcaster turned towards Margot.

'It doesn't matter, Marg, about *that*,' he said, stern, quiet, and reasonable.

'It does matter a great deal – I consider that it matters very much indeed!' Margot retorted with such vigour that both . Victor and Percy gave a slight start of surprise, as if something had pricked them in a sensitive spot, and began to fidget upon their chairs. Percy eased out his wooden leg in a manner that implied discomfort. Victor gave a hurried dry-shave to his face, using his open fist like a loofah.

Then Percy laughed a short and formal laugh, of bitter but indulgent finality. Margot had imported an attitude into the discussion that was so self-evidently confined to herself and to women in general that no response was required or indeed possible (even if she had not been indisposed, as was plainly the case). This merely put an end to all intelligent discourse and so this meeting must adjourn.

He rapped upon the metal table with his knuckles; then he loudly clapped his hands. Then he looked over into the country of Cervantes, at the Civil Guard, who still had him under observation.

'Let's go and have a drink!' he exclaimed. But he discovered Margot's faintly malicious grin fixed on him, informed with a grim purpose. Unlike Victor, he had never seen this aspect of Mrs Stamp before, and he regarded it with distinct aversion. His was the popular response to this aspect of Mrs Stamp. She seemed to him loopy. He looked away and beat a tattoo upon the tin table, meditating upon the manifold objections to admitting women to affairs, and considering what this new face she was pulling might portend if it were not just the intermittent sickliness of the feebler organism. He was cross and uneasy.

'Percy!' purred throatily at him the grinning Margot. 'May I ask you something? Do you mind?'

'Sure! Why not, Marg? Ask away!' he replied with brutal breeziness.

'What I said about Vic's signature is perfectly serious, Percy.'

'Is it? Oh well!' he laughed.

'I cannot allow it to be used in that way. I object! I should like you to understand that – that I object. Very much.'

'Mercy! Why say that to *me*?'

Percy threw his head up in dramatic despair; and Victor with a heavily sedative laugh which struck strangely upon Percy's ears, put out his arm cautiously to surround his wife's slim shoulders.

Percy then heard to his intense surprise his young assistant's voice assume a tone of inordinate saccharine caress.

'My honey-duck is going to put her foot down, is she?' he overheard the muffled murmur, and his ears blushed as they received these honeyed accents on their unwilling drums. 'If

322

they forge Vic's name and make him out a celebrated racke-teer!'

Percy raised his eyebrows and coughed behind his hand. But Margot, grinning all over her face with bitter-sweet caressful reproach, put away her big protector's arm, with a mawkish gentleness dispensing with its muscular comfort, and her high-pitched accents again assailed Hardcaster's harassed ears.

'I shall write to Sean,' she was declaring, 'and explain how I feel about it. It's too much! Victor, you shall not be their *dupe*! I will not allow them to behave in this way. And I think you, Percy, should protect us too. After all *you* are responsible for what happened! We are not here to be made fools of. Vic-tor is not paid for that.'

At this Percy Hardcaster was amazed, and he looked over at Victor for a confirmation of what his ears had reported. But no satisfaction was forthcoming. Victor was as much in the dark as was his friend. His great sunburnt neck was swelling, as he violently dismissed from his throat the voice appropriate to communion with honey-duck, and prepared to reinstate his more accepted instrument of speech. He looked to the im-patient Percy as if a fishbone had caught in his throat.

Two distinct and watertight Margots, Victor considered he could manage. This duality he could master, he had proved it. The technique had suggested itself at once, when the dwarf had upset her. So long as they remained watertight it was all right. He knew from experience that his Margot possessed a second self. That was perhaps why she had second-sight. She was a 'psychic' because she had a *second* psyche. But that was up to a point a manageable oddity. Margot *Number Two* dwelt in a universe apart; and for that he had his little-language all ready. Any situation that might arise he felt competent to manage. He could slip into her wonderland at a moment's notice, and there assume the voice and port of one of its in-habitants. Indeed, was he not an epic figure there, of giant brood? By the mere rumble of his voice was he not able to rout the wicked dwarfs and cantankerous Duchesses that in-fested her Unconscious?

But *this* was quite a new departure. For the two Margots in question had, as it were, coalesced. She had brought out

323

into the light of common day her secret smile, as before – her overstrained imagery as well, without the provocation of an hysterical dwarf, that was the trouble: as if the objects of her fancy belonged outside and not inside at all.

She sought to impose them upon the objective reality. To this, as an artist, he somewhat objected. Here was the *sur-réal* – he had nourished it unawares in his own bosom! And as a man he had to confess that he was at a loss to know how to cope with it. He was even not quite sure, to be frank, that he would take on the job! He was not quixotic enough, perhaps, to take on the delusions of a Quixote. His honey-bird in the full regalia of her private mind sitting down at a café table with old Percy and him and insisting upon wearing her night-dress in public – there was about *that* something he did not like.

Everything had become involved in this brutal invasion of the external plane by the internal plane. Percy Hardcaster even had become for her as it were a wicked dwarf or an evil magician. And this was an advanced sort of nonsense for which Victor felt no sympathy. He looked over helplessly at Hardcaster.

At that moment Madame Mat, carrying her baby boy, came out of the hotel and sat down opposite Percy; Mat followed, sitting down opposite to Stamp. Percy leaned forward and began addressing the baby son of his marxist pal in accents not unlike those which Victor had employed in essaying to comfort his honey-duck. The large and flaccid child observed Percy with sullen alarm. Madame Mat peered round into its face and attempted to hypnotize it into affecting a babyish bonhomie. But it declined to depart from its *Once bit twice shy* approach to society; and as for accepting Percy at his face value, it stoutly refused. At length its mouth puckered. Seeing a howl imminent, Madame transferred it precipitately to its dad's knee, which it rode with some degree of confidence, though still pursued with Percy's insincere attentions.

'*Dis! Qu'est-ce qu'ils disent les vaches?*' clamoured its mother at it, histrionically, putting a bovine mellowness into her voice. 'What do the *cows* say? Tell the ladies and gentlemen what the *cows* say!'

'Moo-o-o-o!' it uttered dolefully, its eye fixed on Percy.

Its mother nodded with approval, for the rest of the party, and laughed for them as well.

'And what do the pigs say? Tell us what the *pigs* say, my treasure!'

Closing its eyes, it gave a series of impersonal grunts. Everyone laughed at its handling of the pig. Mateu and Percy grunted to show they had got the pigs all right.

'Karl! What is it the *sheep* say? What is it the baa-baas say, my lamb?'

It here betrayed its first signs of mental exhaustion. It looked fixedly at its mother and gave her a proper Marxist scowl. Eventually its mother prompted it with a low *baa-a*: and it answered her with a belch which had a *baa* in it somewhere.

Mat rocked it up and down on his knee, pedalling with his foot as if he were seated at a treadle-machine.

'And what do the *ducks* say, my precious?' its mother asked it next. It no longer rode its father's knee in a spirited manner, but slumped backwards and forwards like a horseman who has been disabled and is about to pitch off his horse.

Margot, grinning horribly, leaned forward, occupying the space between the two tables, as she did so; and picking up one of its hands, she asked it with an intimidating hiss as she lisped out the words:

'What do the *ducks* say, darling? What is it? Quack-quack! Say what the ducks say – *Quack!*'

It gave her one wild look, and doubling up and straightening out again in one determined spasm, discharged, all over her arms and knees, its long pent-up bile. Madame Mat sprang to fetch a towel, while Victor drew out a handkerchief the size of an ordnance road-map, and began hurriedly to wipe his wife-let's arms and hands. Grinning with unrelieved intensity, she offered him her fingers and suffered him to clean them between the knuckles, one after the other, with an expression of gloating ravishment.

Percy Hardcaster cast himself up, steadying himself upon his artificial leg.

'Well, let's beat it, Vic, before we have any more accidents!'

You would have thought to hear him that next Mat might

be expected to be sick over Stamp, or perhaps vice versa. He was going to adopt the attitude that his Red friend's baby-son had been frightened by Margot, evidently. Paying for the coffee, he bumped off down the street. By this time it was dark and the lights had been turned on in the Spanish police-hut, and the cloaked figures of the frontier guards had become portentous mediaeval silhouettes, moving to and fro in the shadows beyond the bridge. Margot's epileptic grin swept round, once only, in their direction.

Chapter 4

His unabashed but no longer talkative wife moved forward beside Stamp in the wake of Percy Hardcaster, whom they saw in the distance stalk stiffly into the café. Stamp had his old sports jacket hung across his shoulders, like the Catalan stone-masons, making an abbreviated cape, in the manner of a hussar.

'Aren't you feeling up to the mark, Marg?' he asked her, very confidentially. Had Percy not shown an inclination to be snooty and to blame the wife of his bosom for what was in fact the fault of Mat, in rocking the mooing and baaing brat incessantly up and down, he might have behaved differently. As it was, he curled his arm around her minature waist, and Margot responded by cutting off her smile – but with extreme difficulty.

'I'm well enough, Vic,' she said. 'Do I look cheap?'

She chirruped 'cheap,' one of Agnes's most horrid words; but she used it to mortify herself.

'A bit under the weather, Margot.'

'Under the weather, Victor? I am always under *that*.' She counter-attacked a mosquito with an exhausted levitation of the arm.

'I'm as right as rain,' she said, as if bitten with the meteorological imagery. 'But I must put a stop to all this.'

She stopped speaking abruptly, upon this bald announcement, and neither said anything for a half-dozen paces.

'Somebody has to. I must do it,' she said.

326

Where the he-man would narrow his eyes, Margot opened hers in a glassy stare; and where he would square his jaw, with her the jaw would relax. In order to spring she recoiled.

'Put a stop to what, honey-duck?' Vic cooed, swinging his jacket lazily, punkah-fashion, with an indolent swish.

'You'll think I'm being tiresome, I expect.'

'Of course not, darling.'

'You mustn't mind my having something to say about anything, when I think that it is necessary, will you?'

'Of course not.'

'That's right.'

'So long as you don't upset yourself, Marg.'

'I should be much more upset, shouldn't I, if anything went wrong?'

'It won't. It's all right.'

Margot shook her head (ah, these appealing six-footers, nothing can touch *them*, can it? – or so they think!).

They went into the café and sat down beside Hardcaster. There were plenty of people, of all classes, though all smelt the same to Stamp of French sweat, whether blackcoated or jacketless. This was the clubland of their big village. Panting '*Tout de suite! Tout de suite!*' or '*Voilà!*' as newcomers howled out their orders, the waiters two-stepped with loaded trays or fled to the shelter of the bar screaming *Anon!*

To Stamp's secret surprise it was his one-legged colleague who started the ball rolling – almost with a kick, in fact. For he began with a reference to Margot's recent recriminations.

'What are you uneasy about, Marg?' coming straight to the point, Hardcaster inquired.

'Everything, of course,' she answered at once, inclusively, as if not to be outdone – also greatly to her husband's astonishment. What was the matter with these two people, all of a sudden? He gave it up!

'Everything?' Percy Hardcaster heavily raised his eyebrows, and drowned his artificial surprise in a big slug of 'blonde.'

'Victor has not the same incentive, Percy, that you have to do what he is doing.'

'No?'

'No. He does not believe to start with, in the politics you and Mateu believe in. As you know. He has come out here to give a hand, just *to give a hand*. At Abershaw's suggestion. That was because Victor was hard-up.'

'Quite,' said Percy. 'I understand that. He was hard-up.'

'Very hard-up.'

'In the soup.'

'Yes.'

'Something had to be done. He was down to his last six-pence. I know. Well?'

'Well.' She hesitated, glancing at Victor's michelangelesque profile in pale bitumen, brooding and sculpturesquely unhelp-ful. 'He gives you a hand. And there it should end.'

'And there it *does* end!' Percy announced with controversial vigour. 'Have I asked him to look upon it as anything more than work done for pay: for bad pay, too, I agree? What do you accuse me of?'

'There are risks we did not know about: or I didn't.'

'You knew there was to be a spot of gun-running, didn't you, Marg?'

'I knew what you had undertaken to do, Percy. But I won't let Victor take that stuff into Spain next week. That's what worries me most. I don't see why you should ask him to do that.'

'Oh!'

'It's not good enough, Percy. I'm sorry, Percy. But I am in love with Victor – I can't stand by and allow him to be made a fool of! You have no right to ask him to risk his life. No one is asked to do that for so little money.'

Her face was strained but she was not smiling. Evidently she was expressing herself in this way with a great effort; her eyes were straining forward in their sockets, intent to focus upon a point beyond their range, it seemed; and her lips moved stiffly and numbly, as she forced them to deliver her emphatic mes-sage. It was not easy for her to play this part, and to come out as the opposite number to the masterful male.

'And then on top of everything else this forgery of his signa-ture!' she said.

'Not *forgery*.'

'Call it what you like. To use a person's name without their permission is to treat them as if you owned them. And what is the purpose of it? *Because* there is no apparent purpose *that* does not lessen one's anxiety.'

Victor remained motionless and silent, staring out into the dark street. Percy addressed himself, with eyes lowered, to the preparation of his evening pipe.

'All this arming of Reds means nothing to us; we are not Reds,' Margot proceeded.

'Are you speaking for Victor?' asked Percy, looking up.

'Oh no. But I know what his feelings are.'

'Quite. But putting aside the question you have raised, why are you so hostile to what you call Reds? You don't like the system that dooms him to perpetual unemployment? Of course you don't. Well, some of us kick at that state of affairs. Some of us kick *hard*.'

'You don't kick for Victor's sake.'

'No – not for his *beaux yeux*, I agree. That is your province! But at present you – both of you – have no place in life at all. Victor stands outside of life altogether. As far as other men are concerned he might as well be dead. He is the perfect outcast – more than any tramp. He's as good as dead. That's the fact of the matter.'

'He's as good as dead, to you, perhaps. But not to me. He is life itself to me. I cannot imagine the world without him. You would not be there if he were not there. For *me*.'

'I know, Marg. But I spoke of Victor *qua* artist. He might as well have passed out – he doesn't exist in any real sense. And when I say *real*, I mean real. And I do resent that situation. Believe it or not.'

'Painting is what he lives for.'

'Yes – and he might as well be pushing up the daisies, for all he'll ever get from it! – I know nothing about his powers as an artist. I am assuming that he has great promise. But Art as you understand it is finished. Your sort of art is as dead as the dodo. So what are you going to do about it?'

'Can art die?'

'No, but it must identify itself with life. You are standing outside life. So life passes you by.'

'You'll see we are buried decently, Victor and I?'

'Be serious, Marg! – I like you and Victor. You know that.'

'Victor and I like you.'

'But you and old Vic here belong to a system that is in dissolution. It rots and stinks.

'A system?'

'A political system, see? Like the solar system. *Your* sun is all gone cold: so you keep alive with great difficulty. Your art was the fine flower of a *system*. You understand? The system's finished. Art is the first thing to be scrapped. Always. No one belonging to that system is ever going to help Vic or buy his stuff. (I am assuming his stuff is worth buying – I am sure that it is.)'

'You don't want them to. You would prefer they didn't.'

'But they *don't*. And won't. How do you mean I don't want them to?'

'Oh, you know. Do you want me to explain? Because you want everyone to go under, so that they hate everything terribly, and help you smash things up.'

'But it's not a question, Marg, of what I want. It's what *is*, my girl! All these people want their money for Rolls-Royces. They don't believe in their system any more themselves, or (consequently) in the art of their system. Victor knows that well enough. But you don't know it. Since Victor won't tell you, I have to tell you. It's only fair to you that you should know.'

Both looked at Victor's slumberous profile, and then away again. Percy shook his head, to himself.

'You're not looking things in the face, Marg.'

'Yes I am,' she contradicted him, faintly but flatly. 'All that's no reason to get oneself killed.'

'Who's going to get themselves killed?' he sneered fiercely.

'Or – excuse me then – to lose a limb.' She pointed deliberately at his artificial leg. 'Then who's to say Percy that your system will be any better for painters like Victor than what we've got?'

'I didn't know you were such a politician, Marg!'

'I'm not.'

'You seem to be. I've heard your arguments from people who are politicians.'

330

'My politics are art.'

'Ah, I know where *that* comes from. That's Victor's.'

'You're quite right. Victor has said that. The Reds I meet with Victor have no place for art in their politics – they seem to abominate art.'

'I don't know anything about the "Reds" you meet, Marg. Thank God. They are just a lot of Leftwing intellectuals. They don't count. Forget that crowd.'

'But where's all this leading to, Percy?'

'That's what I was asking myself, Marg.'

'You mean that because ours is a futile existence, painting pictures nobody wants, we might just as well be shot as not? I oughtn't to mind Victor's name being used to cover Sean's schemes and so on?'

'No. His signature oughtn't to have been used. I agree with you. I'm very annoyed about that. I shall ask for an explanation.'

'And I am to encourage him to take any risks you require of him?'

'No. I didn't mean that. Of course I didn't.'

'I don't see it, Percy. I'm sure you're a sincere man.'

Percy Hardcaster bowed.

'But most of your friends are not like you. You know what Victor thinks. He told you that he thought Communism was a racket, like any other racket. Didn't he?'

'That was only an argument. Victor is very argumentative at times.'

'No, Victor thinks like that. If Victor didn't think that way it would be different.'

'I see. You want Victor to resign from this racket, here and now. Is that it? Do you want him to go back to England?'

'I do. That's just what I wish he'd do! But if he won't do that, I want to see that he doesn't do just anything he's asked to do. You know he is a fearless man. So you impose upon him. If I didn't speak like this, Percy, who else is there to say it? No one here. Or anywhere. We are quite friendless. It was no friend who put Victor on to this! His death would mean no more than that of a dog to anyone. To anyone! You are a fanatic. You wouldn't care.'

'You've got me wrong there, Marg.'

'You would look upon it as a sacrifice he ought to make to the Cause you live for, if anything happened to him.'

'It's better to have a Cause to live for, than have nothing to live for, after all!' said Percy. 'Even "a cause" is better than nothing.'

'I daresay. I know you think like that. But there is one person to whom Victor does matter a little.'

'I know there is. I know what *your* Cause is – or *who* it is.'

'Very well. We understand each other, Percy. I am glad we do. I have had my say, Percy. I will prevent anything that looks as if it might make a victim of Victor. Is that plain speech, Percy? Victor is my *racket*. So now we know, Percy, where we are, don't we? And please forgive me for speaking with such frankness. I'm sorry. I had to say all this.'

Several times Hardcaster had glanced over at Stamp, but the object of this harangue – this 'Cause' of Causes – sat gazing impassibly out into the village street, without betraying the slightest sign that he was at all aware of the nature of the conversation in progress. His wife and Hardcaster might have been discussing a new face-cream. But now for a split second his eye flickered back, in the direction of Percy. It consorted with the latter's eye for that compartment of a fast-flashing second during which Percy's had sought his. The calm message set Percy Hardcaster's mind at rest. He smiled very genially at Margot.

'Right you are, Marg, you've got that off your chest! Now have another drink. *Garçon, trois fines!*' he shouted out.

'Not for me, Perce,' said Stamp, as if reluctantly coming to life out of a deep sleep. 'I'll have a double Gordon, if you don't mind, old man. I feel like some fire-water.'

'*Un Gordon, Monsieur Victor?*' cried the waiter. '*Mais oui, Monsieur Victor – un Gordon, Charles, pour Monsieur Victor!*'

A mangy and vindictive cat had stealthily approached Victor's legs, and now it drove its claws through the trousers into the flesh with enthusiastic precision.

'Hey pussy! Cut that out!' bellowed Margot's 'Cause', pushing the cat off with the foot of his other leg.

'That cat is a devil,' Margot said.

'Its claws must be crawling with bacilli,' said Percy, stroking it, and offering it his wooden leg to scratch. He laughed. 'I'm safe! Have a scratch, pussikin!'

Percy was glad he had been right. He had felt sure that this outburst on the part of Mistress Stamp would doubly secure the collaboration of that hero, Victor, in all that might be required of him. He didn't see how it could be otherwise. It was like daring the Digger to risk his skin – for nothing! It was just that *nothing* that *must* do the trick. Not that there was any risk. His *skin* was not in question.

Chapter 5

THE third day after this Stamp, after breakfast in bed, brought out his largest canvas, sixty inches by forty inches. Their bed-room was not large.

'Are you going to start painting, Victor?' Margot inquired, as he pulled the canvas out from beneath the bed.

'What else is there to do? I might as well.'

As he placed things in position Margot stood against the window. There was not much room. The legs of the easel, the table for the palette and paints, and the not inconsiderable Mr Stamp himself – it almost seemed deliberately spread out to his fullest distension – occupied all the space there was, outside of where the double bed stood, and a foot or two for the hot-and-cold washing-sink. She picked up a Hugo's Conversation Course from the floor.

'I think I will go out,' she said.

There was nothing else for her to do, under the circumstances. As it was, she found it necessary to sylph her way through the delicate barricade which had been swiftly thrown up by Victor.

'I hope I'm not driving you out, Marg!' he said. He was slicing off the tumours of caked paint from the surface of his palette.

'Of course not, Victor. Before it gets hot I want to have a walk.'

'It will do you good.'

'I shall go to Pont Romeu, or in that direction.'

'I should. It's hot, peachie. Take things easy, pet.'

'He told me to take life easy!' she quoted, in wistful rejoinder, giving the saddest of carefree tosses to her strangely unmodern head. She left the room, or rather it should be said that she noiselessly eclipsed herself – she almost faded out of it. At all events, Victor looked up, and she was no longer there.

A good solid minute, a slow-moving minute, elapsed, after that, during which Victor continued to attend to his palette; removing, intact, horny craters of pigment, and dropping them from his palette-knife into an envelope. Then he put down, with a suddenness suggestive of an imperative summons, everything, pell-mell. Without looking, he wheeled aggressively upon the door and, opening it noisily, hastened to the farther extremity of the passage, which was terminated by a door marked WATER. Smartly tapping a bridling housemaid's anatomy as he passed her, he entered the lavatory. Slamming the door and ripping-to its bolt, he passed over at once to the window and cautiously looked out.

At watch at this unsavoury observatory, Victor then stood without more movement than a cat on guard at the mouse's funk-hole. Hands in pockets and elbows squared – he had on his jacket, against his custom – he dodged his head up and down, as if anxious to avoid detection.

The window commanded the turnpike which led to Pont Romeu. He had not waited above a minute or two when Margot appeared beneath him and started walking slowly down the road, occasionally referring to the book of French Conversation, which she held open in her hand. She was committing to memory useful remarks, he could see. She seemed well-embarked upon a pleasant educational stroll. The wind imparted to her clothes a meditative, waving, movement. At an even pace the small figure receded. He timed it by the watch on his wrist. In seven or eight minutes it was no longer in sight. The road had a hook in it just beyond the last house in the village.

The high barren wall of rock which was, actually, the very

334

wall of Spain, lay to the left-hand. It was tawny and precipitous and not easy to pass. Behind it lay other walls: walls behind walls, in fact; a mountain wilderness without inhabitants, except for the wild goats, which mercenary hunters went out to kill with machine-guns to sell them to the butchers. And between the trees upon his right were visible the white summits of the French mountains of sport, the high-places of middleclass recreation, though it was too late for ski-ing.

Generally this landscape was served up without music, to his painter's eye; but as he stood at the lavatory window he was now assailed by a full orchestra of appropriate birds, seconded by squads of chickens, which did for the ear what the mountains and the rest of it did for the eye. It was a faultless day. He cocked his eye over at the mountains upon his left. Copybook weather, without a speck of unnecessary cloud. The sun safe for twelve hours of uninterrupted good works. He studied the right-hand skies. Same story. Margot would see no clouds which threatened to fling rain at her, even in celestial play, and the sun would blandly glaze her face old-gold, not skin her alive. There was nothing to cause her to turn back.

She was now ten minutes outward bound and Victor was still at his window, an eye upon the perspective of the turnpike. Abruptly he turned away. Bursting out of the lavatory – his glance as collected but his gait as precipitate as that of a brave man surprised by a dangerous outbreak of fire – passing the simpering maid at a mad gallop, without the customary Clark Gable tap which makes the whole world kin, he disappeared four treads at a time down the hotel staircase. Appearing a moment later at the back door and scattering the hotel chickens, he made for the hotel garage. This faced the main premises across the grass-grown court. The barn-door of this converted garage was ajar and no one was in the courtyard. He entered it at a run.

After a brief disturbance within, there came a mighty purr from its recesses, then an outsize and very handsome dove-grey roadster emerged. Its blunt imposing head appeared unexpectedly quickly for such an important accouchement, riding with drowsy power over the obstructions of the uneven soil. Victor was at the wheel. This monster, as it moved across the yard was gathering speed; it melted ponderously through the ungated entrance at the side of the hotel, bellowing like a pole-axed bullock. A hand waved to it, unnoticed, from an upper window, the words 'Good Luck!' accompanied the flutter of the flesh, with salutation and godspeed. Next moment it had sunk away, with velvet self-effacement, rolling upon a carpet of rich dust, which changed into a low-lying fog upon the road, sucked in at the gateway for some time after the great car had departed.

*

Mateu was in Percy's room at the hotel, when there came a quick knocking at the door. Its tempo was disturbing: the touch of the drummer without was suggestive of very imper-fect nervous control. It had a panic note. Or it had the note of a war-drum. The two Red veterans exchanged dull glances of dour understanding.

Mateu developed on the spot a look of malevolent blank-ness. He lay at full length on the bed upon his back. He did not move. Both were smoking large cheap cigars; and the room was full of a disagreeable aromatic smoke. Margot came in, the fiercest grin to be encountered anywhere outside the walls of a sanatorium chiselling her bloodless face, and her eyes liquid and bright with fever. Grinning at Hardcaster with her head down, she seemed to be roguishly denouncing him from the entrance, as a very naughty youngster, who had been found out, but who was certain to have in readiness a potentially side-splitting alibi. Then she spoke.

'The car has gone!' she said. 'Where is the car?'

'Which car, Marg? Which car did you mean?'

Percy Hardcaster had risen from his chair, and sat down upon the edge of his writing-table. His expression plagiarized the blankness of Mateu's, but, unlike Mateu's, was devoid of malevolence. It was perfectly polite.

'Where is Victor?' she counter-questioned.

'Oh, he left, not twenty minutes ago. He has gone.'

'I thought so. You were all waiting, were you, till my back was turned? That is why he did not go yesterday? If it had not been for me he would have left before?'

336

'Sit down, Marg!' said Percy.

'Thank you. I have no time to lose.'

'Don't be temperamental, Margot!' Percy looked kind. 'There's nothing for you to disturb yourself about.'

'When do you expect Victor back?'

'Tomorrow. Do sit down. Tomorrow. He should be back by noon.'

'He's going a long way then?'

'No. Not so far as all that. He'll probably sleep down there tonight, it's more convenient.'

'He has gone into Spain?'

'I think he may have ventured to do so. With a fellow like Vic there's no knowing what he mightn't do, Marg! He might even risk a trip among the terrible Dons, I think! Don't you, Mat?'

'Is it Figueras he has gone to?'

'Why Figueras?'

'Because that's where you said the stuff, as you call it, had to be delivered. I heard you say so the other day.'

Percy Hardcaster frowned a little crossly at this.

'I don't remember saying anything about Figueras.'

He hastily glanced at Mateu, colouring guiltily.

'I heard you. It's all right,' Margot said. 'I see, that's where he's gone. Will you tell me the address of the people who are taking delivery of those boxes he's got?'

'I wouldn't give you that if I had it here, Marg. Don't be a fool, Marg. You want to send a telegram, that's it, I suppose, saying *Return at once!* Well, you can't, Marg. All telegrams are censored. It wouldn't be in Victor's interest to go sending telegrams. Not to a Spanish address. No. You mustn't do that.'

'I don't want to send a telegram. I'm going there.'

Percy did not reply for a moment, but held her under observation, beneath puckered baby-brows of immature pink, opening his mouth and displaying the fierce chew-hold his teeth had upon his massive cigar.

'You want to go there!' he said at last, in a voice that was intended to be creepily quiet.

'I *am* going there,' she answered, her tone almost threatening, it was so indifferent.

'How are you going?'

'By train. There is a train in about half an hour, I think. I am going then.'

'Very well. What are you going to do that for?'

'Because I will not allow Victor to be made use of in that way – I warned you that I would not.'

'You are going to fetch your husband back?'

'Certainly. To start with.'

'Supposing he won't come?'

'I shall then go back to England at once – that is, if he absolutely refuses to listen to me. I shall go back to England in any case.'

'Marg, listen to me a moment. You've got this all wrong.'

'I'm sorry. I have to go at once. Won't you give me that address? You should give it to me. It is not right of you to refuse. But if you won't, I shall go just the same. That won't stop me.'

'You may make a mess of things if you do that.'

'Not more than they are already.'

'I shouldn't have asked Victor to take that car down there if there had been any danger of the sort you mean. There isn't any. He'll be back here tomorrow. But if you go butting in . . . !'

'I am the best judge of that, Percy.'

'No, you know nothing about it. Otherwise you wouldn't be making all this fuss.'

'You will not give me the address?'

Percy slung himself off the table, and sat down violently upon the chair he had got up from upon her entrance, shrugging his shoulders and waving his cigar.

'No. I will not. Why do you want to be temperamental like this, Marg? It makes me feel like a theatrical impresario. You are being absurd. Victor told me to tell you. . . .'

Margot suddenly turned and left the room. Mateu and Percy burst into a torrent of pent-up Castilian, the latter sweating at every pore and fanning himself with a Catalan revolutionary broadsheet which had been lying upon his table.

'She understands nothing!' he exclaimed.

'*Claro!*' said Mateu.

'She is dumb – she is obstinate. She thinks we are all out to do in her bloke!'

'*Claro, hombre!*' Mateu rolled in impotent displeasure on the bed – it was no business of his.

'She'll get all the police of Cataluña on our track! They've got tabs on us already. She is mad!'

'The police of this country, too! The police of this *village!*'

'I told Victor to leave her at home.'

'You should have told her, Percy, beforehand, before he started with the stuff, and offered them their choice. If they wished to make difficulties, you should have sent them both back by the next train. There are plenty of people! There is no lack of people ready to do these jobs.'

'I know that. There are plenty of tough babies for this work. He is quite unsuited for it.'

Mateu scowled, and grunted between his teeth.

'Still it is *she* who is the trouble.' Percy threw up his hands and bit morosely into his cigar, stuck into a face emptied of expression. 'And it isn't as though she was as much in love as she seems either – with Master Victor – may the devil take her!'

'No?'

'Of course not. She's a bagful of bourgeois affectations. As you see, Matito.'

'Petit Bourgeois high-hatting, goose-stepping and grinning – I have seen it. Who could miss seeing it?'

'Marg – Marg is a museum of bourgeoïseries!'

'Ha! That is not too bad, that! I can *see* that museum!'

'When you see her, you see *it*.'

'She smells of must – as bad as old junk. She disgusts me, your compatriot.'

'She's a secondhand-outfitter of out-of-date attitudes, is Mistress Margot. Sometimes I ask myself where she gets them from.'

'From books! Where they usually get them!'

'I know.'

'From books. From old books.' Mateu snarled as he thought of the printed word. There had only been fifteen years of Communism, but more than twice that number of centuries of

339

fascist authorship. Even when the earth had all turned to Marx, there would still be this ominous shadow of the earth – that is, its time set up against its space – fascist to the marrow, controlled by Athenian and Roman aristocrats. The super-earth, of this dark immortality of *books*! A book was a black-shirted enemy.

'Maybe.' Percy, the book-snob, stared in stolid doubt over Mateu's head.

'Maybe?' sharply echoed him the watchful Mateu. 'Maybe? But she's a Bookworm!'

'Not so much, not so much.'

'But I have seen her with books!'

'You may have seen her with her Bible.'

'Her Bible!!!!' roared Mateu.

'She's a Ruskinite.' Percy smirked and blinked, slyly conceding that she did consort with *one* of the dead devils of authorship, at least.

'A Muscovite!' thundered Mateu, puzzled and incredulous.

'God man, no! *Ruskinite. Ruskin.* A Victorian Greenshirt, who stinks of stained-glass and edelweiss and sweats social-credit, Mat. A proper old burgher – still sells his ten thousand per annum.'

'Ah – I was about to *say*!'

'No, no. But the trouble about old Marg is that she's put her little clock back and sported her little oak. She's a human oyster, is old Marg.'

'She has cut herself off! Out of ladylike conceit.'

'Yes. Outside she's numb.'

'Numb?'

'Perfectly. Look, old horse – me and you, she scarcely sees, smells or hears us! That's a fact. Half the time I doubt if milady knows whether I'm absent or present.'

Percy flushed as he said this, and laughed, to cover, it seemed, his confusion.

'Is she deaf?' asked Mateu, looking up in surprise.

'No. She's *numb*. See?'

'She is numb?' Mateu fingered his limbs, mimicking anaes-thesia.

'That's it,' said Percy. 'Believes she's feeling something when

340

she gets a tickling in her tympanum. When you, Mat, or I, would be seeing red – a good stiff scarlet' – Percy puffed himself out, front-fighter to the finger-tips – 'she, poor mutt, feels faintly *provoked*.'

'That's different, Percy.'

'It isn't. But she can't help herself. The poor girl responds to nothing with great strength, and that's the long and the short of it.'

'Except Mr Stamp.'

'Except Victor? Victor! Why, Victor is just a violent fad of hers!' Contemptuous conviction flashed in Percy's eyes.

'A fad?'

'Just a fad. *Very* violent – unfortunately.'

Percy was beaming and frowning now at his friend. He had perspired profusely in debate. He chuckled: a derivative Spanish chuckle of thick mischief, like a long, rolling, guttural vocable.

'*Violent* – yes!' nodded Mateu.

'A violent fad of hers, that's all. Victor is her private screen star really. All to herself. But a fad. Not a passion!'

'You think not? I don't think that. She loves him very much. It is a passion. A great passion.'

'Not a bit of it! She takes you in – just as she takes in herself. She *thinks* she loves. Which is another story.'

'No, no! You are wrong! Listen! You are wrong!'

'It's all a notion, *hombre*! – that she's got in her head.'

'Not at all.'

'Yes. Victor, he is her big idea.'

'He is a big insanitary parasite. He gets my five hundred goats every time I clap eyes on the big fat tick! He should be squashed out – that way.' Mateu stamped his foot vertically upon the buffer of the bed-panel.'

'He's a common type. A very common type. But she is a very odd fish is Mistress Margot. She's another kettle of fish to Vic.'

'She's a very ordinary girl.'

'No. She's out of the ordinary – and now she's acting "the devoted wife." She does it quite well.'

'She does it well because that's what she *is* – the dirty little fascist doll!'

341

'What is she doing now? Going out in shining armour to rescue Vic! Like Joan of Arc. Like a knight-errant. Why, Victor is her Dulcinea del Toboso, that's about what Vic is! She hasn't got a drop of proper red blood in her body – though I like the girl. I always have done.'

'It's just your little weak spot, Percy. We know that.'

'What. I'd as soon look upon her as a woman as upon my spinster Aunt Jessie up in Stockport. No, but she's a good girl, Margot. Only she's batty. There's no getting away from that.'

'That may be that she's *cold*!' shouted Mateu, spitting quickly (to give Percy no time to muscle in). 'Cold – *yes*. All the English are.'

'The English . . .'

'No, *all*! Their rabbit-teethed women are jokes as women – *qua* skirt, old Perce! She is rabbit-toothed. She is no woman – I will grant you that. But she *loves*! With all her rabbit-teeth she *loves*!' He spat. Then he added: 'As a rabbit loves.'

'No. She is not rabbit-toothed.'

'She is. Noticeably of a perfect toothiness – and that of the rabbit!'

Mateu banged the bedside cabinet with his flattened fist.

'No!'

'Yes!' .

'That's her way of holding her mouth.'

'No! *Caramba* – never!'

'That's an affectation, silly. An affectation of the British.'

'No, señor!' Mateu glared at him.

'I tell you it's a British habit.'

'No, sir, she's toothy!' howled back Mateu. '*Cara – amba!* Her teeth spring out at you!'

'No, sir! She's English: *therefore* you think she must be rabbit-toothed!'

'I deny it!'

'But so it is.'

'Let all that be as you like. *Qué puta!* Let it be that way! I have never seen her fangs. She is toothless! Let it go at that.'

Mateu collapsed himself, and stuck up his shoulders to express hatred of this subtlety. But he was half-laughing at Percy the while.

'Good.' P. Hardcaster was not sorry for a breather. He lowered his point. 'Very well.'

'But she loves that Stamp,' suddenly Mateu clamoured, when Percy least expected it, 'with every cell of her little shrimp of a flat-chested anatomy. Like a dog! You hear me, Percilito! *Like a dog!*'

'Say "like a bitch" and have done with it!' shouted Hardcaster, boisterously rallying, attempting to suggest to Mateu, by means of his broad smile of easy triumph, that he had won hands down. 'And you'll be *wrong!*'

'No, sir! She loves her Mister Stamp. Far more than it is permitted that any *individual* should be loved! Ten times more, Percy.'

'She prefers him, I agree, to the Social Revolution,' the somewhat exhausted Percy was moved to retort. Mateu sat up on the bed and wagged a minatory forefinger.

'You mock at what I have said! Very well. That, Don Percy, is because you too are an Englishman, and at bottom an individualist! That is why.'

Percy flung up his hands above his head, in token of surrender.

'I withdraw – I withdraw! Have it your own way, Mateu! They're both of them a bloody nuisance. That's the main thing. I like old Victor – it's no use. But it's no good trying to get any *sense* into his head.'

'Hardly!'

'Vic thinks he's an artist – whatever that means. They say he's no good even as an artist.'

'And if he were! And if he were!' Mateu was furious at this hairsplitting – of good and bad artists. *La gran puta!* Was not *artist* enough! He seethed with resonant Castilian oaths.

'Exactly. Even if he *were*. You know I'll be blasted if I wouldn't rather he was a fascist – yes, a fascist – than *nothing!*'

At *fascist* Mateu deliberately spat upon the bedroom floor, right in the centre, where no one could miss it.

'*Un fascista es una nada, hombre!*' he frigidly remarked (cooled down to zero in the winking of an eye), as if it were a thing which it should not be necessary for him to have to point out. 'A *fascist* – that also is nothing! A fascist is nothing!'

'No. But it's something one can *dislike*.'

'One cannot dislike nothingness,' Mateu indolently retorted; jerking *nothingness*, presumably, off his right shoulder – where it had alighted – with distaste.

Percy stood up and yawned savagely at Mateu.

'I must go and stop that girl if I can.'

'You will not be able to.'

'No. I suppose not. Wait here till I come back, Mat! *Un petit quart d'heure.*'

'*C'est entendu.*'

'If time hangs heavily on your hands. . . .'

A resentful negative expressed itself sluggishly from head to foot all over Mateu's body.

'No, but if it should, Mat, you can go back to your place and get those cases packed into the car. I would come straight on there.'

'I will stop here,' said Mateu.

'Very well. I shall come up with you tonight, Mat.'

'Very good, but there's no need, Percilito.'

'I will come.

Mateu shook his head backwards and forwards, until the leisurely disgruntled words presented themselves upon his lips.

'I can do the job alone,' he said. 'I shall leave at six.'

'At six? Why at six?'

Mateau shrugged roughly, and began questioning with a pro-testing condescension these boring questions, which were *tontísimos* and might almost have been put on purpose, to tease a body about the time the day gets hot and the eyelids heavy.

'They can see me, can't they, from the police-post across the bridge! They can see me going off in my car. You forget. I am near the frontier.'

'I know that, but I shouldn't worry, Mat.'

'I don't worry.'

'They will be all steamed up about Victor.'

'Perhaps.'

'They will pay no attention to you, Mat.'

'The great Señor Stamp will have so excited them?' Mateu grinned in a very curious fashion up at the pink conspirator from the unpractical North, who gazed down into his sallow face.

'That's the idea. Isn't it. It is, isn't it?' Percy pressed him suddenly.

'That's the idea.'

Mateu squinted down his trouser-leg at the polished tip of his dandy footwear, which he waggled waggishly to and fro.

'No. I shall go early,' he said. 'I shall stop out all night – on the mountain.'

Uncertainly musing, as if the prey of some last-minute doubt, the squat gothic bulk of Percilito hovered in the doorway. Conscience seemed at work. One would have said that Percy was suffering the attack of some bug at least like conscience, if not that scourge in person. Mateu lay quite still.

'Mat,' said Percy, biting the fat edge of a finger-nail.

'What is it?' Mateu looked up, surprised, it appeared, to find his companion still there.

'It has occurred to me, Mat ... you don't think there was anything behind that affair of the signature, do you?'

The raised eyebrows on the bed acted an indolent astonishment.

'What signature? The signing of Stamp's name – are you talking about Stamp?'

'I'm talking about Stamp!' A defensive truculence began to hover about the embarrassed Percy. His chest betrayed a symptomatic swelling.

'That has got me worried, Mat. I had better tell you.'

'You are easy to worry!' Mateu closed his eyes in sleepy contempt.

'Coming together with the other instructions. It was the same mail almost when that turned up. We are ordered to stage this blind in one letter. ... You handle the *real* stuff. Victor. ...'

'Well?'

'It looks as though there might be a sort of connection, doesn't there, between the two things? Stamp comes into both of them.'

'What of it?'

'What of it?' Percy got rather red in the face. 'I shouldn't like old Vic to get in a jam! I'm not so hard-boiled as to stand by and allow that.'

'You and your goddam compatriots. *Quant aux Anglais, tu sais, le copain, j'en ai marre! Stamp! Je l'emmerde Stamp! J'en ai assez de votre mal foutu Stamp. Assez!*'

When the more violent passions were provoked, Mateu preferred the tongue of the French billiard saloon to the idiom of the Castilian house-drain. He knew his way about in the former better than in the latter.

'Very well, Mat. But I'm telling you – I'm staying off any funny business that might turn out that way for Vic. Whatever he is, he's my friend. You get that?'

'Your *friend*? What is that?'

'Never mind what it is. We won't argue about the word friend. But I'm telling you, Mat!'

Percy was now very red. Mateu scowled coldly up at the unalterably good-natured features of this pink English face, contorted to express masterful determination.

'It had struck me, Mat, that you knew something about that Stamp business!'

'Had it?'

'It had. Did you get any instructions – privately – about it? Am I allowed to ask that? Why was I left in the dark? Do you happen to know?'

'I?' Mateu pointed incredulously at himself.

'Yes, you.'

Mateu laughed.

'You are a baby, Percilito! You are a *spoilt* baby. That is worse. All you English are the same.'

'Never mind about the English. We aren't nationalists, are we, Mateu?'

'Some of us behave as if we were.'

'Will you answer my question? Yes or no!'

Mateu looked at him a moment with curiosity. Then he shrugged one shoulder as a private comment, for himself alone. Then he began exclaiming, in a violent tone of cringing mockery.

'Par exemple! Milord Hardcaster *exige*! *Eh, mon Dieu! Votre serviteur, Monsieur le baron! – je me hâte de me rendre à*

346

vos réclamations, si dépourvues de sens qu'elles soient à mon point d'vue! Allez! Vous voudriez savoir, Excellence ...?'

Percy drew out his watch.

'Don't be a fool, Mat!'

'A fool, *Mon Prince*! A *fool*?'

'No, you're no fool! But I must go at once or I shall be late.'

'Late for Mistress Margot! Yes. *D'pêchez-vous!*'

With a harassed half-smile, Percy Hardcaster made his exit, still an angry red. Mateu flung himself back at full length on the bed, his eyes rolling with a sombre excitement.

Chapter 6

I⊤ was half-past four in the afternoon, and Figueras was a matter of a few kilometres away. It was already in sight. The large dove-grey car was leaping at it, in powerful elastic bounds, of transatlantic nervosity. Victor Stamp's eyes were fixed upon its red-light quarter, its hill of Venus – upon which spots that were gipsies moved, appeared and reappeared. They had horses, which they led by bridles, up in the bright and brittle air of the Spanish afternoon. He could see their camp, a fleet of derlict caravans, upon the hillside facing the fort, used as a barracks.

Down upon the road in front of the car, out of a thicket of nuts, stepped a diminutive figure, waving a tired hand. It was a feeble signal. It was like a person waving last farewells in a dream, when the dream is closing, and all its personages are fading into one another as the sleeper tires and is no longer able to hold them apart: an inclusive adieu.

The car rushed past the place where the pale hand still languidly tossed in the dust-storm in the wake of its wheels, but came to a violent halt, a half-dozen yards beyond. Out of the brown cloud came the diminutive figure, all in due course, up to the side of the footboard, stumbling a little, and coughing quietly, repressing the reactions to big mouthfuls of hot dust.

'Victor!' it clamoured mildly, as it advanced.

'Margot!' came back the hail, with somewhat less of a thrill than was customary, while Victor from his seat attended upon her advance, his neck screwed backwards, in phlegmatic expectancy.

'How did you get here, honeybubble?' he burst forth demonstratively, a little fauxbonhomishly.

'How did *you* get here, Victor?' came the pointed rejoinder.

He vaulted out of the car and stood beside his wife, who rubbed her eyelids and gently beat her chest.

'What a lot of dust you contrive to throw up, Victor!' she said, correct and sedate.

'Do I? I lost my way and got behind time. I had to step on the gas to make it. I had a *panne* up in the mountains, too. It's been a bloody day.'

They stood in the roadway gazing at one another. Last seen, this *papier-mâché* figure – a whitish flutter of cotton, a palish, expressionless, wedge of face, a pair of nervous hands – his immaterial wife – was pursuing its way, book in hand, along a French road. Now it had turned up, coming out of a grove of nut trees, only a few hours later, in the middle of a Spanish province.

How had Margot reached this spot – up out of the earth, or down out of the air? The question rolled languidly in his mind as he watched her: he paid no attention to it, he just allowed it impersonally to roll to and fro, as idle questions will. On her side, her manner suggested no consciousness at all of the uncanny velocity these displacements of hers implied. But they just calmly looked at each other: there was no disposition on his part indiscreetly to inquire what had brought her here, or how. That was her business. The why and the wherefore of his being where he was, that likewise was *his* business. His being a world of black and white, composed of clear-cut individuals, it followed that each and all had his own business to attend to, not secretively but as an unchallengeable free-agent and owing no account of himself to any man. And she saw freedom in that way, too.

The big, lean Australian head, as if chopped out of brown indiarubber, showed up well in the Spanish sun. The long, muscular pits of its dimples equably displayed their ascetic lines. The tanned face did not carry about its tan, as it did in

London, as if it were a tiresome advertisement to emigrate and play at the pioneer. Victor was at home here, in a sense. But the small figure in front of him, that was at home nowhere. Yet it did not seem to mind. It looked as if it regarded it as quite as natural to be there as anywhere else. It belonged to Victor, who was its sun and its meridian. At the Pole she would be at home with Victor, as much as it was possible to be that upon this earth.

But this odd self-sufficient dependant could move swiftly too! That tremendous desire of which it was the rash vessel could propel it to some purpose, when the King was in danger – when life itself showed an inclination to slip away!

No business of his as it was, Victor recognized with amusement that this was a singular feat, her turning up as she had. His Margot had beat the band, in the matter of efficient locomotion! She must have chartered an aeroplane! For how had she done it, if not by air? Or she must have arrived like the Egyptian symbol of the psyche. That was more like her than Imperial Airways! Whizzing over the mountains (his memory supplied the picture of a winged *objet d'art* in paint or gypsum), she had dropped down to ambush him just as he was about to reach his destination. She had not wanted him to go – to that she would never have consented. As she would have been opposed to his going, he had been compelled to trick her. Consequently she had projected herself through the air to drop down in his path, staging a timid hold-up. One of his massive dimples smiled, with regretful affection.

He drew this wraith of a small wandering woman towards him, impulsively but in that steady way of the Constant Cowboy – who could not be other than unhurried, though that did not postulate a heart of ice – and he kissed her with an ironic tenderness.

'Margie!' he laughed lazily and gently, in reproachful mockery. 'Why did you come after me, you villain?'

'It is *you* who are the villain, Vic!'

But as he got up against her staring eyeballs, he saw that they were like those of an astonished gazelle that had just been shot at, or those of a distracted monkey which had recently seen its messmates of the tree-tops killed before its eyes, during a foray on terra firma. Her cast-iron reserve brought it about that no dumb animal was in a worse fix than she, at times, or more debarred from imparting its requirements.

He perceived that Margot was the bearer of news. Obviously she was suffering from its suppression – resultant upon her queer canon of refinement. To spill it without warning would be horribly indecent, so she would consider, in the case of any disturbing announcement she had to make. But all bottled-up with something it was plain to see she was. Best to help her to get it off her chest. So he broke the rule of the great open spaces, to eschew inquisitiveness, and to cultivate detachment.

'What has happened, darling?' he inquired, holding her hands, still quizzical because experiencing a sensation of mild guilt. Victor in his most tenderly mocking mood with his honey-angel stood with his eyebrows drawn up and his legs apart.

'I came after you, Victor, when I found out,' she said.

'So I see. You shouldn't have done that, darling.' He gazed at her, saying to himself that he had never expected to reach Figueras. All along had he not felt that something of this sort might occur? He had not been astonished, that was a fact, when he had seen her come out upon the road. He had never believed in his 'escape'! Never for a moment, when he came to think of it.

But that escape of his was a lousy performance – he was kind of ashamed of it too! – it had gone against the he-man grain all right! Turning his sweetheart into a stranger, to be fooled, by himself and a rotten old Red! He had been acting in a way he did not approve of right from the word go. He should never have consented to it. He felt relieved, it was odd to have to say it, to find himself checkmated by his mate. He was on her side all the time, against himself, of course! And he guessed she knew it, too!

'It was just as well,' Margot answered. 'It was just as well I did, Victor. The house you were going to in Figueras is surrounded by police.'

He dropped her hands like two hot bricks – they flew away to automatic service about her meticulous person, immediately

350

proceeding to the expulsion of the dust from hair and clothes. He stood looking at her in astonishment. She might have just said something almost offensive and actually unfriendly. It had been uttered, too, just at a moment when he had been confidingly standing with her, hand in hand, in tender submission to the unwritten law of their love. Why, she might almost have been betraying him to the police!

In his eyes there was almost a glare: it was *she* after all who had betrayed *him*. This was revenge, or had that appearance. It was the revenge of love, if that was love.

'Surrounded. By *police*!' he said in husky protest. 'How do you make that out?'

'I followed Mr Hardcaster, and saw him arrested.'

'Hardcaster arrested! What in hell does that mean, Margot?' He stared at her with fresh incredulity, which furrowed up his face in a displeased frown. 'How did he get here anyway?'

'I will tell you,' Margot said. 'But I think, Victor, there is not a great deal of time to lose. If you don't arrive soon where you are expected, they may come and look for you, I think.'

He had certainly been trapped. For something that called for action had just been brutally announced to him. And here was a notable obstacle to action. It was the obstacle itself that had delivered the news!

Victor turned irresolutely towards the car. Then he wheeled back almost roughly upon Margaret Stamp.

'You're sure you weren't mistaken, Marg?' he asked, as a big man cross-questions a small child, who asserts that she has been the witness of a rape, incendiarism, or suicide.

'Oh, no.' Margot shook her head, refusing him any loophole of uncertainty. 'I am not mistaken. The place is stiff with police. They are Civil Guards.'

'What do they want?'

'I don't know what they intend to do. I didn't stop to ask. But that is no business of ours, is it?'

'Perhaps not,' he said. Victor stood frowning at the ground. He looked as though he were ashamed about something – not what he was first ashamed about – and baffled at the same time.

'Anyhow, Victor, you can do no good – you can only get yourself arrested like Percy Hardcaster. What's the use of that?

351

'No. That's no use. But what made him walk into a police-trap like that?'

'I don't know.'

'You saw it happen?'

'Yes. I was a few yards behind him. I saw it happen. Two men came out of a doorway suddenly and covered him with their carbines. Short rifles – carbines, aren't they?'

'What did he do?'

'Put his hands up over his head.'

'He put his hands up? Well, I can't understand what possessed the old crab to come down here at all. That's what leaves me guessing. He didn't say he was coming. What's it all about?'

'He followed me.'

'Oh.'

'He came to the station at Bourg-le-Comte to try to stop me from going. Then the train started and he jumped on it. Or rather he rolled into it. He rather hurt himself.'

'Oh.'

'Before we left the train, he told me to shadow him. If anything happened, he said to come out here and intercept you. He explained what I was to do. I did so. That's all, Victor. I think he wants you to go back.'

'But how can I go back? They will hold this bus up at their bloody old frontier. Or perhaps before that.'

'You will have to abandon the car somewhere, Victor. We shall have to go on foot, over the mountains.'

'With you?'

'You don't want to get caught. That would be ridiculous.'

'It would be ridiculous. We shall all look pretty silly anyway, shan't we?'

'It was silly ever to come. We look ridiculous as it is. They have made fools of us. But it would be more ridiculous still to go and give yourself up, Victor. To go into that town would be the same thing as giving yourself up. You don't want, Victor, to spend years in a Spanish jail! And I don't want you to anyway, Victor. It is all right for Percy Hardcaster. He's used to that sort of thing, isn't he? He thrives on it. Besides, it's his business. It isn't yours. You are an artist, Victor.'

'Yes, well, that seems the best thing to do.'

'Much the best.'

'Well, jump in, Marg! We'll beat it. You shouldn't have come down here,' he said in a cross voice as he was getting into the car.

'I'm glad I did, Victor.'

'You shouldn't have, all the same.'

'Nor should *you*!' Margot smiled faintly.

There was no answering smile. Victor was *not* amused. Margot had left him no option but to be an angry man. Here he was the man-of-action called upon to *act* – but to act under a bad handicap, and at a time when he was out of conceit, too, to make things worse, with his function. This time she had done something unmargotesque; it had turned him back, so that he had become the original Stamp. For the moment Victor was that. This stranger called Stamp was not her Victor now, she was driving with. It was a strange burly fellow who was rather sulkily detached. Written all over him was *strong and silent*, certainly, but strong and silent against the grain. She shrank into the corner of her seat. She avoided contact with this foreign Stamp, apprehensive of his bulging form, his bilious eye.

The car swept forward over the road, perversely ridged and gouged, and half the time they appeared to be shooting through the air, rather than running along a plane which should have been there but wasn't. On several occasions Margot flew up from her seat like a cork, and was almost lost out of the car. But to this Victor paid no attention whatever: if he had lost her out of the car he would not have noticed it, she felt quite sure. Indeed, almost always when this happened his foot was seen to crush down more cruelly upon the accelerator; and Margot was obliged to cling to the safety straps and other available finger-holds, she was so volatile, to prevent a repetition of this contretemps.

Meanwhile trees, rocks, and telegraph-poles stood up dizzily before her and crashed down behind. They were held up stiffly in front of her astonished eyes, then snatched savagely out of the picture. Like a card-world, clacked cinematographically through its static permutations by the ill-bred fingers of a powerful conjurer, everything stood upon end and then fell flat. He showed you a tree – a cardboard tree. Fix your eye upon this! he said. Then with a crash it vanished. Similarly with a segment of cliff. Similarly with a telegraph-pole.

Her head ached with the crash of images. Every time a telegraph-pole fell down she felt the shock of its collapse in the picture-house of the senses. This rushing cosmos filled her with a bleak dismay. She had not foreseen their mad charge through this forest of objects; and her senses quailed.

Above all she detested this charging beast, that muscular machine. Pounding beneath her, it carried her forward, she knew, by means of unceasing explosions. Very well. But in this act she must co-operate. To devour miles and to eat up minutes, in gulp after gulp, use must be made of *her* organs, so it seemed, as well as its own. Under her feet she had a time-eating and space-guzzling automaton, rather than a hackneyed means of transport, however horridly high-powered. It was *her* time, too, it was gobbling up – under great pressure, in big passionate draughts. What a situation! Victor and this brute were in collusion, he had deceived her for its sake! She disliked its psychological habits even more than its physiological habits, which was saying quite a lot, the latter being disagreeable enough in all conscience. An airplane, she had been told, had none of this crude speeding passion which these things on wheels developed. You could take your hands off it, lounge back to savour the polar scenery of floodlit cloudbanks, beneath the lunar arc-light – perspectives much to her fancy – through which it would continue smoothly to rush, a gentle-manly Pegasus. So they said – she had never tried it. It was the difference between the bird and the quadruped. But this power and effort, frankly plebeian, over against machines for flight, was the difference as well between gas and ether. She hated gas. One bludgeoned your senses away, the other drugged them drowsily under. And she objected to the dentist's habits from his gas-bag downwards. He was a thoroughly disagreeable fellow, like this strenuous machine. Now they dropped down a great hill, however, a mile-long chute, which was a sort of recumbent precipice. That was distinctly easier, though still she felt in great danger from the catapulting habits of her seat.

But this *tearing* of the air was positively uncouth. How men could put up with the wind as they did, she could not imagine. Women in wind-jammers would be quite out of the question! One's ears were converted into whistles, which was a stupid prank, when upon both sides of one's head! Also for two pins it would whistle in one's teeth!

At last Victor seemed satisfied. Furthermore he had emerged from his hostile mood, as it appeared; not quite himself, of course, but a passable imitation. They slacked off somewhat, and she watched the speed-needle go back behind the hundred kilometre mark.

'We'll let her cool,' he said.

'I'm glad of that,' she answered, but without looking at him yet. She would allow *him* to cool down first, a little, too, poor darling. That would be better. But Victor was out for a chat. They still fled along at a respectable pace, but it was possible to converse.

'Old Percy,' said he, with a ghost of a juvenile chuckle, 'always gets left with the baby, doesn't he?'

Victor was decidedly in a better mood! He seemed to feel that possible pursuers had been successfully shaken off, that must be it. Victor identified himself, of course, with this horrible machine, to which he referred as *her*. A pretty lady! A rather disgusting case of mistaken sex! But men will be men. She sighed – a little Virginian echo – a catch of the breath, no more.

He cast a quick look backwards at the crest of the hill behind them.

'No police cars!' he said, with a further propitiatory gargle – a little mirthful tattoo in the throat.

'I hope not.' She found that her voice was gone very weak and her ears sang.

'Not that they would probably trouble much anyway about me. It's old Percy they were after, I expect.'

'I don't think so, Victor.'

'Yes, but what gets me worried, Marg, is that you've probably got old Perce jugged. Now he's done it again and they won't let him go – they'll make him do time. He's for it, poor old bird!'

355

'Percy Hardcaster is able to look after himself – far better than you are, Victor. He will know what to do.'

'Have you got your passport?' he·asked her in a moment.

'Yes. Here it is.' She produced a big strapping passport from a small bag she held, and opened its pink leaves – pink for Great Britain.

Gwendolen Margaret Savage. Twenty-four. Spinster. Eyes, grey-blue. Very descriptive! The rest of the account of her person was there, making her out short and thin.

'They didn't ask you any questions when they examined the passports, Marg!'

'None at all. They always *look* suspicious, don't they? But they said nothing. Here is where they stamped it.'

'That's fine.'

'It's lucky I am not your wife, Victor,' she said. 'The name Stamp, had it been on my passport, would have been quite enough to get me arrested. That occurred to me at once.'

They were passing a farm. A cyclopean barn, fit for the domestic side of the architecture of the pyramid-builders, towered over them. A dog attempted suicide, but Victor prevented it, with an appropriate curse.

'Why should the name Stamp,' he asked, 'have that effect Marg?'

'I think it would.'

'You've got a bee in your bonnet about my name. Really you have, Marg.'

'Have I, Vic?'

'You have that. You have a bat in your belfry where my patronymic is concerned.'

It was back to *Oh, these handsome men!* again: but she had killed all compunction now in her heart, and was prepared to reveal to *any* handsome man whatever how fatal it was to regard his attractive presence as a charm against the shaft that flies by night, or for that matter the more humdrum accidents of the high-noon.

'I am positive, Victor,' she said, following out this new principle, 'that Stamp is a name looked upon by the Spanish police as suspect. For them it stands for a dangerous criminal.'

'Why? What reason have you, Marg, for thinking that?'

356

They were passing through woods. Her face basked in the cool temperature of a cave. She would have preferred to give herself up to this enjoyment; but she strengthened her voice, which had not yet got back its kick, as best she could, by an extra measure of throaty tension, and accommodated him.

'I think the people who sent us here,' she told him, 'have seen to that. They have used your name, Victor, as if you were the head of the smugglers.'

'The captain of the Forty Thieves?'

'Yes, Victor. That sort of thing. Abershaw and Sean have played a trick upon you.'

'A pretty harmless practical joke, darling. You mean that signature? That was a joke, dear. A practical joke.'

'I don't think so.'

'But what's your idea, Marg? That I am blacklisted as Public Enemy No. 1 by the Spanish police?'

'That seems to me probable at least, Victor.'

'But why should all this happen? Why? – why?'

'Because that was what was intended.'

'You think there's been a lot of funny business going on, that's it, is it?'

'I do.'

'But come down out of the clouds, Margie now! Do you want me to believe that the wicked Abb wrote to that big stiff, the police president of Catalonia, and said: "Keep an eye on that man Stamp. He's at the bottom of all this arms smuggling business?"'

'I shouldn't be surprised if that had happened.'

Margot was sitting up stiffly in her seat, like a self-respecting little schoolgirl submitting to a catechism. She answered his questions at once, with no trace of hesitation. At the same time it might have been a geography lesson, for all the emotion that she showed. Indeed, she was more like an exemplary small child who had usurped the functions of the mistress, and was sedately engaged in teaching, instead of learning, by the excellence of her responses.

'From what motive, Marg darling? Only explain that to me – there must be a reason for everything, mustn't there, dear?'

'I don't know, Victor, what are the motives.'

357

'Nor do I!' At last he laughed outright, but very indulgently, at this stiffly erect little figure beside him, and her oracular manner. 'Look, Marg: I'm *nobody*.'

'No, Victor?'

'No. Haven't you got that yet?'

'We don't mean the same thing.'

'I hope we don't always, Margles!'

'But I think I could guess, Victor, at a motive.'

'Well, Marg, let's have it!'

'It's difficult, to put into words. You'd only laugh at me if I did.'

She cast him a moonbeam of a misty glance at this. They had come out of the wood and were rushing through a village, half of which was an orderly waterfall and a sort of rapids. A widish stream made of its street a quay. Several sun-blackened children narrowly escaped falling into the water, as they scuttled out of the path of the car, with its furibund bellow.

To hear that her Vic was a nobody, that amused her a little. She understood, with some precision, that that would not matter even if it were true, as it was not. She had not listened to long talks between Tristy and himself and others for nothing. She had long ago made up her mind that Victor was – well, *a symbol*. Some men are symbols. She knew that. They were the very words even of an argument, in which she had timidly joined (but she had argued *against* the symbolic man); and they certainly abashed her a great deal at the time with all their chatter of symbols. The word 'symbol' then was new to her. And was not her Victor *the symbolic man*, as you might call it, to a fault? She grasped quite well the fact that he *stood for something*. Not for nothing, anything but that. So he could not be a nobody. That was clear enough. She could not in any case have loved a nobody. But she *could* love a *symbol*. And that, as she put it a little hardily, was one up to her. There were some girls who would have shied at a symbol – when they found out it was that.

The lion is a symbol (and Victor was her Richard Coeur-de-lion!) The lion is a symbol of a life that is passed: and in that respect he is much farther gone than the horse. But both lion and horse today were symbols. And she was certainly speeding

358

through a Spanish province now in the company of a symbol. Of a hunted symbol, as it happened, if you could say that: and men were out with their shotguns to shoot it up, upon a hue and cry.

But Victor, *he* poor chap did not know that he was *it*. He had no suspicion of such a thing. He just thought that he was Vic. But *she* knew that he was it – for she had a sort of second-sight. It was a terrible predicament.

Nature had enabled her to see a symbol, where another would just see a pair of trousers, and a lovely brown neck! That was how she had got to know, by second-sight. That was how she had surprised his secret. But it was without, of course, knowing how or why. Perhaps, however, no one was able to decide that.

Supposing, for argument's sake, these people had discovered a Neanderthal Man, let's say, knocking about these villages. What would they all have done? Hunted it, of course. With guns, pitchforks, hammers and sickles – and other symbols too. Well, had not Victor some title to be considered as a Man with a capital letter – as the Kipling Man, for instance? He had that, and he was a fine specimen to boot. (Who was it had called him the Kipling Man – 1930 American model? It was Monty, she felt pretty sure. She recognized Monty's evil tongue in that.) But it was semi-extinct, or it was becoming so. Already Kipling Men were flying in the face of fact – they all had agreed when they were talking about it. It had made her very angry at the time. This sort of Man was in fact an outlaw, at best in a Big Game Park. That was how Tristy had summed the matter up. 'With he of Cromagnon, and he of Neanderthal, the Kipling Man will soon be a skull, and a doubtful femur, and a thing that might have been a rib. Reconstructed, he would figure in the anthropologist's tract.' – 'He may be magnificent, but he is not Marxian Peace!' Victor had shouted, with a big hearty scoff-back that had silenced them. That had brought the debate to an end, and everyone had been ruffled. Victor *would* mention Marx, just to tease them!

How much of this the tendrils of those tender nerves in the small parasite at Victor's side had registered was proved by the intelligent solicitude she had shown him and her cunning reading of the forged writing on the wall. How much she loved this aimless thing! But she was Nature mourning for the mate of her youth. She was the wind sighing on the wart-leaves for its existence among the glacial peaks, after a levelling of all the splendid mountains. She was the sigh of the last rose, and the whisper of the last lily, when the Flower-haters have decreed the extinction of all 'luxury-weeds.' So, and in that symbolical manner, she could respond to the song of the magdalen, brought to her notice by the latter-day wolves, who had suckled her starved intelligence and fed it with Victorian lollypops.

> The red rose cries, 'He is near, he is near,'
> And the white rose weeps, 'He is late';
> The larkspur listens, 'I hear, I hear';
> And the lily whispers, 'I wait'.

*

The road beyond the village was abruptly forced round at right angles, where it came up against a pygmy cliff. They took the corner in an abbreviated spin, without slackening speed. As they came round it Margot was almost lying down, in obedience to the steep turning action of the car, and it was only just above the base of the wind-screen that she first saw the Civil Guards.

Chapter 7

THERE were two Civil Guards. They were not above thirty yards ahead, two figures operatically cloaked, with their carbines half-way up to their shoulders. There was no mistaking them, however, with their strapped and winged flat helmets of black oilcloth. These were the man-hunting gunmen of the law right enough, of the Spanish peninsula, and up to their tricks all right – Margot grinned as she took this in, and saw through their dumb show, as she did on the spot: the men she had always had in the back of her brain of late, and almost *kept* there for that matter, for just this occasion – for just this particular man-trap. True to type as well was their highway-manesqueness – the horrid dressed-up military dolls come to life, at the spot appointed! She had read how they picketed the empty country in times of insurrection, stopping all travellers with their haughty right of search.

One stood just outside the wood, their horses were tethered behind him; the other was planted good and square in the centre of the highway, legs apart. The stiff inverted Prussian V of his legs signified *No Thoroughfare!* as plainly as a red lantern could. He was there for keeps – he was as good as a five-barred gate, and far above flesh and blood, like metal and stone. He did not move – except that his rifle rose above his stomach and then very gradually crept up in front of his chest, like the rising tidemarks of a river in flood. The other waved an arm to signal them to stop, with scarecrow flappings of his black capote. He was a tall man and was provided with an impressive moustache.

'Stop!' as a hollow report her voice summoned Victor. 'Stop!' It was *her* duty, too, to halt him. But it was quite unavailing to shout at *events* – at events three seconds off. As well talk to Time and tell it where to stand! 'Do as he says!' in a shrill bay the genteel organ of everyday broke forth – her neck thrust out rooster-fashion. 'Do as he tells you! Please do as he wants!'

Victor did not stop. There was no Victor there to stop. Or there was Victor – Victor who would not stop; and then there was the man in their path, who would not move. Nothing would shift that stockstill person, helmeted and gunned. He was a fixture, intended to be there – he had *always* been there, stockstill in that road! And he had a bullet to stop Victor at his fingertip. But why would not Victor stop? He would not stop because he *could* not. It was this machine – *it* would not stop: he was attached to a plunging twenty-ton magnet, which rushed to meet the lifted gun.

The magnetic tension could have been broken up at a touch (but by anything *outside* itself, for *she* could have roared and roared again and it would have made no difference), it was so brittle. She watched, in the matter of seconds she had for watching, this mathematical shortening of the space, this telescopic closing-up of the time – of all that separated the man that was a gun, and the man that was a car. There was the deadly instrument – there was the vessel of propulsive power: they *must* meet, they were compelled by their natures to clash. This was a fatality that came into play the moment it was machines, not men, that mattered. But she could see the end of it as plain as two and two make four. And her teeth came out grinning against the shock, like a cat's at bay.

She saw the two Guards get bigger and get bigger. It was as if in a series of blinks, or similar to the jumps of the hands of a large public clock, where the hands were the size of scythes. Now she could *hear* the Guards, or the one that was shouting, he by the side of the road. The other's face was like wood. It was quite expressionless. He was a thick-set young man with a dark blue chin and sharp blue eyes. She saw one of his eyes close up, the lid went neatly down over it; and there was the other at the root of the barrel of the carbine. And as they bore down upon this puppet with its painfully deliberate mechanism, the frantic clamour of their klaxon filled her head to bursting point, in spasm after spasm of menacing sound. She closed both her own eyes as she saw the steel-shutter go down over the Guard's: then she released a long chuckling scream, clawing at her mouth to hold in this offensive outburst.

Screaming and staring she went through that expanding second where time stopped – for her eyes did not stay shut, but when they came open again they had a glaze of sorts, that veiled them to induce in them a partial vision, like that of a smoked glass. Screaming after the manner of an express plunging into a tunnel, she went into it, except that *this* darkness was picked out in vivid patches of violent fact. For all that, it was no longer the light of day, but a highly selective order of blackout. A crude salience was given to items of importance; to the rest it applied its inky sponge. Surrounding the things that were thus picked out, stood a nocturnal haze. What she saw appeared to her in fragments, but in too great detail, for it was incoherent.

They entered the interval of tragic eclipse. The roar of the klaxon whined on her eardrums. She saw the Guard leap aside, as the matador snatches himself away from the path of the bull – but leap too late. She understood that he had leaped too late; too late for something, but she did not know what. An incompetent matador! An inferior Jack-in-the-box! There was an explosion and a dull blow: the blow was him, as he went down. But it seemed to her that it was Victor stamping his foot. As the blue chin sank out of sight, and it sank slowly, there came an explosion, proper to the same quarter. But over to their left something flashed and cracked as well. This was, in fact, the second Guard who was firing. But for her it was merely something like the nearer disturbance – but both simultaneous, so one could not say *echo*. The two happenings ran into each other – things *would* not stop apart. As to that blow the air gave her in the face, she did not connect that with anything. That was a part of the interplay of car and air, of the horseplay of their constant smack and push. Or perhaps a paper bag of wind, that had banged very near to her, to be accounted for if at all under the head of 'air-pockets.' Air-pockets covered a multitude of pops and gusts: and the noises of the wind were legion.

Following upon the first explosion and the buffet that caught the car in the wind, there was a violent lurching see-saw. Its body was badly shaken by this. She clung, her mouth distended in a wide protective grimace, such as the dentist exacts, to her seat. But all this was entirely in order naturally in such a disgusting chaos of Guards, guns, horses, tree-trunks, and the rest of it. They were in the thick of a typhoon. They in their car were like a cork, tossed in some turgid medium – through which, however, they had passed. This storm would stop as swiftly as it had started. That was a way such disturbances had. This one was ending. Or was that not the case? But it was natural they should rock about a little. A bit of pitching and rolling was only to be expected, in this storm of shadows and lit-up objects. She was not at all surprised.

'That fool seemed to mistake us for a bull!' she heard Victor say.

What fool? How a bull? Bulls and fools merged into one another and, in that state, her mind refused them further hospitality. They dropped out of it and were lost in the general welter, where they belonged.

She remarked that on the road in front of them the dust was

spurting up, stung into tiny geysers with surprising suddenness. What was Victor saying? His voice did not carry well in the semi-obscurity (how did it come to pass that the roadway showed up so well? It was quite brightly lit, as if by a head-light).

'He's firing at the tyres,' she thought she heard him say – that's what it sounded like.

He meant the tyres were back-firing, perhaps, which was to be expected of them. Hence, of course, the bumps. Sharp raps upon the car somewhere behind were doubtless the metal crack-ling. Like the reports heard from men's dress-shirts. Victor was stooping forward. She supposed he was trying to see one of the clocks – the time-clock or the speed-clock. Since it had got so dark this was no easy matter. But he was a long while without being able to see what he wanted and she thought she would help him, though her eyes were not too good.

'It's lucky – for us this car is armour-plated!' He was prais-ing the horrid old car now – that Victor was a boy who was fond of cars she had always known. But about this one he seemed perfectly potty – that was why Victor had run away, just to be able to drive it! Silly boy! He had *trompéd* her with a machine!

'Bend down!' he shouted. 'Head down!' That was easy: for they were turning and she found herself flung sideways and very much out of the upright, anyway. At that moment she received a violent blow in the back. She thought Victor had playfully struck her, or by accident, naturally. She looked up.

'That gave the seat a nasty smack!' he said.

'Who?' she asked.

'Same bloke,' he said. 'But it's all right now. It's all over. We're round the bend.'

'Are we?' she said.

'We're out of sight.'

And out of mind, thought she. What did he mean by saying it was 'all over'? That it was getting lighter, perhaps. It *was* getting lighter. Very much lighter. A spasm passed down her body. She felt cold, and began to tremble. What a ride this had been!

*

364

She began violently to tremble – her limbs appeared to rebel against the stolid *status quo* of the trunk. Again a chuckling scream sought to force its way up to her throat. She would not let it. She dug her nails into the palms of her hands, with her teeth she drew blood from her shuddering lip. The ordeal upon her, she had slipped slyly away, out of the front-line. The senses had been under intensive bombardment, but she had not *chosen* to fly. She had been forced back without her permission into her private arcanum. There everything reached her wadded up and muffled in from external shock. So she had sat out the blackout in her ivory tower.

But the catastrophic interval now definitely had passed – she had caught only deceptive glimpses of what was afoot. She had been spared: but now she had come out again. Hurriedly and apprehensively she glanced about her, taking stock. But still she shrank from facts whose impact was *too* rude.

In retrospect she now came to see piecemeal and one thing at a time, what they had passed through, as occupants of this still fearfully speeding car. She understood that they had been fired on – though at first she did not put it quite so plainly as that. She concluded something had undoubtedly happened prior to that – something of a terrible nature, something unspeakably awful, possibly.

At that – at first – she left it. But she did not see now that her original explanation of the *unsteadiness* of the car must be revised.

'What happened to that Civil Guard, Victor?' she asked him, grinning fiercely, as if gloating over what she hoped might have occurred. She flew up in the air as she spoke, smiling most frightfully, like a limerick 'young lady' of the nonsensical Lear. They had risen upon the crest of one of the waves of which this road was composed, and all that had happened was that she was left aloft when the car had settled too quickly for her. But she pinioned herself, to make sure the next time!

'Which one, darling?' Victor asked morosely – his voice sounded very lifeless and dull.

'The one who was standing in the middle of the road. You know the one, Victor.'

'Oh. I think we killed him.'

'Killed him!' she cried almost gaily. 'You don't really think he was killed, do you, Victor?'

She wrung her hands, flinging herself or being flung against the door of the car, smiling roguishly to herself and attempting to look like a lady, under very trying circumstances.

'I'm afraid so,' said Victor. 'It was his fault. We were not to blame.'

'Of course not,' she hastened to reassure him. Poor Victor! 'But do you think he is killed or is he only knocked down? I hope not! I am sure he cannot be! He may be a little injured though. Not much!'

'I should say he must have been killed. Yes. We went over him. We killed him all right.'

'How ghastly – how awful, Victor! How terrible! I cannot believe it! You cannot be sure of that.'

She shook her head very firmly: Victor *would* jump to conclusions.

'One cannot be sure of anything, Marg.'

'I'm sure you can't!'

'He tried to jump aside – did you see him?'

'I saw nothing. Yes, I saw that – at least I think I did.'

'Well, he left it too late. He lost his nerve – that's why he was caught. We smacked him pretty hard.'

She shuddered suddenly and put her face down into the stiffened cups of her two hands. With a wild look cast over the rocky hills which they were now approaching, she retired, numbed once more by the contact with the reality, into her customary brooding retreat. There she would digest this ominous information.

They had killed a Civil Guard! She and Victor. This fact at first stunned her completely. She crouched grinning in her corner, her mind flatly refusing to go on with this. It began to stray and woolgather, entering all kinds of bypaths. It addressed itself to the composition of a chatty schoolgirl letter to Agnes Irons, telling her about the Pyrenees, not hesitating to say how she wished Agnes was there, with her golf-clubs, as she was sure Agnes would find plenty of *bunkers*, and be able to do wonderful mashie shots, and have a *tophole* time. And then she finished her letter to Agnes with lots of love and all the best, and began recalling the last meeting Victor and she had had with Tristram before they had left London; with Abershaw, who had been there, cracking his empty jokes and assuring Victor that she, Margot, did not know it, but that she had been in love with him (that is, with Abb), and had been for some time past – he could even tell her the exact day, if she wanted to know, when she had first fallen for him. 'But don't be sore about that, Vic, old man! She loves you still quite as much as is decent. Only I've come to keep you company – unknown to either you or her. It's because she thinks I'm such a perfect gentleman! You're her perfect man, Vic, I'm her perfect gentleman! We are complementary to one another.'

But while she was brooding over these things which belonged to a remote and peaceful zone of her mind, she was gazing all the time, she found, at an enormous Prussian-blue chin. She could hear the terroristic bellow of their klaxon, accompanied by the whip-cracking and door-banging of rifle-fire. Out of the tail of her eye, meanwhile, she observed a horse arching up on its hind legs with foam decorating its mouth, and the hoarse shouting came to her again of a much-moustachioed dark mouth, strapped down so that it could not open very wide.

Far worse than that, she discovered herself at last watching against her will the floodlit stretch of rust-red road. Plumes of dust were spurting up; but their car (it had left her behind) was rapidly disappearing and had already grown quite small, in diminishing perspective; while in the foreground she was staring down at a disagreeable flattened object. Sprawling in the centre of the road, it was incredibly two-dimensional and, in short, unreal. It might have just been painted upon the earth. But it looked more like a big untidy pattern, cut out of black paper, except for what was the face. That was flat, as well – as flat as a pancake, but as pale as a sheet, with a blue smear where the chin was. It was the chin of Prussian-blue. The flat black headgear of a Civil Guard, likewise no thicker than cardboard, lay a foot away from the head.

Slowly, almost slothfully, within her mind, this novel background for Victor and herself took logical shape. She admitted, a fragment at a time, the components of the scenery for this new Act. The reality which had been shut out would have compelled her, by its maddening pressure, to give it admittance, if she had not met it half-way. So, successively, all the facts that went to make the complete event she allowed to pass inside. She even assisted in the setting-up of this sinister backcloth. At last there was nothing lacking. She saw that the very worst had happened. And after that, and last of all, she perceived, with a darkening of all the horizon of her conscious being, that it was herself that had been to blame! She, Margot, was at the bottom of this adventure! It would have been better if she had been false! It would have been better if she had not cared. It would have been best of all if she had never existed at all!

If she had not interfered, she told herself very slowly, again and again, as if she had been learning a difficult lesson, this would never have come to pass. Nothing so bad as this, at all events. She had made everything a hundred times worse by what she had done. And she had been well-meaning! More than that, she had aimed at something of more positive virtue, like the fortitude of women in the grand rôles of this life, after she had fallen out with her great mentor.

But at this point she fell into a secretive, a soundless, weeping crouched up in her corner, but forced still to cling with one hand to the back of the seat, to maintain herself in position, for the car was proceeding now at a great speed and she was tossed and flung about more like a shopper's parcel than a human being. Her soft sobbing even was made to sound like violent hiccups or short protesting cries, as it jerked out of her breathless body, by the incessant battery she underwent, accompanying the savage onrush of the machine.

So, wildly but softly crying to herself, the life almost shaken out of her body, a period elapsed whose length she would have found it impossible to compute. In the idleness of her despair she remembered the imposing array of all the women in the world in Queens' Gardens – of all those 'Queens' which in an ill-starred moment she had consulted, and she was sure that none had ever been so wretched as herself.

Penelope calmly sitting at home, and the happy calm of Nausicaa – these mocked her out of the pages of her ex-confessor. But there was always the miserable Ophelia, who was the *exception* – alone of all the imaginary women the one who had failed the Man, out of infirmity of character, Ruskin had said. But at least Ophelia had had the sense to take herself off and to be subsequently found drowned in a canal or something. Was not *she*, possibly a more dangerous sort of Ophelia – one who did *not* go away? One who, on the contrary, blundered into action, with her ill-judged and untimely interference? Why had she not left bad alone – since bad as it was, it had not gone so very far and no great danger threatened for the moment? What had possessed her suddenly at Bourg-le-Comte, that she should suddenly take a hand, and begin behaving in a manner that was totally unlike herself? Some evil spirit of that foreign place must have entered into her! It was not *her* Margot who had been acting thus.

But she did not require much persuasion to look upon these parts of the world as infested with occult presences of a most undesirable kind. And from that point in her bitter meditations she drifted into a world dominated by such figures as the dwarf – the aggressive comedian of the Plaza Cabrinetty. Nodding and smiling to herself, she moved within the orbit of his spells.

It grew colder. A ripple of goose-flesh on her arms and thighs announced a change. Her grimacing mouth started to chatter. Whether this alteration was due to the approach of the mountains, or was because of the falling of the night, or whether from some other agency, she did not speculate. For a long time now Victor had not spoken. On several occasions he had stopped and examined a map: and once he had pulled up to take out a cigarette, and had offered her one in silence. Now they were parked upon the summit of a considerable hill.

A good-sized *pueblo* lay below them, mud-coloured, built in the flat and earthy African manner of Spain, upon the hollow cliffs of a wide and waterless river bed. There were two churches. Victor was looking down at it, and then back to his map, spread out upon his knees. Next moment they were off again, with a convulsive haste, rushing down the hill towards the village. They passed it upon their left. It seemed completely deserted. A bridge went over it, across the mud-gulley of the

369

empty river. She stared in terror at this apparently abandoned collection of eyeless dwellings, of crumbling ocherish walls. It must be full of corpses and skeletons, following a visitation of the plague. Or the inhabitants were hiding, inside in the darkness of these mud huts. They were soon out of sight of this stricken spot, however: they continued upon the road that followed the bank of the river on the near side of the bridge. Soon they were climbing a hill beyond. The mountains were now almost overhead. A grey wall of stormy mist obscured the more distant peaks, incessantly scampered over with bold scrawlings of forked lightning, of distinctly Chinese character. The flashes stood out for a long moment like a wayward and demented handwriting. then left the grey rain-wall empty again.

'There's a storm up there,' said Victor, as they came in sight of this phenomenon, and a roar of thunder reached them through the silent evening, hollow and faint.

As if racing towards the scene of the battle, and determined to be in time, they traversed at breakneck speed the last valley of the desertic foot-hills. The soil of this upland steppe was still reddened in the dregs of the sunset. They came to a halt by the side of a frolicsome brook. Beyond this there seemed to be no proper road. A path climbed towards the towering entrance to a repulsive gorge. That was the way to get *in*, for anyone who wished to – who *must* go in among those terrible mountains. Margot could feel their great breath upon her face. She could also feel that they were *there*, in the way that you feel in an unlighted room that someone is there. Their mere size made them *alive*. Was that possible, that *scale* should take with it *life*?

Meanwhile, out of them came a sound like the whisper from the mouth of a Titanic seashell. Of course that was the thunder. Soon they would be alone inside with the storm-gods. It was a prospect that filled her with dismay. For *scale* (not of course, human scale, that appealed to her extremely) was the one thing she could not stomach, and she always felt that she must be crushed by it. At least she would not face it alone. She reached out for Victor's hand and held it in a passionate squeeze. Yet what could Victor do, poor dear? For *Ah, these handsome men!* Victor understood *nothing* of the malevolence of these great blocks of awful matter! He squeezed back and stretched himself.

'This is where we leave the bus,' he announced.

Margot crawled out at his heels. But as she found herself at last on her legs again, she was overcome with exhaustion and semi-collapsed upon the footboard. For some moments she thought she was going to be sick, and bent forward towards the ground, pale and her limbs shaking, in spite of herself.

'Are you tired, darling?' Victor asked her, stooping down and stroking her hair, from which the dust poured out in handfuls.

She nodded her head, perfunctorily at first, and then several times in succession, with increasing emphasis, as a person goes over a penstroke, to give it more precision.

'A little, darling,' she said, cautiously stretching herself from the waist up.

'You must have found it a bit hard-going, Marg!' he said. 'It's been no joy-ride!'

'No,' she said, a blush bursting up in her grey, dust-covered face.

'Still, here we are. We're there. There they are!' He pointed to the mountains.

'I had better rest a moment,' she said faintly. 'It's a very bumpy car, Victor.'

'That's because of the load,' he said.

'I didn't see any load, Victor. I was going to ask you where the boxes were.'

'No, you can't *see* them. They're not visible.'

'Where are they?'

'They're inside.'

He kicked a foot out at the body of it, or rather at the works underneath, below where the footboards ran.

She rose unsteadily and stood beside him swaying a little and supporting herself with his arm. They both stared down at the car. He seemed momentarily almost as much dazed as she was. He passed his hand over his face once or twice.

'Are they *underneath* there, Victor?' she said at last.

He shook his head.

'No,' he said. 'The thing's got a false bottom to it.'

371

'Oh.'

'It's an old bootleg bus. They all have it.'

'Oh, I see.'

Suddenly she laughed shrilly, as the mischievous resource of
the cunning bootleggers appealed violently to her as exquisitely
odd. They certainly were a sporting crowd, their feet on
the sham decks of their machines, passing themselves off as
blameless joyriders. And she and Vic were following in their
footsteps – squatting up there together on their false-bottomed
vehicle all the time. She could not suppress a laugh, she could
not really. It was too killing.

'What a good idea, Victor! What a capital idea, my dear!'

She laughed until a tear or two ran down her cheek. Nothing
had ever struck her as quite so droll. Between them, they were
a scream. If they had been stopped, they would have looked
so innocent. *That* would have puzzled a Civil Guard!

'I'll show you how it works,' he said, a little cheered by her
evident high spirits.

'Do, Victor. I should like to see how it works.'

He opened the second door, into the middle compartment,
where the big bouncy seat was, and after fumbling with the
floor a little, suddenly lifted it up, mat and all. Looking round
by the side of Victor's big arm she saw the cases, all in rows,
in the false-bottom.

Victor bent down and pulled one of the cases up and put it
down on the footboard.

'Some of these are small arms,' he said. 'We might as well
have a gun or two while we're about it.'

Margot turned away. Interfere she was unable to. But *watch*
she could not. Even her impulse to protest had become feeble,
but she could not stand by while he took those things out. They
were engaged upon a path: it had to be followed, where ever it
led. But to stand by with folded hands was not so easy.

She walked a few steps to the side of the mettlesome brook
and looked down at it, observing the clever skipping of its agile
waters as they moved quickly amongst its jumble of ugly
stones, the savage spawn of the big cliffs. Remembering that
abominable torrent which had revealed to her for the first time
the inner truth regarding 'nature,' which she had always, at a

distance, supposed to be so desirable an abstraction; and as a consequence calling to mind how she had been induced to forsake the passive rôle – and to march up into the village to engage in *action*, of all hazardous, foolish things – she arched her neck and frowned down at the ground at her feet, removing her eyes from contact with this bleak and senseless bustle of objectless matter.

An exclamation of Victor's made her turn quickly about. She discovered him gazing into the opened packing case, holding in his hand what looked remarkably like a brick.

She slowly moved back until she stood beside him again. As she glanced at his face she saw that one side of it was twisted up, after the Clark Gable fashion, and conveyed that he had never expected much more of life than was to be found in that burst-open case of firearms, or indeed that fair false-bottom which underlay all the haughty power of that big speed-toy beside which he stood.

'What is that brick, Victor, you are holding in your hand?'

'Oh, just that, Marg! A good honest brick!'

'Where did it come from?'

'Oh, it came from out of *that*!'

'Out of that case, Victor?'

'Even so. It's one of the Smith-Coronas, so to speak!'

'How do you mean, Victor?'

'I mean you were right, Marg, about that crowd. I'm afraid they've fooled us badly.'

'OH!'

'Look at this! There's nothing in those cases. Except bricks!'

She took a step forward and looked down into the packing case. It contained alternatively packing-paper and bricks.

'We've been sent on a fool's errand, Marg.'

'Yes, we have.'

'This must have been only a blind, to draw off attention from Mat. My rôle was to be the decoy-duck!'

He was talking quietly, almost as if in confidence. His voice sounded dead and discouraged. Margot made no comment. Painfully she stood by, and watched the unfolding of these events.

373

'I'd better open a few more,' he said.

He proceeded to haul up out of the hold of the bootleggers' piratic roadster case after case. One and all, upon being forced open, revealed nothing but a cargo of bricks.

'Well, that's that!' he laughed, a sharp short cough of ironic disgust. 'That old devil Hardcaster has parked us here with a load of bricks,' he said. 'And we've croaked a Civil Guard!'

She looked at him quickly, but said nothing; she dreaded anything clear-sighted – most particularly – in place of the traditionally imperfect vision of these starry six-footers. She feared it as much as does the bullfighter a bull which *looks* where he is going when he charges, though not for the same reason.

'I don't believe Hardcaster knew,' she said.

'No?'

'No, it's my impression that he didn't, Victor.'

'But what the hell anyway?' And he turned his back upon the over-tricky car, gaped open in the middle to give up its load of bricks. He fixed his eye, but with less calm confidence than it was his habit to command, upon the less and less inviting-looking gorge, indicated by the shepherd's shack. A strong bellow of thunder brought a frown to his staring eyes.

'I suppose this is the way up they meant,' he said.

But Margot still contemplated the patent car, built for the pawky racketeers. She grinned stupidly at this big murderous dove-grey body, all opened up, like the carcass of a captured shark, and now utterly shown up. Even for Victor it was quite discredited. And at last she laughed outright at the absurdity of it. She laughed loudly and without restraint. A false bottom – a false bottom on wheels; but all full of nothing at all, except packing-paper and bricks! She went on laughing. The joke grew on her, the more she thought about it. She went on laughing more and more.

Chapter 8

PERCY HARDCASTER knew his place. No illusions with
regard to abstract justice troubled the upright cynicism of his
outlook. He 'played the game.' As ever, with an incorruptible
mind, he remained a true 'sportsman.' To *himself*, at least, he
never pretended that he was hardly used. He accepted, for his
political opinions, the status of a game – a game, of course,
of life and death. He would have been more the 'happy war-
rior' certainly, in the class-battle, if he had been possessed of
a more dishonest mind. But fresh hardships only seemed to
have the effect of seasoning his vision. His integrity stiffened
after each fresh buffet of fate. He looked out more bleakly upon
life, seeing it steadily, seeing it whole, and computing his handicap to a millimetre. There was even a certain crisp logic about
finding himself back in a Spanish prison which appealed to
him – it was so grim that it had a logical fitness. Yes, in his
way, and all allowance made for the backslidings of the spirit, he
was glad to be back in prison! Was it not in the last analysis
his proper place? It was what the trench was for the Tommy.

But these considerations did not prevent Mr Hardcaster
from lifting up his voice in protest after protest, floridly delivered, with all the pomp of moral indignation. *And* as he
fixed his flashing eye upon the limb of the law, the passing
turnkey, he did not disguise the presence of the tongue in his
cheek. All must, with him, be transacted upon a basis of im-
peccable veracity. It was never a question of what society
should do to you, but of what society *could* do to you. 'You
can't keep me here!' was what in effect he said. 'By all rights
I *should* be here. But you just can't do it! Let me out!'

He was not let out. But he was not surprised. For he was
only half-fooling when he insisted that they *could* not.

So in spite of protests he still was the occupant of an insanitary, overcrowded cell. His health suffered. After a week he
was still there in the company of a half-dozen insignificant
criminals and vagrants. He was not popular with his fellow-

prisoners. This was partly on account of his undisguised attempts to separate himself from them at all costs, and his loud complaints at finding himself among them, as if he had been of a finer clay. Also his face was of such patently honest cast, so pink, so soap-conscious, that, although harmless enough perhaps, it was not exactly a thing to live with, for a sensitive cutpurse.

But they talked among themselves, and more than anything else his politics upset them. To start with, they were a self-righteous type of politics, full of a disagreeable rectitude they did not relish. But there was another thing. Since his politics were reputed to be so remarkably unconservative, how was it, they asked themselves, that he was left where he was? They felt that he ought, according to all precedent, and if their experience as old jail-birds went for anything – they would certainly have expected him to be lodged in the most luxurious cell in the prison. And they concluded that he must have done something unneccesarily ungentlemanly to find himself thrust in among the likes of them. So at last they cut him. And one pushed his wooden leg out of the way, informing him that he did not own the cell and that he took up too much room. Only an old crone who was a professional beggar was even passably civil to him. This was because, hearing he was English, she thought he must have some money on him somewhere. So part of the time she kept her hand in by holding out her well-worn palm in his direction, and whining loudly for alms. Once he gave her a piece of chocolate, and she immediately spat at him.

Percy's satisfaction at being back in prison was confined of course to his calmer moments, or such times as he was really put on his mettle. He was subject to acute depression for the greater part of the day. He did not see life steadily from morning till night. That would be too much to expect, though he got better as things came to look blacker, as they did very soon. For before long he realized that in responsible quarters – probably Madrid – people were hardening their hearts.

Of course, no pains would be spared to bring pressure to bear in the highest quarters, to have him immediately released. A suitable apology, it would be suggested, should accompany his release. But he was downcast, there was no denying it. He did not exaggerate the influence possessed by the government of His Britannic Majesty. Its legations and consulates, where it was a question of a notorious Communist, cut less ice every day. All this had been gone into again and again. The Spanish republican authorities *would* argue that after all it was impossible that the King of England could be so anxious as he *seemed* to befriend persons of no social standing, except at Moscow, who were, all said and done, his most implacable enemies. The Comintern had decreed him the same fate as for his cousin the Tsar. It was absurd that he should wish to protect its agents!

It was merely national pride, they argued, on the part of these haughty British officials, that was what it was; and when it came down to brass tacks they would not be so offended as all that if these ruffians were not given up. It had been proved over and over again that this was the way they argued. You could not cure them of it. They were hopelessly ill-informed. That vague entity, that all-powerful, *de facto* ruler of Great Britain, which went by the name of the 'Left Wing,' meant nothing to these Spanish boobies. They confused it with the Parliamentary Labour Party, probably! To their backward, provincial intelligence, these unteachable, stiff-necked romantics had no idea at all with whom they had to deal. The world they lived in – the real world, in contrast to the legal world – was to them a closed book.

But Percy, on his side, had no inclination to make the same mistake. He was in a Spanish prison: and these unintelligent, pigheaded *politicos* also were *facts*. Facts had to be faced all round. And this time, he knew, with a Civil Guard killed outright, that the outlook was unpromising. When would he have an opportunity, even, of stating his case? He would be lucky if his case came for trial within the twelvemonth. So Percy's spirits could not but be low. And when he allowed himself to reflect upon the manner of his arrest, and what had led up to it, he sat frowning stolidly at the wall, as downcast as he had ever been in his life. For this man of truth was not in the habit of sparing himself. Indeed, he somewhat enjoyed exercising his incorruptible intellect upon the dissection of Percy Hardcaster. He was like a painter fond of self-portraiture: and his self-portraits were not chocolate-boxes! He hit hard when he hit Percy.

Mateu was right! He told himself that Mateu had been not far wrong about him. Perhaps after all he did somewhat suffer from a weakness that was very common. Women after all were perhaps his weak spot! It looked uncommonly like it. For why had he followed Margot as he had?

Upon the seventh day the turnkey put his head in at the door, fixed his eye fishily upon Percy, then brought his body inside and straddled truculently in front of the seated prisoner. Percy took no notice at all. The turnkey dragged a greasy copy of the morning paper out of his side-pocket, thrust it under Percy's nose, and pointed in savage dumbshow at something it contained. His forefinger stalked backwards and forwards upon a heavily leaded headline, standing here and there for emphasis upon some particularly juicy capital. Then shouting in his prisoner's ear, as if being short of one leg caused one to be hard of hearing, he exclaimed:

'*Muertos! Muertos! Los dos!* Both! The women too! Both of them. Dead!'

Taking the newspaper from the man's hand with the deliberation of offended dignity (professionally assumed, in the natural course of things) and spreading it out carefully – throwing in a slight shake, as if to expel any lice which, seeing where it came from, might be expected to be quartered in it – Percy allowed his eyes to travel over it. They made their way in one condescending non-stop descent the length of the column to which his attention had been so rudely drawn. What his eye took in only deepened his detachment – it seemed even to freeze his face. He also took on a much more offended expression than before.

TWO OF THE GANG. CONTRABANDISTAS. DEAD.
A POSTMAN. PRECIPICE

What nonsense was this, which had been put before him? demanded the poker-face of this proud professional.

In the three seconds – no more – he allowed himself, Hardcaster saw that the bodies of one Victor Stamp and of a woman

378

known as Margot had been found. They were at the foot of a precipice. A French postman found them – proceeding to a mountain village. Assumption: the pair had walked over the edge of the precipice. Probably in a storm. There had been a storm. High passes blocked with snow. Car found in Spain. Shepherd. Bricks. Abandoned. Letter in pocket of corpse. From Stamp's associate. Dangerous agitator – under lock and key. The notorious Hardcaster.

Percy Hardcaster sniffed. He returned the newspaper to the turnkey. His lack of interest was manifest even in the attitude of his artificial limb.

'Thank you,' he said. 'Thanks!'

'Well?' exclaimed the turnkey. 'Well?'

'Your papers as usual are full of lies,' Percy rejoined, stifling a yawn out of politeness to himself.

'You have seen enough? Don't you want the paper?' The turnkey held the newspaper invitingly in his hand, glaring indignantly at his prisoner.

'It is your paper, isn't it?' Percy asked him.

'Yes. Mine.'

'If you will give me back the money you took from me, I would then buy a newspaper of my own.'

'You can have this one!'

'No, thanks. Not one of your lying ones!'

The turnkey thrust the newspaper back into his pocket with a disappointed snarl and had turned to leave the cell when Percy Hardcaster suddenly clamoured, so that the official jumped as if he had been struck and wheeled about upon this alarming megaphone of a man.

'When am I to be moved from this putrid and evil-smelling room where I am kept boxed up with verminous pickpockets?'

An outburst of disapproving oaths broke from the pickpockets.

'Why do I not receive a visit from my consul?' bellowed Percy above the uproar. 'Am I to have no tobacco? I demand to see the governor of the prison!'

But the turnkey had left the cell and slammed the door behind him before Percy had terminated his customary speech.

A heavy silence fell. The pickpockets glared at Percy and Percy at the pickpockets.

Swollen with an affected speechlessness, Percy proceeded to give a sculpturesque impersonation of THE INJURED PARTY. His cell-mates watched him surreptitiously, with an admiration it was out of their power to withhold. Heavily clamped upon his brick-red countenance, held in position by every muscle that responded to Righteous Wrath, was a mask which entirely succeeded the workaday face. It was the mask of THE INJURED PARTY (model for militant agents in distress). Obedient to the best technique of party-training, he sustained it for a considerable time.

But meanwhile a strained and hollow voice, part of a sham-culture outfit, but tender and halting, as if dismayed at the sound of its own bitter words, was talking in his ears, in a reproachful singsong. It was denouncing him out of the past, where alone now it was able to articulate; it was singling him out as a man who led people into mortal danger, people who were dear beyond expression to the possessor of the passionate, the artificial, the unreal, yet penetrating, voice, and crying to him now to give back, she implored him, the young man, Absalom, whose life he had had in his keeping, and who had somehow, unaccountably, been lost, out of the world and out of Time! He saw a precipice. And the eyes in the mask of THE INJURED PARTY dilated in a spasm of astonished self-pity. And down the front of the mask rolled a sudden tear, which fell upon the dirty floor of the prison.